About

Niloufar Lamakan is an Iranian-born author and artist. She moved to the UK as a child and has lived in Islington, London most of her life. She came to writing after careers in tech, design, art, and property. Her debut novel, *Aged to Perfection*, won the Commendation Award at the Comedy Women in Print Prize and was a finalist at the Page Turner Awards. She writes bold, spicy romantic comedies that are unapologetically age-defiant. Her art also explores the connections between age, identity, and society's perceptions of beauty. When she's not painting or writing, you'll find her on the dancefloor.

https://www.niloufarlamakan.com/

 instagram.com/nlamakan
 facebook.com/nlamakan

AGED TO PERFECTION

NILOUFAR LAMAKAN

One More Chapter
a division of HarperCollins*Publishers* Ltd
1 London Bridge Street
London SE1 9GF
www.harpercollins.co.uk

HarperCollins*Publishers*
Macken House, 39/40 Mayor Street Upper,
Dublin 1, D01 C9W8, Ireland

This paperback edition 2025
1
First published in Great Britain in ebook format
by HarperCollins*Publishers* 2025
Copyright © Niloufar Lamakan 2025
Niloufar Lamakan asserts the moral right to be identified
as the author of this work

A catalogue record of this book is available from the British Library

ISBN: 978-0-00-868549-2

Printed and bound in the UK using 100% Renewable Electricity
by CPI Group (UK) Ltd

With love to my family and friends who continue to cheer me on through every twist and turn of my creative path.

PART I
January

ONE

The First Day

Tuesday, 1 January, 10.30am

HAPPY NEW YEAR! It's time for my seventh decade body audit.

Hair on head – longish and honey-coloured because I'm worth it.

Pubic hair – unfashionably natural. I reckon if a guy is lucky enough to be facing my pubes, he's not likely to stop because of a few silver highlights.

Chin hairs – they're so devious. They creep up on you and grow long quietly overnight.

Waistline – pretty trim after my year of travel and trekking. But I can hear my menopause fat. 'I've missed you,' it's saying, 'let me pad you out again. Have some more chips. Ooh, those chocolate brownies look so good.'

Face wrinkles – I don't have any if I don't wear my contact lenses.

Eyes – bloodshot from last night's excesses.

Legs – I should cover them up and stop putting people off oranges. But then again, who gives a damn? I'll wear what I like.

Boobs – nipples still pointing ahead, but is the left boob drooping at a different rate?

Back fat/droop – who knows? What I can't see won't hurt me.

3

Head – still not got the hang of ruling the heart.

Heart – was shattered into a million pieces but almost put back together.

Audit result: not bad. On Instagram, they'd say, 'looking fabulous at sixty'. I wonder if I'll face Catherine Deneuve's 'Arse v Face' dilemma soon? Yes, but I think I'd opt for small arse/wrinkly face. I'll be laughing when I get a wolf whistle from the back and shock when they see the front.

And now – deep breath – last year's love life audit.

Love interests – zilch.

Butterflies in tummy – what are those?

Sex – twice (practically a born-again virgin).

Dating skills – more out of date than the batteries on my vibrator.

Heartbreak – one. A bad one. A really bad one. A really, really bad one.

Emotions – contained. Just about. I'm covering the cracks in my soul with lashings of faux nonchalance.

Audit result: poor. Drastic action required.

Last night, I made a resolution after I did my usual NYE disappearing trick. Not for the first time, I couldn't bear facing that awkward moment at midnight when you have to wait for couples to kiss first before they get to you, the singleton, the odd number, the spare wheel. Instead, I welcomed the New Year sitting on the loo with a glass of fizz, listening to the revellers outside, and shed a few tears. Other women were being cherished on the other side of the door, so why not me? Was I so unlovable? The pain I was an expert at hiding came bubbling up. I ached for a tender loving midnight kiss and longed to be someone's forever love: the one, the missing piece. Over the years, I've spent a few New Year countdowns hiding but I didn't think I'd be doing it when I'm sixty. I thought I'd be sorted by now. One half of a kissing couple. Not still searching for someone to smooch.

I cleaned up my face, applied more lippy, jutted out my chin and decided to start the year with a positive attitude. No more celibacy for me. The world may think I'm invisible and past it because I'm sixty, but I disagree. There's so much I still want to do – make love in a forest, drink martinis in a skyscraper bar in Shanghai, dance in a flash mob, and laugh at Sarah Millican's bawdy jokes till I pee. Being age-appropriate is way overrated. Much better to grow old disgracefully.

Leila gave me the idea for the dating challenge last night. Her NYE party was so much fun, as my vampire eyes will attest. This year's theme was movie characters, and Leila's new house in Hampstead, a huge LA-style modern house with double height entertaining space and lots of glass (a snooper's dream if it wasn't surrounded by trees), was the perfect setting. Three Indiana Joneses were in a manly huddle practising their whip technique. Forest Gump was dancing with Holly Golightly, and the sight of Hannibal Lecter groping Hermione Granger was plain creepy. 'No way!' was all anyone could say as Trey, the magician, smashed Marilyn Monroe's phone with a hammer, then brought it back to life with a gentle rub. And Dragon, the fire eater, nearly set his tiny loin cloth on fire.

Leila was stunning in her Jessica Rabbit costume, her ample boobs popping out and making eyes pop. Grace and Ajay were Ghostbusting, and I was pleased with my space outfit – bikini top and mini skirt made of foil, worn over a gold lurex body suit. Until the foil started crinkling and ripping. I was aiming for groovy Barbarella but ended up a Pound Shop hula girl.

We were having a quiet moment on a sofa, watching the dancing, when Leila persisted with her dating idea.

'Why don't you just try it? One date every week for a year. You might find your soulmate,' she said.

'I know you want me to be happy and I love you for it, but I'm perfectly fine as I am. I don't need a man to make me complete,' I said.

'You might not need a man, but you do need to open your heart again, Sophia Stone. It's been over a year since you-know-who … you run at 100 miles an hour and pretend you're fine, but I know you better. You deserve to be happy and loved.'

'I am happy and loved. I don't need a man for that. And don't mention The Traitor. I DO NOT want to hear his name.'

'We can't let Ro … sorry, The Traitor, ruin your life. He's not worth…'

'Just stop, Leila. Stop.' I showed her my palm, and she backed off about him, but not before reminding me how broken I was this time last year. We were quiet for a bit.

'So, what about the dating idea? Why not just make a New Year resolution and do it?'

'Because one date a week sounds like hard work, and I really need to concentrate on breathing life back into my business.'

'Come on, you don't need to worry about your business. Your clients love you. They won't even buy washing up liquid without checking with you first in case it ruins the magic Sophia vibe in their kitchen. And what about the couple who called you from Colombia to ask if you approved of a wall hanging they wanted to buy for their bedroom?'

'I know. I love it when they come to me for emergency interior design,' I said, smiling.

'See, you'll be fine. And you can always reinvent yourself. How many career changes so far?' She started counting on her fingers. 'There was the PR agency, the jewellery store, the wedding planning company, the management consultancy phase … what was that job you did after uni?'

'Trainee archaeological illustrator. That was a great job. I got to travel around the world and draw ancient artefacts.'

'I was so jealous of you. I was stuck in a dead-end shit job filling in forms for a book wholesaler. But you inspired me to take a risk and follow my dreams,' she said.

'Aw, you never told me that before. It's so lovely to hear I inspired you. And look at you now. A successful sculptor and painter.' We hugged in mutual appreciation. Leila's been a constant nearly all my life. I don't know what I'd do without her.

'Hey, don't forget I'm also lay therapist to my clients so that's seven careers to be precise.'

'OK, then, treat finding a man like one of your projects. I

challenge you to do it. It'll be so much fun, and I bet you'd like more sex,' Leila said, winking.

'Guilty as charged, your honour.'

This morning, I'm clear about what I want. Spending yet another New Year crying in the loo made me realise relationships are not worth the heartache. I'll take on the dating challenge and give it my best shot, but I'll focus on having sex. Sod finding a soulmate. Sod finding Mr Right. Sod finding The One. I don't need to hand over the keys to my heart and happiness to a man in order to enjoy life.

Is it weird to have sex just to avoid feeling too much? Yes, putting it like that does sound a bit bonkers, but millions of people have casual sex just to experience a temporary, often false, intimacy. Why can't I turn that on its head and use sex to avoid intimacy? I have to protect myself from more damage, even if it means settling for less. One day I might rip off the plaster and risk it all again, but right now, I'm taking back control while keeping my soft core well-hidden.

My life is perfect, so why spoil it? I'll stay single and still live life to the full, and if I'm lucky, I'll meet fifty-two sex machines. This year I'll master the art of having marvellous, mind-blowing sex without emotional entanglement. At the end of the year, I will have had the best sex ever and spiced up this year's diary. Win-win. Kill two birds with one Sophia Stone.

To check everything was in working order for my upcoming busy sex life, I dug out my old vibrator from the back of the wardrobe, changed the batteries, and gave it a whirl – nothing like morning sex even if it is with a mechanical toy – and I can confirm I am still a sexual being. A sexy goddess. At sixty. No velour slippers for me, thank you.

P.S. I can't help wondering. Is it actually possible to keep dating, have sex and not fall in love? I'm determined to prove it is.

12.30pm

I couldn't face driving, so I'm on the train up to Harpenden, going to yet another New Year family lunch on my own. I have a love-hate relationship with this time of the year. It's exciting to think about all the positive possibilities a new year brings, but it also makes me reflect on life and I don't always want to face up to some of those reflections.

Mum and Dad are nearly eighty and who knows how much longer they'll be with us. I remember when they both turned seventy, the sense of their mortality hit me hard, and I realised I could lose them at any time even if they are exceptionally healthy. It made me want to cherish my time with them even more. I know I still crave their praise like a little girl, yearning for their attention.

When I was in Bali, the group therapy leader asked me if I felt excluded as a child because my parents were so in love and into each other. And did I feel lonely because I didn't have a sibling for the first ten years? Rubbish. He also suggested I had mummy issues, whatever that means. I do sometimes feel I'm not enough and I have to bite my tongue when Mum obsesses over my weight or looks, but all mums do that, don't they?

My niece and nephew are growing into lovely young adults. I'm so happy Sara's kids bring her joy, though it stings when she lords her perfect family over me. Our sibling rivalry has always been balanced by our once close bond, but recently it's made me feel like the inadequate older sister who just can't get her personal life together. I long for the days she looked at me with admiration instead of reproach. I try to connect with her but increasingly she keeps me at arm's length, probably because she feels guilty for what she did. I wonder if we'll get sweet Sara or sour Sara today.

And me. I'm so lucky I have a great career and loyal friends like Leila, Grace and Ace. On this sixty-first year of my life, I'm entering a new phase and it's daunting not knowing what's ahead. Part of me wants to wallow in the past, to still be angry at

The Traitor for his treachery. For his cheating. For his breaking my heart.

I couldn't talk to Leila about him last night, because even now, over a year since we broke up, thinking about him makes my stomach turn, the bitter taste of infidelity and disappointment lingering in my mouth. Much as I try, I can't unsee finding him in bed – in my bed – with someone else. But unsee it I must. The sharp pain has dulled now, but it still hides inside, waiting to pounce every now and then. He's left a permanent scar and I'm wary of fully exposing it again. I miss that unguarded part of me but protecting myself means living without abandon. I won't let anyone break me so cruelly again.

11.30pm

When I arrived at the house earlier, Dad was putting out the rubbish. He looks frailer, and his hair is the colour of snow. It's hard to imagine he was once a tough young officer leading a platoon of soldiers. My heart broke a little bit.

Sara was exhausting and yes, a total bitch. Forget sweet or sour. We got downright nasty Sara today.

'Decided to spend New Year's Day with your family for a change then?' she said as soon as I walked in.

Jack and Charlotte jumped up excited and gave me lovely hugs after taking their presents. I bought them the clothes they'd asked for, which looked exactly like the baggy sweatpants and top combo they were already wearing. They're not so playful now they're teenagers but still a joy. How can such sweet kids have sprung from Sara's loins?

'I was only away for one New Year,' I said as I gave Mum a hug.

'Hmm. You look good in that dress,' Sara said.

Wow, a compliment.

'Aw, thanks, Sara,' I said, my face warming up.

'I just don't understand why you can't get a man,' she added.

I should have known there'd be a sting in the tail. Mum and

Dad looked at each other, as if to say 'not again'. Mum went into hyper mode.

'Have a drink, darling. And there's food on the table. Don't eat all the chocolates though. You want to keep that lovely slim figure. Come and help me set up this iPad,' she said.

I sat between Mum and Dad for a while and showed them how to use it. Sara was quiet, Laurence watched TV, and the kids were on their phones.

'Anyone made any New Year resolutions?' Mum said.

'I have,' I said.

'Are you giving up chocolate? Do try and keep to it this time, darling. Remember that year you ate a whole tin of Quality Street in two days?' Mum said and puffed out her cheeks, mimicking being fat. Sara laughed – the skinny laugh of someone who's never had to watch their weight.

'No. I've decided to go on a date every week for a year.'

'Woohoo! Go Sophia,' Laurence said. Sara gave him a dirty look and he hung his head in shame.

'That's undignified for a sixty-year-old,' Sara said. I bit my lip and ignored her.

Mum's eyes darted between me and Sara. 'No, it's not. It'll be fun for your sister. Good for you, Sophia,' she said. I showed her a few profiles on a dating app, while Sara stared into the distance. 'Look at all these men, Henry. They all want to go out with our Sophia.'

'That's nice … how's work, Sophie love?' Dad asked.

'I'm seeing a potential new client this week. I hope he's not into wallpaper. I don't want a divorce citing irreconcilable wallpaper differences on my conscience,' I said, laughing.

Sara rolled her eyes. 'Yeah, messing about with wallpaper and cushions sounds very stressful. Being a nurse in a GP practice, now THAT'S stressful, but you don't hear me complaining,' she complained.

'That is complaining?' Laurence said, and Sara glared at him again, so he went back to watching TV.

'Did you remember to bring your travel photos?' Dad said.

'Yes, I've finally sorted them. You'd love the Himalayas, Dad,' I said.

Everyone gathered round to look at my pictures except Sara, who started scrolling on her phone.

'Life's too short to sit through other people's holiday photos,' Sara said.

'Sophia's not other people,' Mum said.

'Tremendous,' Dad said after gasping at the majestic Himalayan mountains. 'Look Betty, love, we could go there for my eightieth,' Dad said as Mum's eyes widened.

God help us.

Sara piped in out of nowhere. 'I don't know why you can't hold onto a man, but I'm just grateful you didn't come back with a new one. I can't take the drama of another breakup.'

I was stunned by her cruelty. She's always had a tendency to be judgemental, but lately her words have a sharper edge. I withdraw more with each caustic remark. I wish we could be how we used to be before resentment built an impenetrable wall between us.

I recreated my NYE disappearing act and hid my humiliation in the bathroom. Is it wrong to want to strangle your sister? Where is the sweet girl who used to save up her pocket money to buy birthday presents for me? The one who fought off a mugger in Barcelona because he'd tried to grab my bag. More than anything, I want that sister back.

Mum came in after a while and gave me a hug.

'You mustn't cry, darling. Don't mind your sister. She doesn't mean it. I think she's going through a rough patch with Laurence. She's so tensed up all the time. Why don't you talk to her? You're so good at helping people with their relationships. You always know the exact right thing to say. She'll listen to you.'

'I've tried, Mum. Sara just makes excuses not to see me.'

'Well, try again. Now fix your makeup, darling. We can't have you looking like that,' she said, true to form. I know she wants me to look my best, but still … at least she approves of my new trim figure, so I didn't have to suffer any 'observations' about my body.

Mum is right about one thing. I am the CEO of Lay Therapy Services PLC. For some reason, people do ask for my advice and listen. How many times have I helped Leila over the years with her husbands? And I can usually bring harmony to my squabbling clients. How come I can give relationship advice to others with surgical precision, when I'm so clueless about my own love life? I should make a concerted effort to apply my brilliant advice to myself. But that's irrelevant now I've given up love for good. My advice to myself is: have fun. And lots of sex.

After lunch, I fell asleep while watching TV and I had one of my sofa dreams. I was in an orgy with fifty-two men in an S&M club, and I said, 'This is going to be the year of amazing sex. This year my sex life will explode. I will be born again. I will not be a born-again virgin. I will get back onto the dick wagon.' I woke up feeling flushed and sweaty. I looked around and there was only Laurence there on the other sofa.

'Did you discover Jesus while you were travelling, Sophia? You were mumbling about the Virgin Mary and being born again,' he said.

Wednesday, 2 January, 6.30am

First day back at work in this new year. I missed my morning routine while I was away. I love my quiet cup of coffee, contemplating the day ahead. Working with my clients gives me a sense of satisfaction that's hard to explain. There's a kind of alchemy in taking their wants, combining different materials, mingling light and colour, and visualising the finished creation. It's like therapy, but with colours, textures, and fabrics.

Some people (like my sister) think my job is mere decorating, but for me, it's more about creating a home that people will cherish. They let me into their lives and homes and, sometimes, even their hearts. I know I'm not changing the world or doing an important job like a teacher or doctor but knowing that I've contributed in a small way to improving other people's lives makes me proud. And I love the look of wonder on my clients' faces when the transformation is complete.

Right, time to get going, otherwise, tomorrow's meeting won't live up to my glowing description.

11.30pm

It's a lovely new year and a lovely new me. I've made appointments for a facial, eyebrow shaping and haircut, to get myself in tiptop shape for the dating challenge. I might even dye the silver pubes pink to spice things up.

To kickstart the dating project, I wrote a poem. There won't be any willies in this diary like my teenage ones (do you remember my poem about Premature Paul in sixth form?). No, this diary will be about proper, plentiful adult dicks. I'm going to call a dick a dick, so to speak.

> *It's time to end the dick drought*
> *Dating more men is what it's all about*
> *Will the dates be fascinating and super fun?*
> *Or will I get more satisfaction from a cream bun?*
> *Will a kiss turn one of them into a prince?*
> *Or will I wish I'd offered him breath mints?*
> *Will he give me his full attention?*
> *Or just be after my pension?*
> *I hope he won't be too old to get it up*
> *I hope he's not a member of the impotence club*
> *I don't mind if he's of the older vintage*
> *If his equipment hasn't suffered from shrinkage*
> *I know I want the ideal man and then some*
> *Or at the very least someone to make me come*

Shelley and Byron have nothing to fear.

Thursday, 3 January, 11.30pm

Went to see a potential client today. Andrew, a tech whiz kid in his thirties, is the embodiment of geek chic. He must have made a mint writing apps if he could afford his amazing waterside apartment near the Tate Modern. He wanted me to design a new kitchen for him and asked if it's possible to have heating under a marble surface. I told him underfloor heating is fine for marble. He stared at the floor for a second.

'What if it's not under the floor?' he asked.

'Where were you thinking of? On the walls?'

'Erm … no … I was thinking under an island worktop? Erm … my partner likes the feel of marble on her skin. You know, on her back?'

'Oh … oh I see.' I paused. 'I've never been asked for that before, but I'm sure I can make it work.'

'I think you might be the woman for the job then,' he said as we shook hands.

Hurrah. After being away for so long, I need more new clients like Andrew if I'm to get my business back on track. Most of my lovely clients have been waiting for me to come back, though I bet the thing they've missed most is not just my design skills but the free couples counselling I throw in as part of the service. The happiest of couples can easily turn into feuding enemies when it comes to deciding on the right shade of white. An interior designer is for life, not just for wallpaper.

P.S. I wish I had someone who cared enough to warm the marble for me.

Friday, 4 January, 11.30pm

I'm all apped up. Joined London Soulmates and Ladybird.

Me

- Height: Can't reach the top shelf
- Age: 60 (should I have lied?)
- Hair: Honey (out of a bottle)
- Eyes: Twinkling
- Physical attributes: Fit
- Education: Swot
- Superpower: Photographic memory for handsomeness
- 'Truly incredible woman,' *The New York Times*
- 'Greatest interior designer of our generation,' *Elle Decoration*
- 'She's my kickass heroine,' *Wonder Woman*
- 'I work hard every day to look like her,' JLo
- 'Our highest scoring member ever,' Mensa
- 'She has a great sense of humour,' Dawn French

You

- Age: 45–61 (just so I can say I'm up for older men)
- Height: Must help with the top shelf
- Education: Swottier the better
- Loves: fun, friends, frolics, films, family, and alliteration

I called Leila to get her opinion.

'Honey, is it a quick one? There's a gorgeous man here longing for me,' she said from her bed and turned the camera to Jude who scowled.

'What do you think of this for my dating profile? *Desired qualities for a man: articulate, adventurous, glass half-full, smells nice, energetic, fit, intelligent, youthful, sexy, confident, funny, attractive, open-minded. Any superpower a bonus.* What do you think? Is that enough?'

Jude scoffed in the background. What's his problem?

'Yes, it's enough. In the same way that Imelda Marcos's shoe collection was enough.' She then grappled with Jude who grabbed and switched off the phone.

Rude.

Is that too much to ask for? I don't think so. I'm getting excited about meeting lots of lovely men. I want someone to long for me. And hopefully there'll be sex soon. Luckily, menopause has not affected my vagina. It's still moist and willing.

Saturday, 5 January, 1.30pm

First meeting of the Brunch Bunch this year. We were missing Grace who went to Monte Carlo on New Year's Day, but Ace is in town after visiting family in Jamaica, and he came along, though I'm not sure why as he kept fidgeting, twisting his wedding band and sighing like he didn't want to be there. Usually, he rocks the 'just got out of bed' tousled look with his carefully unruly afro and silver jewellery, but today he actually looked like he'd just got out of bed, with puffy eyes and a jumper that had seen better days. I put my arm around him and asked if he was OK, and he said he was just tired. When I mentioned his trip to Jamaica, he said, 'Just the usual'. I mouthed to Leila, 'What's up with him?' but she shrugged. We watched him for a bit, but he was distracted and didn't notice.

'Thanks for all the lovely men you tried to palm off on me at the party,' I said to Leila.

I'd been enthusiastic when Leila told me she was introducing me to a few single men at her NYE party and was hoping I'd hit it off with one of them. OMG. How could my best friend think they were good matches for me? I appreciate your dedication to finding a man for me, Leila, but can you please find someone who makes my cheeks flush and my vagina throb? The Divorcee was rather attractive until he started telling me he was exhausted by his children, and desperate to find 'help'. I thought I was being interviewed for the missionary position until I realised he wanted to fill a nanny position. Then there was Cement Man. How much can one person talk about his cement company? Quite a lot, apparently. When he finished his story about an 'absolutely hilarious concrete pouring mix-up', I thought I might be petrified.

And last and least was Dick Pic Man, who decided to Airdrop a picture of himself to me. Later he crept up behind me and whispered, 'Would you like to see the real thing?' Now, I like to look at a penis as much as the next person, but not as a calling card. I overcame my ingrained tendency to be polite and said, 'No, I don't want to look at your shortcomings,' and walked off in a huff.

Leila shrugged and turned to Ace. 'I invited all the single men I know. Malcolm, the divorced one, is interesting. He runs a gallery in Mayfair and might be exhibiting my new sculptures, but she didn't like him.'

'I see. The deal was I babysit his children and he gives you free gallery space?'

'Ha ha, very funny, Sophia,' she said. 'Where do you think she should go to meet guys, Ace?'

'I can't help you there. My last date was with Kelly,' he said, barely smiling, then he looked around with darting eyes.

'You must have done something right. Here you are together, thirty happy years later,' I said. He let out a long sigh, said 'Hmm' then studied the menu even though he'd already ordered.

'Anyway, there's no need for any more matchmaking, thanks. I've registered on two dating apps already, so I'm starting my New Year's resolution as of today.'

'What New Year resolution?' Ace asked.

'Leila challenged me to go on one date every week for a year.'

'That's my girl. You'll find love in no time,' Leila said. She was pleased with herself for talking me into the dating challenge, just like she was at school when she persuaded me to spend my pocket money on crisps so she could win the full set of Troll Dolls.

'Oh no, I'm not looking for love. It'll be pure fun and sex. I don't need the relationship stuff. Ever again.'

Leila's jaw dropped and Ace stared into his empty coffee cup. Sometimes he still looks as shy as he did when we were kids playing in each other's back gardens. He was always the one to look away first when we had staring contests.

'What? Who are you and what have you done with Sophia?' she said, agog, and felt my forehead pretending to check my temperature.

I smiled.

'You're just afraid of getting hurt again. Forget about the past, honey, and look to the future. Anyway, I know what you're like. You'll soon change your tune when you meet someone you like,' she said, satisfied with her analysis of my situation.

She doesn't know the new me. I'm absolutely certain I don't want a relationship. That ship has sailed. I'm through with it. It's done and dusted. I've reached the end of the road.

I didn't want to discuss it, so I started reading out the 'Dick Drought' poem. Ace went to the loo after the first verse, probably embarrassed by the girly talk.

'I love it. You'll be fighting them off, honey,' Leila said, laughing.

'Not sure about that. That's more your department. You always had more boys after you at school than I could dream of, and you're on your fourth husband. How do you do it?'

She wet a finger and sizzled it on her arm. 'Seriously, look at you. Your body was off the scale in the Barbarella outfit. You're smart, you have your own business, and you can write a funny poem. You're an absolute catch. What's not to like?' she said as Ace slid back into his seat. 'She's a goddess, isn't she, Ace?'

Ace nodded.

'I love you guys,' I said.

'And we love you. Your trouble is you're too picky,' she said.

'I lied. I only love you,' I stage-whispered in Ace's ear.

Sunday, 6 January, 10.30am

Two likes!

Just two measly likes. Wow, I am popular. I distinctly remember how it was for Leila when she started dating after she lost Darius. She was inundated with offers and had to narrow her filters to fend them off. When I entered my criteria, the app kept flashing a warning, 'Your chances of meeting The One will increase if you have fewer filters'. It was basically saying, 'You'll never meet anyone if you're that picky, love'. I was being patronised by an app. So, I left it as open as I could bear. And still just two likes – not even a message.

My first liker was recently divorced and said his children had persuaded him to join a dating site. Pity they didn't persuade him to clean up for the photos. All the pictures had been taken on his sofa, wearing grimy tracky bottoms and surrounded by crisps packets, which didn't dovetail with his claims of liking travel, the gym, and good food.

No, I don't fancy dating a crisps receptacle, thank you. I deserve better. I want someone who tries harder to be the best version of themselves. Why aren't I getting a higher quality and quantity of likes? Is there something wrong with me or am I being too sensitive? I know I have to grow a thick skin if I'm going on dating apps, but the approval-seeking Sophia buried deep inside me yearns to be wanted. I must not allow that Sophia to scupper my year of dating. Will get a grip and continue work on cultivating a tougher hide.

The second liker could have been a dream for all I know, but like a lot of others, he wore a hat and sunglasses, so I have no idea what he looks like or what he's hiding. #NoHatsPlease #EnoughWithTheSunglasses

1.30pm

Checked profile. No more likes. Why? Is Leila right? Am I too picky? I don't think so. I just have standards which I'm not going to drop in order to get a man. Much as I want to be picked, to be the popular hot sixty-year-old everyone messages, any encounters have to feel right for me.

11.30pm

Felt sad earlier remembering lovely Darius. Leila was so happy when they got married, especially after the painful divorces from Brian and Ali. It's shocking how life can change in an instant. A lorry's brakes fail, and your husband is gone. I thought she'd never get over it, but she bounced back and started dating after six months. She's just not happy when she's single, and her need to find love overrides everything else.

Still, I wish she hadn't rushed into marrying Jude after just a three-month romance. They were all loved up and cooing over each other on New Year's Eve, and I'm thrilled to see her so happy again, but I'm worried it won't last. She gives her heart so freely. I wish I could protect her from ever getting hurt again, but all I can do is be there if it falls apart. And at the same time, I so admire her eagerness to take another leap, as scary as it is. Maybe someday I'll find the courage to risk my heart again too, but not yet. Not for quite some time.

Seeing them together reminded me of those early blissful years of marriage, when I basked in the glory of James's love, and I was so sure we would be together forever. We were the golden couple: in our twenties, successful, confident, and deeply in love. And when the time came to make our coupledom into a family, we took it for granted that it would work out for us, like it does for millions of others. We were trying for a baby in blissful ignorance that it was never going to happen. When the doctors said I had polycystic ovaries, I had no idea what it meant and that eventually it would destroy our relationship. But after the infertility diagnosis, something shifted between us. The light of love in James's eyes gradually faded, replaced by disappointment and blame.

We'd tried for so long, but after a while, when each month

brought blood over and over again, our hopes and dreams curdled into resentment, sadness, and accusation. He denied it, but I felt his growing bitterness towards me. He blamed me and I blamed myself. In the end, he couldn't forgive me, and he left me for someone who could give him what he wanted most in life: a baby of his own. His flesh and blood to take his genes forward into infinity.

The day I came home to find him gone crushed my spirit. For months, I wandered our empty house like a ghost, sobbing into his abandoned shirts, tormented by my failure and the void where our child should have been. My soul felt fractured, my hopes of a family destroyed. My biggest fear had come true. I was incapable of the most natural thing in the world because my body had betrayed me and there was nothing I could do about it. I pictured myself elderly and alone, with no family to comfort me. Perhaps I didn't deserve a child, or I was being punished for some unknown failing within me. I thought no one would ever want me again, and I was destined to grow old alone without the comfort of love.

I was distraught for a long time but as the months passed, I forgave him, and myself, and let go of my anger. I'm at peace with my body now, not only for how it looks but for what it can and cannot do. I refuse to be defined by an absence, but every now and then, seeing happy couples triggers that old grief, reminding me of the life I could have had but lost. But I believe it also pushes me to live a bold adventurous life. I'm more than the sum of my biology. I can still have a full and happy life, and nurture through my friendships and my work.

The hole in my centre is benign now. It's there but it doesn't hurt. Not often. Time may have eased the pain, but the insecurity has been fixed into my psyche. I developed industrial strength emotional armour so I could avoid ever exposing myself so fully again. Were all my relationships tainted after that? Did the men I was with think me unlovable or did I push them away at the first hint of real intimacy? I wish I knew.

P.S. One more liker but he had no photo. Why do they do that?

Anyway, I don't need a man when my menopausal internal central heating keeps me so warm.

Monday, 7 January, 11.30pm

This morning, I discovered a new white hair on my chin. It had grown at least two centimetres long overnight, the devious creep. I hate that feeling when you rub an exploratory hand over your face and get stabbed by an overzealous protrusion. Even worse, you know it'll jab your friends when you kiss their cheeks. I value the wisdom age has brought, and the way I just don't care about how I look as much as I did when I was younger. It's liberating, comforting, and life-affirming. But piercing insidious fat white chin hairs are a step too far.

TWO

The Opera Buff
___

Tuesday, 8 January, 9.30am

OOH THINGS ARE LOOKING UP. Five likes.

Wednesday, 9 January, 10.30pm

I got home at 7am this morning, head fuzzy and body thinking, OMG, not again. At some point in my life, I'll grow up and be sensible, but for now my brain thinks I'm in my twenties. Unfortunately, my body disagrees. I had to cancel Cassandra and Edward's design meeting because 'I was making an emergency site visit to another project'. Baaad interior designer.

Yesterday, after finishing my dance exercises, Grace called. She said Tayo was sick, and Ajay was looking after him. She had a spare ticket to the opera and begged me to go with her. I've never been interested in opera but thought I should try it at least once. And I'd be helping out Grace, who doesn't get out much. I don't know how she does it, raising two kids and managing a meteoric career. I know she's something big in derivatives, but I have no clue what it entails. Nor does Ajay for that matter, despite being Number One Best Husband Ever.

There was no time for a shower. I discarded my dance Lycra,

pulled on my fitted red wool dress and ankle boots, spritzed on lots of perfume, and hopped on the tube to Covent Garden.

'What's that smell?' the little girl in an astronaut outfit sitting next to me asked while staring at me. I hoped it was my perfume, not exercise juice. Her mum pulled her away.

I got off the tube early at Leicester Square, hoping the walk to the Royal Opera House might blow away the offending smells. I spotted Grace by the entrance. She sniffed as she kissed my cheeks. By 7.15pm, we were taking our expensive front stalls seats, paid for by a grateful client of Grace's, who'd also ordered champagne for the interval.

'Work is an absolute fucking nightmare at the moment,' volunteered Grace. 'My boss is a complete pig. He has not caught up with the twenty-first century. This morning, he said I looked hot in this dress while standing way too close to me. I told him he was invading my personal space and he laughed and said, 'political correctness gone mad'. Sometimes I wonder if it's all worth it,' she huffed.

I thought I'd cheer her up, comedy being my stock response to stressful situations. I'd noticed a man on his own with an empty seat between us. He was studying his programme intently. I nudged Grace.

'Watch this.'

'Have you been stood up then?' I asked.

He looked up, startled. 'No, well, yes, I suppose. Last-minute change of plan.'

'You're in luck. We had a last-minute change of plan too, or I wouldn't be here sitting next to you.' I caressed the empty velvet seat suggestively. He blushed and smiled.

'I'm an opera virgin. You look experienced. Can you give me the benefit of your experience later and fill me in?' I said as his neck turned red. 'About the opera, of course,' I added. I could feel Grace's body shaking next to me as she stifled laughter. Job done.

As the lights dimmed, Grace whispered, 'You're so naughty.'

'He's not bad-looking,' I whispered back, thinking my evening of culture may have dating potential. I took Grace's programme and fanned my hot flush like a fierce flamenco dancer. The Royal Opera House's mixture of ornate gilded mouldings, plush red velvet, and warm lighting made the whole auditorium experience magical. Of course, it helped that there was a little frisson in the air. When the lights came on for the first interval, he smiled back then stared at his feet.

'What do you think of *Carmen*, opera virgin?' Grace said at the bar later, laughing. Her mood was lighter as she poured the champagne. A half glass for her, I noticed. I watched as she went to a quiet corner to call Ajay. As always, she killed it with her work outfit in an expensive-looking fuchsia pink fitted dress and killer snakeskin heels. I wonder what her grey suit brigade colleagues think about it. Not that there was any danger of a Black Nigerian woman blending into a sea of white male faces. And how does she make it to the gym at 6.30 every morning? I only manage to dress myself by 9am.

By the time she came back, I was feeling the effects of the champagne, and I sat through the second part not absorbing much. I polished off most of the bottle at the second interval and wished I'd had something to eat.

'Are you enjoying the show?' I slurred at the man when we returned to our seats.

'Yes, *Carmen* is one of my favourites.' He watched me with amusement while I squinted at him with drunken eyes.

'Your date was foolish to stand you up,' I huffed, then leaned over and slurred, 'I think you're rather cute.' The lights were dimming, and Grace shushed me. She and the woman behind me had to shush me a few more times during the third act, especially when I screamed at Carmen's brutal murder, then sobbed.

After the show, I wanted to go for another drink, but Grace had an early morning meeting. I told her to go on home as I was heading for the loo queue.

'Make sure you text me when you get home, OK?' she said.

'Yes miss,' I said with a military salute, mixing my metaphors. 'Thanks for inviting me.' As she walked away, I shouted, 'I love you, Grace.'

'I love you too, you idiot,' she shouted back, laughing.

When I came out a few minutes later, a man's voice said, 'We meet again.' It was The Opera Buff.

Hello! I thought.

'Can I buy you that drink you wanted?' he asked.

Ooh, he'd been listening to our conversation, the naughty man.

'That would be lovely,' I said, fiddling with my curls.

Earlier I'd thought he was in his late forties, but now he looked older in his clichéd Opera Buff attire of velvet jacket, silk scarf, and fedora hat. But the rosé-champagne-tinted-glasses helped me to overlook the bad outfit. We went to a pub where, over a glass of wine, he told me he was an art dealer. He had Beethoven hair, ruddy skin, warm hazel eyes, and what I later found to be a developing wine paunch. He told me my eyes were sweet and glossy like honey, my pout was pure Brigitte Bardot and my body would make JLo proud, which was probably why, when the pub lights flashed at midnight, I agreed to go for coffee at his place.

His flat was in a converted warehouse. There were colourful canvasses on the white walls and the decor was understated. So why the hammy Oscar Wilde outfit, I wondered as I flopped on the squishy emerald-green sofa. More velvet.

Carrying two cups of coffee, he sat rather close to me, put them down on the Noguchi glass table and announced, 'I want to make love to you to the music of *Carmen*.' I didn't spot any blushing that time. Excited by the prospect of ending the dick drought, I giggled and said, 'Ooh, yes please. As long as you don't recreate *Carmen* and kill me.'

Then I remembered I was wearing the knickers Leila gave me for my sixtieth with 'Full Bush' emblazoned on the front. She thought they were perfect because I refuse to subject myself to the excruciating pain of having my pubic hair waxed. I'm happy with my pubes and if men don't like it, tough. No man is worth that much pain.

Anyway, by that time, The Opera Buff had deftly manoeuvred me onto his bed behind flowing chiffon curtains and was well on his way to removing my dress. I needn't have worried. He grinned with delight at my grooming declaration. It obviously bushed his buttons.

He reached over to the bedside table and pressed on a remote, and magically *Carmen* came on. Had he done this before? I tittered on the bed as he continued his seduction by next removing his own clothes dramatically and throwing them around the room as he sang his way through 'La Habanera'. He tapped and stroked my feet, legs and tummy to the rhythm of the music, ending the crescendo of each verse with a tweak of my nipples and a type of horn noise. That was weird, but I went with it.

I hummed along to the music, gesticulating my arms and legs like a quadruped orchestra conductor in full flow, as I lay on my back, and let him play my body. He kissed me as he drew breath between each verse.

At the end of the song, he went to the wardrobe and threw on a cape (he'd definitely done that before) and rushed at me, mimicking fake bull's horns with his fingers as 'Toreador' started playing. He cradled me like a fallen Carmen and touched his cheek against mine as he sang (ouch, it hurt my ear).

Then he gently lowered me and made love to me. If this had been a movie, we would have had beautifully choreographed orgasms to the song finale, but we passed out from our exertions quickly, and the song climaxed without an audience.

I woke up at 6.30am, glanced over at the sleeping toreador, and winced. I sneaked out, shuddering at the fedora and the velvet jacket hanging by the door, and did the walk of shame to my taxi. I checked my phone. Three texts and five missed calls from Grace. Oh God. I sent her an apologetic text saying I'd passed out when I got home. I didn't want to share my night of opera fuckery just yet.

There was an opera buff who liked to bang
To Bizet's Carmen *as he swung his wang*
He charged like a bull
Gave his penis a pull
And it was over before the fat lady sang

When I got home, Joy was already hoovering. Why had she come at 7am?

'Sophia not come home last night? Been with a man? Sophia looks bad.'

'Yes, Sophia had a lovely time. Thanks for asking.'

She went to the kitchen and came back with a glass of water and paracetamols and put them in front of me as she sniffed at me.

'Sophia need shower,' she said.

P.S. Does last night count as date number one?

Thursday, 10 January, 11.30pm

Despite wincing at the sleeping Opera Buff, I confess my opera initiation was fun. And it was sex for the first time in ages. Hurrah. But I have to admit to being put off by his foppish fashion sense, which surely makes me sound superficial and shallow. I agree I should look beyond the outerwear and concentrate on the man inside. But I also know I wouldn't have let that man inside me if I hadn't been propelled into his arms by copious amounts of alcohol. He seemed attractive in the heady atmosphere of the Royal Opera House, but in the cold light of day, I knew he wasn't for me. And let's face it, the nipple tweaking and horn noises were a bit freaky. No, I will just look back at that night as champagne-fuelled operatic fun of the dick-drought ending variety, never to be repeated.

Friday, 11 January, 11.00am

Just arranged my first Ladybird date for tomorrow afternoon. It's with a very young man (when did a thirty-eight-year-old become 'a very young man'? Where did the years go?). I'm excited and flattered to be asked out by a fit millennial. But that's the wonder of dating apps. Anything or anyone is possible if you're open to it. The trouble is, he wanted to go ice skating and I didn't want to appear unadventurous. But now I'm thinking of all the times I've tried doing anything requiring good balance – skiing, roller blading, skateboarding, etc. – and all I remember is being wobbly, terrified, and falling over. AND I'm sixty years old with menopausal bones.

P.S. Ace has asked me to go round on Sunday. Wants to talk. Hope he's OK. He wasn't his usual bright self last week.

THREE

The Ice Skater

Saturday, 12 January, 1.30pm

GRACE BROUGHT Mia to brunch today. I can't believe she's a teenager already. She's so cute and confident. I couldn't help thinking, if things had worked out for me, I might have a twenty-something daughter or son now, and maybe more younger ones. My daughter could be sitting with us right now. A member of the Brunch Bunch. Wouldn't that be something? A completely different life. I might even be a grandmother and looking after their kids instead of going on a date today. But I can't let myself dwell on that for too long. Thinking of what could have been is surely the path to unhappiness.

I snapped out of it and told them about my upcoming date this afternoon.

'You're going on a date? Aren't you, like, too old for that?' Mia said, then looked perplexed when we all laughed.

I recounted the gory details about The Opera Buff while she was in the loo. Leila was pleased I'd had sex. Finally. Grace was obsessed with the cape for some reason. She said she can't watch *Carmen* ever again.

10.30pm

The best bit about the date was that I didn't break any bones. But that could be because what I did for an hour on the ice rink could hardly be classed as skating. Close up, the rink was huge, the sun was shining, the skaters were happy, and there were loads of kids holding onto cute plastic penguins for balance.

My date said he couldn't believe I'd never tried ice skating, while I delayed the inevitable by taking an awfully long time putting on my skates.

'I'm terrified and a bit rubbish at anything needing good balance,' I confessed.

'Don't worry. I'll look after you,' he said. Sweet.

I stood on the blades, with his help, and thought it didn't feel too bad. He held my hands and I had to look up at him as he was pretty tall. Height, tick. He had light brown hair, cut short on the sides and curly on top, lovely green eyes and a warm smile. Cute face, tick. I was fine with him giving me a double spin. Clutching his arm with both hands, I walked onto the rink heading straight for the side railings for support. It was totally different being on ice. I didn't like feeling so unstable. The idea of skating round the rink with him was appealing, but my hands protested by supergluing themselves to the railings.

'You go round a few times and let me try on my own first,' I insisted, and watched him skate away gracefully while I gripped the sides with both hands for dear life, facing away from the rink and barely managing to stay vertical. Then my feet flailed, and I slipped backwards, fully stretched, belly down, my hands still holding on and my feet trying to run away from me. My arms are toned and strong from carrying my rucksack while I travelled but this was a different kind of workout. Also, how was I supposed to be sexy and flirty from that position?

'Do you need help to get up?' a boy asked (yes, a boy – he couldn't have been more than ten years old).

'Yes, please,' I whispered and reached out with one hand, but he pushed me up by my bottom until I was vertical. I wished I could melt into the ice and disappear.

The Ice Skater whooshed towards me and asked how I was getting on.

'I'm fine, just finding my feet. This is great. I love it,' I lied. 'You go on and I'll catch up.' That wasn't going to happen. If only I could have conquered my fear. I gave myself a pep talk and started, very slowly, to move around the rink still clutching the sides.

'Come on. You can do it,' shouted a dad grinning from the sidelines.

'Come on. You can do it,' copied the little boy in his lap.

I noticed I'd attracted quite an audience. I was a circus clown goofing around the stage with comedy falls while in the main show, acrobats performed amazing feats.

'Just let go. You'll be fine,' shouted a young woman, chuckling.

A rink steward came up to me. 'Do you want to try one of these? It'll help with your balance,' he said, offering a penguin.

The humiliation. I declined. But I wasn't ready to give up. Fired entirely by shame and needing to get away from my 'fans', I skidded around the edge until I came to the open entrance. After several false starts, I let go and rushed for the other side just as a group of five/six-year-olds were being ushered in.

I remember the rest of it in slow motion. As I hurled myself forward, I felt my skates slip backwards, and my arms instinctively reached for something to break my fall. Unfortunately, within my reach were two little boys. I grabbed one with each hand and took them down with me, their bright smiles contorting into grimaces as I did so. Next thing, I was sprawled on the ground face down, half on the ice and half outside the rink. The boys were crying and the other kids screaming as the mums rushed to their children and checked them for injuries. As I got up onto my knees, they turned their fury onto me.

'I'm so sorry, I didn't mean to do that, it was a reflex. Are they OK?' I asked.

'You should be ashamed of yourself. A grown woman using children to break her fall,' one of them said.

'Attacking children, more like,' fumed another.

Relieved that nobody was injured, I let them vent their anger, mainly because I was on my knees and couldn't get up. Then there was a whoosh, and The Ice Skater was next to me and helping me up. He told the mums to chill. It was an accident, and no harm was done.

'I think I want to leave,' I said, defeated.

We got our things and walked in silence to a nearby café where we sat stirring our coffees, neither knowing what to say. He was probably thinking the adventurous date hadn't quite worked out. Then our eyes met, and we burst out laughing.

'Those mums were fierce. They were about to shred you alive.'

'You rescued me from the mama bears. Thank you.' I sighed with exhaustion.

'Taking down two kids in one go. That's impressive,' he teased.

'Thanks for seeing the funny side. And sorry if the date didn't go as planned.' I wondered what he thought of me then.

'There's still time to get to know each other,' he said and winked. That was more like it.

'Do you always suggest sex on the first date?' I smiled and perused him.

'No, I didn't mean that.' He blushed. 'Honestly, a lot of women my age say they want a relationship but, in reality, just want one-night stands. That's not for me. Your profile was different. You sounded more … discerning. That's why I picked you, and I'm glad I did. This may sound old-fashioned, but I'm looking for a relationship and I don't want to rush into sex. I hope you feel the same way.'

Just my luck to find the only man in London who wants to wait for sex. Yes, he was attractive, and I could see myself rolling around with him. But I don't want to break anybody's heart any more than I want mine broken again. I definitely do not want a relationship. I'm not proud of what I did next. While he was paying the bill at the counter, and I was waiting for him outside, a bus pulled up and I jumped on it. He rushed out, calling after me, while I mouthed 'sorry' from the window as the bus started moving.

Sunday, 13 January, 9.30am

I'm aching all over from yesterday's stretching, hanging from railings and pushing over children. It was disappointing I couldn't conquer my fear of losing control, or I might have learnt ice skating. If I'd been a sexy skater instead of a comedy one, he might have got the hots for me and cut to the chase instead of wanting to wait. I acted like a teenager and ran away because I couldn't cope with the kind of intimacy he wanted. I'm not capable of making that sort of emotional commitment right now, but still, I could have handled it better. I should have thought about his feelings and explained myself instead of dashing off to avoid facing my inner turmoil. I texted him and apologised but he didn't reply. Who can blame him? I'm ashamed of myself.

P.S. I wonder if I'd have been a fierce mama bear. Yes, probably.

1.00pm

Joy came earlier. No mention of why she'd come again so soon, but she is the cleaning queen, so I didn't complain. If Aggie and Kim have me on their TV programme to ask, *How Clean is Your House?* I'd say, spotless, thank you. Her timekeeping drives me mad, but I missed her when she went home to the Philippines for a WHOLE month last year. I couldn't bear it if she stops coming now that she's set up her own cleaning company. I'm sure she does my house herself purely for sentimental reasons because I was her first client.

She peeped over my shoulder while I was checking out a profile.

'He too young, too handsome for Sophia.'

Shut. Up.

Going out to escape. I'm sure Ace wouldn't mind me being a bit early.

11.30pm

I walked through Clapham Common and arrived at Ace's half an hour early. As I approached the house, the door opened, and he came out with a younger woman who was wearing pink running gear and had a sleek blonde ponytail. They had a long embrace then looked into each other's eyes, and she stroked his cheek and kissed him on the forehead. It looked very intimate. I felt a body shudder of realisation. He's obviously having an affair, and so brazen to bring her to his house. I always had him down as one of the good guys. Why is he doing this to Kelly? I couldn't bear to confront him, so I hid behind a tree before he saw me, and thought he'd confide in me when I went back at the appointed time.

Ace looked ashen when he opened the door and didn't make eye contact. He made us coffee and we sat at the island eating Digestives. I couldn't bear the tension.

'What's going on, Ace? You look terrible.'

He rubbed the coffee stains on the marble worktop. 'I'm just going to say it … Kelly and I are getting divorced.' He looked up for my reaction. Open-mouthed, I dropped my biscuit into my mug. He fished it out for me with a spoon.

'What? Why? I don't understand,' I babbled. 'When did this happen? Is it because you're having an affair?'

'No!' he said, indignant.

Why was he lying to me? I told him he could tell me anything, but he was adamant he wasn't having an affair.

'Let's just say it was irreconcilable differences.'

'No, let's not just say that. Tell me what's happened, Ace.'

'I can't talk about it. It was … something unforgivable, a dreadful betrayal. She's moved out and my marriage is over. Please don't ask for details. Promise me you won't keep asking questions. I can't deal with it.'

I promised. I wanted to tell him I knew already, to shout at him for being stupid and ruining his marriage, but his eyes were moist and his mouth so droopy, I stopped myself and thought he'd tell me when he was ready. I wanted to console him, but I was also seething inside. I didn't move. He broke the silence.

'Jamaica was great.'

'Was it?'

'Yeah. Two of my orchestra mates went with me and we did a charity gig. Raised £5,000 for the local primary school.'

'You must be proud of yourself.'

'Aunt Cherry was proud. She still helps at the school.'

Awkward silence. I couldn't chitchat like nothing had happened.

'Anyway, I'd better go,' I said, but immediately felt guilty for leaving him. I should be more understanding. When I broke up with The Traitor, I ran away abroad and hid from the questions, so I shouldn't be surprised Ace doesn't want to talk about his breakup.

'I'm sorry about you and Kelly.'

'Thank you. It is what it is.'

It is what it is? How could he be so resigned to it? I wanted to shake him by the shoulders and bring back the kind, caring, spirited man that I know him to be. Or at least I thought I knew.

'Why don't you fight for her? How can you just give up, Ace? I don't understand. Are you sure there's nothing else you want to tell me?'

'You promised, Phia. No questions. There's nothing else to say. I know you always have great advice when it comes to relationship problems, but even you can't help this time. It's over.'

'Your marriage was my one beacon of hope,' I said.

'I thought you said you don't want all that.'

'I don't … no, I don't. Look how upset you are. Love is painful. But … the world has changed since you last dated. It's brutal being single out there and I don't want that for you.'

I looked at him and he was so sad, my heart broke for him a little. 'Are you OK?'

'Not really. It's like I've been dismantled and put back together but some of the pieces were left out. I'm not fully functional. I feel as if I was plucked out of my life and dropped in a new world I don't recognise.' He let out a lingering sigh. 'But I guess it's also a chance for a new life and I'm going to make the most of that. I'll be OK. In time.'

I gave him a long hug. I admire his positive attitude and openness to an uncertain future, but I left his house feeling even more disillusioned with love, and glad to be single. When I got home, I rooted through my desk and found the only surviving photo of my wedding. We looked so happy and full of hope. I regret burning the rest of the photos in a blaze of fury, even though I no longer recognise the grinning woman in the frilly silk ivory dress with the overly teased hair.

FOUR

The Journalist

Monday, 14 January, 11.55pm

EARLIER I WAS SEARCHING through Ladybird (trying not to think about Ace's situation), lost in my fantasy of meeting a gorgeous man, mature in age and personality with the body of a twenty-year-old (ha, if only), when Leila rang. I had a bone to pick with her for twisting the truth. 'You'll have so many men after you,' she'd said, 'you won't have time to keep up with them all.' Hmm, no evidence of that yet.

'It's Jude. We had a row, and he stormed out,' she blurted, followed by a loud sob. 'We went out for lunch today and he was flirting so obviously with the waitress who couldn't have been that much older than Mia. I pulled him up on it when we got home, and he said she was the one flirting with him, and he was just being polite. He said I was paranoid and jealous and needed to get a grip. Then he left. That was seven hours ago.' She sobbed again.

I can't bear to see her cry and joined her in sniffling as I told her it was a lovers' tiff, and I was sure he'd come back when he'd cooled down. I wanted to reassure her, but I have to admit I'm not keen on Jude. There's something about him I don't trust, though I hardly know him, having gone travelling ten days after their whirlwind romance and wedding. But he seems to adore her, and she does him, so I keep my thoughts to myself.

'Do you think I'm paranoid and jealous?'

'No. You were right to voice your concern if it didn't feel right. That's not paranoid. If anything, he overreacted, but he was probably upset.'

'We're always having small arguments, but we make up quickly. The making up is the best bit.' Yes, that sounded like Leila all right. 'This is the first time we've been apart this long since we got married.'

That's exactly what scares me about relationships. One minute you're in heaven, having a romantic meal with your beloved, the next he morphs into Casanova before your eyes. It feels like another person is pulling the strings of your emotions, which makes me uneasy.

'He loves you as much as you love him. I'm sure he'll be back soon and apologise and you can make up again.' That seemed to calm her down.

But does he really love her? Call me cynical, but Leila is quite wealthy, he's fifteen years younger, and I know he's persuaded her to invest £££££ in his recycled handbag startup. I can't help questioning his motives, especially as he was in such a hurry to get married. I hope I'm wrong.

'You don't think he might have gone back to the waitress?' she asked.

'He wouldn't be that stupid. He knows if he misbehaves, you could turn over in bed one night and flip one of your giant boobs over his face and suffocate him. Honestly, he wouldn't stand a chance against one of those weapons.'

She cackled. 'You always know what to say to make me feel better. What would I do without you?'

To cheer her up, I suggested we both pour ourselves a glass of wine while I showed her my matches. I sent her a few of the weirdest profile pictures. There was John, fifty-four, with his arms around a woman whose face had been scratched out. Rory, fifty-eight, had taken a mirror picture with the mobile covering his face, and Peter, sixty, whose photo showed only his forehead. Don't get me started on people who can't even manage to have their picture the right way up. We were still laughing when there were noises in the background.

'I have to go,' she whispered, giggling. 'Jude's back. I think he wants to make up. I'm going to join him in the shower.'

I wanted to tell her about Ace but thought it wasn't the right time. She doesn't need to hear about cheating husbands right now.

OK, back to shopping for men, strictly for sex. No point in searching for love. So much cheating in the world. Too much heartache. I'm better off on my own.

Tuesday, 15 January, 8.00am

After talking to Leila last night, I checked London Soulmates. My first match didn't have a photo, but his profile said he's a journalist, travels a lot and is looking for fun times. I told myself I must be open, and not discount him because there's no picture. I messaged him and he replied even though it was past midnight. We exchanged a few texts before he suggested meeting at Grind in Covent Garden today. I can't find his profile, though, so I hope he didn't change his mind and block me.

And I can't stop thinking about Ace. Texted him to see if he was coming on Saturday but he's now on tour for ten days. He didn't chat for long and sounded down.

Also texted Leila to ask about Jude. They've made out and made up.

11.30pm

Being open didn't pay off. Let's just say, there was no potential for sex. I went into Grind searching for my date. There were only two men on their own. One was about nineteen and the other one was not my type at all. Quite small, unkempt, and slurping noodles. As I walked towards him, he glanced at me then went back to slurping. Phew. I diverted and sat at the next table.

After a minute, a woman I didn't recognise walked up to me. 'Hello Sophia, good to see you. I'm just going to the counter. Can I get you anything?' I thought she was a past client I'd forgotten, so I asked for a latte, and she went off to order while I racked my brain. Was it Sandra in Camden who had the cobalt metro tiles in her bathroom? Or Marianne in Highgate who liked the mad purple wallpaper with giant zebras? I couldn't be sure.

'How is your bathroom looking these days?' I fished when she came back.

'It's … fine, thank you,' she said, hesitant. Was she Sandra?

'And you still like zebras?'

'Erm, yes?' She looked confused. Might be Marianne.

Awkward silence.

'And how's your … husband?'

'I don't have a husband,' she said. Was her husband dead?

'Oh, I'm sorry … for your loss.'

'What?'

'Well, it was lovely seeing you Sa … Ma … Sorry to be rude, but I'm actually waiting for my date.'

'Is this a joke?'

'No! I really am on a date,' I said, indignant. Was it so impossible that I could be on a date?

'Well, unless you're on two dates, I'M your date.' She sighed. 'Let's start again. Hello, I'm Lee.' She offered a handshake, and I took it, as the penny dropped.

'Lee?' I gasped inside and realised that last night's drinks may have impaired my vision somewhat when I picked him. I mean her. How the hell had I ended up in 'women seeking women'? No wonder I couldn't find her this morning. 'Sorry, your profile didn't have a picture … and I…'

She was gorgeous and definitely all woman. Her warm brown hair was in a top knot, and she was wearing yoga leggings and a cashmere jumper casually draped off one shoulder. She was just the kind of person I'd go for, if indeed I wanted to go for a woman. But that's not going to happen. I know what I like, and it involves a penis. She talked about her dating history while I waited for the right moment to tell her about my drunken mistake.

'Are you OK? You seem a bit distracted?'

'I'm fine. Just a bit of a headache,' I lied.

'We should do this another time,' she said, annoyed, pulling her jumper off her shoulder and picking up her bag to leave.

'Don't go. Please. I have a confession to make,' I said. She sighed, raised an eyebrow, then put her bag down. I told her what had happened.

'That's the funniest dating mishap I've heard in a while,' she said, laughing.

'I'm so sorry. You seem nice, and I didn't want to offend you,' I said.

The dating tension having vanished, we hit it off. She told me how her wife had sent her a selfie of herself in bed with another woman by mistake. I told her about The Traitor and how he'd cheated on me in the worst possible way with the worst possible person.

'Jeez, that's awful,' she said.

'It was, but the way I think about it is, if it hadn't been for that prick, I wouldn't have run away and climbed the Himalayas, walked the Inca Trail or seen the amazing Meiji shrine in Tokyo.'

On the bus going home, I got a text from her.

> Hi Sophia, it was lovely to meet you today, even though it was under false pretences. We should go for a drink some time. Lee x

You could have been from anywhere, Italy, US or China
But I wasn't expecting someone with a vagina
I thought I should declare my sexuality
That sex with a woman is not my thing in reality
My confession made me blush
I know I sounded like a complete lush
I wasn't there for a bit of fluff
I wanted something altogether more rough

I must admit you are a fabulous chick
But you lack the prerequisite prick
You are attractive, warm and canny
But sorry, I'm only into my own fanny

I didn't kiss a girl to see if I liked it, but hopefully I picked up a cool new friend.

One more liker today, but nobody I want to like back. His profile picture is spooky. Like a Hitchcock movie poster, with half of his face in darkness.

P.S. At least I have my travel card, so going to dates is free. Have 60+ Oyster card, will date. I'm loving the seniors' discounts and free stuff. cheapskate60s.com

Wednesday, 16 January, 11.30pm

Went to see my favourite clients Cassandra and Edward. They're changing the master bedroom again. I love working with adventurous clients who're willing to take risks, but it's always a challenge to get these two to agree. I'll have to come up with a compromise scheme to keep them both happy.

Texted Sara and told her about my 'women seeking women' date. She said, 'Why do you drink so much?' #Judgemental-SisterAlert. If I do strangle her, would a court of law convict me, given the hugely mitigating circumstances?

Texted Kelly yesterday to ask her about Ace but the texts were not delivered, and her phone just kept ringing when I called. Then I tried to look at her socials, but she's blocked me! WTF? We were never close, but I didn't think she'd erase me from her life.

P.S. I'm still feeling guilty about The Ice Skater. I wish I could just acknowledge I made a mistake, learn from it, and move on, but as usual I'm beating myself up and finding it hard to forgive my bad behaviour. I need to be kinder to myself and accept everyone makes a mistake, but I can't help judging my own actions harshly.

Thursday, 17 January, 11.30pm

It's mid-January and I've managed three dates so far. The first date – unexpected one-night-stand – was with a toreador fond of a full bush. On the second date, my dreams of becoming an Olympic figure skater were dashed. And the third date was lacking the essential equipment.

Sitting here in bed alone, surrounded by empty silence, I'm missing the intimate contented silences of a relationship, and aching to have someone's arms wrapped around me, our legs intertwined. I yearn to experience real intimacy, to be known and be cherished, but past betrayals by The Traitor and others haunt me. There's a longing in me to have someone I trust to see all of me, but the thought of being fully exposed paralyses me with fear. When I first fell in love, I gave my heart oh so freely, but after it was shattered too many times, I hid the broken pieces behind an impenetrable wall of emotional defence. Can I take a risk again? I know I come across as self-assured, and in many ways I am, but if I dig deep, I'm terrified of experiencing that pain again. If I dare to bare my soul, would it survive another crushing blow? Until I feel brave enough to be vulnerable, I'll settle for fun. At the same time, part of me mourns the lack of emotional fulfilment in my life. Will I have to get used to falling asleep alone, in solitary silence?

P.S. I registered on Kindling and messaged a couple of potential dates tonight. Fingers crossed.

FIVE

The Cinema Men

Friday, 18 January, 11.30pm

ONE OF THE Kindling guys messaged me. I've looked at his profile again and I'm not sure. I think in my eagerness to find another date, I'd gone for the 'you never know he might be OK in real life' candidate. He's Italian American – will he be a stallion? – and runs a small members' club/bar. Sundays are film club night when he shows his favourite classics. He's invited me to go along this week. He said he's going to keep the film a surprise but told me he identifies with the main character. I'm intrigued.

Saturday, 19 January, 5.30pm

Another cinema date. He's a writer. Cool. He suggested seeing a special screening of *2001: A Space Odyssey* on Tuesday. Excellent choice, and he offered to book. I like a man who can plan. This date is looking promising.

I'm trying to be environmentally conscious and buy fewer clothes, but the heat of my passion for fashion melted my icy resolve today. It's hard to break the habits of a lifetime. Call me shallow, but I love the ritual of opening the bags, taking everything out, cutting the labels and hanging them in the wardrobe. It gives me a sugar rush, a cocaine high, a dopamine surge. But it doesn't last long, and the new purchases soon disappear in the wardrobe, hidden by previous binges. Must try harder to resist. Anyway, ended up at H&M Oxford Circus, where everyone was so young. Queuing for the changing room, even the people waiting outside for their kids were a generation after me. Is it time to stop shopping in those places? NO. I'm not ready to order elasticated slacks from the *Saga* catalogue yet. I think I'll stick with my goal of growing old disgracefully.

Waiting to pick up Mum and Dad from the train for dinner tonight.

11.30pm

It was lovely to sit round a restaurant table, the three of us chatting, instead of Mum spending all her time cooking in the kitchen and Dad keeping an eye on the telly, although I did spend a significant portion of the evening answering questions about their iPad, which Mum just happened to have in her handbag. Sara always suggests they buy new technology but when it comes to helping, I'm the only one patient enough to answer the same question a hundred times. It's exhausting but I'm so proud of them for wanting to learn.

I took them to Bang Bang to try Vietnamese food. They loved the veggie pancakes, but at one point, Dad swallowed a whole chilli from his curry – his face turned a deep red and tears squirted out of his eyes. Of course, he pretended he had something in his eye, which made me tear up with love.

Watching them together, still in love after all these years, a swell of sadness and regret washed over me about my own failed relationships. Much as I delight in their happiness, I couldn't help but feel a whisper of envy in seeing the connection they share, that warm, fuzzy feeling that I wish I could experience. A twinge of remorse clutched my gut as I imagined the what-ifs and the paths I could have taken but chose to avoid, and I couldn't help but question my own life choices. I know that after James, I always held back a small piece, too afraid of giving all of me. If I'd let myself be more vulnerable when I was younger, instead of shutting off at the first sign of intimacy, would I be happily married now too? What if I'd kept my heart open to the unpredictable twists and turns of love, embraced vulnerability and dismissed the fear that's held me back for far too long? Who knows where I'd be in that parallel universe? Did I burn all my bridges to lasting relationships when, fuming with rage, I made a funeral pyre of my wedding photos? I love sex and, for now, I want it to be enough, but if I find the right man, will I want to let him in?

'They have a sister restaurant in Mayfair. We could go there too if you liked the food,' I said.

'OK, love. Now?' Dad said, reaching for his coat. He is the Undisputed Champion of Misunderstandings. I teared up with love. Again.

Sunday, 20 January, 5.00pm

Cinema Man One texted me the club address and it's in a dodgy part of Hackney. Gulp.

9.15pm

On arrival, I was tempted to get straight back into my taxi but forced myself to stay. Why did I do that? It was a dark and quiet dead-end road with graffitied shuttered commercial buildings, and I was a bit scared. Would I ever get to write another diary entry? And if not, would Elton John agree to sing 'Candle in the Wind' at my funeral, as requested in my will?

I found the purple door with a small neon sign that said Italianoso with a couple of bouncer types smoking outside. Why didn't I run at that point? To be polite, as usual.

I pressed the buzzer and waited while the heavies stared at me unapologetically, then Cinema Man One opened the door. His dark grey hair was slicked back, and he was wearing a black shirt open low at the neck, a pair of burgundy shot silk slim trousers and a leather jacket in a matching colour. Cheesy.

'Hello little lady. Welcome to my humble club,' he greeted me with a classic New York accent. I changed my mind. He wasn't just cheesy but also sleazy, and who the hell was he calling 'little lady'? I was being patronised by a gangster cliché.

The 'club' was one small room and a tiny bar in the corner, a bit like those mid-century Formica cocktail bars people had in their homes in the 50s. The whole place was dark red and dimly lit. It was like being inside a blood clot. The walls were decorated with black and white photos, which on closer inspection were gangster characters from Mafia films. There was Al Pacino in *The Godfather*, Robert De Niro in *Once Upon a Time in America* and others I didn't recognise. I watched my date as he hung my coat and joined me at the bar. In his dating profile, he only had one picture, which was a close-up portrait. It was a good likeness, and his face on its own was attractive. It was the rest of him I hadn't bargained for.

As for the club, there were about a dozen old red velvet cinema chairs that had seen better days facing a mobile screen for the film. A bald man in the front row was fondling a young woman, who was more interested in my arrival than him. A few men stood around drinking spirits, with women in short tight dresses hanging off their arms. It had the feel of what I imagined a gentleman's strip club would be like – with an added gangster vibe.

'With a killer figure like yours, I thought you'd be a Sex on the Beach kind of a girl,' Cinema Man One said, handing me the orange and red drink. It would have been nice to be asked what I wanted, and if that was his idea of flirting, it missed the mark completely. I took a sip. It tasted as sweet as a honeybee's bottom. Oh yeah, and I'm not a girl. This man turned more into a cliché every time he opened his mouth. How did I not pick that up when we texted?

'Hey Sophia, do you have any Italian in you?' he asked.

'No,' I said, knowing what was coming.

'Do you want some?' He roared with laughter at his own joke, and so did a couple of guys at the bar who were listening in.

'Why? Is there pizza?' I said, deadpan. They stopped laughing.

He then told me how this film was his absolute favourite and that he aspired to be as successful as the main character. I gripped my cocktail and wondered when I could make my exit. Then it was time for the film. I made for the back row so I'd have an escape route. The film started and there was Ray Liotta saying, 'As far back as I can remember, I always wanted to be a gangster'. OMG, it was *Goodfellas* and Cinema Man One's idol was Henry Hill. My date aspired to be a ruthless gangster.

10.00pm

Cinema Man One insisted on driving me home. He said it wasn't safe to walk around the area, but I was more scared of him. We were driving through Victoria Park when there was a big thud. We looked at each other, and there it was again: thud, thud. It was coming from the car boot. My heart was racing when he stopped and switched off the engine. The park around us was dark and eerie.

'I'm going to check the boot,' he said. I thought about running but didn't think I'd make it to the main road. I sat gripping my red bag in my lap. He opened the boot and the thudding stopped. A few seconds' silence then his chilling laugh echoed.

'Come and see this,' he shouted from behind the boot door. I got out, still clutching my bag with both hands, and slowly walked down the side of the car and round the back, then turned and looked inside where Joe Pesci was tied up and covered in blood. Cinema Man One gripped my shoulder and put a knife in my hand.

'Finish him off,' he said.

Joe Pesci pleaded with me. 'No, Sophia, no, Sophia, no!'

I woke up on my sofa to find Joy with her hand on my shoulder shouting, 'Sophia, wake up, Sophia!'

Thank goodness it was just a sofa dream, though I wish I could have normal dreams like being naked in public or flying. When I was in the Himalayas last year, it was so cold, I dreamt all my fingers and toes had dropped off. Anyway, I escaped the screening as soon as the film was finished before Cinema Man One could offer me a lift home. I sent him a 'Thank you and good luck with finding The One' text, so I don't think I'll be hearing from him again.

P.S. Why is Joy still here at this hour?

Monday, 21 January, 7.30am

I'm wondering whether I got things all out of proportion last night. Cinema Man One and his club members probably liked to dress up and get into the spirit of the film. Or maybe he's a bit dim and thought he liked the glamour of the Mafia. Sleazy atmosphere aside, it was the thought of being on a date with an aspiring gangster that scared me. If one of my friends was going on a date like that, I'd have told them to run a mile. Yes, I want to be open-minded and adventurous, but I shouldn't be so reckless, especially not out of politeness. But I hope I don't look back after date number fifty-two and decide he was the one that got away. Ha ha. No way.

12.30pm

I was trying on the new dresses that arrived today when there was a clinking of keys from the door. WTF? Joy hadn't finished the cleaning yesterday, but I wasn't expecting her to come back today. I knew she'd have something to say about my new purchases. There was no time to hide them like I usually do.

'Sophia bought more clothes?'

'I'm not keeping all of them. Just trying different things on.'

'Why you waste your money? And that dress. Too short. Too young for Sophia. Why you don't dress your age?'

She shook her head and went off to the cleaning cupboard. It's like having my very own Trinny and Susannah on hand to tell me

What Not to Wear in case my mum is too busy to come round and critique my looks: short skirts make me look short, black makes me look bland, and tight clothes make me look fat. These are but a few pieces of wisdom Mum likes to mete out. And God help me if I'm having a bloated tummy day or not wearing makeup.

Now I'll have to send the dress back or I'll hear Joy's voice in my head every time I wear it: 'Too tight ... Too short ... Too old, Sophia.'

Tuesday, 22 January, 11.30pm

Cinema Man Two was late for our date, much older and heavier than his picture – #DishonestyAlert – not fanciable, and we had a non-date. He hadn't booked so he went to get tickets while I bought snacks and drinks. Apparently, the performance was almost sold out and he couldn't get seats together. I took my ticket and gave him his beer and popcorn as we walked into the dark auditorium. I groped my way to my seat in the front and when my eyes adjusted to the dark, I scanned my row but couldn't see him, though there were a few empty seats. I sat back, snacks ready to go.

When the film ended, having thoroughly enjoyed my solo date, I stood up to look for him and noticed the cinema was half empty, so I headed for the foyer to find him. Did he deliberately buy separate seats because he didn't like the look of me any more than I liked him? As I waited for him in vain, my mind taunted me – not beautiful enough, not charming enough, not enough. Being dismissed so callously after just a glance scratched at old wounds, stirring up that pesky gnawing self-doubt that's always loitering in the background. Even though I knew his rejection said nothing about my worth, I still felt that familiar sting of inadequacy. Would he have stayed if I was younger, thinner, cooler? My inner critic woke up with a start, shredding my confidence. I wanted to sob, 'Why? Why don't you want me?' but I simply walked away, the picture of confidence, while I bled inside. I sent him a text to say I hoped he enjoyed the film, and sorry I missed him at the end. He read it but didn't reply.

Wednesday, 23 January, 11.30pm

OMG, my clients Brandon and Josh. They've always been lovely and so 'together' as a couple, but I sensed an atmosphere today as soon as I arrived at their house. I showed them the flamingo wallpaper Josh had asked for at the last meeting when Brandon was away with work. It wouldn't have been my choice for their scheme, and I guessed Brandon would have a problem with it, but I hadn't expected the fireworks that followed.

'There's no way I'm sleeping in our bedroom with THAT on the wall,' Brandon said, pointing with an accusatory finger at the pink and orange flamingo wallpaper sample.

'Don't be so melodramatic,' Josh said, 'it's cute.'

'You're a design philistine. I can't even...' Brandon said, holding onto his temples.

'And you're a design fascist.' Josh picked up the samples, threw them across the room and stormed out.

I guessed there must have been something else going on between them, and the wallpaper choice lit the fuse. Not an unusual scenario in my world of interior design where you can get up close and personal soon after you've met your clients. Brandon helped me clear up the samples.

'I'm sorry you had to see that,' he said.

'No problem. I can't wait to show you the parakeet bedding I've chosen for you,' I said, trying to lighten the atmosphere.

He smiled a sad smile. 'Will you talk to him please, Sophia? You always know the right thing to say. He'll listen to you, I'm sure.'

I found Josh, tearful, in his study. It transpired that he was upset because Brandon had been away with work a lot lately and Josh resented being left on his own so much. I let him talk it through until he stopped crying.

'He leaves me on my own to cope with everything, then

overrules my choices when he comes back. Why can't I decide for once?' Josh said.

'You can, but marriage is about compromises. I'll find something you'll both love if you come back and make up before I leave. But talk to him and tell him how you feel. He'll understand.'

Josh nodded.

'Nobody ever lost sleep over bad wallpaper, but plenty of people do from a broken heart. Marriage is rarely perfect, but it's precious and it needs to be nurtured with care,' I said.

He nodded again and smiled.

'Though to be fair, if one of you is an accountant and the other a stylist with a big fashion house, why let the accountant make the design choices?' I teased.

He laughed out loud, and we went back to the living room, where I watched him embrace Brandon. I was proud of myself for bringing them together but also a little envious of their love.

Thursday, 24 January, 11.30pm

Went for a drink with my new friend Izzy for the first time since she's come back to London. When I met her and Michael in Peru last year, they'd just got married and were venturing on a year-long honeymoon around the world. I liked them but found it hard to be around their bubble of love and happiness when I was cocooned in a miserable, brittle shell myself. Later, I couldn't believe it when she texted me from India and told me they'd broken up. Tonight, she opened up about the stress of spending 24/7 together for six months and how they just couldn't work through their differences.

'It ended at a train station in Dehli. He wanted to go east to Nepal and I wanted to go south to Kerala. We had a massive row and he walked off and left me on my own. That was the last time I saw him,' she said. 'All that anger and heartache because we couldn't compromise. I was in a daze for weeks afterwards. I was too embarrassed to come back home so I carried on, but it was really tough being alone and heartbroken.'

'I started my travels already feeling numb so I know exactly how you felt. It's true about relationships being all about working through your differences. I made a lot of compromises with my ex-boyfriend, but it didn't stop us falling apart,' I said.

'Why did you break up?'

I thought about giving my usual non-committal answer but sometimes it's easier to be truthful with someone you don't know very well.

'I knew something wasn't quite right. I was never the top of his priorities. His work was more important because he had to impress the boss. His mates absolutely needed him at the pub. And even his ex-wife had to be looked after because she was single and still loved him. There was one time he didn't turn up to my birthday dinner and instead went to console her because her cat was sick.'

'Her cat? That's outrageous,' she said.

'Yes, exactly. I had to explain his absence to my friends and endure their pitying looks. There was always a reason why I came second or even last, and I let him convince me that was normal. Now I feel ashamed for putting up with it and not having the confidence to demand to be treated better. I guess I was in deep and didn't want to change my world.'

'You wouldn't be the first to let your heart play tricks with your mind.'

'Then there was one final betrayal and there was no way I could compromise on that.'

'What did he do?' she asked.

'It doesn't matter now. When he came home from work, he found his empty suitcase and all his stuff in the garden. I wasn't going to pack for him. I told everyone we didn't want the same things and that I'd ended the relationship. The truth was, I was devastated and couldn't work or eat or see my friends. That was why I decided to travel for a few months. Then I could pretend I was fine until I felt better and could come home.'

'Have you met anyone since then?' she asked.

'Nothing serious. I'm done with relationships. What about you?'

'I went to a singles night and met this guy, Mark, who seemed really nice. We ended up back at my place. I thought he liked me, but he ghosted me afterwards. I didn't need that,' she said.

It was good to talk about it even though I didn't tell her the whole truth. I looked at my travel photos again when I got home. Or should that be my running away photos? In Peru at the beginning, in my picture with Izzy and Michael, I have droopy shoulders and dead eyes, but by the time I reach Australia, I'm posing outside the Sydney Opera House with a rowdy group, arms linked and shouting 'cheese' at the camera.

Izzy's experience proves I'm right to just stick to sex. The Carmen experience is the way to go. I'm closing the door to my heart, triple-locking it and throwing away the key. I know I'll be happier that way.

Friday, 25 January, 11.30pm

More lovely free stuff for being sixty. A test kit for bowel cancer from the screening service. Nothing like it for making you feel you're on the downhill journey. You have to smear poo on cards over several days. I'm not looking forward to storing the card in the toiletry cabinet during the proceedings. #ThereMustBeABetterWay

P.S. Doh, Sophia, of course Cinema Man Two bought separate tickets deliberately. Karma for the way I treated The Ice Skater. Why did I feel such a swell of disappointment that I couldn't rationalise away? I didn't even like the man and I don't care if I never see him again, but some fragile well-hidden corner of me craves being chosen. I tell myself I'm happy on my own and I don't need validation from anyone, but the unanswered text ripped open that old wound. Intellectually, I know I deserve more than crumbs of attention from lacklustre men, but my bruised heart doesn't understand. Why didn't he see me, want me, desire me? I know a random man's disinterest does not – cannot – define my worth, but even so, it takes all my strength not to keep plunging into self-doubt.

P.P.S. Yes, I get the irony and I realise I'm just as guilty for dismissing him after just a glance, but I wouldn't have pulled the 'sold out tickets' trick and would have at least given it a chance.

Saturday, 26 January, 9.30pm

Felt a bit fed up today with the dating challenge and the weird experiences so far. I treated myself to a night at home, binge watching Succession with my faithful friends: black pepper Kettle crisps and salted caramel ice cream with a small singleton sized bottle of prosecco. Heaven. Maybe a holiday in the sun with exotic opportunities could banish my dating blues. Who can I go with though? I need another singleton who can get away easily – I don't want to go on my own again. It might bring back unwanted memories of this time last year. I wonder if Ace fancies a holiday. He's having a rough time, and even though he only has himself to blame, I can't help being concerned. I'm angry with him for cheating but equally I can't bear being mad at him. A holiday could be what we both need, and he might confide in me while we're away.

11.30pm

Yay! Ace is up for it. It just so happens he's not doing any concerts in February. We decided on Cuba as weather will be great this time of the year, and it'll be salsa heaven. For me anyway. Ace doesn't have a dancing bone in his body.

Sunday, 27 January, 6.30pm

Just back from the shops. Saw a lovely discounted pink cotton top and couldn't resist trying it on. They didn't have any 10s, so I squeezed myself into a size 8. I liked it but when I tried to take it off, it wouldn't budge past my shoulders. Standing with my arms squeezed upwards brought on a massive hot flush. Gave up after five minutes of battling with the damned thing and went to the till still wearing it.

'It's lovely. Can I keep it on and pay?'

'Yes, but I need to take off the security tag,' said the disinterested cashier with a nose ring.

The security device was fixed to the desk. Cue me, sprawled face down on the counter, and her tugging at the label on the neck to reach the tag detacher. As if that wasn't humiliating enough, she scanned the £5.99 price label while I was there. I cut myself out of it later in the privacy of my own bedroom.

10.30pm

Holiday is booked for Friday. Yay! Heathrow to Havana is ten hours and I can have a catch-up with Ace. Or hopefully a hunky man will be sitting across the aisle from me to get things started.

11.30pm

I'm worried about spending ten days 24/7 with Ace. We haven't been on holiday together since we were children and went on our customary week in Bournemouth every August.

11.45pm

I texted Ace.

> Hi, do you think we'll get on, on holiday?

> Course we will. Where's this coming from?

> I don't know. We've never been on holiday just the two of us. We might get on each other's nerves and fall out.

I know I won't get on your nerves. Not sure about you annoying me though

Oy!

We'll be fine.

He sounds more like himself. Is there a reunion with Kelly on the cards or have things moved to the next level with the ponytailed blonde, in which case why is he going on holiday with me?

I wish he'd talk to me about his divorce. His honesty is one of the things I've always admired in him, and that's why I don't understand him suddenly being a cheating husband. Maybe he's always been a cheater, and this is the first time he's been caught. He'd certainly have plenty of opportunity being away with his job so much. I thought I knew him really well, but maybe I don't. Still, he's been there for me when I've needed him. I want to do the same for him, even if it sticks in my throat.

Monday, 28 January, 11.30pm

There was a guy on the platform at the train station today – in his thirties, kind eyes, and shivering in a puffer coat – sitting at a small table with two chairs, a vase of flowers, a box of chocolates and a sign saying, 'Date while you wait'. The London crowds were diligently ignoring him, and his sad eyes tugged at my heartstrings. I wasn't in a hurry, so I sat with him for a while to keep him company (no dating potential for me). He said he was fed up with anxiety-inducing dating apps and came up with this idea to stand out from the crowd, but it hadn't worked so far. Will I be forced to do something drastic in a few months just to meet men, like play golf, watch football matches at the pub or start doing bar weights?

Tuesday, 29 January, 11.30pm

Peace appears to have been restored in the Brandon and Josh household. They've emailed to ask for other wallpaper options. If ever the design work dries up, I think I might have a future in marriage counselling.

Mum phoned earlier.

'I called All Ages UK and offered to volunteer for driving elderly people for shopping and days out. They were very interested and wanted to take my details,' she said.

'That's good of you, Mum. When are you going to start?'

'I'm not. When I told them my date of birth, I'm sure the woman guffawed at the other end. Then she said I was older than most of their clients, so they couldn't take me on. The cheek of it.'

It must have been tough for her to hear that. She's passed on the 'I refuse to believe I'm old' gene to me, and I'm grateful for it. Better to live life as you want than be restricted by a number.

Wednesday, 30 January, 11.30pm

Today's junk mail included a brochure for stairlifts. It'll be free incontinence pad samples next. One advantage of not having children is that my pelvic floor is intact. I ran to the top of the house without peeing myself and put the brochure straight in the office recycling.

Thursday, 31 January, 11.30pm

Feeling guilty about getting distracted by holiday preparations and missing the final inspection of building work on Emily's kitchen extension. Baaad interior designer.

PART II
February

SIX

The Salsa Teacher

Friday, 1 February, 9.30am

LEAVING FOR CUBA TODAY. And more good news. Emily called and said she loved everything. Phew, got away with that one.

3.30pm UK time (no idea what time zone we're in)

Ace is sleeping like a baby with his head against the window. So much for a good catch-up. Our flight has been uneventful apart from one incident earlier, about which Ace is blissfully ignorant. When he went to the loo, I took the opportunity to get my carry-on duffle bag for an extra jumper. I couldn't reach it at the back of the overhead compartment. A man got up to help me and somehow, we ended up both pulling at my bag and the contents poured out onto the aisle, including my bright pink vibrator. The guy went as pink as the said sex toy and sat down. The young mother in the next row tutted and covered her daughter's eyes.

A steward who was walking towards us picked it up and said, 'Whose is this?' in a loud voice, as he held it at the battery end with just two fingers and a look of disgust. I continued refilling my bag, fully intending to deny knowledge of the damned thing, but the woman with the child pointed at me and said, 'It's hers,' with what I thought was a particularly judgemental tone. Snitch.

I grabbed the vibrator from the steward and said, 'It's for massaging my neck.' He inclined his head and raised his incredulous eyebrows. To be fair, I wouldn't have believed me either.

By the time Ace was back, the commotion had subsided, but he noticed that people in the seats around us were looking and tittering. One actually pointed at Ace, shook his head and whispered into his hand to his companion. The middle-aged woman across the aisle who had earlier been admiring Ace with furtive glances glared at me, then gave him a pitying look before pointedly turning away. Ace looked around, puzzled by the strange atmosphere.

'Did something happen? Why are people staring at us?'

'No, nothing,' I said, not looking up from the on-board magazine. 'They're probably just bored.'

P.S. Must make sure people know we're not a couple, otherwise our chances of finding holiday romance will be scuppered.

Saturday, 2 February, 5.30am Cuba time

Body clock somewhat confused.

When we landed at Havana airport yesterday evening, the arrivals hall was hot and close, and the queues long and slow, but my mood improved at passport control.

'You're sixty years old?' asked the young immigration officer, raising an eyebrow.

I nodded and had a full-on menopausal hot flush.

'You don't look it,' he said, winking and handing back my passport.

'Thank you,' I said, doing Lady Di shy eyes from below my eyebrows. I love this country already.

I consider myself to be age positive and I don't let being sixty get in the way of having a great life, but it still feels good when I'm told I look young – #HypocrisyAlert – but then I'm not claiming to be perfect. I'm a normal woman full of contradictions, constantly fighting against ingrained ideals of beauty and youth, despite being more comfortable in my body than I've ever been. I hope the next generation of women can break free from the pressure to look youthful but the current obsession with plastic surgery and cosmetic enhancements do not bode well for them.

'You look perky,' Ace said. I told him about the passport officer.

'I guess you'll be continuing with your dating escapades while we're here, will you?'

'Maybe, but we're going to enjoy this holiday together. Anyway, you might meet a beautiful señora and leave me in the hotel with only a margarita for company.'

Then I could find myself a señor.

'That's not going to happen,' he said, as if the idea was absurd. I can't work out what's going on with him. Is he fully single now or still seeing ponytail woman? He's an attractive man and he plays the trumpet with the English Symphonic, for God's sake. Women would swoon over him if he let them. Maybe he's feeling guilty and regretful.

It was late when we arrived at Hotel Cubana in Havana Old Town. We ordered some Cuban sausages and a couple of margaritas at the bar to get into the spirit of things. Our waiter winked at me when he brought the sausages garnished with curly parsley. They were artfully arranged into what could only be described as a parade of puberal penises. We stared at the plate between us for a second then howled.

The hotel reception is colonial in style with lots of large planters and high-backed wicker chairs, but the bedrooms' wing has a bare utilitarian feel with a concrete central courtyard where one imagines desperate inmates may have been tempted to throw themselves from a height in earlier times. It's not plush like I'd hoped but the view from my top floor window is a-maz-ing! I can see beautiful ornate buildings covered in a blanket of soot which makes for an eerie feel. Can't wait to venture into the city today. Two hours to go till the restaurant opens for breakfast. Will there be a sausage and two fried eggs display?

Sunday, 3 February, 5.30am

Yesterday, we had a chilled day of falling into a natural holiday groove, ambling through the charming streets of colonial buildings with their peeling pastel-hued paint, and inhaling the intoxicating atmosphere of Havana. Music came bursting out of house windows and cafés alike, along with the smell of local coffee and the faint hint of ocean salt. Colourful 1950s cars gleamed under the Caribbean sun, hinting at a bygone era. The whole place pulsed with a vibrant energy that was utterly enchanting.

Back at our hotel early in the evening, I decided to have a nap before going out for dinner, but I woke up half an hour ago! Some nap.

9.30am

Apparently, while I was in a coma yesterday evening, Ace had gone for a 5K run then come back and made a sightseeing itinerary for today. What a great travel companion.

Monday, 4 February, 5.30am

Yesterday, we had an exhausting day of sightseeing. The Plaza de la Revolución, a sprawling concrete expanse, is guarded by a towering obelisk, and giant steel memorials of the revolutionaries Che Guevara and Camilo Cienfuegos. You can almost hear the echoes of speeches and feel the excitement of the huge parades of the past. The scale and symbolism of it left me dewy-eyed.

More tears were shed at the Cristóbal Colón cemetery, which is breathtaking in a quiet, eerie way. The cemetery is vast like a city of the dead, filled with everything from simple graves to extravagant marble monuments and intricately carved mausoleums. Poor Ace was on tissue duty the whole day.

When we went back to the hotel, I decided I'd have a short nap before going out for dinner. Just woken up. Again! We'll never experience Havana's nightlife at this rate.

I sent Leila a picture of the Camilo Cienfuegos monument, pointing out his resemblance to Ayatollah Khomeini, followed by laughing emojis. She wasn't amused. She can't bear the thought of what that man did to her country. Damn. I am the CEO of Insensitive Friends PLC. Sent her grovelling emojis.

For lunch we were lured into a restaurant by the mellow sound of live music seeping out of its open windows. We ate a simple delicious Cuban meal of slow-cooked beef stew and fluffy rice. The band struck up a dance tune when a man and a woman came onto the dance floor. It was such a joy to see proper Cuban salsa dancing. I noticed that if you put a few pesos in their basket, you got to dance with one of them.

'Come on, Ace. Dance with the lady,' I said.

'Oh no, no, no.'

I kept teasing him, but he escaped to the loo to put an end to my persistence. I called the woman over, put some money in her basket and hatched a plan. She consulted the band and gave me the thumbs up from across the dance floor. When Ace was back, one of the trumpet players came over, handed him his instrument, and gently led him towards the band.

'What's happening, Phia?' He furrowed his brow as he was ushered away. The trumpet player had a word with him, and they both nodded. And just like that, they started playing 'Vivir Mi Vida', and it sounded perfect. I've seen him play classical concerts before but how could he play like that spontaneously with a band he'd met two seconds ago? The other diners applauded while I stood up and clapped vigorously, then felt self-conscious and sat down but continued clapping. I was itching to dance, so when the male dancer came over, I was up and on the dance floor like a firecracker. I was indeed in salsa heaven, but was finding it hard to keep up, let alone look good. As the music built to a crescendo, he tried to lead a double turn, but I misread his intention, pulled in the wrong direction, and fell on my backside.

'Very elegant dancing, Phia,' Ace said when I sat down.

'OK, OK, you win the prize for the best performance.'

He grinned triumphantly.

11.30pm

More sightseeing today, including afternoon tea at the iconic Hotel Nacional De Cuba, full of marble, chandeliers, Grecian-style statues, and old-fashioned faded glamour. The ping from my phone broke the silence in the formal dining room. Not bothering to check the volume, I played the voice message.

'Sophia, washing machine broken. Two G-strings stuck in pipes,' Joy said, as I fumbled to turn the sound down, 'No worry. They not yours. Too small for your ass. Happy holiday.'

Shut. Up.

Old men dropped their sandwiches, genteel ladies gasped, children giggled into their hands, and their mothers tutted.

Later, the atmosphere was more chilled when I finally stayed awake long enough to go for a night out. The club was steamy, dark, and pulsating with rhythm. The heady mix of live music, energetic dancers in sexy form-fitting outfits, and the aroma of Cuban rum was as joyful as I'd imagined. At first, every time a guy took my hand and led me to the dance floor, Ace watched like a hawk as though they were about to abduct me, but he relaxed when he saw my beaming face. Of course, the local women were all over him, but really, dancing is not his forte, and he certainly didn't inherit the dancing gene from his dad. He was embarrassed when a woman grabbed his hips to make them gyrate while the others pointed and giggled. He got annoyed with me when I joined in to laugh at his wooden rumba. Baaad Sophia.

Tuesday, 5 February, 10.30am

At breakfast today, we had a string trio of young music students playing Bach. How lovely is that? I didn't get Ace involved.

After three days (and only one evening out), our time in Havana is over and we're waiting for a car to take us on our three-hour journey to Varadero. It's going to be touristy, but I don't care.

11.30pm

From a distance, our hotel looks like a prison. It's a dull expanse of a square building with lots of small square windows, redeemed only by its peachy colour. I imagined desperate tourists clawing at the windows, pleading to be liberated. But inside it's a different experience. The receptionists are smiley and welcoming, the main bar glows with a warm amber backlight, squishy sofas invite you to lounge, and the lush gardens lead to shimmering swimming pools and the turquoise sea.

We appear to be staying at Cuba's answer to Butlin's. No red or yellow jackets here though. The female entertainers wear tight flirty floral dresses, and the men strut in snug-fitting black tailored trousers – Ooh La La – and colourful drapey shirts. Infinitely sexier than the Hi-de-Hi! crew. The whole team – and there are a lot of them – is led by a character called El Presidente, who is Cuba's answer to RuPaul.

P.S. One of the Ooh La Las is rather gorge.

Wednesday, 6 February, 6.30pm

Earlier, we were relaxing by the sparkling pool, surrounded by palm trees and colourful luscious vegetation, enjoying the warmth of the sun, and sipping Cuba Libres. Ace was dozing in his sun lounger. That man can sleep for England AND Jamaica. It reminded me of one year in Bournemouth when we were playing on the beach, but he kept trying to lie down and sleep, so I took him to our beach hut and, feeling bored, decided to give him a haircut.

He was about three years old and had a long light brown afro which often attracted admiration in the street. His mum couldn't bear to cut it even though people often mistook him for a girl. I searched in my mum's bag for her Swiss army knife – she always had one in case she needed to cut an apple or open a bottle. I pulled out the scissors and set to work on Ace's hair as he slept. By the time I finished, he was like an incompetently sheered sheep with a mullet at the back where I couldn't reach. An hour later, he woke up and wandered over to his mum, who screamed so loudly, a crowd gathered and witnessed me being chastised.

'How could you do that to his beautiful hair?' Mum fumed.

'I was helping him cool down,' I said, weeping and looking sheepish, but not shorn like Ace. She punished me by banning ice cream for the rest of the holiday. No wonder I have a complicated relationship with ice cream. It featured heavily in Mum's reward and punishment regime.

I was woken from my daydream when Ace stirred and noticed I was staring.

'What?'

'I just remembered that time I cut off your hair.' I laughed.

'Ah yes. The hair-cutting incident. Thanks for that. They had to shave my head, and everyone thought I had nits. Mum said she was wary of leaving me alone with you after that in case you decided to inflict some other unwanted favour on me.' He laughed.

'I thought I was being helpful. At least I think I did, or was I just naughty?'

'Erm … yeah, you were always luring me into mischief.'

'But you wanted to be led astray. That's why you followed me to London.'

'Oy!' he said, laughing, and threw his towel at me. I threw it back and we play-fought for a bit until we realised everyone was watching. I'm glad it's not awkward between us. I've forgotten about his cheating. Almost.

P.S. A beautiful new Swedish family came to the pool this morning. Mum and Dad with their teenage son and daughter who were all limbs and blonde hair. They had that uber-pale 'haven't seen the sun for ages' look about them. They slathered themselves in oil and roasted under the sun all day.

11.30pm

El Presidente wore fuchsia pink trousers and a matching satin shirt with giant rainbow-coloured Barry Manilow-esque frilly sleeves, topped with a jaunty gold Stetson hat.

In other The Swedish Family news, when Ace went back to the pool earlier to find his book, he found it balancing on Mummy Swedish's stomach. She suggested with a wave of her hand that Ace should help himself. Then she laughed and called him 'naughty' when he did.

In potential dating news, Gorge Ooh La La Trousers asked me to dance after dinner tonight. His English isn't great, but I think he speaks the international language of looove.

In other nasty sister news, I sent Sara a picture of me and Ace by the pool, captioned 'Wish you were here?' and she replied, 'That bikini's on the small side for someone your age, isn't it?' Her holier than thou attitude makes me want to scream, especially as she's in no position to preach after what she did.

11.55pm

Is Sara right? Should I give up wearing bikinis and opt for more modest one-pieces? I swing from being self-conscious and wanting to cover up to who gives a fuck, I'll wear what I like. I'm mostly at peace with my body now, though it's taken me decades to get to where I can look at myself in the mirror without scowling, pulling in my stomach or contorting my body into unnatural positions to look good. When I was younger, my own self-judgement was worse than any criticism by my mother or sister. I yearned to luxuriate in the sun like other women and display my body without shame, but a lifetime of conditioning would scream at me to zero-in on every new sag, dimple and wrinkle. It was exhausting.

At sixty, I don't care so much now, and despite all those years of conditioning by Mum – that thin is always best – I've won the war with my body. Mum probably doesn't even realise she started it on a summer holiday in Italy, but I haven't forgotten. I remember being awkward, spotty and with enough puppy fat to … cover a Saint Bernard puppy. She was beautiful, glamorous, slim, and a fanatic fatphobe (still is). The other kids splashed around in the pool, but I was deemed too fat to wear a swimsuit.

'No, darling, you can't possibly bare all that flesh. Perhaps next year if you lose weight,' she'd said to me before diving into the pool in her skimpy bikini. When I cried, she bought me ice cream to console me – I still don't get that logic. I gobbled it up and got fatter while I read the Slimming Today magazine she'd left on my sun lounger. When we got home, I went on a diet. For about forty years.

I can't imagine putting so much pressure on myself now. I've managed to stop the constant dieting – yo-yoing from an ideal size 8 to what I thought was an enormous size 12. I've accepted that my identity doesn't depend on the size of my arse. Nor indeed on how I look without makeup. There are enough women in my family judging how I look and dress without me joining them.

And yet, as I re-read Sara's cruel jab about my bikini, I couldn't help but well up with pain and frustration. No matter how hard I try, she finds new ways to make me feel like an inadequate older sister. Doesn't she know I still carry the scars of all the childhood taunts about my body? I long to make her understand how much her judgement hurts, but she twists my words against me. The sister I once adored has gone missing, replaced by this cold stranger who knows just where to plunge the dagger, and how to slap me down for daring to be myself. Some of my old wounds are still itchy, but I refuse to let her scorn steal my spirit. I'll wear what I like, sixty-year-old belly and all, though as old bellies go, it's pretty tight. Sara is so out of order to say my bikini is on the small side for my age. I texted her.

Your mind is on the small side for someone your age isn't it?

Your capacity to take constructive criticism is on the small side for your age, isn't it?

Stop being so judgemental

Stop being so judgemental

You're infuriating

Blah blah blah

Aargh!!

Thursday, 7 February, 6.00pm

I started my salsa lessons in town today. I booked six hours of tuition, and the rep threw in two tickets to see the Buena Vista Social Club, who are playing locally. Ace came with me to check that the dance school was legit. We flagged down a pink open-top 1950s Cadillac with chrome bumpers and cream leather seats and breezed into town. The woman at the school reception perked up when she saw Ace and tried but failed to drag him into the studio for a lesson.

WELL! My teacher turned out to be every bit as sexy as I'd hoped with a tight body, and plenty of Latin swagger. He wore a blue beanie, white sporty trousers, and a white T-shirt, which was striking against his dark skin. I was grateful for the fierce aircon in the studio to help me stay cool from dancing, hot flushes, and the hotness of the teacher. I found it hard to concentrate as his raspy voice and expert hands led me around the dance floor. No wonder the contestants on *Strictly Come Dancing* end up becoming lovers.

Afterwards, I joined Ace by the pool, where a young couple I hadn't seen before strolled past us. She walked slowly and consciously, highly aware of her beautiful body. He followed her, never taking his eyes off her bikinied back. You could almost touch the electricity between them, and the air was thick with lust. I glanced at Ace, who was watching too.

'Bet you wish you were here with a sexy woman like her instead of a middle-aged pal.'

'No.'

'No? Don't you wish you could fall in love and feel that sweet desire again? Those first few months of total obsession? Sex at every opportunity?'

'It sounds great when you put it like that, but it has to be with the right person,' Ace said.

'Didn't it work out with the woman you had an affair with then?' I fished, my heart pounding.

He froze. His nostrils flared and he huffed a long breath.

'I told you I didn't have an affair. And you promised you wouldn't ask questions.' He shook his head, picked up his stuff and went to his room. I am the CEO of Broken Promises Ltd.

I don't want to be in a relationship either but seeing that couple made me yearn for what they had. How divine to be in lust and have beautiful sex before dinner. Oh, to be that young and sexy again. Go away, insecure Sophia. You're not twenty anymore. You're a confident mature woman who's proud of her body.

Latest from The Swedish Family is that after a day of roasting in oil, they are now The Lobster Family.

P.S. Ace was wearing a Speedo today. Not so much a budgie smuggler as a cockatoo hammock. It could have taken centre stage on a Havanan sausage plate. I kept my eyes above the waist, except when I peeked.

11.30pm

I sent Ace a grovelling text, promising no more questions and asked him to join me for dinner. At the buffet, I met a Beyoncé lookalike on her own and invited her to our table. She told us she was a superfan and demonstrated a few poses she'd been rehearsing for the talent show tonight. Her enthusiasm was infectious, and it got Ace out of his bad mood.

After dinner, El Presidente asked us if we wanted to be on the X Factor judging panel for the talent competition. It was random, but hell yeah! So we spent the evening sitting at a desk with two other judges, and scored the acts with numbered paddles. Some guests had entered themselves or their children and were mostly dreadful. Dads who couldn't sing, kids who couldn't juggle two oranges, etc. The Junior Lobsters did a dancing double act that reminded me of Ross and Monica's hilarious over-choreographed routine in *Friends*. Ace was turning into Simon Cowell and wanted to be honest. I had to remind him it wasn't the real *X Factor*.

The last act was Beyoncé, and she killed it. I was transported to 2009, the O2 Arena, and Beyoncé singing 'Baby Boy' while hanging from a harness high above the audience. I don't need to say who got the top score, and the audience gave her a standing ovation.

Friday, 8 February, 10.30am

Over breakfast, we talked about how much we were enjoying our Cuban Butlin's, and I teased Ace about his Simon Cowell act last night.

'Maybe I should enter the talent competition and see how I get scored,' he said.

'That wouldn't be fair. You're a professional.'

'Who said anything about playing the trumpet? I could rap.'

'You? Mr Classical Musician, rapping?'

He thought for a few seconds then started rapping about the holiday, last night's *X Factor* contestants, our performance as judges, and ended with a whispered 'What happens in Cuba, stays in Cuba.' OMG. He was brilliant and so clever. When he finished, people around us clapped and he was embarrassed but thrilled.

'When were you going to tell me you can rap?' I asked, open-mouthed.

He picked up his apple and took a satisfied crunchy bite.

6.00pm

Second salsa lesson this morning. Hot, hot, hot, and steamy. For me anyway. We took a video of us doing the routine and when I showed it to Ace, he said the guy obviously fancied me because he kicked his leg back at the end when we hugged. I hope he's right.

Sent the video to Mum and Dad.

'Lovely looking young man. He likes you. Are you going to have hot Latin sex with him?' Mum said.

'Muuuum.'

'The doctor on *This Morning* said an orgasm a day is good for the heart.'

'Sorry, call coming in. Bye Mum.'

11.30pm

I resisted the urge to matchmake between the waitress and Ace at dinner tonight. I know I should stop projecting what I want onto him, but she so obviously fancies him. We're in quite different places at the moment. I want to have fun and amazing sex and he's given up completely, which I don't understand. If he could have an affair when he was married, why doesn't he want to meet anyone now he's getting divorced? Or is he still with her and that's why he doesn't want to meet anyone else?

Saturday, 9 February, 6.30pm

We played table tennis before coming up to get changed for dinner tonight. I haven't played for a few years, so Mr Super Competitive Ace completely thrashed me. Then he felt guilty and let me win the last game.

In other Lobster Family news, every time I missed a shot and had to collect the ball from near their sunbeds, Daddy Lobster winked at me over the top of his *Fifty Shades of Grey*. Mummy Lobster caught the ball a few times and she caressed Ace's hand suggestively when she handed it back. The Senior Lobsters are now The Swedish Swingers.

11.30pm

Last salsa lesson today. I think my dancing has improved despite having trouble concentrating on his instruction. I can't tell if he likes me or if he's just exuding natural Cuban warmth. I'm looking forward to finding out at the concert on Monday.

In the very exciting meantime, I practised my newly acquired moves with Gorge Ooh La La Trousers after dinner. Ooh La La, Ooh La La. After a couple of dances, he suggested a cooling walk in the hotel gardens where we had a few hot kisses, which did not cool me down at all. Luckily, our waitress was chatting up Ace, so he didn't notice I'd been whisked away. Hot kissing was rudely interrupted by one of the other dancers who called him back to his duties. Sigh.

Sunday, 10 February, 11.30pm

Day trip to Matanzas today. Highlight was the Pharmaceutical Museum, full of porcelain and stained-glass jars. Who knew medicine bottles could be works of art?

Checked work emails and this was waiting for me from Nick and Brittany. They were so sweet during the whole project, and I pulled out all the stops to make sure the refurbishment of their house was finished before the baby arrived at Christmas.

Dear Sophia,
Thank you for making our house so beautiful. You have given us something beyond our dreams. We are so happy and look forward to coming home every day.
N&B

Sara might think interior design is a frivolous occupation, but I feel proud to evoke such emotions in my clients. I shed a few happy tears.

P.S. No sign of Gorge Ooh La La Trousers. I think it's his night off.

Monday, 11 February, 7.00pm

So excited I'm almost hyperventilating. Waiting for the coach to take us to the Buena Vista Social Club concert. I'm wearing a silk fishtail neon pink dress that should look great on the dance floor. Not that I want attention or anything.

11.50pm

Wow, wow, wow. When The Salsa Teacher told me there'd be dancing, I assumed it would be after the concert. I was looking forward to being with him in a social situation where we could get closer. My sexual frustration levels are at an all-time high.

Little did I know that he was providing dancing FOR the show. Halfway through the concert, he came over and called me out from my seat in the audience. Unsuspectingly, I let him lead me towards the stage and before I knew it, we were doing a bolero alongside the band. Me, a dancer for the iconic Buena Vista Social Club. How did that happen? It was all a blur and finished in what felt like a few seconds. Afterwards, he led me back to my seat. I think I floated back.

Ace sat next to me open-mouthed. 'Did you know that was going to happen?'

'No, but now you know you're not the only one who can perform with a band.'

My cheeks were flushed, and I had rivers of adrenalin running through my body. I don't think I took in the rest of the show. When the concert finished, I searched for The Salsa Teacher, wondering if there was a chance for a last night together. When I found him, I thought he was even more delicious dressed up for the occasion with a light blue suit and a jaunty white trilby. I thanked him for the teaching and for tonight's experience. Cue lots of thank you hugs. Not entirely necessary, but a girl's gotta get her kicks somehow.

'When will I see you again?' he asked in his raspy voice.

'I'm going home tomorrow.'

His mouth drooped. More hugging. 'I'll give you my number and you can text me,' he said. Wahey, result. It was great to get his number, but I was hoping he'd ask me to go for a drink or to a club, though he probably wasn't allowed to fraternise with the dance school students. I could see Ace across the foyer, pacing by the entrance. He pointed at his watch, not wanting to miss the coach back to the hotel. I said a reluctant goodbye, wishing I could stay.

Feeling high as a kite on adrenalin and lust – and turned on with no prospect of anyone helping me with it – I caught up with Ace. The coach driver greeted me with a big smile and as I stepped into the aisle, the other hotel guests who were already in their seats clapped and whooped. I took a shy bow and we walked to the back seats as people congratulated me on the performance. The Swedish Swingers slapped our bums boldly as we went past.

My desires may have been unrequited, but it was an unforgettable night. Back at the hotel, I was too pumped to go to bed and suggested a drink at the bar.

'I wish I'd been braver and asked my teacher out,' I told Ace wistfully.

'But we're going home tomorrow so nothing would have come of it.'

'I know, but sometimes it's not about anything coming of it. It's about seizing the moment and going for it. To have experiences to remember and to feel alive.'

I told him I was going to have another drink and he should go to bed, then went up to the bar and ordered a cocktail. The bartender kept looking at me and smiling. He was so cute but way too young for me.

'Everyone is talking about your dancing tonight. They say you dance like a Cuban,' he said.

'Wow, news travels fast.' I thanked him and went back to my seat to savour my last margarita and tonight's incredible experience. I came up to bed feeling contented with a dash of longing.

SEVEN

The Other Ooh La La Trousers

Tuesday, 12 February, 9.30am

I'M ready to leave for the airport, and no longer feeling frustrated. No siree. Last night I was about to get ready for bed (with my pink toy) when there was a knock followed by, 'Room service'. I opened the door to tell them it must be a mistake, but it was The Barman with a bottle of wine and two glasses.

'We celebrate your dance performance tonight?' he asked with a cheeky grin.

Hello! Last chance for a hot Cuban night, I thought, as I invited him in. His pert bottom filled his Ooh La La Trousers so well, his open-neck turquoise shirt revealed a smooth chest like polished mahogany, and he had the cutest smile. He came in, put the tray on the table and made to open the wine, all the time not taking his eyes off me.

'Oh, I forget, what you call it, corky screw? I must go get.' So adorable.

'No, wait. I have a trick,' I said. He was here and I wasn't about to let him leave. I fished in my bag for a lipstick. I took the bottle and rammed the lipstick into it. A little too enthusiastically. As the cork thrust into the bottle, white wine squirted out all over us. I'm a bit out of practice with that trick. I froze, but he laughed and tasted some of it from my lips. I stroked his wet chest and licked him back. Then he poured the wine and, after a sip, asked me to show him my dance moves. We wrapped around each other, his hand warm and firm around my waist as we danced a sultry slow bolero, bodies swaying in unison. I hoped he couldn't feel any wobbly bits. He was hot and taut, and smelt fresh like apples and limes. Our heads were touching, breaths mingling, and hips were weaving in sync to the rhythm of the music. As the track ended, he gazed into my eyes with such passion I thought I would melt.

'Eres la leche,' he whispered into my ear. I had no idea what it meant but it sounded hot. 'It means, you are the milk.'

'Thank you.' Maybe it was lost in translation.

'Eres mi media naranja,' he breathed into my temple. I knew 'naranja' means orange. Was he reciting his shopping list?

'It means you are my other half.' Google translate will be required for this later.

Enough talking, I thought, as the track ended. We stood drinking each other in for a few seconds, then he went down on his knees and his dark amber eyes looked up at me. That was more like it. My boobs would look perter from that angle, but he'd be up close and personal with orange peel thighs. Thank goodness for the soft hotel room lighting. He lifted the hem of my dress, his lips planting soft kisses on my skin as he worked his way up to where I was tingling, before slipping the dress off over my head. I undid his shirt buttons, one by one, stroked his abs and the smooth torso I'd admired from afar. When it got to 'those' trousers, I could wait no longer.

'Take them off,' I ordered him, and he obeyed.

While I watched his magnificence, he put on more music and swaggered over to the bed, crawling towards me and growling like a hungry panther ready to pounce. I think I might have purred. Our bodies came together to the slow sway of bolero, revved up to an acrobatic salsa and finished in an ecstatic final flourish. His lovemaking, like his dance lead, was expert, confident and inventive, and when the time came, I screamed, 'Ooh La La'.

Chilling in bed afterwards, 'You are my cream,' I whispered into his mouth. 'You are my half peach,' I simpered in his ear with a playful slap of his bottom.

This morning, I've been strutting around with a swing in my hip and a spring in my step. It was pure invigorating hot sex, and I want more of it. As I sit waiting for our airport transfer, still trembling with exhilaration, I'm allowing myself to admit I'm ravenous for passion that would make me feel gloriously alive. Since The Traitor, I've been too cautious, hiding my desires behind faux indifference. When was the last time I ignored my fears and followed my cravings? It's time to rekindle that adventurous spirit before it sputters, and to rediscover how delicious it feels to be wanted.

I've decided to resume the dating challenge with renewed enthusiasm. Will the men in London seem too cold after Cuban men? They should make British men do a sort of 'Wooing Women National Service' in Cuba. So, I'm leaving today with passion in my heart and an open mind, looking forward to all the dates awaiting me at home. I may be sixty, but I'm not done with romance and sex yet.

I'm a baby boomer, and still booming
Sexually speaking, I'm still grooving
They say you lose your libido in your sixties
But I'll carry on for as long as I can bend my knees
I want a man who's still erect
A man who can still eject
I want the deliciousness of feeling groiny
I want to get heated and act horny
I want flirtatious sexy conversation
I don't want sex to be just an aspiration
Gods of love, please can I keep my libido?
And have lots of sex with hombres bonito?
My eyesight may be fading but I'm still full of passions

Please God, can I have many more orgasms?

Eat your heart out, Carol Ann Duffy.

Last news bulletin on The Lobster Family. After a week of roasting in oil in the sun, they are now The Walnut Family.

Goodbye and farewell Cuba. You were fabulous.

EIGHT

Cement Man

Wednesday, 13 February, 4.00pm

BACK AT HOME now and trying to stay up to synchronise my body clock, but I feel so sleepy. On the flight back, Ace said I was like the cat that got the cream. I didn't tell him about the cat that brought me room service cream.

When we arrived at Heathrow, I bumped into Cement Man from NYE and agreed to go for a drink with him. Why oh why did I do that?

5.30pm

Was having a lovely afternoon nap and dreaming of The Barman when there was a text ping. It was Cement Man.

> Hello Sophia, it was such happenstance to see you at the airport. Shall we go out for that drink?

No, let's not go for that drink. Ever. And who says happenstance in a text?

> Hi, yes that would be lovely. When did you have in mind?

> How about tomorrow? Are you free?

No way. It's Valentine's Day tomorrow and I'm not spending it talking about cement.

> Sorry, I wish I could, but I have plans. Another time?

Or never. That would be my preference. I have no plans of course. I'm happy for all the couples in love enough to celebrate Valentine's Day but I don't particularly want to watch them doing it. Watching them demonstrate their love, that is. Oh, horrible image of Cement Man in an orgy in my head.

> Not another paramour, I hope. How about Friday? Is that more convenient? I can get us a fabulous table at Coq Riche at 7.00?

Yes, a Friday in the year 2058 would be dandy. Another paramour? Does he think he's my paramour? Who says paramour? At least he'd picked somewhere nice. Wait a minute. Coq Riche. Cock and Money? Oh no, I have an image of him standing on a restaurant table, legs astride, swinging his cock made of £50 notes. A bit like Harry Enfield's 'Loadsamoney' with added penis.

> Yes lovely.

Thursday, 14 February, 11.30pm

Design meeting with Cassandra and Edward. They bickered about the wallpaper options for most of the meeting. She wants florals, and he wants industrial. Cue couples counselling. They agreed on a lovely geometric style with a few flowers dotted on top. Job done.

On my way to the meeting, at least two women were carrying bunches of red roses and for a nanosecond I felt envious. Then I remembered that this time last year, I was walking the Inca Trail in Peru, crying over my high-altitude diet of potatoes and rice, growing my chin hairs (thanks menopause), and vowing never to fall in love again. I'd hacked off my hair to spite my jagged heart. I'd let the blisters on my feet balloon and burst. I'd lost weight and cultivated dark shadows under my eyes. I would have let the insects bite me if there'd been any around. None of it helped. I still felt crushed, and I looked like Edward Scissorhands had done my hair and makeup. I never want to go through that again. Being single isn't so bad. I can choose whatever wallpaper I want.

P.S. No Valentine cards for me but I got junk mail advertising funeral plans.

Friday, 15 February, 9.00am

It's the day of the dreaded date with Cement Man. I must have been wearing my holiday-tinted glasses when I bumped into him at the airport, feeling ultra-positive about dating, and thinking I should give him a go. Just remembering our chat on NYE sends me to sleep. But I'll be open and make the most of it, and hope he has some non-cement conversation.

P.S. On the bus yesterday, the ticket inspector (unlike the lovely Cuban passport official) DIDN'T express disbelief that I'm sixty when he checked my travel card. Did I age in Cuba? #DoesMyBumLook60? Do I care?

6.00pm

Looking good. Smoky eyes, casually tousled locks skimming a berry-coloured cami top over jeans, and killer heels, all topped with an electric pink fur jacket. It's wet and windy outside but I must look hot.

11.00pm

When I arrived, Cement Man was waiting at the bar with a bottle of fizz and an eager expression. He was exactly how I remembered him: dull with a hint of sand. What came first? The sandiness, then the business, or the other way round? His hair was brushed awkwardly to the side in waves that reminded me of sand dunes. He blended so well into the wooden panelling behind him, I may not have noticed him but for the unnaturally white teeth when he smiled and waved. But he was tanned, and it looked good on him. If he wasn't so old-fashioned, he could be nice-looking. I flashed my friendliest smile while in my head I was busy giving him a trendy haircut, putting him in a sharp suit and liking the results.

'You look ravishing, Sophia.'

How sweet. I thanked him and complimented his tan. I was starting to warm to Cement Man with a makeover.

'How did you enjoy Cuba?'

Good start. I let myself hope we were going to have an interesting conversation.

'I loved it. I've decided Cuba is my spiritual home. It's so vibrant and musical, and the people are really warm. How was your holiday? Kenya, was it?' I had a vision of him in a safari suit and hat, blending into the desert sand. Oh no, his penis was sticking out of his shorts. Why did I keep getting these images in my head? Did I have a subconscious longing for him? No. But my imagination was running wild after that first naked image of him.

'It was too hot for me. I found it ... oppressive,' he said. 'I didn't know one could sweat so much. And the flies. Just too many of them everywhere. And I didn't like the food. All that meat – goat and the like. Didn't agree with me. I spent a lot of time on the lavatory.'

Too Much Information.

'Did you like anything about it?'

'Hmm ... yes, I liked the animal safari ... but again, so many insects. And lunch was meat again. Had to use the organic lavatory a few times afterwards. Simply unbearable.'

The bartender must have heard 'heat, flies, lavatory', and grimaced at me.

'Would you like to see some pictures?' he offered.

Yes, anything but lavatory talk.

He took out an iPad from his coat pocket. The folder marked Kenya had 956 photos. He complained through the first few photos as I calculated it would take fifteen hours to go through them all, then he perked up.

'But have a look at these traditional villages. This was the best part of the holiday.' At last, something he didn't dislike. 'It was absolutely fascinating to learn about the materials they use to build their huts.' He clapped his hands and was about to launch into a (probably) long-winded monologue.

Desperate to divert the conversation, I said, 'The views are amazing here.'

'Shall we go and have a look?' he asked.

He was off the bar stool and waiting expectantly before I could reply. We went onto the terrace where it was like being inside a car wash as a fierce drizzle was sprayed around by the howling wind. He was impervious to the weather and to my discomfort, pointing out a long list of London landmarks that had used concrete in innovative ways. He went on. And on.

I was losing the will to live but nodded politely then suggested going back in when my frozen nipples were at risk of breaking through my skimpy top. Stepping inside, the warmth was welcome, but as we walked through the restaurant, there were side glances and tittering in our direction. I spotted myself in the mirror behind the bar. Oh. My. God. My casually tousled beach hair had morphed into an eagle's nest of knotted old strings. I looked like Crystal Tipps on a particularly bad hair day. And my carefully applied eyeshadow was smudged, the smoky eye looking more Alice Cooper than Kim Kardashian. And yes, my nipples were bullets about to be released at speed.

Cement Man pointed at my face and said, 'Oh dear, you seem to have … you look … and your hair…' The most verbose man on earth couldn't find the words to describe my predicament.

I rushed to the loos and was horrified at my reflection in the bright light of the mirror. I tried and failed miserably to repair my hair and makeup. At least the nipples had receded by then. A perfectly coiffured young woman with excessive makeup standing at the next basin grimaced and pulled a face like there was a bad smell in the room. I stuck my tongue out at her in the mirror but went back to the bar feeling a lot less confident.

11.30pm

Just woke up in a sweat, lying on my sofa, still wearing the fur coat, and clutching my telescopic umbrella. I dreamt I was standing in my bedroom, with messy hair, smudged makeup, and giant protruding nipples. Cement Man stood before me in his Y-fronts and proceeded to woo me by pretending to be a builder mixing cement. Shovel, mix, pour. I found it sexy and couldn't wait to get my hands on him. To touch his sand-textured skin and lick it firm. I ran my fingers through his hair and got sand under my nails.

'I want you right now. Take me, Cement Man,' I ordered.

I pulled down his pants with urgency and was delighted to see he was concrete hard. I fell on my back onto the bed with anticipation, but something wasn't right. He was floating above me, and I was sinking into quicksand. He watched laughing as I screamed and disappeared into a bed of wet concrete.

My phone pinged.

> Had a fantastic evening dear Sophia. Do it again soon?

No. I have no concrete plans for that.

> Your talk about cement is incessant
> It makes me want an antidepressant
> I get it, you own a cement company
> But must you buzz, buzz about it like a bee?

You're a successful entrepreneur, yes
But your social skills are a mess
I listen politely and ask a question about cement
But your overlong reply makes me lament
You don't pick up that I'm bored
That I'm not interested in the National Cement Board
I must be nice to you, you're a friend's friend
My God, will this date ever end?
'Another bottle of fizz?' you asked and waited
Oh fuck it, let's just get wasted

P.S. Last night wasn't a complete write-off. While Cement Man was in the loo, the bartender gave me a business card from someone who'd been sitting near us and wanted to meet me. He must like the Alice Cooper look. He calls himself a Wellness Advocate. Exciting.

Saturday, 16 February, 11.55pm

Can't sleep. I could do with Cement Man to send me to the land of nod with his cement talk. He could make a brilliant sleep app. Am I being cruel? He can't help being dull, but he could show interest in other people instead of just enjoying the sound of his own voice. Thinking about it, apart from, 'how did you enjoy Cuba?' he didn't ask me a single thing all evening, so I have no sympathy for him. Told the Brunch Bunch about the date and even Leila was sympathetic, and she's the one who introduced us. Grace was more interested in The Salsa Teacher and The Barman. She said I should totally call one of them and see if they fancy a holiday romance/shag(s).

'If I'm going back to Cuba, I could go for both of them. One for the hotel and one for the town,' I said.

Grace whooped. I love her. She's so feisty and driven and fun with it. If I hadn't gone to that exhibition of archaeological drawings – just to keep up to date in case I wanted to go back to it – I would never have met her. We got chatting about a particularly beautiful drawing of an Assyrian necklace and she was fascinated to hear about the digs I'd been on, so we went for a drink. We immediately hit it off and that was that. She'd just got married to Ajay and was pregnant with Tayo, so it must be fifteen years ago. Happenstance is a wonderful thing, as Cement Man would say.

Anyway, enough reminiscing. I should take their advice and contact The Salsa Teacher or The Barman. Or even Gorge Ooh La La Trousers. Is that something a naïve teenager would do, or a confident woman who knows what she wants and isn't afraid to go after it? The latter, I think.

Then I told them about Ace and Kelly getting divorced and they were in shock. I mentioned seeing him with that woman, but they couldn't – wouldn't – believe he'd have an affair.

'He's just not like that. He's incapable of telling lies for a start. His left eye always twitches and gives him away. And he's not the affair type. He's too lovely and honest for that,' Leila said.

'But I saw him.'

'What was he doing exactly?' Grace asked.

'They hugged and she stroked his cheek and kissed him on the forehead.'

'That doesn't prove anything. She could have been a friend, consoling him. You're jumping to conclusions as usual,' Leila said.

'What do you mean as usual?' I said.

'Honey, it's been a long time since Premature Paul.'

'Who's Premature Paul?' Grace asked.

'Sophia's first boyfriend. She'd been seeing him for a few months. He wanted to have sex and she didn't feel ready. On his sixteenth birthday, she went to his house to give him his present. His mum, not knowing he'd sneaked a girl into his bedroom, sent Sophia upstairs, and she walked in on them having sex.'

'What an arsehole,' Grace said and rubbed my arm in sympathy.

'Exactly. Ever since then, she's been suspicious of people having affairs.' She turned to me. 'Don't let it affect you forty-five years later, honey. And you were better off without him if his nickname was an accurate description of his sexual prowess.' Leila laughed. Grace nodded.

'It wasn't just forty-five years ago, though, was it? It was also The Traitor less than two years ago,' I said.

'I know, and I'm sorry that happened to you, but that's life,' Leila said and gave me a hug.

'Why don't you just ask Ace?' Grace said.

'I did but he denied it and made me swear not to ask questions again.'

'I'll ask him then,' Leila said.

'No! He'll know I've told you. Promise me you won't say anything about him having an affair?' I pleaded and she agreed.

Do I always jump to conclusions? Am I too ready to assume everyone will have an affair if the opportunity arises? Maybe Leila is right. I'm scarred by my experiences and can't let go. I'm pulling at the stitches in my soul to check if the scars will open again, picking at the scab over my heart to see if it bleeds, going back to the times I was hurt, and pressing on the bruises to test if they're still painful. I don't know how, but I must stop it.

Sunday, 17 February, 11.30pm

Met Izzy tonight. She was gushing about her new man, Francis. I'm pleased she's happy again, but frankly he sounds like a knob.

'So, you've had four dates so far and he was half an hour late for two of them and cancelled the third at the last minute?' I said, hoping my summary of the situation would make her see sense.

'Yes, he really wants to see me but it's difficult for him to make arrangements what with his job and everything.'

'Everything?'

'Well … his job. He's a librarian. He finishes his shift at 4pm but he has to stay and put the books back, you know.'

'And that made him late for an 8pm dinner date?'

'Yes. He's so conscientious. The other night he left after we had sex because he didn't want to risk staying over and being late for work the next day,' she said with a dreamy look.

I tried but she didn't want my advice. Why do we turn blind when we get the hots for someone? It's like a curtain of rose-tinted hormones falls and obscures our grasp of reality.

Monday, 18 February, 11.30pm

After the date with Cement Man, I can't help wondering how different it might be to date a hot-blooded Cuban man. If only I could go back and try again. Will The Salsa Teacher greet me with open arms and invite me to stay with him? It's not like I'm after anything serious. Still, it's a long way to go for a shag. Or I could go for the tried and tested and return to the hotel for their exceptional room service. No, I think that was a one-off, and he probably gives extras to a lot of female guests. Lovely as it was, I don't think I'll go there again – the hotel or him.

I'll look at London Soulmates and see if I can get matched with a Latin man instead.

Tuesday, 19 February, 5.30am

I want to be spontaneous and turn up in Cuba to see what happens. There's nothing to stop me. I'm young, free, and single. If it doesn't work out, I can just have another holiday, or I might meet someone else.

11.00am

The universe is looking out for me. A Valentine card came today! From Cuba! It said, 'I'll always want to dance with you'. It wasn't signed but it must be from The Salsa Teacher. He could have easily got my address from the holiday rep. Or it might be one of the Ooh La La Trousers from the hotel. What shall I do? Call them and find out? It's too early in the morning there now. I'm getting the vagina throbs.

11.30pm

Things are looking up here too. I'm meeting The Cuban on Thursday. He's fifty-two, from Cuba (obviously), and works in a salsa bar! What were the chances of that? I'm knee deep in dancing Cubans.

Wednesday, 20 February, 11.30pm

In my sofa dream tonight, I arrived at Havana airport, breezed through passport control, and was greeted by a uniformed driver. I was a 1950s film star with cat-eye sunglasses and a white wiggle dress. I poured a tequila from the limo bar and sat back as the car glided through the lush countryside. I texted The Salsa Teacher and told him we'd be together soon. Finally, we drove along a tree-lined path, arriving at a grand colonial mansion.

He greeted me in a white linen suit with slicked back hair and a handsome expression. We kissed softly as he led me into the centre of the palatial hallway where the staff were lined up. Under the impressive giant chandelier, he dropped down on one knee and opened a ring box with an enormous yellow diamond. Ooh I could finally use my wedding planning skills for my own wedding. But as he raised the box towards me, he had the face of The Traitor. I screamed.

The dating challenge must be affecting my brain if I'm dreaming of marrying someone I hardly know with the face of a person I don't want to see. I either need romance, or I ate too much cheese last night. Either way, the truth is, I called The Salsa Teacher yesterday and asked him about the card, but he said it wasn't him and he had a girlfriend, then his phone cut off. I thought we'd been disconnected by the unreliable Cuban network and called him back, but his pocket must have answered as I could hear him talking to a woman.

'You have great hip action,' he said in that familiar raspy voice as music played in the background.

'I wish I could stay longer and learn more from you, but I'm going home on Friday,' the woman replied in a breathy voice. I could just see him looking mock sad. How did I fall for his act? It's not like I'm in love with him but the insecure little girl inside me longs to be wanted. I'm happy mostly but at times like this, I wonder if being in a couple is better than being out there in the brutal dating world.

Thursday, 21 February, 11.30pm

The Cuban was all flash, all man and all over me, but he wore a wedding ring.

I've decided not to call either of the Ooh La La Trousers. I can't take another rejection. They've likely moved on to other willing tourists. It was all a silly dream. I'm not going all the way to Cuba for a shag. I'll just enjoy the fact that one of them liked me enough to send me a beautiful Valentine card.

Saturday, 23 February, 11.30pm

I had a meeting with Brandon and Josh today. After the drama last time, I wanted to make sure they were both happy with the design. I showed them the 'silver' wallpaper options Josh had asked for in his last email. He picked one but hesitated.

'I like the pattern on this one, but I don't like that it shines,' Josh said.

'OK, I thought you wanted silver,' I said.

'Yes, the colour is right, but I want it without the shine.'

'You mean you want grey?'

Brandon rolled his eyes.

I don't care what Sara says. Wallpaper is stressful.

Sunday, 24 February, 11.30pm

Met Leila at Springfield Park for a walk today. I was waiting for her in my car by the playing fields when a man came up to a tree in front of me and whipped out his penis and had a pee. Did he see me and still do it? I turned away but not before thinking that's the first penis I've seen outdoors since the one on the tango dancer in Argentina last year. Technically, the last time I was near an open-air penis was in Australia, but that was in the dark. My phone pinged. It was Leila.

2 minutes. And I've just seen a penis

So have I!

It wasn't the same penis. She'd seen a flasher two streets away. What were the chances of that? Talking of penises, I'm failing miserably at having lots of sex. I need to up my game and experience more penis sightings on my own terms.

Monday, 25 February, 11.30pm

A rather cute engineer came to upgrade my Sky Box today. He said the satellite dish was too high and I'd need, and I quote, 'the two-man long-ladder team'. I didn't know I needed it, but I want one now.

Thursday, 28 February, 11.30pm

Could have done with the Sky Two-Man Long-Ladder Team today. Site visit to the loft conversion in Pimlico. Had to climb to get into the new master suite. It was just about OK going up through a hole in the ceiling, but after we'd finished the meeting, I peered down that same hole, and could see the void all the way down to the ground floor. I got onto the ladder facing the front, then the back, and various other positions, but I was too scared to climb down. In the end, one of the burly builders carried me down while I squeezed my eyes shut, and whispered 'oh my God, oh my God, oh my God'. Once down, I dusted myself off, and resumed my professional demeanour, pretending nothing had happened while the team stifled laughter.

PART III
March

NINE

Mr Not My Type

Friday, 1 March, 11.30am

HAD a call from my client Lisa. I designed her daughter Hannah's princess heaven of a pink bedroom shortly before going off on my travels. She wants to update some of the accessories. Hannah must be six now. She's such a character and full of wisecracks, so I'm looking forward to going shopping with them. If I had a daughter – if I could have had a daughter – I'd like her to be like Hannah. I wonder if she'd have inherited my love of salsa, or my fat feet or extreme politeness. Maybe she'd have been like Mum: willowy, popular, and fearless. What if she'd got the sharp tongue gene from Auntie Sara? Whatever she was like, I know she would have brought joy into my life, and I would have loved her to the moon and back. I'll never know now.

Saturday, 2 March, 11.30pm

Phoned Sara earlier and invited them all for dinner. She said she's too busy. Yeah right. I'm being nice to her but she's obviously avoiding me. I'm tempted to go over to her house and have it out with her. I'm fed up with her bad attitude, but I miss the sisterly chats we had before she decided to turn into evil Sara. I also miss seeing Jack and Charlotte. I have so much love to give and they're the nearest to having my own children. I can't help wanting to spoil them and trying to be the cool auntie they admire.

Sunday, 3 March, 11.30pm

I went up to visit Mum and Dad today. While I was helping with lunch, I complained about Sara's insults and downright nastiness, but Mum kept telling me to be kind to my sister.

'She made me cry on New Year's Day. Why are you defending her?'

'I didn't want to say anything because she swore me to secrecy, but things are getting so bad between you two, I think I have to tell you.' She hesitated.

'Come on, Mum. What's the big secret? Has Laurence had another affair?'

'What do you mean another affair?' She said, open-mouthed. Shit.

'I meant an affair. Never mind that. Are you going to tell me or not?'

She took a deep breath and said, 'She had a miscarriage.'

'Oh God. When was that?'

'It was a few months before you went off to travel. She'd got pregnant and Laurence was ecstatic, but Sara didn't want a baby at forty-nine and was thinking about an abortion. While they were trying to decide, she went out one night, got drunk, fell down the stairs at home, and lost the baby.'

So that night when she came to me crying and in a state about Laurence having an affair, it must have been a couple of months after the miscarriage. She'd gone through that, and on top of it, Laurence was having it off with someone else. The prick. That must be why she went completely off the rails and has behaved atrociously ever since.

'She's ashamed of what happened,' Mum continued, 'and she thought, with you not being able to have children, and her considering an abortion and then losing the baby like that ... she thought you might judge or resent her. She blames herself. I think Laurence blamed her at first too and they were having a terrible time at home.'

I'm so sad for Sara and Laurence for losing their baby. I can't believe she thought I'd judge her. I would have supported her whatever she'd decided. I love Jack and Charlotte with all my heart, and I've never begrudged the joy they bring to Sara's and all of our lives. I'd be lying if I said I don't envy her for having two beautiful healthy children. I remember seeing Charlotte for the first time in hospital and watching Sara nursing, oblivious to my silent envy. My arms ached to hold my own child, yet I knew it couldn't be so, and the finality of it overwhelmed me, opening an abyss of sorrow. And yet, I also know that the feeling of envy has never been mutually exclusive with being delighted for Sara and loving my niece and nephew with devotion.

Am I bitter and twisted about not being able to have children? I don't think so. I hope not. Yes, it's true that sometimes I still feel a malignant hole in my core, but I work hard on not allowing it to rule my life. Jealousy and bitterness can only hurt me and I don't want to be that person.

Mum begged me not to let on that I know, so I'll have to zip it and be nice next time Sara vents her anger at me. I'll wait until she's ready to talk. It's not going to be easy, especially if she keeps picking at my insecurity scabs.

Wednesday, 6 March, 7.30pm

Today's date was properly rubbish. As if being out there in the dating world and exposing yourself to judgement isn't enough, you have to deal with psychopaths who completely lack any sense of empathy. Dating can be so brutal. I thought it was just on the apps where people behave as though the normal rules of decency and consideration don't apply, but today I experienced it in real life.

My date's profile had a picture of him with a group of men with about a hundred pints of beer in front of them. Not my type, but he said he was a happy, confident man and looking for adventure, so I thought he was worth a coffee. How wrong I was. I arrived early at Coffee Nest. He came in five minutes later, walked up to my table, eyed me up briefly and before I could say hello, he said, 'Sorry mate, you're not my type', and walked out, leaving me open-mouthed and red-faced. It might have crushed a less confident person, but it's not going to crush me, though it still hurts. I'd heard tales of people being horrible like this but didn't think it would happen to me if I was respectful.

Annoying as it was, the experience made me reflect on my own behaviour. Leila used to say I didn't give men a chance to approach me, but I hope I was never as rude as Mr Not My Type. I remember a lightbulb moment a few years ago when I was single – before I met The Traitor. I was at a pub with Grace for her birthday. Waiting for service at the bar, a guy next to me started chatting, and I was giving disinterested monosyllabic answers and diligently not looking at him. Eventually he gave up, but as he walked away, he said, 'You know, you're a babe but you're hard work.' Back at our table, Grace asked me who the dishy hunk at the bar was. I told her what had happened.

'How dare he call me hard work?' I asked.

'He was on the nose though. Don't look at me like that. I've seen three men in here eyeing you up, waiting for an in – a glance or something to give them permission to approach – but you're too aloof,' she said.

I realised then that I didn't want to be that person. I didn't want to be cool and unapproachable, behaving like nobody was good enough for me. That wasn't how I felt. I glanced over at the man and raised my glass, but he looked away.

It occurred to me then that I was still scared of getting hurt again. Was that why all my relationships after James didn't last, fizzling out like spent embers? They all started out well. I'd meet someone who thought I was amazing and adored me, but they could never get close. I wouldn't – couldn't – reveal my soft core. I didn't commit fully because I thought if I showed vulnerability, they could use it to hurt me later. I kept my feelings firmly inside with a giant stopper of nonchalance. I pretended I didn't care and unknowingly sabotaged the relationships. If I didn't commit, then I wouldn't get hurt. Right? Wrong. I may not have let them get close to me, but I still felt wounded and bruised when things went off track. Yet another failed relationship that, somehow, I couldn't explain.

After what Grace said, I promised myself I would be more receptive and open. I worked hard at being present and intimate. To talk about how I felt instead of everything being 'fine'. And it worked, because soon after, I met The Traitor. I fell in love and gave myself to him completely. And look how he paid me back. I know now I'm better off without love. I don't want spiritual intimacy, just closeness of a physical nature. I can cope with that.

After the nastiness of Mr Not My Type this morning, I decided to have a walk in the sunshine, explore the area and forget about the horrible non-date. I walked along Gresham Street, popped into an exhibition of seventeenth-century paintings at the beautiful Guildhall buildings, then headed for Smithfields to find a café for lunch. God, I love London. You can live here for years and still stumble on undiscovered places.

Blissfully unaware I was about to get the second shock of the day, I found a cute traditional Italian café in a side street and joined the lunch time queue of office workers. Looking through the window for a free table, I saw a man and a woman who were obviously having an intimate conversation. She was tearful, and he was holding her hand and soothing her. She had an uncanny resemblance to Grace. The queue moved and I went inside, standing behind Grace's doppelgänger. I noticed she had a pink Miu Miu handbag like Grace's with an identical skull keyring attached to the strap. What were the chances of that?

I texted Grace and said, 'Ha ha, just seen your secret twin. LOL.' The woman's phone pinged and when she picked it up, I saw my text over her shoulder. She read it and put it back in her bag, as I froze on the spot and the man said, 'I don't want to rush you but when are you going to tell your husband? He should know what's going on, and soon', and the woman said, 'I have to find the right time. He's going to freak out. I'm dreading it.' It wasn't Grace's double. It was Grace.

I didn't want to confront her so I hurried out before she could see me. What the hell is going on? Is Grace, the dedicated mother and wife, having an affair? I don't want to believe it but the tableau from the café tells me otherwise. Shit.

Thursday, 7 March, 10.30pm

This morning, I remembered yesterday's awful date and looking at myself in the mirror, wondered what it was that made him think I wasn't his type. What did he see in those few seconds? Perhaps he prefers tall flat-chested women or my skin was too dark for his liking. Was my head-to-toe red outfit too much? Was it my looks? Or am I unaware of something else? Maybe I looked too confident and he wants a mouse. Even though I wouldn't touch him with a barge pole, it's still painful to be rejected so brutally. I must forget about it and not let his nastiness put me off dating.

P.S. I keep thinking about what Sara's been through and how badly she's been behaving. It's hurtful that she couldn't talk to me about her miscarriage. We used to be so close. I feel torn. I'm sad for her but I also want to shake her until the demon squatting in her brain is exorcised and she turns back into the old sweet Sara. I'm managing to keep my fury at bay, but only just. If it weren't for immersing myself in the anger management retreat in India, and all those hours of group therapy in Bali to forget The Traitor, I would be exploding by now.

Friday, 8 March, 11.30pm

Went for a drink with Ace tonight and recounted my experience with Mr Not My Type. I told him I'd been upset at the time, but I was over it now. He listened open-mouthed.

'Wanker,' he said. Ace never swears, but he was quite angry about the whole thing. He shook his head in disbelief.

'Language, Ace,' I said in mock horror.

'You know it's nothing to do with you, don't you?'

I told him yes, which wasn't quite true. I pretend but inside I'm not so good at brushing off nasty comments. He's such a lovely supportive friend, and I was touched by his reaction. I'll do the same for him if he starts dating again, though given how he reacted to my story, he has no idea what it's like being single out there. He's going to need my support.

P.S. Hurrah. Joseph, the architect from the Albion Street project, has recommended me to his clients. They have a house in Belgrave Square, one of the most upmarket postcodes in London. I hope it's a whole-house refurbishment. My favourite kind of project. I love transformations and the before and after photos.

Saturday, 9 March, 11.30pm

Joy came at 7am this morning. I'd forgotten to bolt the front door, so she let herself in and the first thing she did was vacuum outside my bedroom. Why? She banged around until I got up and went out.

'Oh sorry, I wake you? I come early. I'm babysitting Aiden and Ava today.'

How does she manage to do my cleaning, be a nanny to two kids and run a cleaning company?

'Joy loves them but don't want to be nanny every day. Parents are always working late. Children are asleep when they come home. Only I talk to them.'

Why do people have children if they're going to leave them with a nanny the whole time? I know I'm being judgemental, and these things are never straightforward and maybe they have no choice but to work all hours. I just think I would have wanted to cherish every minute with my babies if I had the choice.

Later, on my way back from shopping, I bumped into Joy taking the kids to the theatre.

'What are you going to see?' I asked the children.

'*Matilda The Musical*,' they said in unison. In perfect Filipino accents.

Sunday, 10 March, 11.30pm

I was having a coffee at Café a Deux, minding my own business. Not on a date for a change. A man came in, searched around, spotted me and came over.

'You must be Melanie,' he said, smiling.

'No, I'm not,' I said.

'Yes, you are. You said to meet here. I know it's you,' Mr Angry shouted.

'No, I can assure you, I'm not Melanie.' I didn't raise my voice, but I gripped the cup handle.

'Bloody women. You fix a date, then pretend to be someone else if you don't like the look of him. Bitch.' He rushed towards the door, banged a table, and knocked over someone's strawberry milkshake with his parka.

Once I got over the shock, it made me think of the experiences I've been through so far in my dating challenge. There've been some blinders, but nothing nasty, apart from Mr Not My Type. I suppose there are just as many weird and not-so-wonderful women out there mistreating men. That poor bugger had obviously been on one too many awful dates. When did it become OK to insult people because you don't want to date them? The swipe culture has a lot to answer for. It's bad enough for me but I'm glad I'm not an unformed twenty-something trying to find love.

Texted Grace and arranged to meet her for lunch tomorrow. Phoned Sara and asked her what I should say to Grace.

'Your friends are as bad as you with all their drama. It's none of your business. Why are you sticking your nose in?' she said.

Damn. I shouldn't have done that. Totally insensitive of me given Laurence's affair. I am the CEO of Bad Sisters Incorporated.

Monday, 11 March, 11.45am

On the bus, going to meet Grace. My stomach is doing somersaults. I'll just act normal, tell her when and where I came across her doppelgänger and the pink handbag and see if she admits it was her. Will she confess her affair and confide in me or will she make up some story? Could there be a different explanation for what I witnessed? I doubt it but I hope so. I want to be wrong. I love Grace but I'm fond of Ajay too and wouldn't like to think she's cheating on him. First Ace, now Grace. And possibly Jude too.

3.00pm

Fuck, fuck, fuck. I can't believe it. I was completely on the wrong track. The man with Grace was a colleague. She'd been to an appointment at Barts Hospital on her own because she didn't want to tell her family and friends about it. Afterwards she'd gone to work but had got upset, so he took her out to lunch. She's been diagnosed with breast cancer. She's only forty-five. We cried. She's told Ajay now but doesn't want to tell the kids or her parents yet, so I'm sworn to secrecy. I think the Nigerian in her is avoiding upsetting the rest of the family for as long as possible. She's waiting for a date for surgery. They've caught it early so hopefully that'll be all the treatment she needs. Thank goodness she got the lump checked out.

11.30pm

So sad about Grace. I've been Googling breast cancer all evening. It says eighty-six per cent of women in England live for at least five years after diagnosis. Five years? That's not long. She'll only be fifty then. I thought we were good at treating breast cancer now, but thirty women die of it every day. And the post-surgery pictures are horrible. I can't bear to look anymore. But she's going to be OK. I'm sure of it. She's a fighter.

Tuesday, 12 March, 11.30pm

I'm feeling guilty for thinking Grace was having an affair. Why did I jump to that conclusion? Am I so jaded about relationships that I assume someone is cheating even when they're clearly happily married? Or do I want to believe relationships don't work so I can justify not committing to one myself? Then again, the divorce rate is something like fifty per cent, so something is not right. I'm just a realist. Look at Ace and Kelly.

Dating feels completely irrelevant right now. What if I got cancer? The stats are not good for women my age. If I thought I might die, would it make me want to find love, have more sex, or would I give up and concentrate on my health instead? I might take a break from the dating challenge.

Wednesday, 13 March, 11.30pm

Texted Grace to see how she's doing and she sent a crying emoji.

TEN

Milk Tray Man

Thursday, 14 March, 11.30pm

HAD A MATCH NOTIFICATION ON LADYBIRD. He's handsome in a Milk Tray Man kind of a way. He says he's active, likes travel, and he's looking for someone to spoil. Will check him out. Am I a terrible friend for thinking about dating?

Friday, 15 March, 11.30pm

Ordered some curtains for the Mayfair project. My curtain maker Tanya has set up her own company called Very Well Hung.

Saturday, 16 March, 11.30pm

Went for a lovely walk in Springfield Park. No penis sightings today.

Sunday, 17 March, 11.30pm

Had a drink with Milk Tray Man from Thursday, but he certainly wasn't as smooth or sweet as I'd expected. I introduced myself and asked him his name (his username was Hello Girls, but I let that go). He sighed and just stared at me. The conversation, if you could call it that, went like this:

'Sorry if I've forgotten but I don't remember you telling me your name,' I said.

'Oh, I thought you knew.'

'No, sorry I don't.'

'Are you sure?' he asked.

Did he forget his name and wanted me to remind him?

'I'm sure. I wouldn't be asking you if I knew,' I said. What was his problem? How many times did I have to say it? He shook his head.

'I'm a doctor. Now do you know?'

'An admirable profession, but what's your name?'

Did he have an accident on the way and lose his short-term memory?

'Yes but, do you "know" now?' He winked at me.

WTF? Was I missing something?

'Sorry, you've lost me,' I said.

At that he shook his head, huffed and studied his drink. There was an awkward pause. I made conversation, but I could see he was distracted and not listening. Then after a while, he stopped me mid-sentence.

'You really don't know who I am?' he asked.

For the love of God, how many times?

'I'm Dr Love.'

I raised an eyebrow.

'I've had enough of this,' he said, pushed back his chair, picked up his mobile and walked off.

He'd had enough?

'Tosser,' I shouted after him.

I Googled him when I got home. It turns out he's not Milk Tray Man but had been Mr Z List Celeb a few years ago when he played Doctor Quentin Love in a soap opera called Turmoil in Trevelyan. Where do they get these names? Obviously, his career has risen without a trace. How dare I not recognise him? Tosser indeed.

P.S. Texted Ajay to ask after Grace. He said she's been having tests and seeing different doctors. It's becoming real now, but she still hasn't told the kids or the rest of her family.

ELEVEN

The Guru

Monday, 18 March, 11.30pm

THE HOUSE on Belgrave Square was A-MAZ-ING. The owners were in their early forties and were charm personified. Valentina is from a mega rich tin mine-owning Chilean family and Kenneth is a wine importer (nice job if you can get it, but he's done better for himself in marriage). They showed me pictures of the enormous ranch-style house they'd had built in Chile.

'Wow, that's incredible. Do you live there for part of the year then?' I asked.

'Oh no, that's the barbeque house. The main house is a few hundred yards away,' Valentina explained.

Anyway, the job turned out to be – drumroll – designing a cloakroom! I hereby christen this job Project Toilet. No job too small for this interior designer.

P.S. When I changed handbags for the meeting, I found the Wellness Advocate's card from my date with Cement Man. No other dates on the horizon, so I might as well contact him and see what he's like.

Tuesday, 19 March, 11.30pm

Grace came over tonight for a chat. She said going to the hospital is becoming a full-time job, but the uncertainty is the most difficult part. She's bearing up but wants to know what the future holds for her. They're still doing lots of tests. As expected, Ajay has been a star in supporting and looking after her.

On happier news, The Wellness Advocate was keen to meet when I texted him. I Googled him afterwards. He looks like a white-haired Jesus. Very Zen and calm-looking with piercing green eyes. Definitely worth a date. I think I'll call him The Guru.

Thursday, 21 March, 9.30am

First day of spring, and I have a spring in my step. Meeting The Guru later. He wants to meet at Zen Coffee in Covent Garden. Of course he does.

1.30pm

That was one of the strangest, most intense, and emotional first dates ever. The coffee shop was noisy and crowded but he stood out like an oasis of calm, dressed all in white with a Karl Lagerfeld ponytail, his intense eyes finding mine across the room. I can't believe I didn't notice him at the bar when I was with Cement Man. I introduced myself and sat down but he was mute. He gave me a handwritten note saying, 'the universe told me to have a day of silence today. Let's speak with our eyes.'

'Ha ha, that's the best icebreaker ever,' I said, but he said nothing, continuing to stare.

I was about to say sorry this is not for me, but his eyes were veeery pretty, so I thought, what the hell. I ordered my coffee, verbally. He ordered his herbal tea using the international language of pointing.

'So, do you often leave your card for unsuspecting women at bars?'

Nothing.

'I was on a date when you spotted me, but I didn't see him again,' I said, struggling to continue the one-sided conversation. Heat was rising up my neck and into my face and I felt beads of perspiration over my upper lip. Why do hot flushes always pick the worst times?

I was about to launch into another question when he gently guided my hands down onto the table and put his own over mine. It took a few minutes of locking eyes with him – though it felt like hours – before I could stop the internal chatter of 'WTF is going on?' The light in his bright green eyes was mesmerising and his slightly off-kilter face intriguing.

At first, it was hard to hold his gaze, but as my breathing became regular and my body relaxed, I entered his zone, shutting out the rest of the world, our energies intermingling. It wasn't lustful or urgent but a holistic connection. My pent-up emotions were whipped up into a tsunami, which burst out in slow motion from my eyes. I didn't know why I was crying but it felt good. Then he released my hands, sat back and the spell was broken. Embarrassed by my tears, I went to the loo to clean up but when I came out, he'd gone.

11.30pm

Couldn't do any work this afternoon. Far too perturbed by today's experience. Why did I cry? Was it purely his effect on me, or did he look into my soul? I have so many questions. I Googled 'staring into people's eyes'. Apparently, there have been studies that show ten minutes of staring into someone's eyes can induce a hallucinogenic effect. It sure induced something in me. Why did he go without saying goodbye though? No text since then. I'm drawn to him and want to see him again.

Friday, 22 March, 11.30pm

No word from The Guru. Does a vow of silence apply to texts? I'm restless and hankering after the trippy feeling he created. But given he left unexpectedly, I'm not going to contact him. Did he see something in my eyes that he didn't like? Did I scare him away by being vulnerable and crying? Or is there a devilish side to me I don't know about? Also, was it his effect on me or can looking into anybody's eyes generate that feeling of otherworldliness? Maybe it was because the simple act of looking into someone's eyes is such an intimate experience. I've been suppressing my true feelings for such a long time, it was as if those few moments of intimacy whipped up my emotions and forced them out along with the tears. Am I lying even to myself? Denying my craving for a true connection and not allowing myself to admit I want to love and be loved? I've been pretending not to care for so long I don't even know anymore. But look what happens when I do show my emotions.

Saturday, 23 March, 2.30pm

First Brunch Bunch since Grace's cancer diagnosis. She's been told she needs a lumpectomy and is waiting for an operation date, but more tests are needed to decide if there would be other treatments like chemotherapy or radiotherapy. She had droopy shoulders and a tired expression but obviously wanted a distraction. She and Leila thought I should stay away from The Guru.

'He sounds like a nutter,' was Leila's assessment of him.

'Or a narcissist,' added Grace.

'Or both,' Leila said, 'and I bet he left you with the bill.' How the hell did she know that?

Yes, he was a bit, let's say, unusual. But given we were only together for fifteen minutes, I was surprised to feel such a connection. No throbbing in the vagina department but an experience mostly concentrated above the waist. Anyway, what's a cup of tea between spiritual friends?

Tried the staring thing with Leila but couldn't keep it going for long without fits of giggles, so I did it with Grace. She cried, then we all sobbed.

Sunday, 24 March, 11.30pm

The Guru texted. He said his soul was elevated when he explored my eyes. Just his soul? He's invited me to his next wellness workshop. Doesn't sound like a date but I'll give it a go. I checked out his website and it's a bit Goop, and not my kind of thing. The blurb is up itself and there are lots of expensive products claiming to improve your life, and sex toys with ambiguous descriptions. Where does one insert The Intensifier? The whole set-up feels like it's preying on lonely single women, and the prices are steep. An eyewatering (in more ways than one) £260 for the said Intensifier.

But I'm intrigued by The Guru and looking forward to seeing him. I wonder if we'll get some alone time.

Monday, 25 March, 11.30pm

I got the Project Toilet job. Hurrah! I hope they'll be adventurous. The smallest room in the house is always a great opportunity to be flamboyant. I might not show them the weird ones I've done though, like the guy who wanted it to look like an alleyway or the infinity one where every inch was covered with mirrors.

Wednesday, 27 March, 11.30pm

Phoned Mum and Dad for a chat. An hour and twenty minutes of tech support later! Trying to get a seventy-nine-year-old to hold her phone camera over her iPad so I can teach her how to use her Painting by Numbers app was exhausting. No sooner was that sorted, and she passed the phone to Dad who wanted to know if they should get an 'Anita' like their neighbour had.

'Samuel says Anita's really clever. You can ask her how old

you are and where you live, but your mother's not keen. Have you got an 'Anita' Sophie love?'

Mum shouted across the room. 'She listens to everything you say and puts it on Google. I don't want everyone knowing our business.'

I laughed, but who's going to do my tech support when I'm too old to fathom it? Will I end up lonely and isolated because I can't work out how to communicate with the digital world anymore, and there are no grandchildren to keep me up to date? It's a scary thought.

Thursday, 28 March, 11.30pm

Grace's op is on 15 April.

Friday, 29 March, 11.30pm

Went to see my real-life princess client from a Middle Eastern royal family (I'm not allowed to say which). She doesn't work and has no problem spending the family fortune. She wants a new bed and, as always, wants the most expensive one that money can buy. I told her that the best bed with spring technology to make it the most comfortable sleep would cost around £35K. She wasn't impressed.

'What if it was gold-plated?' she asked.

'It's covered in fabric, so unfortunately it can't be gold-plated. How about a gold headboard?'

'Yes, let's do that. Can we like, also get the springs made with gold?'

Saturday, 30 March, 11.30pm

Here's a fact I didn't want to know. Was watching a programme on TV about menopause tonight. Apparently, your labia darkens as you get older. How do they know, and who's been keeping track?

Sunday, 31 March, 11.30pm

Went shopping with Grace for PJs to wear in hospital. They think she'll be in for one night, which must mean they're not expecting complications. Good news, surely. We went to Harvey Nichols for drinks afterwards. I distracted her with tales of Project Toilet and Dad wanting to buy an 'Anita'. She got quite tipsy and giggled. It was nice.

PART IV
April

TWELVE

The Bus Stop Boys

Monday, 1 April, 11.30pm

GOT A TEXT FROM LIAM, the builder working on the heated marble island job.

> Sorry bad news. Fitted heating under the island marble yesterday but hadn't checked thermostat. Client came home after we'd left decided to 'try it out' and now his partner has burns on her back. Didn't feel the heat while they were at it. Only afterwards. He's threatening to sue.

> Oh no! That's terrible. Will she be OK? I'm coming over.

> They're both at the hospital. I'll let you know when to come. Don't call him. Said not to bother him while she's being treated. He's really pissed with you. Brace yourself.

I tried to ring Liam a few times, but it kept going to voicemail. I was stressed out all afternoon waiting for the call, hoping to God she'd be OK and that they wouldn't actually sue me. Then Liam texted.

April Fool!

Not funny.

Wednesday, 3 April, 11.30pm

I'm so excited. Valentina and Kenneth liked my kitsch tropical paradise idea. Can't wait to start working on it.

Texted Lee of the 'women seeking women' episode to see if she wanted to go for that drink but she hasn't replied. Maybe London Soulmates has delivered for her and she's all loved up.

Thursday, 4 April, 11.30pm

Damn it. It's been three months since I started the dating challenge and I've only had sex twice. What's the point of giving up love for sex if I don't get any? Will The Guru be the third? The dating challenge was for one date every week. I'm not even doing that, let alone having sex once a week. Will have to pack them in for the rest of the year. It might not be one date a week as the challenge demands, but I could aim for fifty-two dates in total.

Saturday, 6 April, 11.30pm

I feel like I've overdosed on oestrogen. The wellness workshop attendees were all female and mostly single going by the questions they asked. The Guru introduced the workshop. No vow of silence today. He is so charismatic, and I could see his audience was entranced. Halfway through his talk, he asked us to look under our seats where we found a delicately wrapped chocolate heart. He was telling us how we should savour life and wanted to demonstrate it.

'Close your eyes,' he said, in a quiet velvety voice, 'place the chocolate on your tongue, close your lips and hug the chocolate inside. Just allow the dark flavour to melt slowly from the heat of your mouth. Feel the rich creamy texture and allow yourself to savour the luscious taste. Let the melted chocolate enwrap your taste buds and send dopamine through your body. Let it slowly fill you with happiness and a desire for wellbeing. Now swallow the melted stickiness of it.'

His voice was as silken as the chocolate in our mouths. The room felt moist and charged with pheromones. We all wanted him. He'd played with us, turned us on, and sweet-talked us to the climax. There was a hush that sounded like a hundred women having a quiet secret orgasm.

He was good at being a Wellness Advocate, and he knew how to push people's buttons. He told us we should do the chocolate trick once a day to boost wellbeing. At the end of the workshop, he came over and stood facing me quite close, holding my hands where they were hanging by my sides.

'Thank you for coming. It means a lot to me,' he said, before he was whisked away by one of his minions with a headset to meet some CEO of a partner company.

Sunday, 7 April, 9.30am

I texted The Guru last night to thank him for the workshop, and he replied saying he hoped I got something out of it. I didn't get what I wanted, that's for sure. I'm now wondering if the first coffee I had with The Guru was even a date. Yes, we had a connection, and I find him attractive, but he hasn't said how he feels about me. Did he leave me his card at the bar that time because he liked me, or was he just recruiting another follower?

P.S. Feeling sexually frustrated. I think I'll invest in The Intensifier.

Monday, 8 April, 12.30am (technically Tuesday, 9 April)

They say you don't get any buses for ages and then two come at once, and that was the case with men at a bus stop tonight. Now officially known as My Lucky Bus Stop. The men were young – late twenties – and there were two of them. One after the other.

I was saying goodbye to Izzy at My Lucky Bus Stop in Soho after salsa at Bar Baile. A tipsy-looking man came up to us and asked for my number. I said no. Who gives out their number to a drunk at a bus stop? But he was persistent and wouldn't go away. I was starting to think why not when Izzy suggested I should give him my number but only if he memorised it. He was repeating the number out loud as he walked away. That was Bus Stop Boy Number One.

Izzy then left me standing smiling to myself when I locked eyes with another young man who rode past on a bike. I was about to get on my bus when someone tapped me on the shoulder. He'd come back to talk to me. He asked me if he could come home with me. Cheeky. I declined but agreed to give him my number. That was Bus Stop Boy Number Two. I was obviously in one of my 'be open to everything' moods. Or was it the sexual frustration of the previous night?

Tuesday, 9 April, 11.30pm

I've had messages from the Bus Stop Boys. All day. They're both keen to see me and shocked when I told them my age, but it didn't seem to deter them. I suspect they just want sex. Should I go for it? I could try one first and see how I feel. I've had two one-night stands since starting my dating challenge (before that was the open-air sex with the tour guide outside his tent in the Australian bush last year). I could do with some no-strings-attached fun as long as they see it in the same way. I don't want anything to do with them if they think I'm desperate or – even worse – grateful because they're young. But I'm not getting that vibe from their texts. I think I'll invite Number One to come round.

Wednesday, 10 April, 11.30pm

Called Grace to see if she wanted any help or to meet up, but she doesn't. I think she just wants to get the surgery over with and not talk about it.

Thursday, 11 April, 11.30pm

Oh boy. Or should I say oh Bus Stop Boy Number One. He came round tonight. He'd obviously dressed up for the occasion, though his navy ankle-length trousers and short-sleeved check shirt were a bit too tight for my liking. I suppose he wanted to show off his muscles. But he smelt nice, and he'd brought a bottle of wine. All good so far. Clean and polite. I was pleasantly surprised that he was good-looking with a shock of blonde hair carefully teased to stand up.

We chatted, flirted and had some wine, but soon started to kiss. I was thinking, what am I doing and why am I doing this? Then I told myself to let go and enjoy it. We were consenting adults, and we could just have a night of passion. We moved quite quickly to the bedroom.

A wham, bam, thank you ma'am later, I was sitting up, with arms crossed and a disappointed expression. I thought he was one of those younger men wanting an older woman who knows what she wants. I hoped he wanted to explore and please, but no. It was all so mechanical, there was next to no foreplay, and he acted like the whole thing was only about his orgasm. He treated it like a microwave meal: no preparation and hoping for a ping of satisfaction in three minutes or less. It was like he was on a rocket going into space, forgetting there was another astronaut on board. Or he might have been following a Sex for Dummies instruction manual that said, 'Insert tab A into slot B. That's it. You're done.' His sex education was at mock-GCSE level, and I wanted someone with a PhD. There was only so much I could do to bridge the gap. I was relieved when he said he had to get up early and left soon after.

I don't remember boyfriends being like that when I was in my twenties. I've heard about younger people approaching sex differently now because of all the porn they watch, but I do hope for their sakes that my experience tonight is not typical of their generation. Never mind the gender pay gap. What about the gender orgasm gap?

Friday, 12 April, 11.30pm

The Intensifier arrived and it's veeery good! Much better than Bus Stop Boy Number One. No word from The Guru. If he can make a room full of women feel orgasmic by eating chocolate, actual sex with him must be super-orgasmic. I want some.

Checked Ladybird and London Soulmates but didn't spot anyone I liked. Have I seen all the available men in London?

Saturday, 13 April, 3.30pm

I was reading *Livingetc* when Joy came down from my office holding The Intensifier. I was on my way to the bathroom to wash it this morning when the office phone rang, and I must have left it on my desk.

'What's this?' she asked.

Gulp.

'Oh, that's for work. It smooths out creases in wallpaper. You know, if it's been fitted badly.'

'Ah, OK.'

'But you should wash your hands in case there's glue left on it. It's not good for your skin.'

I'll remember this moment next time she says something awful to me.

Sunday, 14 April, 6.00pm

Called Grace to wish her luck for her operation tomorrow. She sounded terrified. I told her treating breast cancer is highly successful nowadays. Of course, she's worried about what would happen to her kids if she doesn't come through. Oh God, I don't even want to think about that. She'll be in one of the best hospitals in the country and it'll all be fine. I have a good feeling about it.

All of which makes me think I should stop being sensible and not overthink things. What's wrong with being reckless sometimes? I want to do something to make me feel alive. I think

I'll give Bus Stop Boy Number Two a go. His texting has turned into sexting today so it's time.

11.30pm

BSB Two was keen when I invited him over. Though it was quite spooky when he arrived an hour later, looking and behaving like BSB One. It was a case of déjà view, déjà woo and déjà do. Had they been watching the same YouTube 'how to' videos? Or was it the same porn site? Neither had condoms, and both said, 'no need, I'm clean'. They might just shove it up in a porno but not in real life, thanks. Luckily, I'm responsible.

The sex was … hurried and underwhelming. I tried to spice things up, but he was in a race to the finish that left me on the sidelines. No foreplay, and no consideration for my needs. It was a fast-food drive-thru experience – quick, unsatisfying, and only one person got to eat. Afterwards, I asked him how he was getting home and, to make me feel really old, he said he'd texted his mum and asked her to pick him up.

Never let it be said I don't try new things, but I'm done with young men. It didn't make me feel alive, just disenchanted. For a second, I thought it was me, but I had to remind myself that I'd experienced and fully contributed to good quality sex before, and my recent experiences were lacking in that department. I don't know. Maybe in the end they decided I was too old for them or all they wanted was an orgasm rather than a full sexual experience. Possibly my full bush anti-grooming pubic hair vibe frightened them away. If I'm honest, I didn't put much effort into it either. Neither of them properly, truly turned me on. They were no Ooh La La Trousers. I knew my heart wasn't in it, but I didn't know my vagina didn't want to go for the ride either. I was going through the motions, so to speak, so I have to take some responsibility. Whatever it was, I don't want it again. Meaningless sex is all very well but it has to be good sex to make it worthwhile.

Monday, 15 April, 11.30pm

Visited Grace at the hospital tonight. I bumped into Ajay and the kids in the corridor as they were leaving. He said her operation had gone well and she was resting. Thank God. I tiptoed into her room and watched her sleeping. Then she stirred, winced with pain, and opened her eyes, so I held her hand and told her to go back to sleep.

When The Cute Nurse came to check her blood pressure, I asked to have a word with him, and we went into the bathroom so we wouldn't disturb Grace. As he was telling me about her operation and prognosis, we moved closer, our eyes fixed on each other's faces, then mouths and bodies, and before I knew it, we were devouring each other, grabbing at hair, boobs, bums, and pulling off our clothes.

'Sophia, where are you?' Grace croaked.

We froze, hoping she'd go back to sleep, but she called out again. We both sighed and straightened our clothes and went back into the room. She inspected us with suspicion. He had a few lipstick marks on his nurse's tunic, which was only just long enough to cover his receding excitement. After thanking the nurse for checking her blood, Grace waited till he'd left then turned to me, her smiling mouth turning into an angry slit.

'That's a new fucking low, Sophia.'

'What?' I said, looking as innocent as I could under the circumstances.

'Your hair. And your blouse is done up the wrong fucking way.'

I patted down the stray curls. 'I'm sorry. I don't know what came over…'

She raised her palm and let out a slow breath. 'Stop. I don't want to hear it. I'm lying here feeling shit, with half a breast missing, not knowing if I'm going to live or die and wishing I could curl up and sleep forever, and you, you … are making it all about you. Some fucking friend you are. Aargh.'

'Grace…'

'Just go. I'm too tired for this.' She turned away and closed her eyes.

I'm so ashamed. Why did I do it? Was I overcome by the intimacy of the plush bathroom? Or did the whole hospital situation heighten the sense of my own mortality, and make me want to feel alive? Possibly I yearned to feel desired after the disappointing experiences with the Bus Stop Boys, wanting to prove that I'm still attractive to cute young men. Was it simply too good an opportunity to miss or dismiss? Probably a bit of all those things. I can't explain it, but I hate myself. I'm now officially the World's Worst Fucking Friend.

Tuesday, 16 April, 11.30pm

The Guru texted today. About time.

Hey Sophia, I've missed your positive energy

Hi, nice to hear from you. How's your wellness going?

Very well thank you. I'm planning a 4-day retreat in Crete in June. Would you like to join me?

That sounds interesting. Can you send me the details?

I knew our energies would be aligned.

How exciting. A retreat in Greece sounds fabulous. He must be interested in me after all, and he's been waiting for the right opportunity to spend quality time to connect.

P.S. Haven't had the guts to call Grace. Need more time.

Wednesday, 17 April, 11.30pm

What the hell is happening with my friends? Went to a 'singles party' for thirty-eight to fifty-five-year-olds with Izzy. She has realised Francis is a knob and ditched him. Good. We were both slightly out of the age range at either end, but reckoned it would be OK. We booked the tickets about two weeks ago, but tonight I didn't want to be there. How are you supposed to know that in two weeks' time at that appointed hour, you'll feel like being on show and acting flirty in a room full of other single people searching for love, sex or whatever it is they're looking for? Sometimes these parties feel like a cattle market where people stand around displaying their assets and hoping for a buyer. You need to be in the mood to put in the hard work.

The event was in one of those huge plush bars in the City where one room had been cordoned off with red rope to make you feel like celebrities. We bought a bottle of wine and sat down for a chat, not playing the self-promotion game. A few brave guys tried to interject, and we made polite conversation but didn't encourage them, so they moved on.

'What's the point of coming and not talking to anyone?' Izzy asked.

'You have to be in the zone for these things and I'm not feeling it tonight. Sorry. Do you mind?' I asked. I felt guilty and relieved when she said it was OK and we could enjoy a girly night instead.

'Oh my God. Is that Jude?' I said, looking at the guy in the corner whispering into a woman's ear. 'Yes, it's him. What the hell is he doing here?' Jude must have felt my eyes burning through him and looked over to me. There was a tiny hint of annoyance on his face, which was quickly hidden with a smile as he strolled towards us.

'Hello, hello, what are you doing in this part of the world?' he asked, all casual.

'We're here for the singles party. What about you?'

'I was having a drink with a friend in the other bar and on the way back from the Gents, I spotted a colleague and came to talk to her. What do you mean singles party?' he asked, looking around.

'This room. This is a singles party. You know, where single people come to meet?'

'Really? I didn't know. I just wandered in. Someone might have picked me up.' He laughed.

I listened to his explanation sceptically and wondered if I should give him the benefit of the doubt. After all, it was the end of the evening and the red rope had been removed. It was feasible he could have come in to see his friend.

'Manners, Sophia. Are you going to introduce me to your friend?' he asked.

I introduced Izzy but when I turned to her, the colour had drained from her face, and she barely whispered hello.

'Let's take a picture to send to Leila,' I suggested and took out my phone. As we looked into the lens for a selfie, I locked eyes with him. My expression must have said, 'I'm onto you'. There was a flash of rage on his face before he caught himself and grinned for the camera.

'I'd better say goodbye to my colleague,' he said. We watched him strut over, whisper something to the woman, and go to the other bar.

'What's the matter, Izzy? You look like you've seen a ghost,' I said.

'I sort of have. That was Mark, the guy I told you about, that I had a one-night stand with back in January, but he obviously doesn't remember ghosting me. Is he a friend? And why did you call him Jude?' Her eyes were tight, and her face flushed by then.

'I called him Jude because that's his name. He's my friend Leila's husband. Are you sure it was him?'

'Absolutely. I had no idea he wasn't single, let alone being married to your friend. We live in a city of millions, and I manage to pick him.'

'Oh, he can be a charming little shit. They've only been married about eighteen months. She thinks she's in a fairytale romance and doesn't know she's living a lie with a devious, philandering husband. I can't believe he's so heartless and selfish to do this to Leila. Actually, I can believe it. I've never trusted Jude. What a complete and utter bastard, going round picking up random women for sex.' Rant over, I turned to Izzy who looked stricken. 'Oh no Izzy, I'm so sorry. I'm not blaming you. It wasn't your fault. I'm just furious with Jude.' I gave her an apologetic hug while I extracted my foot from my mouth. How do you feel about him now? Do you still like him?'

'No, I think he's a little shit too,' she said.

'Do you think I should tell Leila? She loves him so much. I can't bear to see her heartbroken.'

'I'm hardly the best person to ask, but I'd throw him under the bus if I were you. He deserves it. Would Leila want to know though? Some people don't. They want to pretend it hasn't happened.'

Leila's going to be devastated if she finds out. What should I do? I'll put the pic on Instagram and let Jude explain it to her. I don't want to be the messenger who gets shot. Also, did he truly not remember Izzy or was he pretending? If he didn't remember her, he must have a lot of one-night stands, but if he did, then he's a very good actor/liar. Either way, it's bad news. I wish I hadn't gone to that blasted party so I wouldn't be sitting here grappling with my conscience. And we didn't even meet any men.

11.40pm

I've posted the pic, with 'guess who I bumped into?' tagging Leila and Jude.

P.S. Must practise my selfie angle to make my not-so-button nose look smaller.

Thursday, 18 April, 7.30am

Did I do the right thing posting that pic? I'm not at all sure, but wouldn't it have been a matter of time before Izzy would come to some party or other with me, and meet Leila and Jude?

Leila's comment on my post popped up. 'Small world, isn't it? We had a good laugh about it last night.' Obviously, she didn't suspect a thing and I felt uneasy replying with a few laughing emojis. She has no idea his devotion could be an act. Or possibly she does but is not acknowledging it. Relationships are so complicated. People want different things from having a partner, and their wants can often be opaque or dishonourable.

11.30pm

I've been on edge all day about the Jude thing. I texted Izzy to see how she was and asked her exactly when she'd had the one-night stand with him. It was 14 January and, according to my diary, that was the day he had a row with Leila and disappeared for hours.

Friday, 19 April, 11.30pm

I arranged the surprise for Mum's birthday. I was all happy about my genius idea until I texted Sara to tell her about it, and she said she's not coming to the party because she has to work an out-of-hours' shift.

> Are you serious? You're going to miss Mum's 80th?

I'm serious.

> Can't you get someone to cover?

I could but I don't think I should. It'll look bad.

> But she'll be upset and how will it look to her friends if you're not there?

Don't lecture me Sophe. You were away for nearly a year, and now you're too busy having it off with all and sundry on your embarrassing dating challenge, so don't pretend you're the dutiful daughter

> That's so unfair.

That's so unfair.

She's so infuriating. If it wasn't for what she's been through, I'd go round and give her a piece of my mind. Ohm. Ohm. Ohm.

Saturday, 20 April, 1.30pm

I felt so awkward with Leila at brunch today. She's blissfully ignorant of her husband's exploits. Am I a terrible friend or a good friend for not telling her? She's been so happy with Jude, and I don't want to be the one who destroys her happiness. But surely, she must have spotted the clues. There are always clues.

No Grace today. She's at home recovering from the operation. Fingers crossed that's sorted her. We sent her a selfie to say we missed her. I told Leila about the nurse, and she laughed like a hyena, then told me to go visit Grace. Today. I'm not going to tell Grace about cheating Jude. She has enough to worry about.

On the bright side, Ace is in town and joined us. He's been diversifying from classical music, and he enjoyed the jamming session in Cuba so much, he's been rehearsing with a Latin band! I know I embarrassed him at the time, but it's turned out great and you never know where it might take him in the future. Sophia strikes again. He invited us to their gig next week, which'll be great, except Leila wants to bring Jude. I can't face him.

Ace noticed I was a bit off and asked me about it after Leila went to her yoga class. I swore him to secrecy and told him about Jude.

'I can't believe it. Why would you get married and cheat on your wife so soon after?' he said.

'Because he's an arsehole and can't keep his dick zipped up? And we don't know if it's a one-off. Leila said he was openly flirting with the waitress that day.'

'Men like him give us all a bad name.'

I raised my eyebrows and inclined my head. He didn't react. He's in no position to pass judgement on other cheating men. Then I felt awkward, so I told him about my Cement Man date, and he laughed heartily which I thought was a bit unnecessary. Why does he take such pleasure at my dating disaster?

11.30pm

I was too ashamed to tell Ace about the bathroom incident, but I did make myself visit Grace at home today. Ajay welcomed me in, and tried, unsuccessfully, to hide a grin.

'Your shirt's done up wrong,' he said. I looked down then remembered I was wearing a T-shirt. I got flustered and splashed his hair and denim shirt as I put my dripping umbrella away.

There was the hubbub of a party upstairs, and the sweet aroma of the hot spicy food laid out on the dining table. I went up to Grace's bedroom and hovered by the door until I was spotted by her mum Oni, who held out her arms, shuffled towards me and hugged me hard, squashing her ample breasts against me.

'Sophia dear, what have I done to deserve this? What did her father do to be punished by God? What did my daughter do to get this nasty disease?' she asked in her exuberant rhythmic Nigerian accent. She whispered the word 'disease' as though saying it quietly could make it disappear.

'It's not anybody's fault, Oni. It could happen to anybody,' I said, but she just sighed and shook her head. Grace was hugging her drain bottle, sitting up and looking surprisingly well, which was lucky as her family were in full-on 'Nigerian auntie' mode. There were nine aunties surrounding her bed in small groups. Some were chatting, laughing, knitting, or eating, and all of them seemingly oblivious to Grace, who was texting and ignoring the mountain of food on her tray.

'No Sophia, God is punishing us. I don't know why. Why?' Oni continued.

This prompted a few of the aunties to join in. They raised their arms to the heavens, threw their heads back, and asked, 'Why God?'

'Why do you make this woman suffer?' asked another auntie. The others repeated it in unison in an orchestrated performance. How did they decide who says what and in what order? It was like a Catholic wedding where the congregation knows exactly how to respond to the priest's pronouncements while the non-believers look perplexed.

I went over to Grace, who shifted to her side to sit up, and four of the aunties jumped up with cries of 'What is the matter? Let me help you. You must eat. Are you in pain?'

I caught Grace's eye as I took in the theatricality of the situation and we both laughed, which made her wince with pain. Cue more fussing. She gave me a tired smile, and whispered, 'I love them, but I wish they'd give me some peace.' As if by magic, Ajay appeared and said Grace needed rest. The aunties grumbled but were subdued as they left the room. Grace said the doctors were pleased with her progress and she was feeling better, if a little low.

'I'm so, so sorry Grace. I don't know why I did it, but I know it was insensitive and selfish. I love you so much and would never want to hurt you. Will you forgive me? Please?'

She took a long look at me. 'It was an awful thing to do but … I probably overreacted after the effect of the anaesthetic. I can see the funny side of it now, especially the bulge under his tunic. I couldn't help looking in that area each time he came to check on me.' We burst into laughter.

'Seriously, what's going on with you? You're the most considerate person I know. It's so unlike you to do something like that.'

I told her about the Bus Stop Boys and not being sure whether I feel like a confident cougar or a saddo being used by young men for easy sex.

'They should be grateful you even looked at them. It's not your fault they were incompetent and can't appreciate a good thing when they see it.' She hesitated and looked serious. 'But promise me this: only do what makes you happy, not just to win the challenge.'

I promised. It was good to get her reassurance and not dwell on self-doubt. What is going on with me though? It's only April. Am I done with seeking only sex already? Is it really what I want?

Sunday, 21 April, 11.30pm

Grace's forgiveness and a good night's sleep have done wonders and I'm feeling positive today. The Guru sent me the hotel details for the retreat. The place looks amazing – a mixture of Greek/Scandi minimal style, set in beautiful, lush gardens with sprays of magenta bougainvillea and to-die-for views of the Mediterranean. Familiarly wonderful. I think I'll go. At worst, I'll have a lovely relaxing holiday in Crete and if things work out with The Guru, it could be REALLY good fun.

Tuesday, 23 April, 11.30pm

Grace has had the dressing removed. It doesn't look as bad as the pictures they showed her before surgery, but it was still a shock. I wanted to meet up, but she said she's not up to it. Surely going out and having a distraction would help? I guess everyone deals with it differently. I thought Grace would be her usual uber-strong self, but she sounded down. I'll send her some lovely gifts to cheer her up.

Wednesday, 24 April, 11.30pm

Called Mum this morning to wish her a happy eightieth birthday. She's super excited about her party on Sunday and gave me a long list of instructions for things to bring. I'm in charge of decorating the hall she's hired for the occasion. It's a pretty basic community hall, so I'll have to dig deep into my bag of interior design tricks to make it presentable. I'm hanging lots of lengths of white muslin and fairy lights to cover up the nasty bits. It's used as a nursery during the week, though. I don't know how I'm going to hide the ball pit and children's toys.

Thursday, 25 April, 11.30pm

Been writing my speech for Mum's party. I'm getting nervous about it. Why did I let Dad talk me into it? I suppose it was quid pro quo for his contribution to the party. I need to say what an amazing person she is but also be funny. What if it's a complete flop? I don't want a repetition of that time I started a thank you speech over drinks at the end of a build project, when the extremely drunk hen party sitting next to us heckled me so badly, I had to give up halfway through.

THIRTEEN

The Fetishist

Friday, 26 April, 5.30pm

LOOKING FORWARD to going to Ace's gig tonight but not to seeing cheating Jude. Or should that be Judas?

Saturday, 27 April, 10.30am

Leila, Jude, and I met up in Soho yesterday to see Ace and his new band. The club on Dean Street had lots of red velvet, dimmed lighting, and black and white photos of bands. Same look as Cinema Man One's film club but without the menace and sleaze.

While Jude was at the bar, I told Leila the gory details about the Bus Stop Boys, and we were giggling in a huddle when he came back.

'What's so funny?' Jude asked.

We both said, 'Nothing,' and burst into laughter again. He looked annoyed and asked me to shuffle across, so he could wedge himself between us. Then he turned his back to me and was all over Leila, doing his best to make me feel like a spare part. I couldn't bear to look at him acting like a loving husband.

When Leila went to the loo, I decided to confront him.

'Did you really not remember Izzy the other night?' I asked.

'Who's Izzy?' He's a good liar.

'You know, my friend at the singles party, that you had a one-night stand with and then ghosted?'

'She must have me mixed up with someone else. I'm a married man, you know.'

'Yes, an important detail that you conveniently forgot to mention, Mark. It's no use pretending, Jude. I know what happened.' My heart was thumping in my chest.

He shrugged his shoulders, peered around, then turned to me. 'What are you going to do about it?' he hissed.

I don't know what I was expecting but I certainly didn't think he'd admit it so quickly.

'You have to tell Leila. Or I will.'

We both clocked Leila walking back towards us. He smiled, leaned close, and hissed into my ear again, 'You do that, and you'll never see her again. I'll tell her you've been throwing yourself at me and I've been rejecting you. Who do you think she'll believe? Sad old single Sophia or her loving husband?'

Leila came back and wedged herself between us. He pulled her in close and kissed her, giving me a menacing look over her shoulder. I faced away from them and picked up my drink, but my hand was shaking.

Sad single Sophia. I didn't know alliteration could be so cutting.

The band came on then and we whooped and whistled. Ace was cool and casual in the new setting and in his element. After a while, Leila said, 'Don't look but the cute guy two tables to the left is checking you out.'

I was still feeling rattled, but I played along. I didn't want her seeing I was upset and asking questions. I waited a minute, then casually glanced over and caught the guy's eye. Yes indeedy, he was cute. Sitting alone, his long legs sticking way out from under the table and only a tiny hint of a middle-age spread. With his chiselled jaw, close-cropped hair and sharp clothes, he reminded me of Jamie Foxx. And yes, he was a fox.

He nodded at me, and a few minutes later walked over,

crouched next to me, and introduced himself. 'If your friends can spare you, would you join me for a glass of champagne?' he asked in an American accent, pointing at the ice bucket on his table. 'It's too much for one person but it's a special occasion,' he said. I hesitated.

'Please, it would make the evening complete to share a birthday drink with a beautiful woman. And if you don't mind me saying, it looks like your friends want to be alone.' I looked at Leila and Jude, who were absorbed in each other again and thought, what the hell? I moved over to his table, and after getting me a glass, we toasted his fifty-seventh birthday. The band went off for a break then.

'Are you here for work or pleasure?' I asked. The pleasure was all mine.

'I'm visiting from Florida and thought I'd check out this place. I'm a professor of philosophy at Miami University. I'm giving a series of lectures at UCL on the meaning of modern love.' Of course he was.

A babe with brains. Basically, my ideal man. He was charming and complimentary about my blue silk dress and gold sandals.

'Would you mind if I eat? I had so many students talking to me in between lectures that I had no time for lunch today,' he said as the waiter arrived with his food.

'How's your steak?' I asked after a few minutes.

'It's OK, a little tough,' he replied as he struggled to cut a piece off. As he did so, his knife slipped, and the contents of his plate went flying off the table, with most of the buttery crushed potatoes ending up on my foot. He apologised profusely and before I could protest, he got down on the floor and used his napkin to clean my foot.

Then he looked up at me and said, 'I could lick it completely clean if you like.'

Gulp. My first thought was, how dare you? Then, why not? I nodded.

It was dark and he was partially covered by the tablecloth so I couldn't see what he was doing. My eyes popped as I felt his warm wet mouth envelope my big toe and his lively tongue swirl around it. It was an odd experience but not without pleasure.

Leila mouthed 'WTF?'

'I think I got it all off and there's no damage to your sandals,' he said as he got up and sat back in his seat. 'You have delicious feet,' he said, smiling.

My feet are on the, let's say, plump side, wide, and a nightmare to fit into the average shoe. In a warm club, wearing sandals, my toes were like trussed-up sausages trying to break free by sizzling against their shackles. The small toe had managed to escape and poke out triumphantly between the straps. Why did he think my feet were nice? Usually, it's my chest area that attracts the most attention, which is lucky, as I have a fractious relationship with my legs, they not having grown as long as I'd expected and wanted.

The band were back on, and we settled down to listen. But I couldn't help thinking about the lovely sensation I'd felt on my toe. Was he a foot fetishist? Did he get his kicks from sucking toes? That was something I'd never tried before, and quite fancied experiencing. So halfway through the set, purely for research purposes, and ever so gently, I knocked over my glass in the direction of my feet and a stream of red wine rushed over the table and poured onto my toes which just happened to be right under it.

'Oops,' I said, acting mock coy with my hand on my cheek and locking eyes with him. He narrowed his eyes at first, then a gleeful smile.

'Oh dear, let me wipe that for you. And your beautiful gold sandals are covered in red wine,' he said, getting down on his knees.

Once again, I couldn't see what he was doing, and then, there it was, hot and moist. My big toe had entered his mouth, and he sucked it freely and luxuriously. It was quite a turn-on and I wanted more of it. When he'd finished, he sat back in his chair, and I nodded with approval.

'I wonder, are you prepared for your lecture tomorrow?' I asked.

'Yes, I think so, why?' He narrowed his eyes again.

'In my opinion, you haven't practised enough. You need someone to help you rehearse it. You know, help you lick it into shape?' I couldn't believe what was coming out of my mouth.

'Yes, I think you could be right. My speech is back at my hotel if you'd be kind enough to let me … practise on you.' My toes were tingling. 'You could kick off your sandals and relax while I perform it for you.' OMG, so sexy.

He paid the bill while I sipped my wine and anticipated the pleasure to come. I felt guilty about not waiting for Ace and Leila and just managed to text them to say I didn't feel too good and had to go home, before grabbing and kissing him as the taxi arrived at his hotel. Once inside his room, I draped myself on the sofa and wriggled my toes. He took off my shoes, handling my feet like precious works of art. I squirmed with pleasure as he worked his magic.

A light lick, kiss and delicate touch all over my right foot first, becoming more passionate as he saw my delight. He licked across the top of all my toes, which tickled and tantalised in equal measure. Then he took in all of my big toe and sucked in a rhythmic movement. I didn't know feet could be quite so erotic. My other toes got the same action, one after the other, each being cherished and pleasured with equal enthusiasm. He kissed my ankles and licked slowly down to the top of my toes, then teased me as he traced his tongue between each one.

I was already ecstatic and wanting to move onto the rest of our bodies, but like a pro, he did the same to my left foot. That was the most epic foreplay ever. The Bus Stop Boys should take note. It whetted my appetite and drenched me in lust. I grabbed and pulled him up towards me and kissed his mouth. The sex afterwards was probably average technique-wise, but the starter was so amazing it elevated the main delicious course.

I didn't even care that my feet weren't freshly washed and nor did he. I'm glad I went with the flow and invited myself to his room. I'd like to do it again, though I have a feeling I've already experienced the master, and anyone else would be a poor second.

In the morning, I had to leave for an early meeting. Pity he was catching a flight home after the lecture. I would have liked to experience him again. He's clever and erudite, good-looking with a hot bod, and has superb tongue skills. But Florida is too far. I'll have to think of the experience as an initiation gift that could keep on giving.

> Ooh I'm glad I met a foot fetishist
> I didn't know toe sucking was on my fantasy list
> I knew we were both in the flirty zone
> But I wasn't expecting to have my toes blown
> I was shocked that soon after saying hello
> You got down and intimate with my big toe
> But our desires were soon aligned
> And I wanted contact of the footsy kind
> You said your steak and potatoes were nutritious
> But you thought my toes were more delicious
> As you did what you do best, my eyes were shut
> I fantasised you'd eat steak off my butt
> I admired your skills as a philosopher and ethicist
> But I mostly enjoyed you being a foot fetishist
> You were so erudite, sexy and just my type
> Should we try long distance sex on Skype?

P.S. Been Googling foot fetishism. Yes, he was an expert.

12.30pm

I texted Ace to apologise again for leaving early and he asked how I was feeling. I'm a liar, liar, liar. I'm the CEO of Pants on Fire. And I'm ashamed.

I was pleased to hear the gig had gone well and they'd been asked to play there again. I'll send him a congratulations card.

Haven't heard from Leila. If she'd seen me leaving with the Fetishist, she'd have texted by now for the gory details.

And fucking Jude. He was the model loving husband last night. Does he love her and still sleep with other women?

11.00pm

The Fetishist texted me before his flight to say how much he'd enjoyed last night and that I should look him up if I'm ever in Florida. Nice idea but unlikely to happen.

I've put the finishing touches on Mum's birthday speech. Fingers crossed it'll be a hoot. Early night tonight. Driving to Harpenden in the morning to help with the party.

P.S. I've booked a pedicure for next week.

Sunday, 28 April, 11.30pm

Oh. My. God. The party started as The Betty Appreciation Society and ended in high drama. When I arrived at Mum and Dad's this morning, Dot was icing Mum's birthday cake. Why oh, why? Let's just say, lovely friend as she is, Dot can be a bit airheaded, and baking is not her forte. I expect she volunteered, and Mum didn't have the heart to say no.

'My granddaughter Maddison did a lot of the work. Didn't you, Maddie?' Dot asked the surly-looking teenager in Doc Martens hiding behind a curtain of dark hair and staring at her phone. Maddie raised her head, rolled her eyes, grunted, and went back to her mobile.

'Yes, she's been such a help. She even popped to the shops because I'd forgotten the tamarind for the cake,' Dot said in a showy loud voice. Then she turned to me and whispered, 'She's fourteen, and a bit, you know, introverted. My daughter thought it might help if she mixes with other people. All she's done is go to the shops but as soon as she was back, she went straight to the sofa and her phone. I had to rifle through her bag to find the tamarind, and she didn't even buy the right amount.'

Maddison stood up like a meerkat surveying her surroundings, bit her lip and darted around searching for her bag. She rummaged through it several times and, not finding whatever it was she was looking for, sat down and mumbled 'shit' under her breath.

Then the birthday girl made her entrance looking fabulous in an elegant emerald-green 1950s dress, à la Roland Mouret, her shiny white hair in a loose bun. She hasn't passed those tall willowy genes onto me. Dot and I clapped. Maddie glanced over for a second. I'm furious Sara couldn't (or wouldn't?) come to her own mum's birthday party. She said she had to cover for the out-of-hours service at work, and I think Mum believed her, but I'm sure she just didn't want to make the effort to talk to Mum's friends. I don't know many of them either but that's not the point. We'd be there to support Mum, not worry about the guest list. It's not about us but about Mum and what would make her happy. Sara should have at least tried to put her feelings aside for just one afternoon for Mum's sake. I'm trying to be sympathetic, but she can be such a selfish cow.

'Have fun,' Dad said as we were leaving, then winked at me. Usually, he's happy to be left in peace with his sudoku, but he was perky today. I winked back. When I was little, he was always playing tricks on Mum and winking at me to let me in on it, and I'd wink back just like today. I forget he was only eighteen when they had me.

The hall twinkled with the decorations I'd arranged, and there were flower displays and sheer curtains cordoning off the ball pit and hamster tube in the nursery playing area. Dot's cake took pride of place at the end of the buffet table. I hoped it tasted better than it looked. Mum had invited forty of her 'closest friends' for a girls' party and floated around greeting them and being adored by her gushing fans.

I wonder if I'll have so many people coming to my eightieth birthday. I might have to up my game to reach Betty's popularity levels. The chatter and giggling got louder as more women, in their forties to eighties, arrived. It quietened down a little as the guests did their best to make a dent in the huge buffet. In the meantime, my hot flushes were becoming turbo-charged, what with the excitement of the surprise and feeling anxious about my speech. Then it was time.

'Ladies, ladies,' I shouted and waited for hush. 'Mum, I have a surprise for you.' I nodded to Maddison, who rolled her eyes and pressed play on 'Leave Your Hat On'. Dad appeared at the entrance wearing his old army uniform and cap, carrying a baton, and still looking dapper at seventy-eight. The guests went wild and started clapping and whooping. He did a sort of shuffling swagger into the hall, rolled his hips, and did a Rod Stewart-style dance bouncing at the knee, holding his arms aloft and shaking his baton suggestively. He looked down at himself, then at the audience and back, licked his index finger and sizzled it on his chest, just like I'd shown him in the Chippendales videos. Then he started to undress, pausing for effect at each item of clothing. Off came the belt, which he thrashed on the floor before giving it to a lady near him, then kissing her hand as she blushed. He lassoed his tie over his head and threw it to the audience. A few ladies elbowed each other to catch it. He slipped off the jacket and put it over Mum's shoulders before the trousers were whisked off in one move, tearing the Velcro apart.

The women were beside themselves, laughing and screaming as each discarded piece of clothing was thrown their way. He took off his shirt, still bouncing from one foot to the other and was left wearing just his cap and a khaki romper suit with Property of Betty emblazoned on the front. Everyone was clapping and screaming 'Henry, Henry, Henry'.

I was so proud of him. OK, so it wasn't so much a Chippendale strip but more like dad-dancing, but I was glad the show had gone to plan. I was about to thank him, but he went over to Mum, put his cap on her head, took her hand to stand up and tried to lift her, to gasps of delight from the audience. That was not in our script. It was so romantic for a second, the two of them staring into each other's eyes. Eat your heart out, Richard Gere. Then he started wobbling and losing his balance, this time to gasps of horror. It was the quick thinking of the dishy hall manager who rushed over, caught Dad's back, and steadied him that saved the day. Phew. What a hero.

We served tea and cake to calm things down, then it was going to be my turn. Dad was a hard act to follow, and I wished I'd gone before him. I told myself it was a friendly audience, so I'd be fine. After about forty minutes or so, I girded my loins and went for it.

'I want to say a few words about Mum to mark this important birthday. She's eighty today. We think. She stopped celebrating her birthdays around the age of thirty-two. Mum, that's forty-eight birthday presents you could have had.' I laughed. A few people smiled politely. Wasn't as funny as I thought then.

'She may be eighty, but she certainly has more energy and determination than the rest of us. Her long shopping days are legendary. She won't come home until she's seen every piece of clothing at House of Fraser,' I carried on to mildly amused faces. 'She's always the first to arrive and last to leave a party.' A few titters. They were warming up. 'For her seventieth birthday, she persuaded me to go for a skydive with her. Mum did a great jump, but my bum somehow got glued to the seat and the only jump I did was from the plane's steps to the tarmac. She's a braver woman than most.' Some people were giggling. That bit wasn't meant to be funny.

'She loves her garden and has some happy feathered friends. Her favourite is a robin called Christopher'—tittering was getting louder—'apparently, he's been coming for food every day for about thirty years'—shrieks of laughter this time. 'She has her own unique way of looking at the world, and always encouraged me and Sara to be uncompromising in how we lived.' There was howling laughter and chatter by then. WTF? Why was that so funny?

I persevered and told a few more anecdotes about her eccentricities. 'Elastic bands from chickens to tie your hair anyone?' I asked. They were laughing so much I couldn't hear myself. It was hard to keep going over the din. I thought I'd stop while I was on a high and ended with, 'She's the kindest and most forgiving person I know, always lending a helping hand to anyone in need. That's why we all love her, and she has so many friends like all of you who are here today.' I was expecting clapping for my finale, but they were all laughing and ignoring me, so I slipped away to the kitchen where the dishy hall manager was trying to talk to Dot.

'We need to start clearing up,' he said.

'Clearing up?' Dot mumbled, struggling to keep her eyes open.

'What's going on here?' I asked. 'Did someone put vodka in the tea or something? They all look out of it.'

'We don't keep alcohol on the premises, so unless you brought it…' he trailed off.

No, we hadn't brought any.

'Maddison, you've been in the kitchen the whole time. Do you know anything about alcohol being served?' I asked. Maddison stared at her Doc Martens.

'It wasn't my fault,' she whined.

'Come on, Maddison, what have you done? Spill,' I said, starting to panic, wondering how they were all going to get home.

'I bought the tamarind for the cake … and Granny didn't give me a chance to give it to her. She took it out of my bag. Only she took the wrong packet. She has no clue.' She rolled her eyes.

'Come on, spit it out,' I said.

'It was hash.'

They were all high. I didn't know whether to be angry, worried or to laugh. Dot was snoozing draped over a table by then, and back in the hall, it was slow motion mayhem. Three people were floating on top of the multi-coloured balls in the ball pit, staring blankly at nothing. I could see others struggling to get through the transparent hamster tube. Two women were on rocking horses, each lifting a giant sponge hand with great effort to land slowly on the other's head, bursting into high-pitched giggles on impact. One woman was crying while being consoled, and at least three people were dozing across chairs. It was an enactment of a hippie student party, but by elderly people in a children's nursery. Apart from Mum and Dad, that is, who were quietly canoodling in the corner.

Maddison, the hall manager, and I were the only ones who hadn't eaten the cake.

'What can we do?' the dishy hall manager asked.

'Just have to sit it out,' Maddison said and shrugged her shoulders.

'Maybe some water?' I suggested.

'I'm not throwing water over a load of pensioners,' he said. He was cute but a bit dim.

'To drink,' I said. Doh.

Maddison went round with jugs of water, and I started clearing up the mess, including grabbing a plate off a woman who'd helped herself to more cake, while the hall manager coaxed out the sleeping women in the hamster tube. Luckily, the buffet was still plentiful and got eaten up once they all got the munchies. After a while, people started sobering up and looking bewildered. One woman asked jokingly if we'd put vodka in the tea. So many said they'd had the best time. I was relieved there were no injuries.

'Thank you, Sophia Lovely, for that hilarious speech. I've had a fantastic time. It's been a day to remember. And the cake was so unusual. I must ask Dot for the recipe,' Mum said, as she floated away with Dad on her arm.

I thanked Dot for her help as she and Maddison left. Then Maddison ran back.

'Can I have the money for the hash?'

'I'm sorry, you must have mistaken me for someone who buys drugs from a fourteen-year-old dealer,' I said. She stomped off.

The dishy hall manager was clearing up and looked as exhausted as I felt, but still quite attractive. I was about to go over when I spotted a glint of gold on his left hand.

P.S. I bet Sara will regret not coming.

Monday, 29 April, 7.30am

Ha, ha yesterday!

7.35am

Can't stop laughing.

11.30pm

Mum's birthday party was fantastic. She was proud of me, and Dad was proud of himself. I'm so happy.

P.S. I've started getting targeted ads for foot fetishism. 'Buy foot fetish shoes at toe-riffically low prices, from £3'. Foot fetishism is surprisingly affordable.

Tuesday, 30 April, 7.30pm

Called Sara to tell her about Mum's eightieth and asked if she'd spoken to her and Dad since the party, which she hadn't.

'So how did it go then?' she asked reluctantly.

'It was fabulous. Everyone laughed at my speech, we had hash cake, got stoned and the stripper snogged Mum.' Put that in your pipe and smoke it.

'For God's sake,' she said and rung off.

11.30pm

Got a message from a man I'd liked on Ladybird a few days ago. He has long hair and was wearing a loud red shirt in his photo so I'm hoping he'll be a bit unusual or maverick. Will text him tomorrow.

P.S. No word from The Guru. Has he changed his mind?

PART V
May

FOURTEEN

Mr Cocky

Wednesday, 1 May, 7.30am

JUST TRIED to reply to Red Shirt Man, but he's deleted me! Did he expect an immediate reply? I don't get upset by idiots anymore, but the cumulative effect of the rejections is starting to mess with my head.

Thursday, 2 May, 11.30pm

A short Kindling date at Holy Grind today. I sat at Mr Cocky's table, and he asked what I wanted to drink. When he came back from the counter, he put my latte on the table and handed me a banana.

'I didn't ask for a banana,' I said.

'I thought you could show me how much of it you can get into your mouth in one go,' he said and winked.

WTF? Was this guy for real?

'Really?' I huffed and rolled my eyes.

'We may as well find out now what you can do for a man of my size.' He winked again.

Is it just me attracting the peculiar ones? How could he think it was OK to have that as his opening gambit? Who would play along with that?

'You're disgusting.' I pushed back my chair, picked up my bag and headed out. I was halfway down the road before I noticed the banana in my other hand.

Friday, 3 May, 11.30pm

Valentina and Kenneth loved my designs for Project Toilet. We're going to have dark green palm print wallpaper, including on the ceiling, pebble tiles, green loo (back in fashion), a basin carved out of rough stone, and a driftwood mirror. The *pièce de résistance* will be the cistern in the form of a fish tank, with real tropical fish. Each time you flush, it looks like the fish are about to disappear down the pan, but as the water drains away, they stay in their protected compartment, oblivious to the illusion. Minimalism is dead. Long live maximalism.

Saturday, 4 May, 3.30pm

No Brunch Bunch again today. Ace is away for three months. Leila was going to lunch with Jude, and Grace is still at home. I've tried to get her to come out with me, but Ajay says she's concentrating on getting well and hasn't been seeing anyone much. I miss her.

11.30pm

Went to a colleague's birthday party tonight. I was on my own and didn't know anyone. A couple came in, stood next to me and she went to get drinks.

I made conversation. 'Hi, I'm Sophia. How do you know the birthday girl?'

He looked fearful. 'My girlfriend's gone to the bar,' he said.

Sunday, 5 May, 11.30pm

It's only 5th May, but this month has been rubbish so far. One rejection, one unwanted sexual advance, and one snubbing. Project Toilet is the one thing keeping me going.

Tuesday, 7 May, 11.30pm

The Guru sent me the details for the retreat. He wasn't planning a retreat with me but running one for a group of twenty. I must have got it all wrong. It costs £3,350.

Wednesday, 8 May, 11.30pm

Been miserable today. I told The Guru the retreat was expensive, and he said, 'You can pay in instalments.' I feel so foolish I was taken in by him. He's a conman on the make, preying on single women who are hoping for his attention. And I fell for it. I wanted him and allowed myself to believe the feeling was mutual. Looking back, there were no real signs that he was interested in me as anything more than a client, but I read what I wanted into his actions. I think I'm busy in June after all. I left him a terrible review, which made me feel much better.

Thursday, 9 May, 11.00pm

Mum called this morning and asked me to go to an appointment with her but didn't want to give me details over the phone, and she hadn't asked Dad to go with her for some reason. She doesn't normally invite me out on a weekday. I hope she's not sick and coming to see a doctor. But why wouldn't she ask Dad to go with her? She didn't sound worried, but I am. I called Sara and asked if she knew anything about it, but she didn't. I want to ring Dad but don't want to upset him.

FIFTEEN

Mr Snappy

Friday, 10 May, 3.00am

I'VE BEEN Googling 'common illnesses in the elderly' and frightening myself. Mum's always so robust and healthy, I can't bear it if she's sick. We're meeting in Soho. Why there? Maybe it's a private clinic. My mind is racing with the potential scenarios, all equally horrendous.

11.30pm

I didn't get back to sleep this morning. Was feeling terrible and looking awful with dark shadows under my eyes when I arrived at Ground Café to meet Mum at 9.30am. She was so stylish in her black palazzo pants and a drapey top with horizontal black and white stripes, finished off with a cashmere coat and pristine trainers. I hope I'll look that good when I'm eighty. Who am I kidding? I don't look that good now.

'Hello, Sophia Lovely, thanks for coming.' I love it when she calls me Sophia Lovely. She likes to tell the story (and I like it too) of how she came up with this pet name for me. Apparently, by the time I was three years old, I would pick my own clothes in the morning, inspect myself in the mirror and ask, 'Sophia lovely?' Ha ha, not much changed there.

'But what's the matter? You look so pale. Why didn't you put on some makeup?' she said.

I didn't rise to it and said I was tired.

'You've been very mysterious, Mum. Where are we going?' I asked, dreading the answer.

'You'll find out soon enough.' We finished our coffees, and I followed her down Old Compton Street turning into Wardour Street, halfway down which she stopped at a door and rang the bell. Just a door with a bell, no brass plaques with names of doctors with letters after their names. My mind was racing by the time the lift doors opened on the second floor.

'Surprise,' Mum said with a huge grin and jazz hands. We were in a studio and people were preparing for a photoshoot.

'Hello Betty. You're looking gorgeous today,' said a rather attractive man with a camera around his neck. I guessed he was in his late forties, with thick salt-and-pepper hair, cut short like Steve McQueen's in *The Thomas Crown Affair*, black jeans and a T-shirt emblazoned with the Rolling Stones' hot lips image. I perked up from my insomniac lethargy and wished I was wearing makeup.

'Thank you,' Mum said, blushing. 'This is my daughter, Sophia.'

We shook hands. I watched him walk back to the set and thought, *you can point your telescopic lens at me any time.*

'Mum, what is going on here? I thought we were going for a doctor's appointment. I thought you were sick. I didn't sleep all night, for God's sake,' I blurted.

'I'm sorry, Lovely. I didn't mean to worry you. I wanted to surprise you. A few weeks ago, I went to a birthday party at my new friend Phyllis's house. Her son'—she nodded towards the man—'is a fashion photographer and he asked me if I'd be interested in modelling swimwear for *Pour Vous*, and that's why we're here. I wanted someone with me, and your dad doesn't approve, so...' she trailed off, apparently realising that her mystery-making had gone a bit too far. 'I'm sorry.'

I teared up with relief and hugged her. 'That's fantastic, Mum. What a great opportunity. Trust you to breeze into a modelling job.' My mum is a swimwear model at eighty years old.

'Also'—she paused—'he's single.' She winked and tapped her nose.

What I thought was going to be one of the worst days of my life was turning out to be rather fun with hunky-man potential. Coffee and pastries on the table. Don't mind if I do. A large coffee, one pain au raisin and one pain au chocolat later, and I started to feel human again. I nosed around the studio, having surreptitious glances at Mr Snappy and trying to radiate nonchalant sexy vibes.

Mum came out of makeup and joined the other models for an inclusive group shot. She was wearing a red one-piece, gold sandals, red lipstick, and hoop earrings, wind machine blowing her long white hair, all of which was stunning against the newly applied fake tan. Yes, she was the oldest of the models there, but she looked the part. After a while, I sneaked out and found a cool shop in Greek Street, where I bought some makeup and a T-shirt with the words 'Free Hugs' on the front. I slipped back into the studio, makeup applied, wearing my new T-shirt, and sat watching Mum being photographed in a hot pink swimsuit and matching sarong. I was feeling a bit more confident, a bit more myself. At the end of the day, prosecco and beers came out and Mr Snappy came over and invited us to stay for drinks.

'I'm exhausted, Lovely. I'm going to catch the train home and see if your dad is still talking to me. Why don't you stay?'

'Your mother is such a good sport and for an amateur she acted rather professionally. I think *Pour Vous* will be pleased with the images,' Mr Snappy said, after Mum had left. Then, as if he'd noticed me for the first time, 'I can see where you get your looks from. And yes please.' He nodded towards my emblazoned chest.

Hello, was he flirting? I perked up one more notch and gave him what I thought was a pouty smile, then regretted it at the sight of my reflection in the mirror behind him. Still haven't mastered the art of the pout. He left me to mingle with the team, and apart from a few stolen glances, we didn't interact much. As the party started to wind down, I went to say goodbye.

'Why don't you stay a bit longer? I'd love to take some shots of you.'

'Erm … I'm not sure,' I said, remembering I hadn't washed my hair this morning.

'Stay, it'll be fun.'

'But I'm not dressed for a photoshoot.' I was torn between wanting to stay but being afraid I'd look awful in the pictures.

'Trust me, you'll look great.'

'OK,' I said, hesitant but excited at the prospect of spending time with him.

When we were alone, he sat me on the floor, with my pleated neon pink skirt fanned out around me, then shone a light directly over my head. He showed me the first few snaps, and they were beautiful. Go Sophia. I relaxed then and got into it.

'How about one without the T-shirt?' he asked.

'Do you want me to wear something else? I don't want to wear anything my mum wore. That would be weird,' I said with a laugh that came out as a snort.

'No, I was thinking in your bra. You have a marvellous figure.'

My face flooded. Where was he going with this?

'No, I don't think so.' I was acting cool but feeling flustered.

'I want to do an arty shot. Warm light from a single dimmed spotlight bathing your body, black background, and you framed by your neon pink skirt. It'll be tasteful,' he persisted.

Come on, Sophia. Where is your spirit of adventure? Mum would do it. Why not you? Why not show off your toned figure?

'OK. As long as you promise it'll be stylish.'

'I promise. Absolutely.'

I peeled off my T-shirt and thanked the lingerie gods for guiding me to put on a pink lacy bra this morning.

'Wow, the pink bra and skirt sure zing in this light. And your silver necklace reflects light beautifully around your face.'

'It's an old one I designed myself when I had a jewellery store,' I said.

He whistled. 'Creative and a businesswoman. Why did you stop designing?'

'It just took its course and one day I decided I wanted a change and sold the business.'

It was nice chatting and I felt more comfortable, my confident posture returning. We peered at the shots in his camera viewer – standing so close, I felt the warmth of his breath – and the pictures were indeed arty.

'Now without the bra?' he asked, and I obliged, by then acting like Kate Moss, shaking my hair out, posing with my arms raised over my head and looking straight into the camera. 'If you don't mind my saying, your breasts are a knockout. Can I ask how old you are?'

'Thank you,' I said, ignoring his question.

'You didn't answer my question.'

'Not that it matters, but I'm sixty,' I said, jutting out my chin.

'Oh, sixty? Really?'

'It sounds older when you say it.' I laughed but he didn't. He fiddled with the setting on his camera and took a few shots on autopilot. No more flirting.

'I think we're done here,' he said, without looking at me, as he started packing up.

I got up and pulled on my clothes, suddenly feeling very naked. I needed to get out of that place and away from him.

'If you want copies of the photos, leave me your address and I'll send them on,' he said over his shoulder.

'Send them to my mother.' I rushed to the lift, which took forever to come up. I kept the tears in until the lift doors had closed.

Saturday, 11 May, 7.30am

I don't know why I allowed myself to be taken in by him. And a photographer to boot. Aargh. What a cliché. It's not as if it hasn't happened before. I get pursued by a younger man. They think I'm great and we're getting along fine. Then the 'how old are you?'

conversation pops up, and suddenly, I've gone from perfect to past-sell-by-date, like that time when Jilly set me up with her friend at a party. She knew my age, but he didn't. We were having a nice chat and he seemed keen. When I came back from the loo, he'd disappeared. Jilly said he'd asked her my age and decided I wasn't for him. In his forties, he was probably looking for someone to have children with, and I would have been a double whammy being older and infertile. I should give up on young men and date an attractive older man so I can take the youthful high ground.

10.30am

Mum phoned.

'How are you, Lovely? Did you enjoy "the shoot"?' I could just see her saying this in quotation marks, pleased with herself for using the right lingo.

'You looked gorgeous, Mum. I'm so proud of you.'

'Thank you, Lovely. It's a shame your dad doesn't feel the same way. He hasn't talked to me much since I told him about the modelling job. It's so unlike him to sulk like this. I think he imagines I'm going to be an international supermodel, travel the world and leave him on his own. It's flattering, but there's no need for the silent treatment.'

'Are you going to be an international supermodel?'

'I did enjoy it and I wouldn't mind at all if I was asked to do it again.'

'Go Betty, go Betty.'

Mum giggled, then asked me about Mr Snappy and I told her he was too young for me.

'I'll talk to Dad if you like. Persuade him to be more supportive? You know he adores you. He can't stay mad at you for long.'

'Would you, Lovely? You are a good girl.'

I melted in the glow of praise. Then I wished she'd told me I was gorgeous when I was younger. I wished she didn't think I

165

looked ill without makeup. I wished she didn't give me that look every time I reached for a chocolate. I wished I was enough.

1.00pm

Joy turned up two hours late. It's like she can smell heartache. She didn't follow her usual cleaning routine, but instead hovered around me, polishing the coffee table to within an inch of its life.

'Ah Sophia, you look sad. Had a bad date again?'

I scowled.

'Maybe you give up dating, ha? You too old.'

Water off a duck's back.

'How's Jasmine doing? She must be about fourteen?' I asked.

Her face lit up and she got her mobile and showed me a picture of her daughter in her school uniform. 'Yeah, she's a big girl now, and clever in studies,' she said.

So, she's a single mum, runs a cleaning company, does my actual cleaning and nannies in the week. Superwoman.

Sunday, 12 May, 11.30pm

Sara didn't ring to see if Mum was OK. You'd think she'd be worried after my call on Thursday. I texted and told her everything was OK and about the modelling. She just said, 'Yes I heard.' I despair. I want to shout at her and shake her by the shoulders but of course I mustn't upset her. Sometimes I just want to tell her I know about everything and be done with it.

Called Dad and mentioned Mum's modelling to see why he's being so grumpy about it.

'I'm not being grumpy. If your mum wants to go galivanting, that's her business. Who am I to stop her? I'm only her husband,' he said.

I told him it was a great opportunity, and he should be proud of her, but he didn't want to talk about it. What the hell is happening with my family?

Monday, 13 May, 11.30pm

Andrew, AKA Mr Sex on the Kitchen Island emailed to ask if it was possible to have heating under the decked area outside the kitchen. How many more areas are going to have heating for sex? Though it could become my interior design USP. I could change my company name from SinteriorS to SexteriorS. I've only just realised SinteriorS sounds like an S&M club. Why didn't anyone tell me?

SIXTEEN

The Networker

Wednesday, 15 May, 11.30pm

WENT to Izzy's company party for their clients tonight. It was meant to be a networking event and I was hoping to find contacts or clients, but I ended up meeting someone I liked. I think he liked me too as he made a point of telling me he was single quite early on in our conversation. He's not good-looking and he wears boring business suits – just normal and lawyery – but he was charming and funny, and conversation flowed. Chemistry is everything, and I sensed the mixed chemicals between us would be explosive. The Opera Buff may not have looked right for me, but I'm not superficial and shallow. We bonded while we watched the people on a mission to consume as much free booze as possible. I gave him my card. It was a networking party after all.

Thursday, 16 May, 11.30pm

I've been having butterflies all day because The Networker asked me for a date. I Googled him and found his company's website. Looks like he's a big cheese. Texted Izzy and told her about the date. She didn't know him but said she'll ask around.

Saturday, 18 May, 3.30pm

I asked Joy to tidy up my wardrobe, but I'd forgotten that the joke blow-up man I bought for Leila's hen night was in there. She brought it into the kitchen with a look of utter pity on her face and put it on the table under my nose. He was deflated and shrunken.

'Oh Sophia, you sad. You have a plastic man.'

'It's not mine,' I shouted after her as she left the room.

I remembered how much fun Leila's hen night was, and how pleased I'd been to find the 'plastic man' in a joke shop. When I took it home, I rang Grace and said, 'If I die in my sleep tonight, and my family find a blow-up man in my cupboard when they're clearing out my house, please tell them it's for Leila.'

Tuesday, 21 May, 8.30pm

Izzy texted.

> Hi Sophia, bad news. I joked to a colleague that we were networking AND matchmaking at our party and told him about you. He'd had a meeting with your guy that day. Apparently, he was talking about his wife and four kids and going to Florida in the summer. Sorry

> Are you sure it was him?

> Yes absolutely.

> Devious git.

Was he wearing a ring that night and I missed it? I feel cheated on, and I haven't even been on a date. I marvel at his deceit for telling me he was single right at the beginning, before even I had an inkling that I was interested in him. Is it any wonder I always suspect people are having affairs? I like to think I'm an honest straightforward kind of a person, so I'm surprised when people are so devious, to the point that I doubt myself and think I must have got it wrong. It's naïve, I know, but I don't want to be cynical either.

Wednesday, 22 May, 11.30pm

The Networker emailed to say he was looking forward to seeing me tomorrow and where did I want to meet? I felt like saying, 'And are your wife and children joining us?' Instead, I said, 'So am I.'

I have no intention of turning up. I told him I've always wanted to go to the One Below Zero bar. He emailed and said he'd booked it. I know they charge £50 per person before you even drink anything.

Thursday, 23 May, 6.30pm

He emailed asking where I was. Silence is golden. He'll be paying the £100 bill about now.

11.30pm

I'm not going to waste any more energy on him. Will forget and move on. And I must, absolutely must, stop being overexcited before getting to know someone. Thank God Izzy found out before it was too late. I might have grown to like him and how would that fit with my sex only plan? Was Leila right? Am I deluding myself to think I'll be happy with just casual sex? I've got so good at hiding my feelings I don't think I know any more.

SEVENTEEN

The Neighbour's Son

Friday, 24 May, 11.30pm

I'VE BEEN FEELING low after The Networker deception, and no dating prospects on the apps. I need a bit of TLC. I've arranged to see Irene and Ana for afternoon tea. They sounded super excited about it. I have such fond childhood memories of them. Me and Sara spent a lot of time in their garden next door, playing and being fed cakes and biscuits. How sweet were they to even put a gate on our dividing fence so we could go in and out easily? Irene must be about eighty-six now and Ana was four years younger – practically a toy girl. Our parents were so open-minded for that time. The other girls in the street weren't allowed to go near them in case they were 'turned into lesbians'.

Saturday, 25 May, 11.30am

This morning, Joy arrived wearing one of the jumpers I'd given her. It was a bit tight around her pudgy belly.

'It looks better on you than it did on me,' I said, purely to be nice.

'Yeah, maybe it's 'cos you're fat,' she said as I choked on my coffee.

Now, the sun is shining, I'm on the train to Totnes and looking forward to seeing my honorary aunties.

5.40pm

On the train going home. Had a good journey down taking in the beautiful West Country scenery. When I got to the Magic Sip Teashop, I watched Irene and Ana through the window as they chatted, their heads close, until they spotted me and waved. They're always so together. It's lovely. I don't know how Irene still manages to be meticulously groomed. Her hair had been dyed blonde and was coiffured to within an inch of its life. Her nails were painted red to match the lipstick on her angular face, and she was wearing her signature string of pearls and a yellow twinset. And she's still so upright (she doesn't just have a stiff upper lip), although she has more sharp edges now.

Ana, on the other hand, couldn't be accused of over-grooming. She's all mushy curves, wild grey hair, bushy eyebrows, and her pudgy neck and arms are covered in clashing metal jewellery. She fits right into the Totnes' bohemian ways. I remember being a bit frightened of her when I was little. Back then, she still had her robust Russian manner before Irene softened her, but the accent is still there. On paper they would be a terrible match – Irene with her aspiring upper middle-class English ways, and Ana a free-spirited Russian gardener. But love works in mysterious ways.

'Darling,' Irene and Ana greeted me in unison.

'I keep my finger crossed for your train to be on time,' Ana said.

Irene pursed her lips. 'Fingers, Ana, not finger,' she whispered under her breath.

'I didn't touch anything,' Ana said.

Irene tutted and turned to me with a beaming grin, flashing her too-white dentures.

'I had a lovely walk from the station,' I said.

'Ah yes,' Ana said, clapping her hands like an excited child. 'Did you see the wailing willow tree? The blossom, so beautiful.'

Irene tutted.

Ana poured me a tea and leaned over conspiratorially, beckoning me to look inside her voluminous patchwork bag. 'You fancy some wodka in your tea, dear? I have the hip flask,' she said, tapping her nose. I nodded.

'So, my dear Sophia,' Irene began. I knew what was coming and dropped my sandwich distractedly.

'Buttery fingers,' giggled Ana. Irene gave her a resigned look but didn't correct her and turned to me.

'Have you seen any of the men you met on your travels since you've been back?'

'I'm sorry, Auntie, but no, I haven't,' I replied, feeling slightly ashamed to disappoint them. 'I'm working on it though.' I told them about the dating challenge.

'In fact,' I announced mischievously, 'I had a date with a woman a few weeks ago. She's a journalist, really cool and great company.' They both stopped mid-scone, and stared first at each other, then at me. I blushed and they probably thought it was because I was being coy, not that I'd made a twit of myself on that date.

'My dear, we had no idea,' Ana said.

'I'm pleased for you, as long as you're happy, dear,' Irene said.

I couldn't hold up the pretence and told them what had happened.

'For a minute I thought we could go on a date double,' Ana said, and burst into laughter.

'Ah, how times have changed,' Irene said. 'You don't have to hide your ... sexuality,' she whispered, 'like a guilty secret nowadays. It wasn't so easy in our time.'

Ana nodded in agreement.

'You know, I leave my country and my family when eighteen years old. I think, it would be different in England. I can be free and open, and not afraid I will be arrested for loving woman. In England, the police, they're not interested. But people judge. They make fun when they see lesbian woman. So, I decided never to tell anyone, but then I met Irene,' Ana said, and reached for Irene's hand.

'Oh, please tell me the story of how you met. I know it by heart, but I love hearing it.'

'Yes, it is an excellent story, my dear, isn't it?' Irene said, delighted to share her anecdote again. 'I used to take my foreign students for a drink in the local pub after class sometimes. You know, to show them the British way of life and practise speaking English. One night, there was a big group including Ana. She was so beautiful and bubbly with a mane of curly black hair. Later, one by one, the other students left, until it was just me and Ana.'

Ana interrupted. 'I went to bar to get wodka, to show Irene how we do it in Russia. She look at me from behind, I could tell.'

'I was trying to be discreet, but I couldn't help it, and I knew I was falling for her, but I didn't know if she'd be interested in me. While she was at the bar, I noticed her open bag with a magazine's corner sticking out. That's great, I thought. She's reading to improve her English, just as I'd suggested in class. I pulled it out, curious to see what it was,' Irene said.

'It was *Playboy* magazine,' Ana jumped in again. 'I find it under bed in hotel where I work after class. I read it a lot. Veeery good for my English,' she bellowed, and winked at me.

Irene glowered at her for pinching her punchline, then turned to me with a smile and said, 'The rest is history, as they say.'

'It's such a sweet story. Sixty years later, you're still together. I've given up on love.' I sighed.

'So, you not going to see the woman again?' Ana asked.

'No. I think I prefer penis after all,' I said, and we all giggled. 'I've been on lots of dates though.'

I told them about my dating experiences so far:

- An opera buff who made a bull of himself.
- An ice skater who wanted to wait.
- Two weird cinema encounters.
- An exceptional room service experience.
- A teacher who turned me on (to dance).

- A concrete date that bored me stiff.
- A Cuban with a glint of gold.
- A brutally honest type.
- A guru who performed magic with chocolate.
- The fast young men who didn't wait for me.
- A professor of footology.
- A caress interruptus incident in a bathroom.
- A banana-brandishing boor.
- An ageist arse.
- And a devious married man with an exceptionally large bar bill.

'That sounds exhausting, my dear,' Ana said.

'We should introduce her to our neighbour's son,' Irene said to Ana, who nodded and clapped her hands.

'His name is Anthony, and his son is also Anthony, but they call him Tony. Anyway, Tony moved back down here to be near his dad. He's a lovely man and he's single now. You'd like him, Sophia.' She took out her mobile and searched for a long time, as though searching for the meaning of life itself. Finally, she found Tony's number and made me promise to contact him.

We finished our tea, and I stood up to gather my things and head to the station. 'It's been a tonic spending time with you. I'm going to carry on dating and find fulfilment if not love,' I said, tearing up. I'd missed them so much. Everyone needs aunties like Ana and Irene. We hugged goodbye and as I left, I said, 'Tony, here I come.'

'I hope you come with whoever you want,' Ana shouted after me as Irene winced. I giggled and bounded off.

Feeling buoyed, I texted Tony.

> Hi Tony, this is Sophia. My aunties/your neighbours Irene & Ana may have mentioned me? They suggested we should meet up if you're up for it.

Hello Sophia, did they? That's good of them. I'd like that. I don't get out much these days

We'll have to do something about that! I live in London. Do you ever come up? Or we could meet in the middle somewhere?

A day out in London? yes I'd like a day out in London I can catch any train after 9.30am

Hmm, sounds like a homebird, but he has just been through a divorce.

That's fine, how about Tuesday at 6.30pm near Paddington Station? I know a nice Italian for an early dinner. I'll text you the details.

Yes, I shall look forWard to that I'll go to the station tomorrow and buy my ticket. nothing fancy for food please.

Pizza is hardly fancy. Oh, my lovely aunties, have you paired me up with an oddball? I thought about asking for a photo or his surname to check him out but decided it might be fun to make it a blind date.

11.30pm

I've booked a table at Giovanni's for Tuesday. Feeling a bit excited but mostly apprehensive.

Tuesday, 28 May, 11.30pm

I sat in Giovanni's with a glass of red courage and waited. Tony's train was getting in at 6.15pm so there was plenty of time for him to make the five-minute walk to the restaurant.

'I hope the beautiful signorina is not kept waiting for much longer,' said the swarthy waiter with a husky voice. That place is such a cliché. I love it.

'You can always join me to make me feel better if he doesn't turn up,' I flirted, and his face flooded. It's so cute when men blush.

At 6.40pm, no sign of him, and no response to my texts. Then an elderly man came in looking worried and exhausted, and on seeing my bright blue dress, smiled and shuffled towards me. Very slowly. With a stick.

WTF? Then the penny dropped. Not getting out much, bad texts and going to the station to buy his ticket after 9.30? I was on a date with Anthony Senior! The waiter helped him sit down, then smirked at me as if to say, 'I don't think much of the competition'. By then, I'd processed my shock and asked Anthony Senior about his train journey.

'Oh goodness, I'm feeling puffed out. I must have taken a wrong turn out of the station and got completely lost. My son told me to use the map on my phone, but I don't know how to work the blooming thing. By the time the nice young lady helped me find this place, I'd been walking for ages. My knees are giving me gyp.' He sighed long and hard.

We small talked for a while.

'It's lovely to be here with you, Sophia, but can I ask why Irene and Ana suggested we meet? Are you in the pottery business like me? If I can be of any help, just say the word.'

'How shall I put this? I thought I was coming on a date with Anthony Junior.'

It took a second or two, but he started laughing and so did I.

'Anthony Junior will be jealous of me. Wait till I tell him.'

He told me about the family pottery business, and I gave him the highlights from my travels. He was a total sweetie. We had dinner. Nothing fancy, of course. And we shared a bottle of wine. It was a pleasant evening despite the mix-up and lack of romance potential. I walked him to the station, worried he might stumble after an alcoholic evening. Before putting him safely on the train, we took a selfie on his phone and sent it to his son. Let's hope the son is interested and is as lovely as the father.

Thursday, 30 May, 1.30pm

Took Lisa and Hannah to a specialist supplier this morning to shop for princess stuff for her bedroom. As the lift doors opened and Hannah had her first sight of princess heaven, she whistled and said, 'Oh fuckerty fuck.'

Lisa said she didn't know whether to be mortified or proud of her for using the words in the right context.

I wonder if I would have been a disciplinarian type of mother. No, I think children should be allowed to blossom in their own way. If I had a Hannah in my life, I would let her flourish and be herself, not attempt to tame her with too many rules. Even if it involved saying the odd 'fuckerty fuck'.

Friday, 31 May, 11.30pm

Boy am I glad May is over. It started bad and went downhill. The alarming statistics are:

One ageist rejection, one time-based rejection, one unwanted sexual advance, one snubbing, one deception, and one case of mistaken identity.

On the positive side:

One lovely project (even if just a toilet).

BRING ON JUNE!

PART VI
June

EIGHTEEN

Mr Full of Himself & Mr Beard

Saturday, 1 June, 1.30pm

BRUNCH BUNCH TODAY. Grace came for the first time since her surgery. She was quiet and slightly droopy at the shoulders. She'd gone back to work this week but couldn't cope, so she's having more time off. I told her about the mix-up with the two Anthonys and that made her laugh, and wince from the scars. I'll arrange something nice for us to do together when she's feeling better.

Leila asked Grace about Monte Carlo. She's planning a surprise holiday for her wedding anniversary in October. Oh Leila, if only you knew.

Monday, 3 June, 11.30pm

Rubbish Ladybird date tonight. Mr Full of Himself went on and on about how he was the top salesman in his company, got a massive bonus – small dick? – and he has a Porsche – small dick? – and he's going on holiday to a five-star hotel in the Bahamas – small dick? I wasn't impressed and won't be sizing up his dick any time soon.

Tuesday, 4 June, 11.30pm

Project Toilet is on hold. They're going back to Chile for a while. Boo.

Wednesday, 5 June, 11.30pm

Date with Mr Beard at The Diner tonight. He ate a giant stacked burger, chips, onion rings, sweet potato fries, and a side of pancakes with cream, while his tongue constantly searched around his beard for escaped crumbs. I was mesmerised and repulsed. THEN, although I'd only had a skinny burger, he wanted to split the bill in half. No way.

Thursday, 6 June, 11.30pm

Ace called. I don't usually get a call when he's away. He sounded fed up and said he wasn't sure if he enjoyed his job and the travelling anymore. He's a bit young to retire but he's thinking about it.

Friday, 7 June, 11.30pm

Izzy texted this morning. She was panicking about going to her friend Matilda's wedding tomorrow and pleaded with me to go as her plus one. Michael is going to be there, and she doesn't want to be Izzy-no-mates when he's bringing his new girlfriend. I was reluctant at first as I won't know anyone but decided to go for Izzy's sake, though I do think she should be taking a pretend boyfriend, like in a romcom, instead of a middle-aged pal.

Thinking about her situation reminded me of what it was like for me in my forties after things went wrong with James and I was single again. I dreaded going to weddings. I was always pleased for my friends and hoped that their marriages didn't end up in divorce like mine, but each wedding was a reminder that I'd failed at the game of love and failed at my marriage. James was the love of my life, and I remember thinking I was going to be blessed with happily ever after, but life had other plans for me. No viable eggs meant no babies, and eventually, no James. I was faulty goods. I've never understood how he could leave like that. Sometimes, it still hurts twenty-odd years later. Get a grip, Sophia. No point in looking back. The future is bright.

NINETEEN

Mr Delicious

Saturday, 8 June, 5.00pm

WAITING for Izzy to pick me up in my red-hot dress. It's an evening wedding so it won't be going on all day like an interminable fairy tale. Hopefully, there'll be lovely food and drink (freeloading60s.com) and a hunk. #SexStarved60s

Sunday, 9 June, 7.30am

The wedding was UBER-glamorous with the London skyline in all its glory as the backdrop to the ceremony on level 39 of The Gherkin. We both teared up at the bride's whimsical dress as well as when they said I do. I realised the tears were for the joy of seeing two people in love. I wasn't crying for me. There was no sadness in me for being single. I have a good life and I'm enjoying it. I wouldn't want to get married even if, by some miracle, I meet Mr Right.

Thankfully, Izzy and Michael had been seated away from each other, so there was only one awkward moment when the four of us came face to face as we headed to the upstairs bar.

'Hello Izzy,' Michael said breezily, as if they were still good friends, 'and Sophia, I haven't seen you since … Peru.'

Izzy said a meek hello and shifted on her feet, looking uncomfortable. It broke my heart seeing her like that. I couldn't have him acting smug and thinking she was sad and lonely without him, even if she was feeling exactly that.

'I don't know the beautiful newlyweds, but I begged Izzy to bring me as her plus one. Her gorgeous young man had to go away on a last-minute work trip to the US. It was a shame, wasn't it, Izzy?' She furrowed her brow then caught herself.

'Yes, an important meeting he couldn't miss,' she said.

'But his loss was my gain. I've always wanted to see The Gherkin.' I was pleased Izzy didn't let Michael see she was still hurting. We reached the upper level and were relieved when they wandered off.

'Thanks Sophia, you genius.'

I gave her a hug and we clinked our glasses.

Dinner was exquisite. The creamiest burrata and heritage tomatoes to start, turbot with watercress and pea mash, and chocolate tart with raspberries and white chocolate sauce. Matilda's dad gave a heart-warming speech and then it was the best man's turn. OMG. He gave a speech fit for a raucous stag party, with stories about the groom's many conquests and their adventures in Amsterdam's red-light district and coffee houses. The top table were squirming in their seats, with frozen smiles, but the best man was oblivious. There was a pause, alas not to wrap up but for dramatic effect. He held up an innocuous-looking Tesco carrier bag containing a gimp mask and a whip for the wedding night. One of the grandmas whooped. Matilda's mum had had enough by then. She stood up, head tipped and smile fixed, hugged and thanked him and gently pushed him back down on his seat mid-sentence. There was a mass sigh of relief, followed by a moment's hush before the DJ saved the day by playing 'Embarrassment' by Madness.

But the speech drama aside, the most exciting part was the gorgeous man sitting at the next table. I could see him out of the corner of my eye (as he could me) and thought, hello! He was in a slim cream suit with white leather sneakers and had salt-and-pepper slicked back George Clooney-style hair and a thinnish beard. And wow, such a sexy smile. After coffee, as soon as Izzy went off to chat to her friends, we locked eyes, and he came over and introduced himself.

'Isn't it a stunning view?' he asked.

He was stunning. And hot. Tsss.

'It sure is delicious,' I said, looking at him instead of the view. 'What a lovely wedding.' I was trying to stay cool and hot-flush-free but being menopausal is much like being a teenager when you meet someone you fancy. Your hormones take over and you turn into a sweating lobster.

'Did you enjoy the food?' he asked, while looking handsome.

'Oh, absolutely delicious, especially the chocolate tart.' I'd savoured the richness of it in my mouth. Exactly what I wanted to do to him.

'Matilda asked me to help her with the menu. I'm a friend of the family. And you? How do you know them?'

'I'm an imposter. Well, I came as Izzy's plus one. Are you a chef?' He had all the right ingredients, put together in the most appealing way.

'No, I don't make the food. I eat it and write about it.'

I wanted to eat him and write about it.

'A restaurant reviewer? What a delicious job.'

'You like delicious things, don't you?' He was definitely flirting with me. 'I love your dress by the way ... how shall I describe it ... it's ... delicious,' he said, turning up the heat.

Then he checked his watch and picked up his mobile. 'It was lovely to meet you. I'm afraid I must go. I have to submit an article before midnight.'

Damn. He left as I hid my disappointment, but before he was out of sight, he stopped and walked back.

'I was thinking. Would you like to have a delicious dinner one night and discuss all things delicious?'

Cheeky. But yes.

'That sounds fun. You can help me broaden my food

vocabulary.' I didn't want to look too eager. But yes, yes, yes, yes, as Sally said to Harry in the New York diner.

4.30pm

He just texted and asked me to dinner at his house. Hurrah! Going to have a lovely long bath and pamper myself now.

11.50pm

The taxi dropped me off at an apartment block on the river near Tower Bridge. Flat no. 25 was the penthouse. Gorgeous, foodie, and rich. Jackpot. He looked so handsome when he opened the door, wearing a floral shirt and white jeans and smelling of expensive cologne. I wore a blue satin slip dress that swished beautifully as I walked in my silver sandals. I left a red lipstick mark on his cheek. The apartment was softly lit with a warm sensual feel. The Bee Gees were singing 'How Deep is Your Love?' Was he trying to tell me something? I headed for the terrace and took in the twinkling London skyline. He followed, and standing close behind me, reached around my waist and offered me a glass of champagne with one hand, caressing my arm with the other. I took a sip. He swept my hair back gently and nuzzled my neck as we watched the flickering lights, our fingers intertwined. This guy knew how to woo a woman. Then he led me to the dining table.

'I've prepared a surprise tasting menu for you.' Ooh, what a great idea. 'But I have rules, and you must obey them.' He sounded so confident and masterful my stomach turned to jelly.

'I can't wait. What are the rules?'

'You must guess the main ingredients of each dish, or you'll forfeit an item of clothing.' I was ready to agree to anything but remembered I was only wearing four things. Not that I minded taking them off, but that would only take us through half the meal.

'I agree to your rules, but I have some rules of my own. If I guess right, you have to forfeit two items of clothing.' I knew that my refined palate would have him stripped naked in no time.

'You're on.'

He walked to the open plan kitchen and brought over two dishes. I took a mouthful as he watched.

'Tuna, spring onions and lemon,' I said. He sighed and took off his shoes.

The next course was equally easy. Beetroot, walnuts, stilton cheese. I even guessed the reduced balsamic. Socks off.

The third course was tricky. I guessed beef with artichoke and tarragon sauce, but it was venison. He eyed up my dress, but I took off my sandals instead. He raised an eyebrow.

The fourth course was prawns with chilli and tomato. Easy-peasy-lemon-squeezy. Squeezing was what I wanted to do to him. He stood up, undid his cuffs and shirt buttons slowly, and threw his shirt across the room. Then he took the waistband of his trousers and yanked them off in one move. Was that the scratchy sound of Velcro?

He got up to get the next course and I watched his delicious body. Firm and smooth, exactly as I'd imagined. And he was wearing Calvin Klein shorts. Of course.

I guessed pheasant for the next dish, but it was partridge. I reached down the back of my dress, undid my strapless bra and in one move pulled it out from under my dress and held it up high, before throwing it aside. It landed on the sofa on top of his shirt. Even our clothes couldn't wait to get together.

The first dessert course was a chocolate tart with a twist. There was another flavour I couldn't work out. It turned out to be basil. I lifted my dress and slowly pulled it over my head, releasing and flicking my hair – ouch, a little too violently.

So, there we were. He in his Calvins and me in neon orange briefs to cover our modesty. He brought out the last course. Strawberries and cream. He led me to the sofa, where he dripped the luscious dessert onto my breasts. The cream started to melt, and the strawberry pieces slipped down the sides of my chest as they oozed their sticky juices. He licked and kissed me, his face smeared with strawberries and cream.

I woke up to find I was lying on my sofa, gripping a spilt mug of tea over my chest. I'd been snoozing after my hot bath. Wishful sofa dreaming. Or was it a prophecy and going to become reality when I see Mr Delicious next week?

Monday, 10 June, 11.30pm

Dad phoned earlier and said an envelope had arrived for me.

'Who's it from? Did you open it?'

'Oh, no, no I didn't open it. I didn't look inside at all. Really, I didn't.'

'That's OK, Dad. I thought you might have opened it by mistake. Who is it from anyway? Is there a stamp or address?'

'Oh no, no. I didn't open it at all, but it says Soho Photography Studio on it.'

Shit. He must have seen my topless photos. Thanks Mr Ageist Arse.

Tuesday, 11 June, 7.30pm

Spoke to Mum. She has another modelling job. Go Betty! Mr Snappy (AKA Mr Ageist Arse) introduced her to an agent. Is there no end to her talents? I'm pleased for her but worried about Dad. He was hoping the modelling was a one-off, but now she has a second job, he's been grumpy about being left at home on his own and giving Mum the silent treatment.

Wednesday, 12 June, 11.30pm

Texted Sara and asked if they all wanted to come to me for her birthday but she was evasive as usual, and said she'd get back to me. I won't hold my breath.

Thursday, 13 June, 1.30pm

Just had a text from Mr Delicious confirming the time and his address. Hurrah! I suppose it's OK to go to his house on a first date?

Saturday, 15 June, 2.00pm

Brunch with Leila. She'd spoken to Grace but apparently, she didn't want to talk about her health and changed the subject when Leila asked. I worry Grace is not coping and she's bottling up her feelings. Time to send her more flowers and chocolates.

Leila talked about investing in Jude's startup but she's not sure if his recycled bags are a viable business proposition. Oh God, if he's a serial cheater and they break up, she'd be heartbroken AND lose her money. If I hadn't found out he's a total knob, then I wouldn't be in this indecision hell. Life is so complicated.

4.30pm

Sitting on Leila's sofa, I was trying to tell her about Jude, but my mouth wouldn't cooperate. Finally, I gathered my courage and blurted it.

'I have something to tell you. It's awful and you're not going to like it.' I was shaking.

'Don't look so worried. Whatever it is, it can't be that bad.' She was so calm and happy, and I was about to shatter her life.

'Jude's been sleeping with other women,' I blurted and braced myself.

'Is that all? I know, honey. We have an open relationship.'

WHAT? When did that happen? It's so not like Leila to share her man. Jude must have forced it on her.

'You never said. Are you sure you're not angry?'

'No, I don't mind at all. In fact, I'll let you into a secret, honey. He sometimes brings his women home, and we have threesomes.' She winked.

'Really?' I asked, wide-eyed and open-mouthed. I felt relieved but how come I didn't know about her new predilection?

'We're always looking for fresh meat.' She paused. 'Maybe you want to join in next time?' She ran a finger over her glossy lips.

I screamed and sat bolt upright on the sofa. It was a prosecco-induced afternoon nap that ended in a horrible nightmare. Or wishful thinking that Leila won't be angry. I'm never lying down on my sofa again. My dreams are becoming wild.

Sunday, 16 June, 10.30am

It was a balmy evening, so when I arrived at Mr Delicious's Bethnal Green Victorian terrace last night – not quite the penthouse flat he had in my dream last week – I imagined an intimate evening in the garden surrounded by romantic fairy lights. He greeted me at the door wearing a long cream silk kimono. Were we having dinner first or what?

'Did I miss the memo about dress code?' I laughed. The kimono, stopping short of his ankles and open at the neck, revealed his furry chest and legs, and when he stepped back to let me in, it opened, revealing other hairy parts. I'd got the hairiness wrong in the dream too but hoped the evening would involve strawberries and cream. Preferably eaten off my body.

On the way to the kitchen at the back, I caught a glimpse of the dining room which had a long table but only one chair. The back of the house had been extended with sliding doors revealing a cute garden. No fairy lights, but there were Japanese lanterns spreading a warm glow, a small wooden table with a vase of peonies, and two chairs. It was all different from the dream but equally romantic.

I sat at the breakfast bar watching him arrange the sushi on a beautiful blue and white porcelain dish and pour saké into shot glasses. Ooh, sushi, saké and sex.

'You might have gathered that I'm doing a Japanese dinner,' he said, looking pleased with himself.

I gushed about his culinary skills and admired the lights as we took the food and drinks out into the garden. I didn't mention not being keen on sushi. The food was not important. He was enough for me. Do balmy evenings make everyone horny?

'This is for starters. I have Nyotaimori planned for the main course.'

'How lovely.' I had no clue what Nyotaimori was, but it sounded adventurous. 'Is it a tasting menu?' I asked, hoping.

'Sort of,' he replied and smiled.

There was plenty of flirting over sushi, and the saké was slipping down smoothly. We even had a kiss before he went off to prepare the main course. A sweet kiss on a warm evening left me eager for what was to come. I Googled Nyotaimori as soon as he'd disappeared. Wikipedia said:

Nyotaimori – often referred to as 'body sushi', is the Japanese practice of serving sashimi or sushi from the naked body of a woman.

I didn't know the name for it, but I had heard of this practice, or art form as it's called. Though it can look beautiful, I think it's degrading for women to be used as a food platter or an ornament. In any case, I didn't want a third person on the date.

He'd been gone a long time, so I Googled 'how long does it take to arrange Nyotaimori?' and ended up looking at the images instead. I don't know which was more disturbing: the ones of people prodding at the poor woman's pubic area with chopsticks, or the ones trying to pick up sushi with their mouths. I was thinking how the main course was looking less appealing when he called me.

'Dinner is served,' he shouted.

I went inside and into the dining room. Double OMG. It was Nyotaimori all right, but with a twist. No beautiful young woman in sight. Mr Delicious was serving the food on himself. Triple OMG.

'Wow, this is … unexpected.' Why did he go and do that? It didn't follow the aesthetic when the prawns were nestled in pubic hair, and the scallops were snuggled in chest fur. By then, I knew why there was only one chair at the table. I wanted to run out, but instead I sat down. I can take politeness to extremes.

'I suggest you start in the chest area and work your way down,' he offered, pointing his hand up and down his body as if to say, 'Knock yourself out, babe'.

I picked a tuna sashimi from the least hairy part of his chest. Weren't you supposed to put a palm leaf or something under the fish? I inspected it quickly for hair and put it in my mouth. It was indeed delicious. Emboldened, I took a piece of salmon, this time further down his chest. Again, it was beautifully fresh and tasty. But then. Was that a chest hair in my mouth? I quickly took it out and carried on. The plump scallop above his navel was so fresh and went down without any hair garnish. I picked one of the cod pieces near his groin, which started to stir on being touched (the groin, not the cod). I put the fish in my mouth and there it was again. A hair. Oh no, yuk. Two hairs. Even I couldn't take politeness this far.

'Sorry, I just can't,' I said meekly, and pushed my chair back. He flinched, sat up quickly and got off the table with bits of fish and vegetables flying off him. He stood for a second, naked with a semi-erect penis framed by pieces of seafood still stuck to his body, then rushed upstairs. I waited for ten minutes thinking he'd come down once he'd cleaned up, but he didn't reappear. I called up to him from the bottom of the stairs but no reply, so I left. I texted him in the taxi.

> It was lovely to see you again. Thank you for all the effort with the food. Sorry about the main course. S x

He didn't reply. Hairy sushi aside, I liked him. I wonder if he'll see the funny side of it today and call me.

> *Your sushi made me feel juicy*
> *The omega 3 made me want to be a floozy*
> *Sensual pleasure of the slippery cool kind*
> *The kind that makes you want to grind*

Ginger and wasabi are so warming
I'm looking forward to you performing
All those vitamins raise my energy
Sushi and saké, like us, have synergy
Let's dip into something saucy
Let's get hot together, you and me
Wait, is that noodle on your nipples?
Pollack on your penis, and bass on your bollocks?
Wait, is that chest fur in my sashimi?
And that? Is it pubic hair in my zucchini?
I've gone right off the sushi, saké and sex feast
This Japanese foreplay is now ceased

Monday, 17 June, 11.00pm

Nothing from Mr Delicious. I guess his ego was too bruised to face me again. He was brave enough to display himself as a food platter and I liked his confidence, being a sucker for a confident man as I am. I don't think I would have the guts to do something like that. I would fret about where my boobs might end up when I lay down, or feel the need to shave off the pubes, in which case I'd worry about the shape of my fanny. *Naked Attraction* has a lot to answer for. I never knew there are so many different shapes and sizes! Anyway, it's a shame he was upset about the hair incident. BUT onwards. #TooHairyAnyway

Tuesday, 18 June, 11.30pm

I persuaded Grace to come for a walk on Hampstead Heath today. Finally. Ajay bought her the cutest Yorkshire terrier called Terry, so we took him with us. She said she can't face going back to work and she's concentrating on getting better. I never expected Grace to be like this. I thought she'd accept her condition and deal with it like she deals with other problems: directly and efficiently. But it's turned out very different.

P.S. We stopped and talked to lots of people with dogs. Lots of men with dogs. I might have to borrow Terry for a flirting walk.

Wednesday, 19 June, 11.30pm

Texted Sara to wish her happy birthday and ask if she liked the flowers I'd sent. She just said, 'Yes thanks.' I despair. Will she remember my birthday?

TWENTY

The Hot One

Thursday, 20 June, 5.00pm

LOOKING FORWARD to the Material Build party tonight. It's a good way of passing a couple of hours seeing the latest designer collections, networking with other people in the industry and enjoying lovely food and drink. It'll be a good party even if it is in a building supplies showroom where we'll be surrounded by screws, glues and loos.

I'm wearing a knee-length plunge neck (low but tasteful, of course) yellow dress. Bold colour blocking is always good for standing out in a crowd.

Izzy is coming as my guest. It'll do her good to meet new people and forget about Michael. And I'm meeting Kai, who'll be there with his surveyor colleagues. He's my party partner in crime and I haven't seen him for ages. I'm so glad I kept in touch with him after our Mayfair project finished all those years ago.

Friday, 21 June, 12.30pm

Yup, it was a wild party all right. The wine was flowing, and the canapés were tiny. Bad combination. Will you ever learn, Sophia? AND if I wasn't menopausal, I would have said I must have been on heat. I spotted loads of attractive men to approach and flirted my way around the party.

At one point, I spotted a good-looking man standing alone. He had floppy brown hair and the most sparkly green eyes. Matteo turned out to be Italian and was on a shopping visit to London for his company. Emboldened by his friendliness, I was about to tell him his eyes were beautiful when he mentioned how much his wife loves London. Doh Sophia. Should have checked the ring finger earlier. I made my excuses and went back to Kai and Izzy.

'Who was that hunk?' Kai asked.

'That's Matteo, from Italy. And yes, I thought so too, until the wedding band glinted.' I scowled.

'If he's alone in London, you could "entertain him",' Kai suggested with a cheeky grin. I told him that wasn't my style and thought of Leila and her lying cheating husband.

'You're projecting what you want to do with him. But I'm afraid he referred to his wife, not husband, so you're out of luck.' Kai was unamused. He went off for a smoke while Izzy and I walked around the showroom. When we reached the final display, which looked out onto the back lane, we spotted Kai through the floor to ceiling glass. For some reason I decided to do an exaggerated disco dance and Izzy joined in. Then we blew kisses at Kai and walked away. We thought this was hilarious, but Kai was horrified and mouthed, 'What The Fuck?'

On the way back to the party area, we giggled as we followed the red wine trail we'd left on our way in. At least it wasn't a carpet showroom. We re-joined Kai and his colleagues who were standing in a group. One of them was about six foot two, blue eyes, dark hair grey at the temples, and an athletic body. Like a tall pale Rob Lowe, and just as dreamy. I thought his colouring was Irish, and hoped he'd have a lovely accent to go with it. I will call him The Hot One. He was holding court and people were laughing. I like a funny man who can work a crowd. On seeing me and Izzy, they all sniggered.

'We all enjoyed your window display,' declared The Hot One. I narrowed my eyes.

'Didn't you see all the people smoking out in the lane when you decided to display your dancing skills?' Kai said.

NO, WE DID NOT. Izzy and I looked at each other, mortified. I was hoping to sidle up to The Hot One and engage in some serious flirting. What must he think of me? I was fighting a hot flush when he came over.

'I had no idea there was an audience. It was a joke with Kai,' I said, my face crimson by then.

'Don't worry about it. You were very entertaining.'

Away from the pack, he was shy, and yes, there was an Irish lilt to his voice. I smiled and looked up at him as he bent down to talk to me above the din. The redness spread to the rest of my body.

'In that case, you're welcome. No charge for the show.' My eyes smiled back at his shiny pools of blue. I was starting to get my composure back and feeling charged with lust. He was H. O. T. HOT.

'Are you a surveyor like Kai?' I asked.

'No. His old firm were clients of ours. Although, I do know how to survey an asset.' Thinking that was a corny chat-up line, I raised an eyebrow.

'I'm a property lawyer. I help protect people's assets and rights. It's interesting work but the hours are insane.'

'You make it sound like you're a superhero. Truth, and justice, and the British way.' I did a Superman pose looking into the distance. He laughed. 'It's a bird. It's a plane. It's Property Lawyer Man.' I did a scream pose and squeaked, 'This looks like a job for Property Lawyer Man.' He was howling now.

'What about you? What kind of superhero are you?'

Superman and Superwoman are the extent of my knowledge about comic books, but Superwoman would have been too obvious. Then I remembered a character I read about in an article about cool feminist heroes. She was perfect.

'I think I'd be Suzie,' I said. He narrowed his eyes. What he didn't know was that Suzie, a librarian, has a superpower. Whenever she has an orgasm, time stops for her, and she gets up to no-good when the world around her is frozen. She meets Jon, an actor, at a party and discovers he can do the same. They decide to sexploit their powers as a couple and start their career as sex criminals. 'She's a comic book character with a special superpower. You should look it up.'

'So, your family must find it difficult if you're always working late at the office,' I fished.

'No, I'm divorced but I try to see my twins as often as I can. They live with their mum.'

He told me the twins were about to have their sixth birthday. I said I was young, free and single, and told him about the married Italian incident.

'I'm glad he was married. You're talking to me now.'

I melted.

'I'm glad too.' I did my Lady Di shy eyes while I sipped my wine.

'Does that mean you might say yes if someone asked you out for a drink?'

Yes, yes, yes. 'Hypothetically, if someone asked me out for a drink, and they were super-hot, I might say yes.'

I gave him my number, and thought it was a good time to make an exit as I could feel the effects of the wine. I didn't want to start off the encounter doing something embarrassing. Then I remembered I'd already done that. Later, I had a text from him asking if I got home OK which was nice. Then another saying he'd found Suzie, and that Property Lawyer Man might want to give up lawyering and become an actor with a special superpower. That made my tummy tingle. And my vagina. I managed to text 'good night' and 'Let me know when you want to go for that drink' before falling into a deep happy sleep.

11.30pm

I was hoping to get a text from him today but nothing. We were all a bit drunk last night and I want to be sure he's interested enough to initiate a conversation in the light of day and ask me out properly. I don't want to chase him. Might have to ask Kai, but he's not the most discreet of people, so I'd better play it cool for now. Still, a poem would be appropriate.

> *You fell into my life like a meteorite*
> *Cor, you are a bit of all right*
> *Boom, wham, zap, pop, kapow*
> *You're giving me the throbs now*
> *You look like a man of steel*
> *With extra superhero sex appeal*
> *Your looks are an absolute marvel*
> *Your eyes the colour of blue marble*
> *If you kiss me, I won't raise an objection*
> *I won't say no to a whole-body connection*
> *You are The Hot One, the caped hero of justice*
> *I want coitus with you, not interruptus*
> *I want our bodies to be legally binding*
> *I want them to soon be grinding*
> *I hope you are a sexual daredevil*
> *The kind that will make my bed dishevel*
> *I'm looking forward to feeling your deposition*
> *Or better still an unrefusable proposition*

Saturday, 22 June, 1.30pm

Only Leila today for the Brunch Bunch. I told her about The Hot One and how much I liked him. I confessed that my sex-only rule was about to be broken as meeting him had made me reconsider my intentions. She listened patiently as I babbled.

'That's fabulous, honey. Go for it and have some fun. But remember you've met him once. Don't jump in and decide he's the one for you before getting to know him. I know what you're like.'

Yes, she knows exactly what I'm like. She can see I'll throw myself in, convinced he's the perfect man for me way too early, then get upset when it goes wrong. She's trying to protect me from ME. But I'm not too old to learn new tricks. I can handle this, though I should listen to her advice. I'm probably reading too much into a random drunken conversation. Or did his eyes twinkle when he looked at me?

'I know. You're right, but we really did have a connection.'

'So why do you think he hasn't followed through and asked you out yet? He did imply he was going to do that, didn't he?' She wasn't going to let it drop. She was applying logic because she knew my logic had vanished. She was asking the sort of questions I would have asked if it had been her. She's right. As the CEO of Amateur Counselling Services PLC, I should give myself the best advice possible, except I seem to have morphed into a teenage intern on a summer holiday work placement. I have no clue.

'I think he might be shy,' I offered.

'Honey, he's a commercial lawyer. They don't come in shy models.'

'He could be waiting a while, so he doesn't look stalky.'

'Hmm … be careful, OK?'

She was right. I am going to be sensible, and not get too excited or it'll end in tears. Now all I must do is apply that advice to my actions. I can't believe that overnight I've gone from 'I never ever want a relationship again' to being this excited about the slim possibility of one.

To shut her up, I showed her the poem about The Hot One. She grabbed my phone and started reading it out loud, pushing me away when I tried to retrieve my phone. When she'd finished, there was a hush and people were looking. I noticed the old couple next to us, him with his mouth open and her smiling. She winked at me.

11.30pm

No text from The Hot One. Damn. Why hasn't he got in touch? I wonder if I should take matters into my own hands. It's the twenty-first century, and I should practise what I preach about equality. I shouldn't have to wait for a man to ask me out, but I don't want to appear desperate either. This is why I find relationships so hard. You're entirely at someone else's mercy. You can't control how they feel or behave, but their emotions and intentions affect you. Tomorrow I'll do a bit of swiping and see if anyone can take my mind off him. Yes, I'll keep my options open.

Monday, 24 June, 11.30pm

Messaged a couple of people on Kindling but my heart's not in it. I can't be bothered.

Tuesday, 25 June, 11.30pm

Lisa sent me a lovely picture of Hannah posing in her new princess heaven bedroom, holding up a 'Thank you, Sophia' sign. She's adorable. Moments like this make my job so rewarding.

If I had a grandchild her age, I would design the most beautiful magical bedroom for her. It would have animal murals on the walls, stylish furniture, and lots of fairy lights. If only.

Wednesday, 26 June, 4.30pm

One of Leila's friends is having a launch party on Friday for her new book called *Pubic Hair Etiquette*. It'll be fun to hear her do a reading and catch up with a few friends over a drink. I think I'll invite The Hot One. It's just a casual social invitation. Not a date. This way if he doesn't show any interest, I won't have the embarrassment of being rejected.

11.30pm

Hurrah! Kai and The Hot One are up for it.

Friday, 28 June, 5.30pm

It's the night of the book launch. Maybe tonight I'll get together with The Hot One. The anticipation is killing me. I'm fed up with all the disappointing dates and just want a sex machine who adores me.

Saturday, 29 June, 9.30am

I thought I'd created the perfect scenario to pick up where I left off with The Hot One, but my cunning plan didn't work. He arrived late, though he made a hell of an entrance. He stood at the bookshop door, took in the room with smouldering eyes, then swaggered across the room towards us in a sharp navy suit and adorably ruffled hair. Marvin Gaye's 'Let's Get It On' played in my head. I looked at Leila and mouthed 'Wow', but she raised a nonplussed eyebrow. Later, my hopes were dashed as, apart from complimenting my green tea dress and a quick conversation in which he told me the author sounded up herself, I hardly got near him. In fact, it felt like he was avoiding me, and then he left early.

I'm annoyed with myself for reading too much into our last conversation. He certainly didn't show any spark of interest this time. Why did he come? Or did I play it too cool and didn't give him a chance to get close?

P.S. The best bit of the evening was the author reading. The blurb on the book said that 'Ellie Anderson (28) has a degree in social anthropology with a special interest in aesthetics'. When she was introduced, she folded her leather-clad legs onto the chair, closed her eyes and took such a long dramatic pause that the worried bookshop owner was about to intervene. Then she took in a few slow breaths and finally read her book's introduction:

> *To bare, or not to bare, that is the question:*
> *Whether 'tis nobler to remove and suffer*
> *The slings and arrows of a waxing regimen,*
> *Or to take arms against a full bush*
> *And by opposing end them. To shave—to laser,*
> *No more; and with a removing cream we end*
> *The pain of the thousand shaving nicks*
> *That flesh is bare to: 'tis a Brazilian.*

The Hot One had a point. But it was interesting to hear what drives pubic hair grooming choices, from one man shaving his pubes to make his penis look bigger, to a woman shaping and colouring hers as a form of artistic self-expression. Of course, we all wanted to know what style of pubic hair the author had, but nobody dared ask.

1.30pm

Had a The Hot One debrief with the Brunch Bunch. Leila had a chat with him last night but didn't pick up any vibes about me. Damn. She also said, and I quote, 'Anyway, why are you so obsessed with him? He has a good body but he's no oil painting.'

I beg to differ.

11.30pm

Kai texted this afternoon to say thanks for the invite. But nothing from The Hot One. Right, that's it then. It's not going to happen with him, so I'm going to do some swiping before bedtime, and go back to plan A and looking for sex. I'm not cut out for this relationship lark.

Sunday, 30 June, 10.00am

Leila is sixty today. How did that happen? How have I known her for nearly fifty years? I remember going to her twelfth birthday party. Her family had recently moved from Tehran to Totnes. Her mum had tried her best to make the party 'English friendly', but the kids had never heard of Kookoo or Khoresht or Piroshki and refused to eat. Even though Leila couldn't speak much English, I knew we'd be friends for life the first time she made me laugh by mimicking one of the arrogant older school boys behind his back.

She's rejected all suggestions of a birthday party, so I'm taking her out for lunch at The Wolseley, then delivering her back to Jude for dinner. I hope he's got something amazing planned. She deserves amazing. Anyway, I'm going to forget about cheating Jude and have a fabulous time with my best friend.

7.30pm

We reminisced and laughed so much and got through two bottles of fizz.

'Do you remember our holiday in Goa? Was it in the 80s or 90s?' Leila asked.

'The one where we were both recovering from a breakup?'

'That's the one. I'd been consoling myself with food and you'd been punishing yourself by starving. So I was heavier than usual and you were a lollipop, and people thought you were my daughter,' Leila said, wide-eyed and open-mouthed.

'Yes, and I remember the taxi driver who took us everywhere. One night we got back to the hotel and as we got out of the car, he looked us up and down, inclined his head from side to side and said, "Oh lovely. One big. One small".'

We both shrieked and other diners stared, so I gave her my presents. A bottle of sweet cider to remind her of the first time we got drunk at the church disco, a *Maths for Dummies* book – I'm sure she still thinks a times table is a table for a clock – and hair products – styling our hair must have taken up sixty per cent of our teenage years. And a glamping weekend in Dorset, to which she said, 'You know I hate camping', but she accepted graciously when I suggested she should try something new in her sixty-first year on this earth.

When I took her back home, Jude was all smiles while Leila told him about our day, but behind her back, he gave me the evil eye. What the fuck? I'm starting to think it's not just that I caught him misbehaving but that he's jealous of me. He envies my closeness and friendship with Leila and can't stand to see her so happy around me. The green-eyed monster has reared its head. What will it do next?

11.30pm

WELL, WELL, WELL, things are looking up with The Hot One. Feeling happy and optimistic earlier, I decided I needed to know one way or another if The Hot One was interested. I'm a modern independent woman after all and I shouldn't have to sit around and wait for a man to approach me.

> Hi, have you had a good weekend?

Hi, I'm working today. How was yours?

> That's a shame, but I suppose Property Lawyer Man's work is never done. There are assets out there to save!

Ha ha, yes, I guess so

> I've been celebrating Leila's 60th today

Lucky you. Sounds better than being in an office all day.

> Those clients won't save themselves.

Ha ha. You can tease me if you want

> I did have a lovely time, but I was a bit distracted

Why was that?

> I imagined you in a superman outfit

Was it a good image?

> Oh yes, super.

Then he asked me if I wanted to go away for the weekend which was a way over the top response. I wonder if he likes me, or he just wanted company. Or sex. Either way, it was too much and then some.

BUT we now have a date for the following Monday. Yippee. I'm good at taking the initiative, so why didn't I do it before instead of fretting about whether he's interested? How long should I wait before having sex with him? I don't want it to be a one-night stand. I like him too much for that. Stay cool, Sophia. You haven't even been on a first date and you're planning the next one. Get a grip.

PART VII
July

TWENTY-ONE

The Hot One Again and Again

Monday, 8 July, 7.30am

D DAY TODAY. My first date with The Hot One. I hope he texts soon, so I know what we're doing tonight. I took the initiative and made the date come about so I'm not going to chase him today. SO EXCITED.

11.30am

Still no text. He should have contacted me by now.

1.30pm

No text.

2.30pm

I can't bear it.

4.00pm

Right, I need to know what's happening.

4.15pm

Fuck, fuck, fuck. I texted him only to be told he has an emergency with his kids and can't make it. I was full of adrenalin in anticipation of the date and now I feel like I've had it punched out of me. I would have been disappointed but accepted it if he'd told me he had an emergency, but to wait until I contacted him? That's rude. Was he even going to tell me?

10.30pm

Went for a walk to shake it off. The people of Islington obviously don't believe in curtains. There were so many happy families round dining tables and a few couples having candlelit dinners. I know it's not an attractive attribute, but I felt envious. Early night for me. Let's hope our date on Wednesday will make up for it.

Tuesday, 9 July, 11.30pm

I was hoping he'd call with an update but nothing. Is the emergency ongoing?

Wednesday, 10 July, 4.00pm

He texted to say he had to work late, and shall we go out on Friday? Aargh. I'll give him one more chance.

11.30pm

I suppose he couldn't help it if he had to work. He can't just walk away. Fingers crossed for Friday.

Friday, 12 July, 10.30am

He's booked the restaurant and we're all set for tonight. Butterflies in my stomach. I hope he's as charming as I remember from the party.

6.30pm

Spent all day on a building site getting filthy. After much scrubbing in the shower, I'm ready for The Hot One.

11.30pm

I'm in heaven. It was a perfect date tonight. Going to bed to dream of him.

Saturday, 13 July, 1.30pm

Woke up to the memory of my lovely date last night, which made me feel energised and positively skip to 'Born to Grind'. I walked in with a huge smile on my face.

Leila took one look at me and said, 'I take it the date was good?'

'Oh yes. You could say that. In fact, it was perfect. He'd booked Le Petit Bistro in Islington. How did he know it's one of my favourites? Anyway, we talked all evening about our lives and childhoods and all sorts of things, until the restaurant threw us out. And we had a kiss before parting.' I grinned.

'You're like a teenager, Sophia. No, like Cinderella after she's met the prince.' Grace giggled.

'You can laugh at me all you like. I haven't been this happy for a long time.' It was true. Finally, I felt like I'd connected with someone who was on my wavelength. Someone who appreciated me. Someone I think has relationship potential. AND he is so exceptionally sexy. Those dazzling blue eyes, kissable mouth, and legs that go on forever. I don't know how I managed to keep my hands off him. I can't believe I'm saying this, but I don't want to rush into sleeping with him, because I want more than just sex. Gasp.

I think I want a proper relationship. Am I doing the right thing? I thought I didn't want emotional entanglement, but I seem to have done a complete turnaround. Something has awakened in me, and I want more. I want to love and be loved. Is he going to be the one who entices me into coupledom?

3.30pm

Joy took one look at me and said, 'Why you grin like that? You look silly.'

I ignored her, but she kept staring at me suspiciously. I'm sure she polished the coffee table three times.

Sunday, 14 July, 11.30pm

Haven't heard from The Hot One. Should he have texted by now?

Monday, 15 July, 5.30pm

He wants to meet up on Wednesday. Yay! I've been so happy all day. Even demanding Cassandra couldn't dampen my spirits. She told me she'd changed her mind about the master bedroom design and wanted me to come up with a new scheme. I know she'll love it when it's done, but she's afraid of making the wrong decision, so she plays delaying tactics. Usually, I'd use my best interior designer/therapist skills to reassure her but today I said, 'No problem. I'll do a new scheme,' and floated out of the meeting.

Wednesday, 17 July, 5.00pm

We're going for a romantic picnic tonight. The food and the fizz are all packed in an ice bag. Now I'll make myself delicious!

11.55pm

WOW, WOW, WOW. Tonight's date was the best. I'm so turned on and tingling all over that I can't sleep. We found a lovely spot near the lake and spent the evening draped on a blanket, flirting and frolicking. Sitting in the middle of all that natural beauty, his eyes glinted, and he looked at me like I was the most beautiful creature there. There were still people wandering around the park, but we were in a bubble of lust that blurred out everything and everyone around us. I hadn't felt quite like that for a long time, that depth of desire – and yes, even a hint of potential for love. I reached out and caressed his shoulders and arms as he lay back on his elbows. He sat up and held me around the waist. I felt protected and wanted.

By the time I opened the picnic, I was all fingers and thumbs, and flustered with a pink face. I managed to get the tuna salad dressing all over his T-shirt. Then I popped the prosecco cork, which hit him – comedy style – on the forehead just above his right eye.

'I probably deserved that. Sorry I didn't have time to bring anything, but I knew you'd be all over it.'

I said it was OK, but it would have been nice if he'd brought something.

We walked through the park, our hands naturally finding each other. We kissed again, a long and lingering goodbye kiss as I stood on my tiptoes, and he bent down to reach me.

'Ever since we met, I hoped for this,' he said, holding me around the waist with no intention of letting go.

'Did you?' I asked, then teased, 'It's a good thing I made it happen then.'

He protested it wasn't true and that he'd done the running. 'Whoever it was, we got to the right place,' he said, and kissed me again.

'What's that?' I sniffed. 'Is that Eau de Tuna I can smell?'

He laughed and shook his head, and I noticed the beginnings of a bruise around his eye.

I think I'm falling for him a little.

Thursday, 18 July, 11.30pm

Went to see potential clients in Camden today. The couple and their two teenage daughters were charming, but the house was obviously ruled by their three creepy-looking crinkly pink sphinx cats with piercing blue eyes. I could see the evidence of their mess and destruction on the carpets, sofas, and beds. The cats sensed a nonbeliever among them and showed their discontent by puking up on the stairs as I was being shown around the house. The owners thought it was terribly funny and said it happens all the time. I need the money, but I don't want the job. Everything will be destroyed by the cats.

Was hoping for a 'Thank you for the lovely picnic' text, but nothing. I'm sure I didn't imagine the connection between us. Or am I jumping ahead too much? No, I'm certain he likes me. He looks at me with such warmth and longing. Anyway, life's too short and he's gorgeous. Why hold back?

Friday, 19 July, 5.30pm

The Hot One texted this afternoon and wants to meet up soon. He said he didn't want to wait too long to see me again. We have a date on Sunday. I can't wait to see and touch him again. No sex for a few dates though. It'll be better to wait and get to know him. I sound like The Ice Skater. I still feel guilty about him.

Saturday, 20 July, 2.30pm

'What's the latest with The Hot One?' asked Grace as I sat at the table.

I told them about the picnic date. Leila was being cautious again and telling me to calm down and not jump the gun. Grace found it amusing and kept laughing. I know she's been down lately after her cancer surgery, so it was great to see her enjoying herself. But as soon as I asked her how she was recovering, she broke down and said she'd had a meltdown last week because she might need chemotherapy. She was fretting about Ajay and the kids and her career, on top of worrying about how her body will cope with it. Personally, I think she should give up her job. She doesn't need that level of stress on top of everything else.

I felt guilty to have been gushing about dating while Grace was suppressing her emotions. But I'm going to her next appointment with her, so I'll have a chance to be a better friend then. Hopefully, there'll be some good news for a change.

Ace was quiet. He was probably fed up with listening to me going on, or is he regretting causing his marriage breakup now he knows what dating is like nowadays? I wanted to catch up with him on his own, but he's off abroad again tomorrow.

11.30pm

The Hot One has booked Terrazza in Highbury for tomorrow. He has good taste in food. And women, of course. They do a tasting menu. Oh, how I'd love to play strip tasting menu with him, like in my Mr Delicious dream. We could play pretend stripping and imagine we're getting naked. That would certainly hot things up. He'll be ravenous for me after that.

Sunday, 21 July, 11.30pm

I'm in bed (on my own) and trying not to float away. It was sexy, fun, and perfect tonight. The Hot One sizzled in jeans and a blue T-shirt that set off his eyes beautifully. He leaned forward and nodded when I suggested the strip tasting idea. The waiter was perplexed when we said we didn't want him to announce each dish, but did want to keep the menu for reference. The food was tasty and The Hot One even tastier. The game was better than in the dream, less dramatic but more intimate and seductive. Sometimes, keeping your clothes on can be more erotic. He kept my gaze while we were eating and watched my mouth as I guessed the ingredients. Not an out-of-body experience, like with The Guru, but an altogether more sensual and romantic one. At first anyway. Then we descended into uncontrollable laughter as we tried and failed miserably to do dirty talk.

'I like your shorts,' I said, after I'd imagined him taking off his trousers, 'but I wasn't expecting Latex on the first date. I think you should take them off.'

'I like your bra, but I wasn't expecting nipple tassels on the first date. I think you should take it off,' he replied.

'And that piercing on your … erm … do you take that off at night?' I asked.

'No, but I think you'll enjoy it.' He winked.

Neither of us knew where to take it after that so there was a slightly awkward pause.

'It's Sophia, isn't it?' said a Phil Mitchell lookalike with an impressive beer belly as he came over to our table. 'I didn't recognise you with your clothes on,' he said in a geezer accent, with leery eyes and leerier grin.

'I'm sorry. Do I know you?' I said.

'I came to the life drawing class you modelled for,' he said, putting life drawing in quotation marks with his index fingers. 'I was with the stag do.'

'Oh.' I blushed like a ripe peach.

'Good to see you, even with your clothes on.' He laughed as he walked away.

I picked up my spoon and stabbed my panna cotta as The Hot One tried to hide his own wide grin with his hand. I'd done the class as an act of defiance after I broke up with The Traitor. I wanted to feel that my body was beautiful and worthy of capturing on canvas. But the stag party were hideous and were thrown out after making lewd comments. It was horrible.

'He looked like a nightmare student,' The Hot One said but didn't ask any questions, as he could see I wasn't entirely comfortable with the revelation. I like him even more now. He's playful and brings out the mischievous in me. Despite feeling sexually charged by the end of the evening, I said no when he asked to come home with me. I'm managing to control my sexual urges so far, and my heart is fluttering away and wants to fall in love. How did I go from 'only sex' to no sex unless it's a relationship? I'm going from one extreme to the other, I know. I've remembered what it's like when you meet someone you really want. The butterflies, the luscious thoughts, and that lightheaded, breathless feeling of lust. Leila was so right about me changing my tune as soon as I meet the right person. Obviously, I've been in denial, telling myself I don't need love and pretending to just want sex, when all along I yearned to be in love.

Monday, 22 July, 6.00pm

Mum called so I asked her for advice on the Leila and Jude situation. She thought it was best to keep quiet. These things have a habit of working themselves out and one should not interfere in someone else's marriage. I decided to take her advice and promised to practise my best Jude-friendly face for next time.

'Mum, you're so lucky you've never had to worry about anything like that with Dad.'

'Hmm…'

'That didn't sound convincing, Mum,' I joked, confident that Dad would never be unfaithful.

'What? Sorry, Lovely. I'm a bit busy. Must go.'

She rung off. Why is she so busy? Or did she say that because she didn't want to talk about Dad? Come to think of it, she didn't reply to my comment. Surely not? Don't be silly, Sophia. Not Dad.

11.30pm

Dad phoned as I was about to have dinner. A nice surprise. Today was blessed with much parental attention. He loves it when I call him, but both he and Mum think I live such an amazing life that under no circumstances must it be interrupted by something as mundane as a phone call.

'So, what are you having for dinner, Sophie love?' he asked.

It's funny how, as a family, we find no phone call is complete without a rundown of recently consumed food, meals about to be eaten, or indeed the menu planned for the next meal. I'm sure that didn't help my teenage puppy fat problem.

I told him I was making a Jamie aubergine bake and he said he won't bother me then. I had to shout to stop him hanging up. Then he asked me about dessert, and I told him ice cream because I knew he'd like to hear that. Dad and his ice cream. It always makes me laugh when he listens patiently while a waiter tells him about all the exotic ice cream flavours available at a restaurant, and then he says, 'Vanilla please.' Every time.

He said he'd had toast and cheese for dinner, and I asked why Mum hadn't cooked.

'She did, but,' he said then hesitated, 'you may be aware, we're not talking much, so I ate alone in the kitchen.'

It was worse than I thought. Things must be bad if he's missing out on Mum's cooking.

'What's the matter, Dad? Why aren't you talking to Mum?'

'I don't want to involve you kids. I'll handle it.' Typical of Dad's stiff upper lip attitude. I persisted but I knew from his tone he wasn't going to tell me.

'I'll tell you one thing, though. I've joined a ballroom dancing club for the over-seventies. I'd forgotten how much I enjoy dancing. We're rehearsing for a performance at the local care home. I'm doing a rumba with Consuela.'

Who the hell was Consuela?

'She's one of the women at the club. From Spain. She's seventy-two and shoots from the hip when it comes to the cha-cha-cha,' he said, sounding more cheerful.

I didn't like it at all. He hasn't been this excited since I took him to the Red Arrows show a couple of years ago.

'Is Mum going dancing with you?'

'Oh no, Sophie love. She's far too busy with her international modelling career to come dancing with me.'

There it was. He was trying to console himself (or should that be Consuela himself?) with a Spanish temptress who's jiggled her tassels at him. I'm sure there's nothing to it, but Mum and Dad need to talk.

Wednesday, 24 July, 7.30pm

Phoned Sara to discuss the situation with Mum and Dad.

'Hi sis. Have you time for a chat?'

'Really, Sophe? It's seven o'clock. I'm busy getting dinner ready,' she said.

'Sorry, I didn't think.'

'You never do, Sophe, do you? You think everyone is footloose and fancy free like you.'

'I wanted to talk about Mum and Dad, not about my marital status.'

'That's a relief,' she said with an impatient sigh, then screamed. 'I can't do this right now. The burgers are burning.' She managed to evade me again, though burning burgers were a new excuse.

I texted her later and suggested a drink tomorrow and she agreed. That was something, I suppose. I hope she's ready to talk. God knows I am. And why is SHE calling ME inconsiderate?

Thursday, 25 July, 6.30pm

Waiting for Sara to arrive. Just had a text from The Hot One, saying he's leaving work and will see me later. I reminded him we were meeting tomorrow, and he sounded disappointed. How sweet that he was so desperate to see me he was wishing it to be today? I'm all warm inside. I hope Sara won't be in a bad mood again tonight.

11.30pm

Sara marched in with a slit for a mouth, her jaw set hard and her knuckles white from gripping her bag. I hoped she was nice to her patients. I decided I would be easy-peasy-breezy and relaxed, whatever her attitude.

I bought a bottle of wine hoping she wouldn't be in a rush to get home. Laurence could get his own dinner and feed the children for a change. He's the one who had an affair, so shouldn't he be making it up to her? I think he'd be OK with helping more around the house, but lately Sara likes to be a martyr and do everything herself. I suppose it's her way of coping with the guilt.

'Are you on a bender tonight then?' she asked when she saw the bottle. I ignored that comment. I tried to make her laugh and reminded her of the first time I got her drunk on red wine when Mum and Dad had gone away to Norfolk to see Auntie Susan. Sara must have been about fifteen. We were dancing around to Irene Cara's 'Flashdance' in the front room, and I decided it was time she was initiated into the red wine club.

'I don't remember the music, but I do remember feeling dizzy after the second glass,' she said with a scowl. No matter how nice I was to her, she was prickly back.

'You were going, "Sophe, Sophe, I can't feel my legs. Sophe, why is the room spinning?" It was so funny.' She was still glowering. I wanted to shake her by the shoulders.

'Yes, then I spent the next hour draped over the loo being sick.'

Why couldn't she just enjoy the memory with me? She had to make it sound like I'd done something terrible to her.

'It wasn't a great initiation, but we did have fun together when we were young, didn't we?' I asked.

'Yeah, we did.' Her pursed lips turned into a tiny reluctant smile.

I reminisced about how happy I was the day Mum and Dad brought her home from the hospital. Everyone thought I'd be jealous, but she was so cute with her dark curly hair, and at ten years old I could appreciate having a baby sister.

'Anyway, what's the important thing you wanted to discuss with me?' she asked and looked at her watch. I poured her another glass of wine.

'I'm worried about Mum and Dad. You know she did a swimwear shoot?'

'Yes. Dad told me. What was she thinking? Getting her kit off at eighty years old? She should act her age and cover it up. And going out galivanting, leaving Dad on his own. No wonder he's upset.'

'I went to the shoot with her, and she was stunning and graceful. Stop being an age-fascist.'

'I should have known you'd approve,' she said, rolling her eyes. 'I'm surprised you didn't join in and do a double act.'

'And what would be wrong with that?' She always did know how to pick at my insecurities. She knows I swing from being proud of being sixty to not wanting to mention my age at all. I know that's contradictory, but I'm not claiming to be perfect.

'An eighty-year-old and a sixty-year-old undressing for the camera? I bet only perverts will want to see those pictures.'

She hasn't always been like this. We used to be close, but it's been awful lately since she did what she did. She must still feel guilty about it, but she doesn't know that I know, so why is she being horrible to me?

'Anyone would think you were one hundred not fifty with that attitude. Have you not heard of the body positivity movement? Or have you been too busy cooking dinner to pay attention to what's going on around the world?'

'Don't have a dig at me because you don't have a husband, Sophia.'

'Actually, I'm dating a lawyer and it's going great.'

'"Actually, I'm dating a lawyer",' she said. 'Oh, just act your age,' she spat out. She picked up her voluminous bag, put her mobile in, stood up and gave me her 'I'm extremely disappointed in you' look.

'Where are you going? We need to discuss Mum and Dad.'

'Why don't you talk to Mum and tell her to forget the stupid modelling idea? Leave me out of it. I'm done here. I'm not going to listen to you lecture me about my marriage.'

She walked off and left me wondering how and why it all

escalated. Why is she mad at me when I've done nothing wrong? She's ten years younger than me but acts like she's older. She treats me like I'm not a mature adult because I'm not married with a family, but I'm not defined by my marital status. I've been through a lot myself, but my experiences and challenges have been different from hers. I've had to deal with divorce, living my life without a partner's support, being cheated on, and – the big gaping black hole in my life – accepting I'll never have children. I love Sara but lately I don't like her much. #HadEnoughOfJudginess

Friday, 26 July, 5.30pm

I hope it'll work out with The Hot One. I have a good feeling about it. And about him. I've been dating for seven months (how did that woman on the radio find her husband in three months?). Yes, seven bloody months! And it's been one disaster after another. Can I bear to carry on dating and hoping? It all seems like a lot of hard work for no return. But if this one doesn't go anywhere, I don't know if I'll be happy with being single again. Will I want to go back to only looking for sex or not bothering to look at all? Now I've had a taste of what I could be missing, it does feel like my life is lacking something. I regret not trying harder to meet someone before. I've been happy, but now feel I could have been happier. And that makes me sad. I can't bear the thought of a lonely old age.

But why am I getting sad? I have my hot date tonight. I'm going to cook a main course, so we can have sex for starter and dessert.

Saturday, 27 July, 11.30am

The Hot One lived up to his name. He's just left and I'm staying in bed to savour our night of passion. I can't stop grinning. We managed all of twenty minutes of chat – or should that be foreplay? – before we ended up in bed. We started out touching on the sofa, where my bra somehow came off before my dress, Joey Tribbiani style. We kissed softly at first then passionately. He had no middle-age droop trouble in the trouser department. Phew, what a relief. He was equally sexy naked as he was in his light blue jeans and Comme de Garçons T-shirt with a red heart logo. Was he trying to tell me something?

His body was slim and taut, and I wanted to touch all of it. When his largeness was revealed, I wanted to say, whoa, let's talk about this. He was XL or possibly XXXL. But he was gentle and considerate, and we took our time until it worked. It helped that I found him so bloody attractive and had no trouble being ready for him. I was hungry and he was the buffet. I wanted a bit of everything and to go back for seconds.

After a while we stopped for dinner, then went back to bed and did it again. I could feel he was strong, so when instead of rolling over to change position, he stood up and took me with him, I thought he could probably take his arms away and I would still stay up. Like a Barbie mounted on a lollipop stick! I savoured touching his smooth chest, good enough to eat off – put that in your pipe and smoke it, Mr Delicious – his rock-hard abs, thighs that could crack a walnut, and the bountiful penis. In the morning, it was bliss to wake up next to him and caress those perfect sinewy shoulders and arched back. We made love again, and I felt calm and happy afterwards. I think there's a real connection between us. Definitely physically, and hopefully a connection of the hearts soon. #Shagtastic #AmfallingForHim

P.S. I think his penis deserves a name of its own. I've christened it Junior.

Wow you are a sight to behold
My temperature has risen threefold
You are an object of desire
My body is singing like a choir
My skin totally tingles
You're as yummy as a box of Pringles
Anticipating your sensual crush

Brings me out in a hot flush
You look as tasty as a chocolate Hobnob
Ooh you've made my vagina throb
Please can we touch again quite soon
Wow, you're making me swoon
I want Junior to be mine, all mine
Oops my panties have fallen down
I had you as a starter, main and dessert
Now I am a culinary expert

5.30pm

Joy was on time and on cutting form today. Could she have been more misnamed? Firstly, she came into the bedroom before I'd had a chance to tidy up after last night's acrobatics.

'Oh, what you do in bed, Sophia? Such a mess for Joy.'

I was too happy to get annoyed and just smiled while she yanked off the sheets.

'And what's this?' She pointed at a stain on the sheets as she gave me the evil eye. Oh God, was there nothing this woman would be too embarrassed to say? I blushed, and she tutted.

I escaped to the kitchen to make lunch. She came in five minutes later and put the sheets in the washing machine as she glared at me, then noticed the dirty dishes from last night.

'Oh Sophia, did you cook? You know how to cook?' she asked and did her best surprised expression.

'Yes, I can cook.'

'But why you use everything in kitchen? Such a mess for Joy.'

Such a diva.

Meeting Izzy for drinks tonight. Will have lots to tell her. Will she notice my awkward bow-legged walk courtesy of Junior?

11.30pm

I must have been glowing with pheromones tonight. I had three men chat me up, but I wasn't interested. I resisted talking about

The Hot One though. I didn't want to drive Izzy mad. On the way home, I texted him and asked how his Saturday evening had gone. Then I threw caution to the wind.

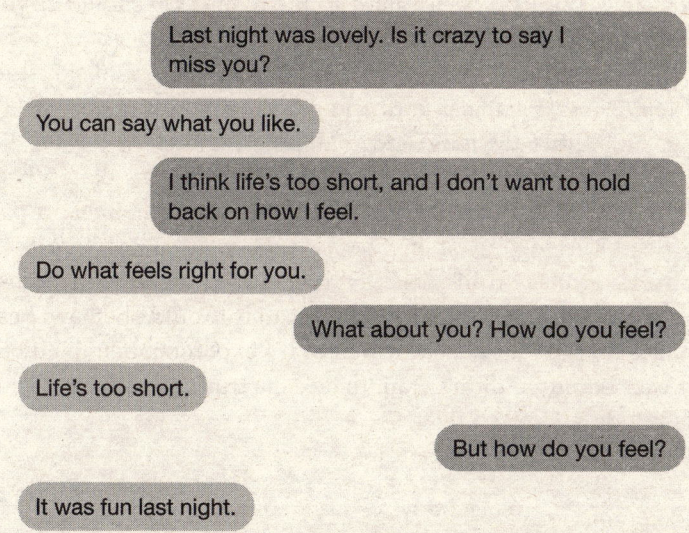

> Last night was lovely. Is it crazy to say I miss you?

> You can say what you like.

> I think life's too short, and I don't want to hold back on how I feel.

> Do what feels right for you.

> What about you? How do you feel?

> Life's too short.

> But how do you feel?

> It was fun last night.

WTF? What did that even mean? Is he saying he only wants to have fun? I told him before that I wanted more than that. A proper relationship. Wish I hadn't texted him. I didn't reply.

Sunday, 28 July, 10.30am

I woke up feeling deflated and doubting my feelings. I read the text again and he definitely hadn't gushed back at me. Could I have got it all wrong? Didn't he feel the connection I felt the other night? HeLikesMe.com or HeLikesMeNot.com

11.30am

He called to ask if I was OK as I hadn't replied. I told him I didn't appreciate his text. He said he wants to talk and explain his situation. Whatever that means. I feel like curling up in bed for the rest of the day. #SodYou

11.30pm

Leila called earlier to invite me for dinner next Saturday. She said it was ages since I'd been round to them, and we should have a proper catch-up. If I'm honest, I've been avoiding going to her house because I don't want to see Jude. And I feel so disloyal for not telling her what her husband's been up to and that he's a lying, unfaithful, devious, and manipulative dick of a man. If I was married, would I want to know if my husband had been unfaithful? I'd like to think yes. But then I also remember a past boyfriend turning up at my house one night with what were clearly love bites on his neck. He persuaded me that the marks were a reaction to the seafood he'd eaten for lunch. Now I can admit to myself that I chose to accept his explanation, implausible as it was, because I didn't want to face the truth. Would Leila want to face Jude's deceit?

Monday, 29 July, 11.30pm

Mum texted asking for my aubergine bake recipe. Said Dad had mentioned it. She'd put three aubergine emojis in her text.

At least they're talking.

Tuesday, 30 July, 11.30pm

Not heard from The Hot One yet. Went for a drink with Izzy and told her what had been going on.

'Do you remember Francis, who I dated for a while?' she asked.

'Yes, the knob who messed you around right from the beginning.'

'And do you remember you wondered why we go blind as soon as we get the hots for someone?'

She raised her eyebrows and tilted her head. She might as well have said, I rest my case. Shit. Is that me now? Completely blind and being messed around? Right from the beginning? Am I ignoring the red flags? I don't want to repeat the mistakes of the past. I need to think.

Wednesday, 31 July, 11.30pm

He wants to meet up on Friday. Does he want to have a 'talk'? What did he mean by his 'situation'? He's definitely divorced. I know that from Kai. So what could it be?

PART VIII
August

TWENTY-TWO

The Hot One Continued

Thursday, 1 August, 11.30pm

WENT to Grace's appointment with her today. The great news was that she doesn't need any more treatment. Fantastic. She'll take some tablets for the next few years and be monitored. She was so relieved she burst into tears. I took her for a coffee afterwards. I know what it means now when people say someone looks like a shadow of their old self. She said she'd gone back to work but couldn't handle it and will probably stop again for a while. I think she's mostly recovered physically but mentally she's finding it hard to go back to life before cancer.

It's scary how life can be turned upside down at one stroke. It certainly makes me think about what matters to me. What is important in my life? I feel I should just be grateful for being healthy, and regard everything else as a bonus. It's easier said than done, though, when you're hankering after someone, and you don't know where it's going. A new relationship is like standing at the gates of heaven, with the other person playing God and deciding whether to let you enter the inner sanctum. Even if he does let me into his heart, what will life be like with him? Will it be beautiful forever, or will he eventually send me to the gates of hell?

Friday, 2 August, 6.30pm

The Hot One is coming over. I hope he's not going to end it. I want more of Junior.

Saturday, 3 August, 11.00am

It was a lovely evening. And we even had a bonus round of sex this morning. No 'talk'. I should have asked him, but I was enjoying myself and didn't want to go there. I didn't want to face up to whatever was on his mind.

We went to bed pretty much as soon as he arrived, then cooked dinner together. While we were eating, he confided in me about his childhood. He talked about his mum's depression and how it made his life miserable as a child. There was little laughter or happiness as she was barely managing to cope from day to day. He said he found it hard to feel loved in his adult life as a result. I felt sorry for him but so glad that he shared that. Doesn't that mean he feels a connection with me?

11.30am

OR was he telling me he didn't want a relationship because he can't love or be loved? I wish I was a mind reader. #AnyTipsPaulMcKenna?

2.30pm

Can't stop thinking (and grinning) about this morning. It was so good, I feel moved to write another poem.

> *The way we kiss is steamy*
> *And it's making me hot and creamy*
> *My hand reaches under your belt*
> *You're pleased to see me, I detect*
> *I'm impressed – that's some wood*

You possess a fine manhood
Though it is on the large side
I'd still like it thrust inside
It's like a super-sized giant sausage
I can't help it, I want to pay homage
It's very long and very fat
M&S don't make them like that
We are working up a sweat
And you've made me very wet
Now I think I have your full measure
And you're giving me so much pleasure
Wow I'm starting to lose my head
I bet I'm going very red
My pulse is racing much quicker
I think you've pressed my trigger
I forget myself and scream
And feel pleasure in the extreme
If I smoked, I'd have a cigarette now
That was great, wow, wow, wow

7.00pm

Got an email from the House of Sphinxes saying they've decided to go with another designer. Was it because I didn't show enough love for the cats?

Off to Leila's for dinner. Looking forward to seeing her but not Judas Jude.

Sunday, 4 August, 10.30am

I hate Jude. And Leila. Last night, I arrived at their house having decided to stay out of their marriage like Mum suggested. We had a few drinks before dinner, and everything was fine. Leila had cooked a delicious Shirin Polo with buttery rice, oodles of dried fruit, nuts and saffron, and melt-in-the-mouth lamb shanks. We were catching up on our news while we ate.

'How's the dating challenge going? Spill. Every. Thing,' demanded Leila.

'You know I've been seeing The Hot One?' I gushed, 'I like him, but he works all hours, and any spare time has to be for his kids. It's difficult to make time for us. I think he's into me though.' My cheeks warmed up.

'That must be tough, honey,' Leila said.

'Are you sure it's his work that makes it difficult? Or is he just not that into you?' Jude asked.

You'd know about deceit, Jude.

'No, it's his situation,' I said, staying calm.

'At least while you're with him, the rest of London's male population is safe from your cougar advances and your dating challenge,' he said without a hint of humour.

'That's not nice,' I said. My body tensed.

'Jude, stop teasing Sophia.'

Taunting, not teasing.

'I think he's lucky to have you, honey. I hope he can sort out his problems, and you two can live happily ever after,' she said cheerily. Jude didn't comment, so I changed the subject.

'How's it going with the exhibition preparations?' I asked Leila. 'Have you found an art gallery to work with yet?'

'I…' started Leila, but Jude interrupted.

'No, she hasn't. Poor babe,' he said as he rubbed her back. 'She's having to bankroll the exhibition herself because no one will take her on.'

He was taunting Leila now, and I didn't like it. How dare he talk about her like that? She's had several successful sculpture exhibitions way before he came along. I wondered why he was putting her down. Despite being a cheater, or because of it, he's usually supportive of Leila's work.

'But that's OK, isn't it? If she pays for the exhibition herself, she'll get to keep one hundred per cent of the profits,' I said. Doh.

'It's just that, apparently, we have enough money to pay for an exhibition that might make a loss, but we don't have enough money to inject into my business that's about to take off into the stratosphere. What do you think? If there was a cool brand selling amazing handbags made of recycled materials, you'd buy one, right?' He was addressing me but looking at Leila.

I was thinking, you've picked on the wrong person for support, mate. And good for her if she's refusing to finance his business. I know that he, unlike Leila, hasn't had much success with his past ventures – like when he opened a flip-flop shop in Sheffield in the middle of winter. He's reached the age of forty-five without any evidence of a career.

'Can we not discuss that tonight, please? I want us to have a lovely dinner together,' Leila said.

'But I only need enough to do the launch and then the money will roll in, babe,' Jude insisted.

'I'm sure Sophia doesn't want to hear the details of our finances. Right, anyone for pudding?' Leila stood up and went to the kitchen.

'You were no help. I thought you'd want your friend to make money from a successful business,' he snorted at me.

'And why would I want to help you extort money out of my best friend when I know you've been cheating on her?' I hissed, keeping an eye on the kitchen door.

'Oh, you're not still going on about that, are you? It was nothing. I'd had a row with Leila, had too many pints. That's all. Nobody died. Nobody got hurt.'

'But it wasn't once, was it? I hear you're quite a Casanova on the singles party circuit,' I spat out.

'What do you mean?' He twisted his wedding band around his finger.

'I'm on the singles scene in London, as you reminded me earlier. I hear things.' I hadn't heard anything.

'Do stop the amateur sleuth act. You're not good at it. You don't know nothing about me.'

'What about the singles party last Thursday then?' I was bluffing. All I knew was that there was another party in the City.

'Why? Were you there? Anyway, it was just a drink.'

So brazen. Even if he hadn't been with another woman, he'd gone to the party with that intention.

'And somebody did get hurt. My friend Izzy that you bedded then ghosted. And how about your wife? She'd be devastated if she finds out.'

'At least I'm not a desperate sixty-year-old trying and failing to find love. You're pathetic. Going on dating sites and picking up men all over the place. At your age. But nobody wants you. Do they?'

Did I really look like that to other people? I felt my cheeks heat up as tears nipped at my eyes, even though I knew he was just playing a power game and trying to make it about me rather than his bad behaviour.

'Here we go, orange and cardamom cake, made by my own fair hands. Cream or ice cream, Sophia?' Leila put the dishes on the table, then saw my anguished expression.

'What's the matter, honey? Are you crying?' She came over and hugged my shoulders. 'Jude, have you been teasing her again?'

'She's had too much to drink. As always. Just leave her be. She'll sleep it off.'

'Come on. What did you say to her?'

'OK, OK,' he said, putting his palms out. 'I wanted to save you the upset, babe, but you leave me no choice. I'm embarrassed to say it, but Sophia made a move on me while you were in the kitchen, and she got upset when I rejected her. There. See what you made me do?'

'What?' She looked at me, then at him. He shrugged.

'Is this true, Sophia?' She took her hands off my shoulders.

'No, of course it's not true,' I spat out. 'I was going to tell you that your husband has been sleeping with other women. He's fabricating this to divert your attention.' I sneered at him. 'See what you made me do?'

Leila slumped into her chair and looked at us, one then the other.

'Is this true?' she growled at Jude.

238

'No, of course it's not true, babe,' he said. 'She's drunk and desperate. She'll say anything to get out of it. Let's just forget about the whole thing. I won't mention it again if she won't.'

So magnanimous. I could see Leila was starting to believe him.

'He's lying. He's playing you. Surely you can see that. I can prove it,' I said, my confidence returning. I didn't want to drag Izzy into it. She'd done nothing wrong, but I had to convince Leila. 'That day when you had a row with him over the waitress, he went to a singles party and had a one-night stand with my friend Izzy. You can talk to her if you want.'

'She's lying, babe. I went to see that special screening of *Star Wars*. Remember?'

'We can call Izzy. Right now,' I said, offering my phone.

'No, wait a minute. I remember Jude hinting that you were flirting with him before. On a couple of occasions, in fact, and you've been acting weird around him for a while.'

He'd been clever – preparing her for this eventuality.

'That's not true. I wouldn't do that to you, Leila. I've been weird around him because I knew what he'd done.'

She narrowed her eyes and gave me a disbelieving look. A look that said, 'you're guilty'. I WAS guilty. Guilty of not being as devious as Jude. Guilty of not anticipating how the truth could unravel. Guilty of not believing how nasty people can be when protecting themselves. I should have told her earlier. I felt wet tracks down my face.

'I think you'd better leave.'

I looked up, thinking she was addressing Jude, but no, it was me. She turned away, shaking her head.

I stood up. 'You're a deluded coward, Leila. You two deserve each other,' I said, before picking up my bag and banging the door shut behind me.

I was drenched by the time the taxi came, and as I was getting in, Jude stuck his head out of the upstairs window and shouted, 'And don't come back, you evil witch!'

Me and the driver stared up into the rain at him for a second before driving off.

'Do you want to go via the offie, love?' he asked.

I nodded. What a thoughtful man.

Monday, 5 August, 10.30pm

I went to a site visit today and one of the builders said, 'Cheer up, love, it might never happen,' except it has. I texted Leila this morning wanting to talk but she hasn't replied. Is she so desperate to have a man that she chooses to believe his lies? She didn't even ask about the proof I offered. That would mean learning the truth, and she obviously doesn't want to do that.

I texted The Hot One and asked him to come over after work to keep me company, but he's working late. He has an early morning meeting tomorrow so he can't stay the night either. I wish his employers wouldn't impose on him so much, but he's too conscientious to refuse. I thought he'd jump at the chance to look after me. I could have done with some TLC tonight and he's not there for me. Is this how it's going to be?

I'll tell Grace and Ace about Leila at some point, but I can't face that right now.

Tuesday, 6 August, 7.30pm

I sent The Hot One a picture of two sets of bra and pants next to each other – cream and pink lacy number vs. hot red satin – and asked him which one he wanted me to wear next time he comes over. He said, 'Wow.' That should give him a nudge to arrange another date.

11.30pm

It worked. He's coming round tomorrow.

P.S. He chose hot red satin. Men are so predictable.

Wednesday, 7 August, 7.00pm

Shit, shit, shit. He's cancelled. Said he was so stressed about work he wouldn't be able to relax with me. Bollocks! Surely if you feel stressed, the best thing for you is to be with someone who cares about you. And have sex. I was looking forward to going out tonight, and it's too late now to try and organise something else. #FeelLetDown

10.00pm

Going to bed early tonight. Couldn't sleep last night fuming about Leila. I texted her.

> Fuck you! You disloyal fucking excuse of a friend.

She didn't reply. I called her and left a long voice message saying I was so disappointed in her, that I didn't know who she was anymore, and she was welcome to her cheating lying devious husband.

Thursday, 8 August, 5.00pm

Had a sweet text from The Hot One apologising for last night and wanting to make it up to me. I could do with being appreciated.

11.30pm

His company's offices on Fetter Lane were as plush as I'd expected. The receptionist called The Hot One and gave me directions to his office. I was happy he'd asked me to meet him at his work. That surely showed he wanted his colleagues to meet me. The few people still working in the open plan area examined me as I strutted towards his office. As soon as I went in, he kissed me passionately and started grabbing at my dress. I told him I couldn't. What if someone heard us or walked in? But he said to relax. He couldn't wait, and we could be quiet.

The danger was a turn-on, and I thought, what the hell. We started undressing each other frantically. He swept away the stuff on his desk and lifted me onto it and himself onto me. We could have been caught at any time and that made it more exciting. I climaxed quickly and just as he was about to burst, the door opened, I turned my head to see the intruder, and something dug into my cheek. I screamed.

I touched my face and there was a dent where I'd fallen asleep on my TV remote.

Friday, 9 August, 6.30pm

No dreaming about The Hot One tonight. I'll have the real thing. I don't know how I'm going to sit through dinner. I've been in an 'about to have an orgasm' state all day just thinking about him. And about Junior. He pushes my trigger, but he likes to do the same things every time, sometimes in the same order. I hope he'll be more playful this time and take my mind off Leila.

Saturday, 10 August, 11.00am

He arrived an hour late last night, by which time I was on edge and annoyed. We went for a meal, and he was distracted, rambling about work and what a tough week he'd had. Didn't give me much of an opportunity to say anything as he was completely wrapped up in himself. Not exactly 'making it up to me' for the other night.

When we went back to my place, it was straight to bed and, regardless of everything, the sex was amazing. This morning he was livelier, so I put last night's distraction down to a bad week. I was starting to relax and wonder why I'd got so worked up about everything.

'You know I like you,' he said. 'You're great company and I'd like to see more of you to do stuff together. And you're independent. You don't need anyone to make you complete. I like that about you.'

I thought that was so sweet, and exactly what I wanted to hear. I kissed his forehead and told him I liked him too.

'It's so hard at work at the moment and it often affects my personal life, working long hours and not being able to plan anything. But I need to put in the hours to protect my partnership. You understand, don't you?'

Yes. Sort of.

'And, you know it's not easy with my ex-wife. Trying to co-parent the twins. She's not always accommodating. Regardless of how she behaves, and how I'm feeling, I can't let it affect the kids. They're my top priority. They have their mum and she's a good mum. I don't want to confuse them. Do you understand?'

'Yes of course I do. You're a good dad and that's one of the things I like about you.' I kissed him again and he was happy after that. #HotDad

11.30pm

Ace texted to say he'll be in Valencia at the end of the month, and did I fancy going? Hell yeah. A few days of sun, sand and music is exactly what I need. Would The Hot One like to come along and make it sun, sand, sex and music? Is it too soon to think of going away together? If I'm being sensible, then I'd say yes. But what's wrong with being reckless for a change? A few days of 24/7 together, away from his work and commitments, might be what we need to bring us closer. After all, he did ask me to go camping with him for our first date. I'm sure Ace won't mind.

P.S. No Brunch Bunch today. I was spared the humiliation of Leila refusing to talk to me. I was hurt before, but I'm pissed off now. Ace couldn't believe it when I texted him that Leila wasn't talking to me. He called me straight away and let me vent. It was a bit awkward talking about cheating though. When is Ace going to tell me exactly what happened with Kelly?

'I don't know him well, but I've always thought Jude is slippery. Leila will come to her senses soon,' he said.

I'm not sure about that.

Sunday, 11 August, 11.30pm

Been thinking about what The Hot One said. Why did he make a big thing of it and say, 'Can we have a talk?' as though it was something serious, when all he said was that he liked me, and his kids were a priority? I wouldn't want a man who doesn't put his kids first. I've told him that already.

Anyway, I think we're OK. Sort of. It's bliss when we're together but in between the times we see each other, there's no communication. I don't know how to take that. Maybe he wants to take things slowly. I don't want to keep contacting him if he doesn't want it, but it upsets me that he seems to forget about me when I'm not in front of him.

I wish I could talk to Leila about all this. She'd help me think it through. I miss having her in my life. When is she going to realise Jude is a knob? Texted her to say we need to talk. She read it but hasn't replied.

P.S. I told him about my dream in his office and asked if he wanted to recreate it. He said no way. He's not as playful as I thought.

Thursday, 15 August, 6.30pm

Dinner with The Hot One tonight. I hope he's not going to be stressed. Even if he is, I'll soon help him relax.

Friday, 16 August, 11.30pm

He was late again last night, which wound me up, but I relaxed after a while, and we had a nice evening followed by great sex. I was so tempted to ask him about coming to Valencia but decided to wait and ask Ace first.

Saturday, 17 August, 2.30pm

Grace was looking much better today. I told her and Ace about Leila and asked if they'd heard from her. They hadn't. Terry growled.

'That must have hurt. You've been friends for so long. I bet she's too embarrassed to contact us. She must know deep down that you're not lying but she doesn't want to face it,' Grace said.

'Why does she want to stay with him anyway if he's been unfaithful?' Ace asked.

Ironic.

'She's never been good at being on her own. She needs a man by her side. I suppose, as Jude is her fourth husband, she really wants it to work. And she doesn't care if she's a total bitch.' Terry's ears pricked up and he wagged his tail and barked.

'There's no excuse for her behaviour but I bet she's upset about you,' Grace said.

'I bloody well hope she's suffering,' I said.

It was a relief to know they supported me, but eventually I changed the subject and told them about The Hot One being a bit unreliable. I asked Ace if it was OK to take him to Valencia. He twisted his mouth and glanced at Grace, then said it was fine. Grace gave me a quizzical look. Ace left soon after to meet a friend.

'What?' I asked as Grace continued staring.

'Are you sure that's a good idea? Taking someone you've just met on holiday with Ace?'

'What's wrong with that? Firstly, I may not have gone out with him many times. Yet. But I like him and it's a natural progression to go away together. Secondly, I'm sure Ace will like him once he gets to know him. Don't worry, it'll be fine.'

'But you've been complaining about how he never calls you. Doesn't that tell you something?'

'Exactly. It'll give us a chance to spend time together and get closer.'

'If you say so,' she said, and shrugged. Terry barked.

It'll be fine. We'll come back from Valencia all loved up.

P.S. Is Leila going to cancel her Brunch Bunch membership for good?

11.30pm

Asked The Hot One about going to Valencia. He wasn't sure at first but couldn't resist my powers of persuasion. It's going to be great.

Sunday, 18 August, 11.30pm

Forwarded the flight details to The Hot One, then texted him in case he hasn't checked his emails.

> Hi, emailed you the flight details. It'll be so much fun!

> Thanks. Yes seen your email.

> Not much packing to do. Mostly bikinis and lingerie for me.

> Sounds good.

> Just thought. Should I have bought a separate ticket for Junior?!

> Ha ha

> Let me know where you want to meet, OK?

Monday, 19 August, 11.30pm

Went to see a client who wanted me to prepare her flat for sale as it wasn't attracting buyers. As soon as I walked in, I knew she didn't need an interior designer. She needed a cleaner. The sofa had suspicious yellow stains, there were splodges of food around the kitchen, and a layer of grime over everything. The smell of cat was accompanied by floating furballs. The worst place was the bedroom, where a beautiful pristine white Persian cat sat on a navy throw covered in hairs. The smell was so strong, I almost gagged. I employed my best interior designer diplomacy and suggested a freshen up.

She was pleased she didn't have to redecorate and agreed to buy a white throw to mask the hairs. At least sphinx cats don't moult. I asked Joy to give the place a spring clean.

Tuesday, 20 August, 7.00pm

Had a text from the Persian Cat Lady saying Joy is allergic to cats.
Joy texted to say, 'I'm not cleaning that house. It's too dirty.'
Sent Persian Cat Lady another company's name.

11.30pm

No word from The Hot One since Sunday. You'd think he'd want to talk and plan our holiday. I had to text and ask if he was still OK with the travel plans for tomorrow. He apologised and said he'd been busy and will have a look at my email again. It drives me mad – and makes me miserable – that he doesn't text me other than to arrange to meet. But it's so nice when we're together. And I miss Junior.

Wednesday, 21 August, 6.00pm

He finally texted this morning. Better late than never. I'm so excited. He's coming round tonight, and tomorrow we're flying off to Valencia. Weather forecast is scorchio, and we're going to relax, have uber-scorchio sex, and enjoy quality time together. I can't wait.

7.30pm

Damn, damn, damn. He's doing an all-nighter at work, so he's going to meet me at the airport tomorrow. It would have been nice to get up and get ready together and go away like a proper couple. I hope he's not going to be too tired for our first night away.

Thursday, 22 August, 9.30am

Waiting in the departures lounge for my flight. I want to scream and howl. The Hot One texted this morning and said he needs to work on an urgent case and can't come to Valencia. He couldn't even talk as he had to go into a conference call. Surely he's allowed to have SOME time off. Ace will be rehearsing most days and performing in the evening, so I'll be on my own. Sun and sand sans sex for me then.

11.30pm

Fuck, fuck, fuck. All the excitement and energy has been drained from me in torrents of tears. I was about to go and meet Ace for a drink before his gig when there was a text from THO – I can't bear to call him The Hot One anymore. The prick has dumped me. By text! How could he do that to me? Some bullshit about 'I have to concentrate on my work, and then there are the twins,' and how it wouldn't work 'trying to juggle everything'. BULL. SHIT. Millions of other people juggle work, kids and relationships. Why can't he?

It's callous and cowardly to finish a relationship by text. I must have got it all wrong. He wouldn't be treating me like this if he had any feelings for me. I couldn't face telling Ace, so I made an excuse. My eyes are too swollen for going out. I've downed everything in the mini bar to knock myself out, but I still can't sleep. What a shitty holiday this turned out to be. I hate him but still wish he was lying next to me here. If only there was a switch for turning off feelings.

Friday, 23 August, 11.30pm

I told Ace I couldn't see him because I had 'tummy trouble' so he wouldn't ask any questions. I'm not ready to talk about it. Spent the day going back and forth from my terrace to the mini bar. I'm in no state to see anyone. The waiter who brought up my room service did a double take at my swollen eyes, crumbled mascara, and hair like a furball. I did a triple take at my reflection in the mirror later.

I phoned Grace and cried down the phone for about two hours. She was lovely and listened to me ranting and asking, Why? Why? She resisted saying she'd told me it wasn't a good idea. Oh Sophia, why don't you ever learn? I did exactly what Leila was worried about, and what I told myself I wouldn't do. I jumped in with both feet, allowed my feelings to run away with me, thinking he felt the same way. I must have been blinded by love. Or more likely by lust. But is it wrong to allow your feelings to flourish? To not try to hold back and to feel free to enjoy them? Is everyone else so afraid of love, they hide their feelings? I can't be the only one who feels like this.

I must have checked my phone a hundred times for a text from him. Maybe he was having a bad day and couldn't cope and will change his mind, but nothing. I drafted several texts ranging from 'how can you do this to me?' to 'you utter shit', but I didn't send them.

This is exactly what I didn't want to happen. I was happy enough being single and living my best life. As soon as a man comes into the mix, I end up being miserable and heartbroken. I don't need this. I should get some sphinx cats so when I die, they could eat me and put on some much-needed weight.

Ace has been texting and checking up on me, offering to bring food and drink, but I put him off. He is the sweetest man. Perfect boyfriend material. Except for the cheating, of course.

Texted Leila and told her what had happened, and she replied, 'Sorry to hear that.' Just sorry to hear that? How many times have I supported her through her relationship breakdowns, and when I need her, I get just a 'sorry to hear that'. I threw an empty mini vodka bottle across the room and shouted, 'Cow!'

Saturday, 24 August, 3.30pm

I couldn't put Ace off anymore. I felt so guilty, and it didn't help that, as the poster boy for the orchestra, his face was on a billboard across the road from my balcony. When I met him for lunch today, he gave me a funny look, then reached over and patted down the knot of hair at the top of my head. I was managing to pretend everything was fine until he asked about THO, at which point I turned into a blubbering mess. He paid the bill and ushered me towards the beach for a walk along the shore.

'Why does it always go wrong for me?' I asked between sobs.

People on their sunbeds were hauling themselves up to see who was howling.

'You've met guys who weren't right for you, that's all,' he said.

'But what did I do wrong? I know he was having a rough time at work, but I thought we were good,' I whined.

'It's probably nothing to do with you. It's more likely something about him that's not right, and from what you've told me, it sounded like he made you miserable most of the time anyway.'

'Yes … that's true. But have you ever met someone and thought she's the one for me, and you just wanted to go for it?'

He didn't reply, but after a while he said, 'You deserve to be with someone who loves you unconditionally. Someone who puts you first and makes you happy, not someone who keeps you guessing about how he feels and doesn't turn up to be there for you.'

He is so right. That is exactly the kind of person I need. He escorted me back to my hotel but not before suggesting I have a coffee in a nearby café. I looked through the window and declined. The chairs were too hideous for words. We need more men like Ace in the world, but with better taste in chairs.

10.30pm

Spent the evening on my terrace. Feeling exhausted from the drama of today and the self-inflicted misery. Didn't make it to Ace's concert again. I'm the CEO of Worst Friends on Earth United. I didn't want to risk sitting in the front row and blubbing through the performance. I will get a grip and go tomorrow.

No text from THO to see if I'm OK. THE PRICK. I hate him but my hands and lips are yearning for his body.

Grace texted and said she'd met Leila for brunch today. She wanted to call and tell me about it, but I said I was too upset already.

TWENTY-THREE

The Italian – Not So Stallion

Sunday, 25 August, 10.30am

FEELING BETTER today and less sorry for myself. And things are looking up at the hotel. Made it to breakfast this morning, but was a bit tearful over my scrambled eggs. I noticed the solo man at the next table was watching me. He reminded me of Stanley Tucci – not classic good looks, but there was something attractive about him.

'Why are you crying? You're too beautiful to cry,' he said in a sexy Italian accent.

I thanked him for the compliment and told him it was a matter of the heart and I'll be OK. He was charming and sympathetic, and we chatted for a while.

'What you need is a relaxing day by the sea. I know a secluded beach off the tourist trail where you can get a natural tan. Why don't you join me there later?' he asked.

It has to be better than another day of moping in my room. So that's what I'm going to do this afternoon.

Monday, 26 August, 5.00am

Just when I thought things couldn't get any worse. It's like I forced myself to think of the worst things I could do to make me even more miserable, and then did them.

My taxi driver gave me a lecherous look when I gave him the address of the beach yesterday afternoon. It didn't take long to understand why. My Spanish isn't great but even I could work out what 'Playa Nudista' meant. Before I could turn back, my Italian friend spotted and beckoned me. I sat next to him in my sarong, clutching my bag and trying to keep my gaze above his waist.

First Worst Thing: The Italian used his ample Roman charm to persuade me to go nude, flattered my ego with compliments, made me laugh, and then invited me back to his room for afternoon delight. I accepted. If I'm being honest, all I could think was, yes I'm going to have sex and that'll show THO. Revenge sex will be sweet. Or so I thought.

Back in his room, our suntan lotion and sand-covered bodies entwined, and I started to enjoy myself. But when we tried to move on from foreplay, it ended in him looking shell-shocked and saying, 'That's never happened to me before,' and me rushing out half-dressed. Was it my fault? Did I do something wrong? I felt undesirable and unwanted. I couldn't even have revenge sex with an Italian Stallion.

Second Worst Thing (the worst, worst thing): Went to meet Ace after his concert, had too much to drink and started sobbing again, so Ace took me to a quiet corner to calm me down. He ordered coffee to sober me up, but I still had a glass of wine in my hand and carried on drinking. He consoled me while I cried on his shoulder and prattled on.

Then I looked up and into his eyes, and I don't know what came over me. He was being so nice and protective, and I was upset, and needed comforting. I kissed him. On the mouth. And I think he kissed me back ever so slightly, but I can't be sure. When I pulled away, I was already feeling ashamed of my behaviour and regretting what I'd done.

He looked at my anguished expression, stroked my cheek with the back of his hand and said, 'It's OK. Everything'll be fine.'

What was he supposed to do? Push me off? He's too lovely to do that. I came to my senses, ran out and went back to my hotel as he called after me to go back. What have I done? I can't face him today. Will go to the airport early before he has a chance to come to me. I'm so ashamed.

11.30am

On flight home. I cannot believe yesterday. First, I managed to make an Italian Stallion go limp. Then, as if that humiliation wasn't enough, I went and ruined things with Ace. I don't want to lose him as a friend and I'm afraid he'll be uncomfortable around me now. I texted him before I left.

> I'm so sorry. I should never have done that. I'm all over the place. Will you forgive me? Can we just forget it and never mention it again? Please?

He took ages to reply, or it felt like ages.

> No need to apologise Phia. We're good. xx

I don't deserve him. He should be shouting at me for getting out of control and putting him in a difficult position. Thank God his flight is tomorrow. I couldn't have coped with two and a half awkward hours in the air together.

Tuesday, 27 August, 11.30pm

Grace came over to give me the lowdown on what Leila had told her on Saturday. Apparently, Jude has convinced her that he hasn't been unfaithful. She remembered that night back in January when he disappeared for a few hours. He'd come home and said he'd been to the cinema, and she believed him.

'He said Izzy must have mixed him up with someone else. Can you believe it?' Grace said. 'And … she said you've made passes at him several times. She's upset about that and waiting for you to apologise to both of them.'

Once I stopped screaming, Grace said she thought Leila was fooling herself. 'She knows the truth deep down, of course she does, but she's not going to admit it. I'm so disappointed in her. She's lost all judgement.'

'She's upset? More like delusional. If she thinks I'm apologising to that little shit, she's really lost it.'

'And … sorry, but she said she wants her Versace top back.'

Good to know she values her Versace top more than our friendship. When I got home, I stomped around, banged a few doors and smashed the Abigail Ahern vase she'd given me for my birthday. Then I found the silk Versace top I'd borrowed from her a few months back. I cut off the straps and shredded the hem. I put the pieces in an envelope, stuck all the stamps I had on it and posted it to Leila before I could change my mind.

Feeling sorry for myself on all fronts and could do with some TLC. I want to go to Mum and Dad's but don't want them to see me like this. Will ask Irene and Ana if I can visit them for a couple of days.

Wednesday, 28 August, 11.30pm

No text from Ace. He probably hates me for putting him in such an awful position. I keep remembering how he sat there as I threw myself at him. Too nice to push me away. I hope to God I haven't ruined our friendship.

I've eaten two sharing bags of black pepper Kettle crisps and a box of four (full size) mint Magnums. I'm going to die sad and lonely AND fat. At least the cats will have a feast. To top it all off, my neighbour opposite was at the window with little Jessica in her arms looking at a bird in the tree outside. They saw me on the sofa, in my underwear, and surrounded by crisp packets, ice cream wrappers, and empty cocktail cans. Jessica waved. I really must replace the broken blind.

P.S. Is it terrible of me to admit I quite enjoyed the kiss?

TWENTY-FOUR

The Right Neighbour's Son

Thursday, 29 August, 12.30pm

ON WAY TO TOTNES. I decided to invite Ace down for a BBQ on Saturday. He hasn't seen Ana and Irene since he moved to London. It'll be neutral territory and we can talk. I can't put it off.

P.S. I so enjoyed cutting up the Versace top.

11.30pm

So lovely to see Irene and Ana today. Being with them always reminds me of happy childhood days. We had afternoon tea, then a walk – though at their pace I can hardly claim to have done any exercise – and back home for dinner and telly.

They were acting like rampant teenagers tonight. Irene patted Ana's ample bottom every time Ana walked past the sofa with more nibbles for us while we watched *Mary Queen of Scots*. At first, I didn't know where to look but then I joined in, each of us taking a different buttock and howling with laughter.

'Stop it, you. I'm not a pork, you know,' she said. More laughter from me and Irene. Ana pretended to be annoyed while she smothered a giggle.

When the film got a bit sad and Ana started crying, Irene went over to her, hugged her and kissed her on the cheek. So sweet.

'I wish I could find a relationship like yours. I thought having meaningless sex would be enough for me but apparently not. And it's not like I've had lots of that either,' I said, feeling sad again.

'But you can find love, my dear. There must be lots of men who'd love to go out with you. You must look for them,' Irene said.

How many times have I heard that?

'I'm tired, Irene. I don't know if I have the energy to carry on looking,' I said. I should buy three white Persian cats with a matching throw.

'You have years ahead of you. Look at us. We're steel in love. And we do sex,' Ana announced, too loudly.

'Sophia doesn't want to know that,' Irene admonished Ana, then turned to me. 'Only when my hip isn't playing up.'

Too. Much. Information.

Friday, 30 August, 6.30pm

We went to the shops to buy stuff for tomorrow's BBQ. OMG, Ana's driving! She was in fourth gear straight out of the drive and went through 1,001 roundabouts without gearing down. The car spluttered and jerked while I sat at the back feeling hysterical with equal measures of fear and laughter. As for her parking. She was oblivious to the long line of cars waiting for her to manoeuvre into what was quite a large space. Back and forth, back and forth. #WantToHide

Irene and Ana are still hoping for romance between me and the neighbour's son. I'm seeing Anthony Junior for a drink tonight, though I don't think I'm ready for dating yet. In fact, I've been thinking I might give up the dating challenge. I've done eight months of it and here I am, a runaway and miserable. I was happy in January and now I'm not. What's the point? #DatingSucks

11.30pm

Tony was lovely. Not in a fanciable way but easy to talk to and a good listener. We ended up having a heart to heart. I told him I was fed up with the dating challenge and didn't know if I wanted to risk being heartbroken again. He told me about his divorce. It wasn't dramatic. They'd just grown apart and once the kids left home, there was no joy.

'One of my neighbours,' he said, 'was still working hard in his sixties, ignoring his wife's pleas to retire, and saying, "Another year and we'll have enough money to travel and relax". He finally retired on his sixty-sixth birthday but the following day, he was killed in a car crash on his way to the golf club. That was a wake-up call for me. I decided to live a more honest life and be true to myself. That was when I asked my wife for a divorce and moved here.' He told me I could meet someone tomorrow and still have years of happiness ahead of me. Wasn't that worth the effort?

'I've only just met you, but I can tell you're a determined person. Why give up now?'

He was right, of course. You never know what's round the corner. Look at Grace getting cancer at such a young age. And Leila is sure to have heartbreak around the corner. If Tony's been in an unhappy marriage for years and still believes in love, how can I give up after eight months? I must look to the future, not over my shoulder.

Saturday, 31 August, 11.30pm

Ace came over for the BBQ today. It was awkward at first. At one point, while everyone was eating, he said he wanted to talk so we sat on the swing away from the others.

'Look, about Valencia…' he said. 'I know you were in a bad place and a bit drunk, but I want to know … does it mean you … oh this is so difficult … erm … can I ask…' He was looking down at the grass. He obviously wanted to find out if I had feelings for him, in which case it would be too awkward to continue being friends. I couldn't bear it. I had to stop him saying anything to make things worse.

'Look, Ace, I was all over the place and yes, way too drunk. There's no excuse for the way I behaved. I don't want to lose your friendship. Can we please forget about it? Pretend it didn't happen and go back to how we were?'

He hesitated, then smiled a sad smile and said, 'Forget about what?'

Tears fell down my cheeks and I hoped he meant what he said.

'Don't cry. You've done enough of that lately. Come here.'

He put his arm round me, and I let my head rest on his shoulder as the seat swung back and forth and we watched the BBQ for a while.

Then I exhaled and said, 'Anyway, imagine if we got together after all these years. What would people think?'

'Yes, imagine.'

We walked back to the BBQ, and I sat with Ana while Ace talked to Anthony Junior. I glanced over a few times, and they were deep in conversation. I was glad he was enjoying himself. Probably bonding over football or something.

PART IX
September

TWENTY-FIVE

The Entertainer

Sunday, 1 September, 6.30am

CAN'T SLEEP for worrying things might be awkward with Ace on the train today. It'll probably take time to go back to where we were before the kiss.

When I was saying goodbye to Tony yesterday, I thanked him for the advice in the pub.

'I hope you find someone soon, Sophia. Although sometimes a person can miss what's under their nose,' he whispered, nodding towards Ace.

'And there was I thinking you were a perceptive relationship advisor,' I teased him. 'No, we're old friends. Nothing is going to happen there.'

'Think about it,' he said, smiling.

11.30pm

Everything was fine on the train, but as I looked at Ace across the table from me, I couldn't help thinking about what Tony said. Was he saying I should go for it with Ace because he's a lovely guy? Or was he telling me Ace has feelings for me? They were talking for a long time at the BBQ. Did Ace say something to him? He's never given me any hint of being interested. If he is, has he always fancied me or is it only recently? Did it start in Cuba? Or was it because of my drunken kiss in Valencia? I must be a bloody good kisser.

No, the whole idea is mad. I think Tony wanted to make me feel better by suggesting, 'Don't be sad. Here's someone you could go for.' He doesn't know the history behind our friendship, so he probably misinterpreted affection for romantic love. Anyway, I couldn't possibly go for someone who's cheated before.

Leila, where are you? I need to talk to you. How much longer are you going to be a complete bitch?

Monday, 2 September, 11.30pm

Right, new month, new week, new Sophia. Starting today, I'm not going to moon over THO anymore. I must stop feeling like a sad victim. I checked the diary for how many times I'd seen THO, and it was seven times. How can I feel this bad over someone I've only seen seven times? It's completely ridiculous and I must stop it. Today. Now!

It's been ages since I checked the dating apps, and I've found a few potential matches. The problem is, do I go back to looking for just sex? CAN I even go back to looking for just sex now that I'm hankering after a relationship again? I don't know. I'll just wait and see what happens. No need to decide yet.

What I do know is that my heart is not in it anymore. I started the year full of hope and looking for fun and sex, but my dating experience so far has been abysmal. Then I met someone who changed my mind and made me crave a relationship again. I let him build my hopes up, but it ended in exactly the manner I was trying to avoid when I set off on the dating challenge. I'm unhappy and heartbroken. Maybe I should just give up men. Life would be less exciting but easier. And I wouldn't have to keep up the pretence of enjoying the dating challenge.

Tuesday, 3 September, 11.30pm

Felt a bit sad again today but pulled myself out of it. I searched the internet for techniques to help. There's one where every time you think of the person you want to forget, you imagine them floating away from you until they turn into a tiny dot and disappear into oblivion. I liked doing that. Yeah, fuck off into oblivion THO.

Wednesday, 4 September, 11.30pm

Ooh, a match on London Soulmates. He's attractive, though a bit young at forty-two. It'll probably be OK if someone is in their fifth decade, just not in their third. No more Bus Stop Boys for me. His profile says he's in the entertainment business. Intriguing. Is he a singer, juggler, dancer, or actor? So many possibilities. And he says he wants a lady (I object to that word, but I'll overlook it for now) for fun and an ongoing relationship. I sure could do with some fun.

Thursday, 5 September, 11.30pm

I pushed THO into oblivion at least twenty times today. Also feeling sad about Leila. It's been a month since that horrible row. She's still ignoring me. I wonder if she'll come for brunch tomorrow. I miss her but also feel angry about how she's treated me.

Arranged to go for a drink with The Entertainer, though I'm not feeling it today. Can't get excited about dates anymore. Invariably, I end up disappointed, so I'm conserving my energy for now.

Saturday, 7 September, 2.30pm

Leila not replying to Brunch Bunch group texts either. Grace was down in the dumps about work, so we drowned our sorrows with a full English, maple syrup pancakes on the side and a bottle of prosecco. It worked liked magic. We decided to plan a spa trip.

11.30pm

I don't know whether to be disappointed, insulted, indignant, or all of the above. My date did not cheer me up and I can't be bothered to write the details. It's not worth the ink. I've written a poem about it. Enough said.

You were delicious like Tom Hardy
In coming forward, you weren't tardy
Your body was built like a fort
All hard muscle and rippling taut
I wanted you to coo in my ear
And be my best date of the year
'Let's have plenty of food and drink'
You said to me with a wink
You suggested a holiday in a luxury resort
On a yacht in the sun where we could cavort
You told me I was such a sexy sort
And our bodies should together contort
The bill came but you were somewhat short
You wanted me to pay and be a good sport
'I can't believe this,' I retorted
'I wanted a king, not to be consorted'
To my dismay, you snorted
And said it was fair play for being escorted
The penny dropped and I was distraught
He thought his time was being bought
Oh no, I had dinner with an escort
Abort, abort, abort

P.S. Another failed date made me think about THO. Pushing-into-oblivion count off the scale tonight.

Sunday, 8 September, 11.30pm

Should I take it personally that an escort thought I might want his services? I suppose he's using a free dating app to pick up clients. And there must be some women who take him up on it. Good for them if they get what they want out of it. But it's not for me. I have plenty of friends for company, and The Intensifier in case of a sex emergency.

Monday, 9 September, 11.30pm

I have to say I'm disillusioned with this dating lark. How hard does a woman have to work to find a decent man? Or to find satisfying sex for that matter. I don't know how much longer I can continue with disappointment and disaster. There are still four months of the dating challenge to go, though.

I've never been a defeatist and I'm not going to start now, so I'm not quitting the dating challenge, but I have low expectations for the next few months. I won't be getting excited and pumped full of adrenalin in the run up to dates, only to crash horribly afterwards. I will save my energy and excitement until I meet someone that offers some hope for either an enjoyable or meaningful time.

TWENTY-SIX

The Submissive One

Tuesday, 10 September, 11.30pm

ANOTHER DAY. Another message. Another date arranged. It's not worth writing about him until I meet him. I'll decide then if the date deserves a detailed description.

Wednesday, 11 September, 11.30pm

Had a sad call from my client Daniel. I met him when he'd just moved into a house with his fiancée, Maria, and wanted me to arrange a surprise for their return from honeymoon – a backlit white onyx wall behind the bath, etched with their initials. Corny but sweet. Now they're divorced, and his new girlfriend wants it removed. You never know how relationships will pan out. I keep thinking, I could meet someone, fall in love and live happily ever after. The glass-half-full in me believes that. But of course, that's not real life.

Thursday, 12 September, 11.30pm

It was a mad date. I won't be seeing him again – for reasons that will become obvious in the poem – but it did make me giggle afterwards. For all the wrong reasons. I might be practising openness and want to experience new things, but there's a limit to what I'll be open to when it's presented to me in the first five minutes of a date.

You look like a pretty regular guy
But that impression is certainly awry
How sweet, you brought me a gift
I wasn't expecting one so swift
Maybe it's chocolate or perfume
I open it and you say 'vroom, vroom'
The shock makes my chin drop
And my eyes involuntarily pop
Where did you buy these beauts?
It certainly wasn't in Boots
It's a gift of handcuffs covered in fur
I don't know what to say, er…
There's more – a black satin eye mask
To keep you in the dark during the task
You lean over and whisperingly quip
'Back at my flat I also have a whip'
I swiftly drink my Colombian blend
This date is definitely at an end
'I have to go,' I say, 'it's half past six.'
'Keep the gifts, hope you find your dominatrix.'

Friday, 13 September, 11.30pm

Went dancing at Bar Baile with Izzy tonight. A properly hot guy – I'd guess in his forties – chatted me up. Somehow, we got talking about the gender orgasm gap, and he told me that he is an expert at giving orgasms, and did I want him to prove it? Yes please.

Saturday, 14 September, 8.30am

Waiting for Grace to pick me up for our spa day. Really looking forward to a girly day of pampering. I expect to come out rejuvenated and ready to vroom, vroom.

Sunday, 15 September, 7.30pm

The spa hotel was beautiful with acres of neatly landscaped grounds, a cosy restaurant, and an amazing outdoor pool – thank you to the weather gods for arranging the hot sunny day. Over brunch, we checked out the pamper menu and planned our day. I wanted to relax in the sun by the pool for a bit while Grace had her facial.

'Interesting bikini,' Grace said.

'Isn't it? Bandage bikinis are so in. Do you like the colour?' I asked, inspecting myself in the mirror.

'Lime green wouldn't be my choice, but it looks good on you,' she said. The twenty-something me would have fussed about non-existent excess flesh hanging over the straps, and Mum would have certainly had something to say about it. But now, I don't care. It's liberating. Mostly.

At the pool, there was just one guy doing laps. As I settled on my sun lounger, he swam towards me and said hello. We chatted and flirted for a while. A bonus I wasn't expecting. Though I did think it would have to stop as soon as Grace came out. I couldn't risk a repetition of the hospital bathroom incident. The day was for me and her to enjoy on our own.

I swam for a few laps, then he came over again and we were talking as we stood in the shallow end. There were a few other people there now and a couple of children diving in and out of the pool. I noticed he kept looking down at my body surreptitiously. It was lovely to be appreciated at first, but I started to feel uncomfortable as he kept staring for a second then looking away.

'I hate to tell you this, but your bikini…' he said, nodding at my body. I looked down and was horrified to see it was completely see-through and the strips of Lycra were not quite where they were supposed to be. On this occasion, I wished I didn't belong to the 'full bush' school of aesthetics. It was like I had a black poodle trying to escape out of my bikini bottoms, and my nipples were out and proud.

'Oh my God!' I shrieked and doggy-paddled to the edge of the pool. I hauled myself up and got out, only for the bra to get dragged down by water collected in the cups, revealing way too much boob. I stood on the side of the pool for a second trying to cover my modesty with my hands and ran over to my sun lounger. The rest of the day is a complete blank and I only know what happened from what Grace and Ace have told me.

Apparently in my hurry to get to my towel, I tripped over a discarded flip-flop and hit my head on the edge of a bench as I fell. I was knocked unconscious, and they had to call an ambulance. Grace had run out of her rudely interrupted pamper session, her face covered in green algae, and screaming, 'oh my God, oh my God, the blood,' as she hopped in circles in hysterics.

They checked me out at the hospital, said I was OK but had a concussion and should stay overnight for observation. Grace called Leila and couldn't get hold of her, but she got through to Ace, who came and took over from her as Ajay was going away and she had to go home to the kids. Thank God she didn't call my parents. She knew I wouldn't have wanted to worry them.

Now I'm writing this, I wish I'd been conscious to see Algae Woman freaking out over Full-Bush Woman and her poodle.

Monday, 16 September, 3.00pm

Feeling better today, but what a weekend. Our pamper day certainly wasn't relaxing, especially for poor Grace having to deal with my accident. She's always in control and I can't believe she fell to pieces. I think after what she's been through, her tolerance threshold is low.

Ace stayed last night to make sure I was OK. Apparently, I

drove him and Grace mad at the hospital with my short-term memory loss.

'Why am I in hospital? What happened?' I'd ask, touching my bandaged head.

'You fell and bashed your head, but you're OK,' they'd reassure me.

Then a few minutes later, 'What's happened? Why do I have a bandage on my head?'

'You slipped and knocked yourself out.'

'Did I? Are they going to operate?'

'No, you'll be fine. They're keeping you in for observation.'

A few minutes later, 'Why am I in a hospital bed?'

And so on and so on.

8.00pm

Leila came round earlier. She'd been on a weekend retreat and hadn't turned on her phone till earlier today. Ace let her in.

'About time,' he growled at her before he left us to talk.

She stood at my bedroom door, looked at my bruises and started crying. She came over and gave me a hug, but I didn't hug back, so she sat at the end of the bed.

'How are you feeling, honey?' I didn't reply but carried on staring at the mascara stain on my white duvet cover. 'When I listened to the frantic messages from Grace, and the thought of losing you...' she trailed off. 'I came as soon as I heard.'

I glanced up at her, then went back to the stain.

'I've missed you so much. I'm so sorry. I've been a bitch,' she said.

I locked eyes with her and said, 'I won't argue with that. I don't know how you could do that to me. Like fifty years of friendship count for nothing.'

'I'm truly sorry.'

'We've never once let men come between us,' I reminded her.

'I'm so stupid. I knew you wouldn't have made a move on Jude. Ever. I know he's not faithful. But I don't want to lose him.'

'You knew he was unfaithful? And you still chose to believe him?' I was right. She'd known all along but has been pretending it was all my fault.

'I'm pathetic, I know. You're so strong, but I'm not. I know you were looking out for me. You always have. I've been vile. So shabby and cruel. Please forgive me.'

'I've been miserable, and I needed you in Valencia. You abandoned me,' I said, my eyes dribbling.

'I know, honey. I'm so sorry. If it's any consolation, I've been miserable too. There's no one else I can giggle with the way I do with you. You know I love you, don't you?' She came over and hugged me hard.

'Ouch, mind my bruises.'

'Sorry. Will you forgive me? You can't stay mad at your bestie forever. Will I make you a cup of tea? Go on, go on, go on, go on, go on,' she said, in an Irish accent mimicking Mrs Doyle.

We laughed, our cheeks still wet with tears, and I gave her all the gory details of my fall. She said she couldn't bear it if anything had happened to me. She asked me to forgive her again.

'OK, OK. I suppose you've grovelled enough. I forgive you. You're here now and I didn't die.'

I asked her about Jude.

'I've been acting like nothing happened, but I don't know how much longer I can pretend. I can't decide what to do,' she said. 'I've missed your wise advice.'

'What's more important? Keeping him despite his infidelities or letting him go because he's making you unhappy? That's the choice,' I said. She nodded.

'And … sorry about your Versace top,' I said. We burst into laughter.

P.S. Just had a flashback of coming round after my fall. I opened my eyes and saw Grace, The Algae Woman, leaning over me and I screamed.

Tuesday, 17 September, 10.30am

Starting to feel human again. Ace has been wonderful at looking after me. He keeps me hydrated, bustles about the kitchen making meals, dabs ointment on my scratches and generally anticipates my every need. He's so generous and kind-hearted, with a core of goodness. He is a 'good man'. A short phrase with such a big meaning. A good man who drops everything to help a friend in need, shows his love by caring for people, and forgiving others' stupid mistakes. That's why I've trusted and treasured him as a friend for so many years. If I didn't know him, I'd say he's too good to be true.

I can't help remembering what Tony hinted at and wondering whether Ace rushed over to the hospital because he's a good friend or because he has feelings for me. Or both. I need to work it out somehow. But then again, he's not Mr Perfect. I don't know the circumstances, but he did cheat on Kelly, and I couldn't possibly be romantically involved with someone who does that. Not after The Traitor. I can't put myself through that kind of agony again.

In other romantic news – or lust news – The Orgasm Expert has been texting and wanting to know how I'm doing, which is sweet. I do get fanny flutters every time I hear the ping of his texts – how can a ping be such a turn-on? – but his banter is annoyingly limited.

Wednesday, 18 September, 11.30pm

Told Sara about my accident today. She was annoyed that nobody had told her before, but then it doesn't take much these days. She might be angry about not being contacted earlier, but I wonder if she would have rushed over to my aid like Ace. Anyway, the accident seems to have softened her and she's coming over tomorrow night. I haven't seen her since she walked out on me at the pub back in July.

Thursday, 19 September, 11.30pm

I was happy that Sara was coming to see me tonight. She brought me chocolates and looked concerned sitting across the sofa from me. Like the old Sara. It was all going OK until I started to confide in her about my love life. That flicked a switch, and the disapproving, judgemental Sara was back in full force.

About the bikini, she said, 'You should wear age-appropriate stuff.'

About Mr Snappy, she said, 'What do you expect if you get your tits out after five minutes?' I let that one go too.

I giggled as I told her about the Bus Stop Boys, and thought she was bound to laugh about the mum picking up one of them. But no.

'For God's sake, Sophe. What the hell are you doing bringing home young men less than half your age? It's undignified.'

It's not like I've deliberately chosen to be single. Even after all the horrible experiences, I'm still looking for love. Probably. I wanted to make her understand how hard it is to find love, especially at sixty years old. I wanted her sympathy, not judgement, so I told her about THO and how distraught I'd been about the whole saga.

'It's not surprising he dumped you. You can't keep chasing men and expect them to respect you. You have to play hard to get.' That was below the belt insensitive. I saw red.

'You criticise me, but you don't always play hard to get, do you, Sara?' My heart was thumping in my chest, and I felt the colour drain from my face.

'What are you talking about? I've been with Laurence for the last twenty years and we're way past playing hard to get.'

'Just Laurence? There hasn't been anyone else? Anyone at all? Not even once?'

'No, nobody,' she said, but she was hesitant.

'At least I didn't sleep with my sister's boyfriend,' I shouted. It was her who turned pale this time, then she blushed deep.

'What do you mean?' she asked in a timid voice. The penny had dropped.

'I saw you with him. In MY bed. Didn't you wonder why he disappeared out of my life straight after your visit that night? I threw him out the next morning. His pathetic excuse was that he didn't know I'd let you sleep in my room. He said he'd got into bed and had sex with you, thinking it was me. Did you not wonder why I went off to travel round the world all of a sudden?'

'Why didn't you tell me you knew?' she asked after a pause, shell-shocked.

'Because I knew you were vulnerable. You'd found out Laurence had an affair, and you probably needed to prove to yourself somebody wanted you or to get revenge. He … The Traitor just happened to be there. It could have been anyone. I knew you were drunk and had probably lost all judgement. And because you're my little sister. Lovers come and go but sisters are forever, even if they behave as badly as you did. We always said sisters forever, didn't we?'

She looked at me for a moment as her eyes filled up, then picked up her bag and headed for the door.

'Don't run off, Sara. We need to talk!' I shouted as she banged the door behind her.

I should have set fire to her aura like the witch doctor in Peru told me. Instead, I took a hallucinogenic, mind-altering, gut-wrenching, foul-tasting magic mushroom concoction in Colombia, because another witch doctor said it would help me come to terms with what she'd done. I fucking hate mushrooms!

Friday, 20 September, 11.30pm

Been texting Sara all day. She's read them but she's not replying. I've been walking around the house, slamming doors and kicking cupboards. Anyone would think SHE was the wronged party. I protected her from the shame and embarrassment of what she'd done with The Traitor by not acknowledging it. Do I get any thanks? No.

But … if I'm completely honest, the other reason I kept quiet was that I didn't want to face the fact that I'd spent three years of my life with a man who could do that. I loved him and thought we would grow old together. I wasn't going to admit he didn't love me. I'd had my doubts for a while. I knew it deep down but chose to ignore it. I didn't want to be the wronged woman, so I brushed it under the carpet. Now I know that wasn't the right thing to do. It was bound to explode at some point. I should have had a massive row with Sara at the time and tried to put it behind us. He wasn't worth losing my sister over. What do I do now? I don't need this heartache on top of everything else.

Saturday, 21 September, 11.30pm

Met Leila for brunch. She thinks I should leave it for a while, let Sara cool down and hope she comes to her senses and apologises soon. She's probably right.

Leila told Jude she'd made up with me. Apparently, he brushed it off and said he's forgiven me anyway. He's been particularly attentive to her since then. I bet he's worked out she's onto him and wants to throw her off track. The little shit.

TWENTY-SEVEN

The Orgasm Expert

Sunday, 22 September, 11.30pm

JUST GOT HOME after a drink with The Orgasm Expert. I needed a bit of fun and distraction from my troubles and boy did he provide it. He's not much of a conversationalist but hey, you can't have everything. I haven't fancied anyone this much since THO. They do have similar bodies, all lean and tall but this one is olive-skinned – a definite improvement on THO's almost translucent white skin. I shouldn't be comparing, but THO still hasn't bought a one-way ticket to oblivion.

Back to The Orgasm Expert. I realise he didn't tell me anything about himself except his supposed skills in the orgasm department but surprisingly I don't care that I know nothing about him. I asked him about his job and where he lives, etc. but he was evasive and what little he did tell me didn't ring true. So exactly what does a business consultant do? The conversation was dull and felt like it was from a *Dating for Dummies* book, so I wasn't sure if I wanted to stay for long. THEN, he leaned over and kissed me slowly and luxuriously. He touched my back and a couple of his fingers strayed under the hem of my top and sent ripples down my body. It was electric and I knew I wanted more of it.

Monday, 23 September, 11.30pm

More texts from The Orgasm Expert, wanting to demonstrate what he does best. He's coming round on Wednesday. I hope he'll want a marathon, not a sprint. I hope it's a slow-cooked meal for two, not a takeaway for one. I hope he's read the *Kama Sutra* not *Sex for Beginners*.

Thursday, 26 September, 11.30pm

There was no time for writing a diary last night. No siree, I was too busy having orgasms. He certainly did not disappoint. Three times. And each time with a different technique.

Technique One, Finger – Just the right amount of pressure and speed so it didn't feel like an electric sander. No other body parts touching which made it more intense. AND he got down on his knees and watched the action close up. I felt like saying, hey I want to see what's going on down there.

Technique Two, Tongue – He should patent that tongue action. It went up, down, round, in and out, not leaving any nooks or crannies un-nibbled.

Technique Three, Junior, mark II – He seemed to operate at 360 degrees, and he's obviously mastered the right position for optimum orgasm-giving to within 0.01 degree.

He smiled to himself every time it happened, as though his purpose in life was being fulfilled. None of it was out of the ordinary but somehow, he knew how to perform it to perfection. I christened him well as The Orgasm Expert.

Friday, 27 September, 8.30pm

Phoned Sara on the landline and she picked up but hung up when she heard my voice. WTF? Leila is right. I'll leave it for a bit. She's bound to realise at some point that I'M the injured party.

Saturday, 28 September, 11.30pm

Grace told me she was thinking of leaving her job. She said she's had it with all the stress, and that having cancer has made her rethink her priorities. She wants a less stressful job but has no idea what, only that it has to be joyful.

'What about a dating agency for middle-aged people? Going by my abysmal experience, we really need someone with a personal touch that puts some thought into matching people with similar passions. The apps are OK if you like digital dating, but maybe it's time to go back to meeting in real life. And think of all the love and joy you'd be spreading.'

'I don't know anything about running a dating agency,' she said.

'You're great with money and people, and you have a massive brain. You can work it out. And I can help you with PR. You know I had a PR agency before I met you, right?'

'No, I did not! You amaze me, Sophia.'

While we talked about the possibilities for a new business for Grace, people kept stopping to pet Terry and we'd stroke their dogs, chat for a bit, and move on. And that's when it came to me.

'A dating agency for dog owners. You could call it Date Hound or Puppy Love. Or Pooch Passion. Or Dating Walkies. Brilliant. Yes?'

Grace laughed and said she'd think about it.

Sunday, 29 September, 10.30pm

I had a lovely weekend with The Orgasm Expert doing the kitchen to bed run. He sure has lots of energy and can perform at the drop of a hat. Or should that be at the drop of a skirt? His conversation was quite limited, though, and consisted mainly of making lists about things he could see in front of him.

'I like this Chilean wine,' he said at dinner. 'Wine can be from lots of places – Californian, Australian or Argentinian. There's also Bavarian and French.' OMG.

'I like Italian food,' he said, after I cooked pasta. 'There are different foods from many countries in London. Indian, Chinese, Italian. There's also Thai, Japanese and Turkish.' Double OMG.

I prefer his sexual repetition habits. After he'd gone, I realised that this is the first time I've fancied someone without feeling any attachment or emotions towards him. Not that I don't care about him but enjoying sex with him doesn't need an emotional commitment from me or him. It just means I don't need to have the whole of him. In fact, I find it surprisingly liberating to enjoy amazing sex with someone who doesn't have relationship potential. He seems to like me, but I don't know if his feelings are engaged either and he is obviously hiding his true life from me, so I think that makes us even. If nothing else, I've achieved my New Year's challenge of mastering marvellous, mind-blowing sex without emotional entanglement.

PART X
October

TWENTY-EIGHT

The Orgasm Expert Again and Again

Tuesday, 1 October, 11.30pm

HAD a text from Cement Man inviting me to his engagement party. Leila gave me the lowdown. Apparently, he met and fell in love with a woman in the – wait for it – cement business! Even Cement Man has met someone who wants to marry him. I'm happy for him. Everyone deserves to be loved. But I'm also a little jealous. I want to ask, what's wrong with me? Why doesn't anyone want to marry me? Have I been the architect of my singledom, or have I just been unlucky? Begone, green-eyed monster.

Thursday, 3 October, 11.30pm

Went to check on progress on Cassandra and Edward's bedroom only to find the expensive tropical jungle wallpaper that went all the way up the vaulted ceiling had been hung upside down.

Friday, 4 October, 11.30pm

Leila and Jude are going to Monte Carlo tomorrow for two weeks. I don't know how she can stomach it.

Sunday, 6 October, 11.30pm

The Orgasm Expert came round for some afternoon delight, which is our thing now. We did have one conversation today about the phenomenon of super-orgasms, which featured in a documentary earlier in the week. Never mind three orgasms. Some women have up to 100 orgasms at each sitting – so to speak. I remember one of them saying, 'Oh I was tired last night. I only had thirty-four orgasms. I've been known to have sixty-two.' The Orgasm Expert said he'd like to meet one of those women. I said I'd like to know who was doing the counting.

I think neither of us thinks this – having fantastic orgasms – is going to develop into a relationship. We never make plans or do stuff together. We meet occasionally and it's purely for sex. And that's fine. But is it enough? I thought I just wanted sex until I met THO. Now I'm confused. I'm still going to have other dates and see what happens.

Tuesday, 8 October, 11.30pm

Had a video date with Mr Horizontal tonight. I did my makeup, got changed and set my mobile up on a stand in front of the sofa with a glass of wine to hand, so it would be as near to a real date as possible. He, on the other hand, was wearing a ripped T-shirt (not cool, just old) and was lying in bed. I wanted to say, 'Really? You can't even be bothered to sit up?' I was perky and ready to mingle but his energy was so low that, after about twenty minutes, I deflated like a plastic puppy with a slow puncture. Anyway, it wouldn't have worked. The interior designer in me could never have slept in that bedroom. #MankyDuvetCover #ClashingWallpaper #MyEyesHurt

Wednesday, 9 October, 11.30pm

Jude keeps posting lovey-dovey holiday pictures of him and Leila on Insta. He makes me sick. I've unfollowed him.

Friday, 11 October, 11.30pm

It's OK having a sex buddy and no relationship. I'm self-sufficient. I don't need a prince to rescue me. This could be the way to go. I'm not missing out by not having a partner in life.

Saturday, 12 October, 1.30pm

Ace came to brunch today, which was lovely. I didn't realise I'd missed him so much. After the concert in Brussels next week, he's not touring anymore. He said he'd had enough of living out of suitcases and wanted to spend more time at home with his friends, and to jam with his new Latin band. He's buying a flat in Bermondsey and wants me to help him decorate. I'm looking forward to seeing him more often. He was so good to me after my accident, and he puts so much into our friendship. I really appreciate his kindness and generosity. Now he needs me to help set up his new life and I want to do my best for him. I appear to be more excited than usual at the prospect of a new project.

I think Grace is much better and finally starting to feel like her old self again. She even said she's thinking about my doggie dating idea.

Sunday, 13 October, 11.30pm

The Orgasm Expert wanted to see if he could turn me into a super-orgasm woman, and who was I to deny him that pleasure? I won't need to do any exercise for the next few days. I must have burnt a whole week's worth of calories. I had to admit defeat after four. My muscles gave up and I felt like I was more likely to pee than orgasm.

Afterwards, we had a couple of glasses of wine and pizza for calories as he listed the different types of pizza – margherita, four cheese, ham and mushroom, and on and on and on. Then he went onto types of pizza base – deep pan, thin crust, calzone. I don't know what goes on in his head when he lists things, but I wish he'd stop. Sometimes I kiss him just to stop the lists pouring out. The sex is sooo good, but I don't know if I can bear the conversation, or lack of it, anymore. I think we're coming to the end of the road with this arrangement. Or should that be the end of the list?

Monday, 14 October, 11.30pm

Project Toilet is back on. Hurrah! I'd better start looking for an aquarium.

Wednesday, 16 October, 11.30pm

Ace got the keys to his new flat today, so I went round to have a look and celebrate with him. The views were spectacular, but the place was in serious need of updating. The oak kitchen cabinets had turned orange, and the bathrooms were altogether too beige. The previous owners had left behind a beaten-up leather sofa and two red bistro chairs.

'So how do you want to decorate your bachelor pad? All black leather and red satin sheets with remote control dimmers?' I nodded in the direction of the sofa.

'That sounds like something I definitely don't want,' he said, wrinkling his nose.

'I'm teasing you. We're not in the 80s. Bachelor pads can be quite tasteful these days.'

'Who said I want a bachelor pad? No, I want something cosy and inviting to come home to, but not boring. Do you know what I mean?' he asked.

'When you say inviting, who are you thinking of inviting? Laaadies?' I wanted to know more. He laughed and didn't reply so I persisted. 'Really, as your interior designer, I need to know what kind of activities will be going on in each room, so I can design for purpose. For example, should the master bathroom have one basin or two?'

'Definitely two. And enough wardrobe space for two,' he said.

'You've changed your tune. Have you met someone?'

'I just want to futureproof.'

'Are you futureproofing for anyone in particular? Should I speak to her?'

He didn't reply but opened the champagne, and we walked around and talked about the design. After a few glasses, I felt braver.

'Come on, Ace, you can tell me. Who is it?' I said, leaning on the black granite island.

He looked at his glass and ran a finger around the rim. 'My divorce came through today.'

'Oh, I'm so sorry.'

'Don't be. It's over and I'm moving on. I'm feeling optimistic. New flat, new life and all that. And you never know, maybe a new relationship.'

'That's a good way to think about it,' I said, 'but, do you wish you hadn't been unfaithful, and you were still together?' He gave me a puzzled look. 'Are you still seeing the woman you had an affair with?'

He let out a long breath. 'I told you before. I didn't have an affair.'

'But you said Kelly left because of a betrayal.'

'Yes, but I didn't tell you I was the one who'd been unfaithful. You just assumed I had. It was Kelly who had an affair.'

I put my hand to my mouth in disbelief. Had I misjudged him all this time? Come to my own untrue conclusions? Why do I always think people are having affairs?

'Why didn't you say anything? Surely not out of loyalty to Kelly if she betrayed you?'

He picked at the limescale around the tap. 'If I'd told you, it would have made it more real. I didn't want to face the truth, because … remember I went to Jamaica for New Year? It wasn't just to do the charity concert. I wanted my aunt's advice … because the affair was with … my dad.'

'Whoa! Your dad? Kelly and your dad? How?'

'I think I told you he had that car accident and broke his wrist about a year ago. I was away with work, and I was so grateful to Kelly for looking after him. Apparently, she cared for him a little too well. Our marriage wasn't perfect, but still … it was a double betrayal.'

'How did you find out?'

'One time I caught an earlier flight home because she said Dad was taking her out for dinner to thank her, so I thought I'd surprise them. I got to the restaurant and saw them holding hands and looking into each other's eyes. They couldn't deny it. Afterwards, she said she was sorry, and could we try again? I did try but I just couldn't get past what they'd done. I haven't seen Dad since then.'

'That is … a lot. It's fucked up. You poor love. All this time you've been coping with that, and I thought you were the one who'd behaved badly. I'm so sorry.' Then I remembered the ponytailed woman at his door. 'But that day when I came over and you told me about the divorce, I saw you kissing a woman on the doorstep. That was why I assumed you'd cheated. Who was she?'

He shook his head. 'That was Juliette, Cliff's wife. I didn't know how to tell Cliff about Dad, so I asked her to do it for me.

'Juliette? Your brother's wife?'

I am an idiot. I am the CEO of Jumping to Conclusions Ltd, with a first-class degree in Wild Judgemental Imaginations.

He told me the affair had gone on for a few months, but they stopped seeing each other after Ace found out. Then he admitted their marriage wasn't working and, in a way, it was all for the best. He could start a new chapter of his life. I gave him a long hug. As I drew away, our faces close, we locked eyes, and I panicked and pulled away. I felt sad afterwards, for Ace and for myself. I'd been wrong about him and blamed him when I should have trusted him. I'd projected my own insecurities onto him when he was suffering and needed my support. I should have been a better friend to him, like he is to me. I messed up, big time. Now he's divorced and he's met someone and decided to stop touring to be with her. It must be serious if he's planning a cosy home for two. I'm pleased for him after what he's been through, but I don't know how to feel about it.

And why is my default conclusion always that people are having affairs? Did Premature Paul plant a seed of doubt in my mind for all future relationships, and The Traitor finished off the job and made me bitter and twisted? There was a time I only thought the best of people unless they proved me wrong. Now I assume everybody is a cheater. I must try harder and not let past experiences continue to rule my thoughts.

P.S. I admit, I was wrong. It looks like Ace is perfect after all.

Thursday, 17 October, 11.30pm

It's Ace's last concert tonight in Brussels so he'll be home for good tomorrow. I'm really looking forward to having him around and spending more time with him. I've been working on the design for his flat today. I kept stopping and wondering who would be living with him there. I don't know how I feel about helping him set up a cosy nest so he can move her in. Whoever it is, she'll be lucky to live with Ace. He's such a caring, thoughtful and supportive man. The kind of man who's exciting yet reliable, talented and humble, honest but not cruel. Am I jealous of her? Yes, I probably am. That's exactly the kind of man I want in my life.

To distract myself, I checked Ladybird to find I had a match. His profile says he wants a dog lover, and his black miniature schnauzer does look cute.

TWENTY-NINE

The Dog Lover

Friday, 18 October, 7.30am

QUITE EXCITED AS I ended up texting The Dog Lover last night. He's obsessive about his dog Dexter, but let's see. I'm meeting him for a drink after work tonight. It's been ages since I had a date.

11.30pm

Dexter was as adorable as his photo (his owner didn't look too bad either). In the pub, people kept stopping and petting him – Dexter that is – and the bar staff brought water and treats. Note to self: borrow a dog for pulling? Anyway, it was going OK, and we were on our second round of drinks when Dexter, who'd eaten most of my crisps, took a liking to me and climbed onto my right leg and started humping.

'Can you get him off me, please?' I asked The Dog Lover who was unperturbed.

'He likes you. Crisps are his favourite. He's saying thank you.'

'I mean it, please get him off me.' It was embarrassing. Dexter's fans were looking and laughing.

'Just relax. He'll stop in a minute,' he said. Was he serious? Was I supposed to wait till his dog finished humping my leg?

'Please make him stop. This is not consensual,' I said, quite loudly as I tried to shake him off, but Dexter was holding on like my leg was the love of his life.

The Dog Lover reluctantly peeled Dexter off me and put him under the table. Presumably, he finished himself off on his owner's shin.

'Dexter's just cuddly and he gets excited. When I still lived with my ex-wife, he used to sleep between us in bed. And sometimes'—he sat forward and grinned—'if me and the missus were, you know, getting amorous, he'd join in.' He laughed as though this was the sweetest thing and not at all strange.

'What do you mean, join in?' I asked, not sure I wanted to know the answer.

'You know, if I was on top, he'd climb onto my back, and bark as we went at it. Sometimes, he'd peer over my shoulder and look at my wife and a bit of dribble would fall onto her,' he said, smiling wistfully, and patted Dexter who was now sitting next to him and eyeing up the rest of my crisps.

I finished my drink and stood up. 'It was nice meeting you. And Dexter, but I'm not as much of a doggy lover as you wanted,' I said.

I hope he finds a suitable applicant for the doggy position.

Saturday, 19 October, 11.30pm

In other dog news, went with Ace to pick up his new dog Winnie, the most darling cockapoo puppy. The two of them together are adorable. He cuddled and kissed her. Then I cuddled and kissed her. I felt like we should be kissing and cuddling each other too, and there was an awkward moment when we were really close, but we stopped and both snuggled Winnie instead. I sort of wish we hadn't stopped. Is that weird? Maybe it was my excitement of seeing Winnie. I could grow to love this little one, but I hope she's better behaved than Dexter.

Sunday, 20 October, 11.30pm

Spent the afternoon with The Orgasm Expert. I don't think the sex makes up for our incompatibility anymore and I didn't feel as turned on as usual. The chat before sex was a passion killer. How can you feel sexy when someone is listing their junk mail? There were vouchers for the local pizzeria (he could tell them a thing or two about pizzas), a brochure for a foot massage machine and leaflets for fast cash loans. Please, make it stop.

Will he be upset if I finish it? I don't think he has any feelings for me either but probably enjoys the no-strings-attached sex. I also think our arrangement is a bit of a distraction for me and I want to be free to find a real relationship. I'll try harder if I don't have orgasms on tap.

Monday, 21 October, 11.30pm

Met Grace tonight. She's handed in her notice to her super high-powered job.

'I never appreciated how precarious life can be. After everything I've been through with the cancer, the surgery and all the anxiety, I want to go all out and enjoy every single moment,' she said. 'And, I think your doggie dating idea could have legs.'

Yay. She's thinking about Cupid Corgis or Matchmaker Mutts. She wants me and Ace to help her with a test event. I could ask The Dog Lover if I can borrow Dexter. He's bound to get off with someone. Or I could turn up without a dog and share Winnie with Ace so people might think we're together and leave him alone. It's selfish of me, I know, but I don't want Ace to meet anyone. He's like a secret treasure I want to keep to myself, but then it wouldn't be right to sabotage Grace's event.

Wednesday, 23 October, 7.30am

MY BIRTHDAY! I'm sixty-one today. It's such a huge number it scares me, but I'm cool with myself. I'm sorted. I'm resilient. I think. I've been through a lot lately. After months of travel, I immersed myself back into London life and picked up my business again. I've been on good dates, bad dates, funny dates, and downright ugly dates. I've had my heart broken, had a lot of orgasms and nearly died of a flip-flop related accident. But I'm good. Onwards.

P.S. Jude is coming to my birthday dinner on Friday. Why?

11.30pm

Mum and Dad called to wish me happy birthday. Separately. Nothing from Sara.

In other birthday-related news, this morning I asked The Orgasm Expert for a birthday orgasm, and he obliged using his finger and tongue techniques. I hadn't intended to end our sex buddy arrangement today but afterwards, over coffee, he picked up a chocolate digestive and said, 'There are lots of different biscuit types…' I wanted to shove a bourbon into his mouth to make it stop. No more lists. I set him free to bring orgasmic joy to other women. #TakeHimOffMyHands #WillMissTheOrgasms

It was very grown up and amicable. We both knew it had run its course. No arguments, tears or expectations. Just lots of pure liberating sex and then it was over. At the beginning of the year, I wanted sex without emotional entanglement but didn't know if I could do it. Now I've mastered it, I'm not sure it's what I want. It feels too empty.

Thursday, 24 October, 11.30pm

Joy came – two days early – and spotted my birthday cards.

'How old are you?'

'Sixty-one,' I said, and watched her eyes pop out of their sockets. She does that every year.

'Sixty-one,' she repeated. 'That's old. When do you retire?'

'Not any time soon,' I said.

'Yes soon.'

Friday, 25 October, 9.30am

Phoned Dad to wish him happy birthday. Seventy-nine today. He's been a wonderful dad to me despite being so young when he had me. His family has always been his priority, and of course he's worshipped Mum for over sixty years. Lucky Mum.

But today he sounded down in the dumps. Relations seem to be getting worse between him and Mum. He's spending a lot of time rehearsing with Consuela, and Mum's been doing modelling again. I know they love each other, so if they don't sort themselves out soon, I'll have to intervene.

I'm going to try and forget about that for tonight and enjoy my birthday dinner.

Saturday, 26 October, 10.30am

Last night, I went for drinks and a meal for my birthday with Grace and Ajay, Leila and Jude, and Ace. It was the first time I'd seen Jude since the row back in August. He's the last person I wanted to have at my birthday dinner, but Leila said he wanted to apologise and make things right, so I agreed for her sake. He pretended nothing had happened, but I couldn't help being cool towards him. I went to the bar to order drinks, and while I was being served, Jude came up and offered to help. I thought he was trying to be nice, so I accepted.

'Still single then?' he asked, ignoring the drinks on the bar.

'Yes.'

'I hear you got dumped by text. He must have thought a lot of you to do that,' he said. Of course he wasn't being nice. He was deliberately trying to upset me, and he was succeeding.

'Leave me alone, Jude. You're here because of Leila and I don't need your commentary on my love life,' I said in an emphatic whisper. I was surprisingly calm even though inside I was fuming, and my eyes were filling up. I still feel raw from the episode with THO and don't need my nose rubbed in it.

'No need to be unfriendly.' He put his arm round me. 'You can always come to me if you fancy some cock.'

'Fuck off, Jude.' I tried to push him away, but he still had his arm round me, and I was trying to wriggle out of his grip when Ace walked past.

'Hey, hey, what's going on here?' Ace asked. 'Are you OK, Sophia?'

'Jude insulted me then propositioned me.'

Ace turned to Jude, who was holding his palms up and backing away.

'She's delusional. And desperate. Every time I talk to her, she thinks I'm making a pass at her,' he said and smirked.

'Oy, stop that. You apologise to Sophia right now,' Ace said, just as I lost it and slapped Jude. I should be ashamed of resorting to violence, but I'm not. I'm glad I did it. He deserved it. And I liked seeing a red handprint glowing on his smug face.

He felt his cheek, and his cocky expression changed to disbelief as he snatched my wrist. 'You bitch.'

'Don't you dare touch her. Just get out, Jude,' Ace said and made a grab for Jude's arm.

'Don't be like that, Kenny G. I understand. You're jealous she came on to me and not you,' Jude said. 'You know she's blown every trumpet in London except yours, don't you?'

By this time, Leila, Grace and Ajay had seen the commotion and had come over.

'Come on, babe, we're leaving,' Jude said to Leila, turning to go.

'No, you're not,' Ace said as he pulled Jude's shoulder back and punched his face, right in the spot where I'd slapped him. I enjoyed the punch too.

The look on Jude's face was priceless. He felt his cheek again and a trickle of blood oozed out of the corner of his mouth. 'Come on then. Let's go outside, Kenny G. I'm gonna smash your face so you can't blow anymore.'

The two of them went outside before the bar manager got to them, with me and Leila grabbing at them to stop, and Grace and

Ajay following. Outside, they locked horns for a few seconds and grappled with each other. Then Ace pushed at Jude's chest, and he fell to the ground, but before they could carry on fighting, Leila managed to drag Jude and make him walk away.

Ace rubbed his knuckles, and shouted after him, 'Kenny G plays the saxophone!'

Dinner was muted after that, but I was happy not to be looking at Jude's face anymore. What story did he spin to Leila when they got home? I'm sure he'll try and squirm his way out of it and say it was all a misunderstanding. Will she believe him this time?

Going to call Ace to see if his hand is OK and to say thank you for being a hero. Seeing him defend me like that warmed my heart. I've always wanted someone who puts me first and supports me. I can see Ace would do that for me. How lovely would it be to have him by my side the whole time to look out for me? And for me to look out for him. Now I know he's not a cheater, it changes everything. I'm seeing him in a different light. And I'm getting unexpected but not entirely unwelcome vagina throbs.

P.S. When I was pulling Ace away to stop him fighting Jude, I breathed in his aftershave, and it reminded me of Valencia and that lovely kiss.

11.30pm

Leila called to apologise for Jude. She said they'd had a terrible row on Friday night when they got home. As expected, Jude had told her he was being nice to me, and I misread it as him coming on to me. He was furious she hadn't backed him up. I told her what he'd said to me.

'I'm sorry about that. He's having a tough time with his business and probably took it out on you without meaning it. He's my husband, Sophia. I have to support him.'

Not if he's a complete dick, you don't. As far as I'm concerned, I'll be ecstatic if I never see his ugly mug again. I hope Leila will see sense soon.

Grace texted.

> How are you feeling? Sorry about your birthday dinner. Jude is a fucking nightmare

> I'm OK thanks. Isn't he just? I wish Leila would admit it to herself and get rid of him

> Yeah but will she?

> I have no idea.

> He must have a giant dick or something! Ace was a hero though. Never seen him so angry.

> Yeah, he was my knight in shining armour.

Sunday, 27 October, 10.30am

I realised that Friday was the first time I'd seen Leila and Jude together since our falling out. Things were different between them. Not as carefree and tactile as before. Can a leopard change its spots? I have a feeling Jude's always been a manipulative nasty cheater and he's not about to change. Why did he want to come anyway? To be horrible to me for putting doubts about him in Leila's mind? Did he want to prove to Leila that I wanted him by pretending I'd made a pass at him again? Or he might want to cause a rift between me and Leila. Or all three.

11.30pm

I can't help thinking about Ace on my birthday. He came to my aid and there was no doubt whose side he was on. I'm so independent and I can look after myself, but it was nice to have someone to protect me and be there for me. He's such a good friend. But did he behave like a friend or someone who's in love with me? Ace is Ace. Can I think of him as a lover, now I know he's not a cheater? I'm starting to think maybe I can. #FriendsToLovers?

Monday, 28 October, 11.30pm

I had a sofa dream about me and Ace, dressed in matching beige macs, black trilbies, and dark sunglasses, and following Jude to take pictures of him with another woman. We showed them to Leila, and she kicked Jude out. We were laughing and singing 'Good riddance'. Then we hugged and were about to kiss when I woke up.

That may be a good idea. Deep down, Leila knows what Jude is like and must be struggling to choose her next move. Seeing the evidence could help her decide. I don't want to upset her, but I think Jude is doing that already and she may be happier without him.

P.S. I wish I hadn't woken up when I did. Now, I can't help wondering what a proper kiss with Ace would be like. Not one where I'm drunk and out of control, but a romantic one when we're both into it and it's a lovely lingering smooch. Hot flush alert.

Tuesday, 29 October, 11.30pm

Ace brought Winnie over and we went for a walk on Hampstead Heath.

'I wanted to thank you for the other night. You were a complete hero,' I said.

'He had it coming. I've never trusted Jude.'

'But you went above and beyond. You could have got hurt.'

'Not by that little squirt,' he said rubbing his still bruised knuckles.

'I've never had anyone fight for me like that. It was quite exciting actually.'

He smiled with adorable twinkly eyes. 'Well, I don't want to make a habit of fighting, but you know I'll always be there for you, don't you?'

'Yes,' I said and thought about how much I wanted that.

I stroked his knuckles then caught myself and told him about my dream and asked if we should enact the sleuthing. Winnie barked her approval. She'd look good in our detective outfits.

Ace said, 'Don't be absurd.'

I curved my mouth down in mock sadness and looked up at him with puppy eyes. He laughed and pulled me in for a hug. It was so nice, I stayed there as long as I could. Then later, as I played with Winnie, I caught him gazing at me with an expression I couldn't quite place. Was it tenderness? Or even longing? It stirred up unexpected feelings inside me that I quickly suppressed. I'm sure it was wishful thinking. He was probably thinking I'd be a good dog-sitter if he goes away. Still, I rather enjoyed the look.

PART XI
November

THIRTY

The Greedy Piggy

Friday, 1 November, 11.30pm

ONLY TWO MONTHS left of the dating challenge. At least I had some fabulous sex last month. Apart from lots of orgasms, The Orgasm Expert has given me a sense of freedom. I don't want to go round having gratuitous sex all the time, but it's comforting to know I can if I want. I suppose I'd better trawl the dating apps. Time is running out. Those years as a management consultant have left their mark on me. My brain is tuned into objectives, outcomes, deadlines, and key performance indicators. The project-lover in me wants to make the dating challenge work. But how will I measure success? Is it the number of dates, the number of shags, or meeting a soulmate? Somewhere back in the summer after The Hot One, I probably should have done a proper project review and set myself new goals. I'll just have to go with the flow. I can't give up now. I've never been a defeatist and I'm not going to start now.

Saturday, 2 November, 11.30pm

Went to see Mum and Dad today. They put on a show for me, but the atmosphere was frosty. Every time Dad mentioned Consuela,

Mum went to the kitchen. I followed her and she said she'd done a small modelling job and Dad was being grumpy about it. I'll be forced to stage an intervention if they carry on like this.

'Why is he being so difficult? I can't take much more of it,' she said.

'Come on, Mum. How many other people can look amazing enough to be modelling at eighty? And you're married to a man who has adored you from the minute he set eyes on you. Life is great.'

'Yes, but…'

'You know, one time, I asked Dad why he never talks about his childhood. He told me it was a tough miserable upbringing, and he was unhappy as a young man, but everything changed when he met you. It was so romantic. I wish I had that,' I said, to remind her how lucky she is in life.

'Ah, your dad was so dashing when we met. His love changed my life too. My childhood wasn't so happy either. You were too young to remember Grandma, but she was so overweight. Over the years, the bigger she got, the less she looked after herself. I used to dread her coming to the school gates or parents' evenings. The other kids would take a look at her and be vicious with their teasing. She had the weight problem, but I was the one bullied for it.'

Why had she not told me that before? It all made sense now. All those years of being told to stay slim and look my best. She was projecting her fears. She was trying to protect me from the pain she suffered. The weight of criticism lifted from my chest, and I felt a surge of love for her.

'You're right, Lovely, I am lucky. And you … you may live a different kind of life, but I'm so proud of you. You're talented, clever and beautiful, and I have a feeling that very soon you will meet someone who will change your life for the better.'

'Are you really proud of me?'

'Of course. You should hear me when I talk about you at the Monday coffee mornings. The other mothers get so jealous.'

OMG. I've been waiting for those words for so long my emotions squirted out of my eyes and I howled.

Sunday, 3 November, 11.30pm

Jude texted. Called me a marriage wrecker and told me to keep my nose out of it. I told him his marriage would be fine if he didn't offer his dick around so much.

Monday, 4 November, 11.30pm

I've been messaging ClubLover tonight. He's fifty-two, a film producer from LA (is that just a hook?) living in London. He has an outdoorsy relaxed vibe and perfect Californian teeth. His profile said he's adventurous, likes jazz trios and club sandwiches.

> Hi ClubLover, is that your name cos you love dancing or club sandwiches?

> Well hello Sophia, we could do both at the same time if you like

> That sounds fun. I love dancing. And a great club sandwich.

> I aim to please. In triplicate!

> You're making me hungry.

> We'll have to do something about that

> Ha ha

> Care to get together and discuss our favourite all time club sandwiches? Maybe we could recreate them sometime?

> Let's do it.

> I warn you though. I'm a greedy piggy as you British say.

I love a bit of food flirting/banter. We're going to meet in Soho on Thursday.

Tuesday, 5 November, 11.55pm

Went to Ace's bonfire night/housewarming drinks tonight. I arrived early to give him a hand but found he already had a helper. He introduced her as his neighbour Jacqueline. She was all perfume and false eyelashes, with too much boob on show.

'Hello Sophia, do call me Jacquie.'

'Hello Jacqueline. Do you live in this block?'

'Yes, I'm on this floor, a couple of doors down. I met Ace when he was viewing the flat, and after he moved in, I brought him a welcome plant. And now here I am.' She looked up at him with adoring eyes.

'Yes, here you are.' I forced a smile. It's not like me to take a dislike to someone so quickly, but I did with her for some reason.

'Wasn't that kind of Jacquie?' Ace asked. I nodded.

'Jacqueline, is your husband or partner joining us tonight?' I asked.

'God, I hope not. I divorced him last year.' She laughed. Too loud. 'I found my flat after I got rid of him and I'm so glad I did.' She eyed up Ace, who was pouring me a drink. She was barking up the wrong tree. Not Ace's type at all.

'Jacquie's been helping me get everything ready. Isn't that nice?'

I wasn't sure about her at all. She was obviously on the lookout for her next husband and wanted to get her mitts on Ace. Not while I'm around to protect him. She so isn't his type.

I was relieved when Leila arrived on her own. I didn't need two people to annoy me tonight. Apparently, Jude wanted to come so he could apologise to me in person but had to work late as he had a big contract to prepare for his bag business. Yeah right.

It was a lovely party, and I especially enjoyed it when Ace came over and put his arm around me while we were all on the terrace watching the fireworks on the horizon. He's done that hundreds of times before, but this time it made me tingly and giggly. I looked up at him and he gave me a warm smile, but I went back to watching the fireworks in case he could tell I was having fanny flutters. What the hell is going on, Sophia?

The only downer was the helpful Jacqueline interrupting people's conversations with, 'Nibbles anyone?' every five minutes. I'd had enough of her by the time the party finished.

'I'll help you clear up, Ace,' she said when the three of us were left in the kitchen.

'Isn't that nice, Ace?' I said. 'But you've done so much already. I'll take it from here,' I said, and waited, hoping she'd leave. She said she wanted to help and carried on tidying up, so I went to take the bottle of wine in her hand, but she held on to it and it tipped, splashing a massive red splodge down her face and dress. We all froze.

'I'm so sorry, let me clean that for you,' I said. Inside, I was pointing and laughing.

'It's OK. It's probably time I went home anyway.' She kissed Ace on the cheek before saying goodbye.

'She was only being neighbourly,' Ace said after she'd finally gone.

'Yes. And the rest. Didn't you notice she was fluttering her eyelashes at you? I know she's not your type, so I was helping you get rid of her.'

'Were you? I got the distinct impression you didn't like her. It's not like you.'

Was that what I was doing? Protecting Ace? I don't know where all that came from. She'd been nice to me all evening, but she rubbed me up the wrong way for some reason. Grace must have noticed, too, when she asked me why I was giving Jacqueline the dagger eyes. I told her I didn't know what she was talking about.

We were drying the glasses side by side later when Ace said, 'So what is my type?'

'You know, someone fun, loyal and positive. A happy, creative, adventurous woman with a sense of style.'

'Hmm.'

'I don't think you know what you want,' I said.

'Yes, I do. You just don't get it.'

More like he doesn't get it. If we weren't friends, I'd say I'm much more his type than Jacqueline.

Anyway, I can't wait to get started on re-designing the flat with him. God, a terrible thought. The second basin isn't for Jacqueline, is it? Surely not? She's so wrong for him.

P.S. Winnie agreed with me about Jacqueline and growled at her every time she walked past. Good doggie.

Wednesday, 6 November, 11.30pm

Texted Leila to see what she thought of Ace's flat. She loved it but thought it needed my magic touch to give it sparkle. Of course.

> What did you think of his neighbour Jacqueline?

She was nice enough.

> I found her a bit too much. Quite annoying.

Yes, I noticed.

> She got on my nerves. She was all over Ace. So shameless.

And what would be wrong with that? They're both single.

> She's not his type, that's all.

Really? Anyone would think you were jealous.

Me?! Jealous? Why would I be jealous? Don't be ridiculous.

Good night xx

Thursday, 7 November, 7.30pm

It was cold outside, but I regretted wearing so many layers while I searched in the busy bar for The Greedy Piggy. I was glowing with perspiration and about to give up when I spotted him in a booth. He reminded me of Owen Wilson but with a perfect nose.

'Well, hello Sophia. Welcome to club sandwich,' he said in a chilled Californian accent as smooth as cream.

'Hello to you too,' I said breathily.

I took off my layers, then sipped the margarita he'd poured for me, licking the salt from the glass rim without losing eye contact.

'That dress … does it for me. I'm into you. You know what I mean?'

I nodded. I could get used to being adored like this. Ding-dong!

'So, you're a designer? I hope you have some designs on me for tonight.'

I giggled. 'I'm always full of designs.'

Then a tall woman with a cascade of red hair over her milky shoulders slid into the booth. She put an arm round him and kissed him on the mouth. WTF?

He leaned over and said, 'Our trio is complete. What do you think, Sophia? She's beautiful, isn't she?' He looked into her eyes.

What the double fuck? Were they some sort of exhibitionist couple?

'Yes, she's beautiful.' I couldn't help being polite. 'But I don't understand. What is the trio for?' I asked, irritated, just as the penny dropped.

She reached under the table and stroked my thigh. I pushed her hand off.

'It's cool, man. We all love a club sandwich, right?' he checked.

'No, we don't,' I said, standing up and collecting my many things.

'Are you angry, Sophia?' he asked raising his eyebrows.

Of course I was fucking angry. I didn't want to be an extra. I wanted the starring role.

I finally got all my stuff together. 'I'm leaving,' I pronounced, sticking out my chin and intending to storm out, but the bar was completely packed, and nobody was moving. 'Sorry, sorry, can I get through? Sorry, excuse me,' I continued until I was outside.

Who knew what club sandwich meant? Not me. Now I'm sitting outside a bar with a drink and wondering if I was too hasty. A threesome is something I've never tried, but how would it work? Who does what? God, I sound like my aunt asking with genuine interest, 'What do lesbians do?' My phone pinged.

> It's all cool. If you change your mind, we'll be at my apartment soon.

He texted me his address, which wasn't far. Maybe I should stop being so prudish and try something new.

11.30pm

I hesitated outside his apartment door but forced myself to knock. He opened the door, looking buff in an exceedingly small pair of black hipsters. He stroked my back as he ushered me in, and the hairs on my neck stood up. I could see into the bedroom where his –girlfriend? Wife? Sex buddy? – was magnificent in golden lingerie, draped over the bed. They were both so sexy, I thought, go girl, enjoy.

The Greedy Piggy and his piglet pulled me to the bedroom where she unfurled my scarf, pulling a few hairs out with it. Ouch. They removed one glove each, one finger at a time. She tugged the ribbon tie on my coat at the wrong end, winding it into a tight knot, and grappling with it before reaching into the bedside table for scissors and cutting me out of it.

As he took off my cardigan, there was so much static I imagined my hair sticking up in a halo. I touched it and I had imagined right. I quickly smoothed it down and returned to our *ménage à trois*.

One more layer to go before I was in my underwear like them. Piglet pulled up my dress, but it got stuck, my arms shooting upwards and the dress covering my upper body and head. He intervened with a hard tug, and it came off. Ouch, that nearly took my arms off.

Damn. I'd forgotten about the nude shapewear. I bet she doesn't even know what shapewear is with that body. He yanked it off over my head. Only the thick tights left. I pulled at them before he attempted it, but I lost balance and fell. When I stood up, they were kissing and caressing, their limbs tangled. Had they gone off the club sandwich idea after the awkward dance of the seven veils?

I climbed onto the bed to get in on the act, caressing his back, cupping his buttocks and licking his ear but it was like I wasn't there. I lifted my right leg over them and pushed myself up and over to the other side, ending up spooning her and kissing her neck but she was equally engrossed in him. I reached over to fondle a breast as he pulled her tight to him and my hand got stuck between their chests. I was the chicken in the club sandwich, except they'd decided to have a BLT. I pulled my hand just as he released her, and I fell off the bed.

I woke up with a thud. I had indeed fallen, but it was off my sofa. I remembered coming home and thinking I'll lie down for a minute. I was still wearing all my layers and must have been thrashing around from the heat. I think my subconscious was telling me threesomes are not all they're cracked up to be. Either that or there is something seriously wrong with me if I'm being rejected in my own sexual fantasies!

I think I'm coming to eat club sandwiches
But you want me as filling for different positions
You advocate the pleasures of a ménage à trois

Isn't that a bit ooh la la?
You're cute but she is excess to my needs
I'll take you on but only if she recedes
The way you two inspect me low and high
Makes me feel like a piece of ribeye
You look like you're ready to eat
And to you I am just fresh meat
Into your bed I may want to hop
But not with another woman on top
You want me to join your sandwich club
No thanks, I'd rather eat lunch in a pub
You tell me to be open and live free
But you're after a vagina spree
You look at us both with impish glee
You're a truly greedy piggy

Friday, 8 November, 11.30pm

I re-read The Greedy Piggy's profile and texts to search for clues I might have missed about his intentions. I did some Googling, and it turns out:

Club sandwich = threesome sex, of any combination

Jazz trio = jazz is all about tension and release and is often compared to sex

P.S. Will I get targeted ads about club sandwiches?

Saturday, 9 November, 1.30pm

I told Leila about The Greedy Piggy wanting a threesome, and about my dream. Only I didn't tell her it was a dream. Leila said, 'I didn't think you'd go for that kind of thing, honey,' and she laughed and nodded knowingly when I confessed the truth.

Ace arrived and asked what we were laughing about but I didn't want to tell him about The Greedy Piggy, so I just tapped my nose. I don't want to talk about dating with him. It feels wrong somehow, and I can't imagine him going for a threesome any more than I would. Then I had a hot flush imagining him and me in a threesome except the third person was invisible.

I plucked up the courage to ask Ace about Jacqueline.

'So, is there something going on with you and Jacqueline? You looked quite cosy together the other night. Is the second basin for her?'

He shifted in his seat and took a long gulp of juice before replying. 'No, it's not for her. We're just neighbours,' he said, sounding on edge. Could it be he didn't want me to think there was anything between them because he wants me instead? I didn't dwell on that unlikely possibility for too long, though the thought of it gave me palpitations.

11.30pm

Thinking back to Ace's party, I know I wasn't nice to Jacqueline. Did I engineer spilling red wine on her by getting into a tug of war? I feel ashamed of how I behaved. That's not the type of person I am or want to be. Is Leila right? Am I jealous? If I'm honest, I think I probably am. It's the same feeling I had when Ace asked for the second basin. I don't like the thought of her or anyone else using that basin. But do I want it to be my basin, now I know he's not a cheater? I need to work it out. AND he needs to declare his real intentions for that basin.

THIRTY-ONE

The Widower

Thursday, 14 November, 7.30am

DATE WITH A BARRISTER TONIGHT. Hope he doesn't turn out to be a devious married arse like the last lawyer. Gosh, that was back in May. It seems like a thousand years ago when I was still eager about the dating challenge, writing about everything in great detail, and analysing every date. Now I'm jaded and can't be bothered. I'm going on dates purely because I don't want my project to fail. If Ace gets it together with that Jacquie woman, I'll be the only singleton again. I must stay positive. Tonight could be the night.

4.30pm

On the way to meet Izzy before my date. She said it was urgent and will tell me when I see her. Very mysterious.

11.30pm

Izzy told me she'd gone to a singles party the night before and surprise, surprise, Jude was there. He didn't notice her of course. Too busy working the room until he hit the jackpot and met a woman who was interested in him. Things got quite steamy between them, and after a while, they left together.

'I'm not proud of what I did,' Izzy said, 'but I wanted him to get his comeuppance. For deceiving then ghosting me, cheating on your friend and being so awful to you.'

'What did you do?'

'I followed them. Out of the bar, on the tube and to her house. And I took photos. I probably wasn't discreet, but they were all over each other and didn't notice. Am I a terrible person?'

'No, you're not. He deserves everything he gets.'

She showed me the photos and they were indeed incriminating. I have a dilemma again. Do I tell Leila? I remembered what happened last time but is she ready to hear the truth now? We pondered my predicament, trying to anticipate what Jude might do. I can imagine him saying it was just a colleague and she'd come onto him, or he was seeing her home because she was drunk, and she kissed him. Anything to make himself the innocent party. But the pictures were clear. You could see it was him kissing a woman as they went into her house. Surely, even Jude couldn't wriggle out of that. I had the evidence, and I didn't need to go sleuthing with Ace and Winnie in matching detective outfits. I would decide what to do in the morning.

But I still had my date, though I didn't feel like it by then. He was waiting for me at the bar when I arrived. I thought he must have come straight from work as he wore a black suit and white shirt and a sad expression. To liven things up, I told him about some of my funnier recent dates but couldn't get through to him.

'So, what's your relationship background? Have you ever been married?' I asked.

'I'm a widower,' he said, and his mouth drooped at the corners even more.

'Oh, I'm sorry.' I paused, then changed the subject. 'Did you come straight from court?' I asked, pointing at his suit.

'No, I didn't go to court today. I was at a funeral.'

'I'm sorry, was it someone close?'

'Yes, my wife,' he said, and started weeping.

'I'm sorry. It was your wife's funeral today?'

'Yes.'

'And you're out on a date?' WTF? What kind of psycho goes on a date after his wife's funeral? I started getting my things to leave and was thinking I could throw my red wine over him.

'No, wait. Don't go. We were separated. You see, she left me for another man a year ago.' I sat down again. 'I was upset at first but then I was angry and hated her for it. Then she … she was killed in a car accident. I thought I could finally move on…' He was trying to choke back the tears. 'I thought today was going to be the first day of being free of her, but now … I think I still love her,' he sobbed.

What the double fuck? So he'd asked me out to make himself feel better and he's telling me he's still in love with his dead wife who left him for another man?

I had no energy to be angry and I just wanted to come home, but by then he was crying so much I felt sorry for him and didn't have the heart to leave. I bought him a drink, gave him my tissues, and consoled him for twenty minutes until he'd calmed down and I could make my exit. I've so had it with the dating challenge. I can't take another knockback or more nastiness. Or any more nutters.

Saturday, 16 November, 10.30am

Got a text from The Widower.

Him: Thanks for looking after me the other night. I'm buying if you fancy meeting up next week.

Me:

Sunday, 17 November, 11.30pm

I think I'll tell Leila. She'll listen this time. She has her doubts about him anyway. The pictures will just confirm them. I know what I'd do in her shoes. I'd kick him out. I certainly wouldn't want to hold onto a cheater. But Leila's different. She's gone from one relationship to another ever since school. I love her but I'm glad I don't need a man to make me feel complete. In fact, I don't know if I need or want a man ever.

Monday, 18 November, 11.30pm

Went to Argentinian Tango with Izzy. We'd had a few dances when a guy in his late seventies asked for my hand. We started to dance cheek to cheek, and he was a good leader, so I was enjoying it. After a while I could tell he was exhausted as his breathing got heavier. Next thing, there was a gulp and a clack, and something fell between us. We stopped and stared at his dentures on the floor.

'I'll go and wash these,' he said as he picked up his teeth. I went back to Izzy, who pointed to my shoulder where there was a damp patch on my shirt. Dribble? Flying spittle? He returned five minutes later and, flashing his newly rinsed teeth, asked me to dance again. I declined, but the perky elderly woman with the unnaturally even teeth next to me was delighted to oblige.

Wednesday, 20 November, 5.30pm

I'm nervous. I asked Leila to come over. She probably thinks I want to talk about my love life but I'm going to show her the photos.

11.30pm

She was upset but surprisingly calm. I think she'd suspected as much for a while, so it wasn't a shock. She's staying with me tonight. She told Jude she'd had too much to drink and couldn't drive, so as not to raise his suspicions. It's awful for her, but she knows what she must do.

Thursday, 21 November, 6.30pm

Leila phoned. She's done the deed. She went home this morning, cleared their joint bank account, and took her investment money out of his business account. Thank God I told her when I did, or that money would have disappeared into his startup contracts tomorrow. She packed a bag for him and told him to get out when he got home. He tried to play the innocent party, but it didn't work this time. I'm sad for her but happy he's out of our lives.

Friday, 22 November, 11.30pm

Some happy news at last. Project Toilet was completed this week, and I went to meet V and K today. They're delighted with the design but not as much as their four-year-old who's been flushing the illusion cistern many, many times a day.

Sunday, 24 November, 11.30pm

Went to Grace's doggie dating test event. Not sure how she did it, but there were about thirty middle-aged single people all cooing over each other's dogs on Parliament Hill and having a fabulous time. Grace brought Terry and she looked like she was enjoying herself, even making friends with one dog lover. I'm proud of her for being so resilient. I borrowed Dexter, who did what he does best by trying to hump other dogs and human legs with equal vigour. I had to leave early before he started a fight. Ace and Winnie were a big hit of course.

'Oh my gosh, you're a musician. How wonderful. And your dog is so cute. Like her owner,' gushed one woman, who was the twin of her grey Afghan hound.

I nudged Dexter towards the woman, and she walked away in disgust as I laughed on the inside. Much as I want Grace's business to succeed, I was relieved when Ace said he was only there to support Grace, so I hope he didn't exchange numbers with anyone after I left. Snarl.

Wednesday, 27 November, 11.30pm

Tried a circuit training class today so I could wear my lovely new floral workout outfit. I was standing tall and feeling sexy in my skin. While we were waiting to go in, I noticed Mr Fit checking me out.

'I haven't seen you here before,' he said with a gorgeous smile.

'No, it's my first time. You look like you're a regular though.' I nodded at his biceps.

'I am, but you must work out, yeah? You look pretty fit in that outfit,' he said as he scanned my body.

I giggled and blushed. The teenager in me is never too far from the surface. I went into the class thinking I must bump into him on the way out. The class was hell. Not wanting to be defeated, I kept up with the running, weightlifting, crunching, rowing, planking, and on and on. By the end of it, my top was completely soaked, hair was frizzed out, and I was walking with the stoop of an eighty-year-old. The cute guy walked past with a look of disbelief at my transformation. I looked at him and thought, I'm just too tired.

Friday, 29 November, 11.30pm

Still aching today.

Saturday, 30 November, 1.30pm

Leila and Ace were already there when I arrived for brunch. She was surprisingly upbeat even though Jude had gone back yesterday to pick up some stuff and been nasty about her withdrawing her money out of his business. Then she told us that she'd gone to a top firm of lawyers about her divorce yesterday and ended up agreeing to a date with one of the partners!

'I can't believe it, Leila. How do you do it? How have you managed to arrange a date in your situation?' I asked.

'I could tell you, but then I'd have to kill you,' Leila said unhelpfully.

What am I doing wrong? I could take a leaf out of that Jacqueline woman's book and ingratiate myself on one of my neighbours. I could get a tight short dress, flaunt my boobs, and walk around the neighbourhood asking, 'Nibbles anyone?' I know I'm being mean about her but God, I hope there's nothing going on between them. I can't bear to ask Ace.

P.S. He was wearing a casual cashmere sweater and looking particularly wowy. I held my hands on my lap under the table to stop myself touching him. It was agony.

THIRTY-TWO

Mr Platonic Peck

Sunday, 1 December, 11.30pm

ELEVEN MONTHS DOWN. Only one more to go. No dates on the horizon and no prospect of being coupled up by the end of the year. In November:

Was called a marriage wrecker.

Invited to be the chicken in a club sandwich.

Actually wrecked a marriage.

Consoled a date about his dead wife.

Finished Project Toilet. Hurrah! Thank God for the beacon of light and hope that was Project Toilet. I will miss it.

Shall I give it one more push and go for a few dates in December, or do myself a favour and give up? I don't know if I have the energy or the inclination to carry on with the dating challenge, especially now I'm distracted by thoughts of Ace. But then I can't be sure if he has any feelings for me, so I probably shouldn't be too hopeful on that front.

I thought I was doing all the right things: using apps, being open to people, grasping every opportunity, and yet eleven months later, here I am recovering from a broken heart and not having had much sex to write about. I can't decide what to do next.

11.45pm

Come to think of it, Leila and Ace were awfully cosy when I walked in yesterday and they didn't reply when I asked what they were talking about. Oh no, no, no, no! Are they getting together? She said she had a date with her lawyer, though, but maybe that was to throw me off the scent. Or Ace could be seeing Jacqueline AND Leila. And Leila is seeing Ace AND her lawyer. They're both cheating on their lovers. Everyone is seeing everyone except me.

Monday, 2 December, 11.30pm

Leila and Ace together? No way. Or yes way?
    Texted Leila.

Just wondering, are you seeing Ace?

When?

Any time

What are you talking about?

Are you 'seeing' Ace?

You've really lost it.

You were so cosy the other day

Honey we were talking about you.

What about me?

You know, dating etc.

Nothing specific?

I need my beauty sleep. X

Phew. Maybe Ace told Leila he's in love with me. I like that idea much better. In fact, I love that idea. I want to ask Leila, but I know if I do, she'll start teasing me and I'll feel awkward when we're with Ace. I need to work out a way of finding out how he feels.

Tuesday, 3 December, 11.30pm

Had a message from a guy on London Soulmates being complimentary and wanting to talk. He's divorced with a seven-year-old daughter. I'll go on one last date.

Wednesday, 4 December, 11.30pm

Had my hair and nails done, ready for the Christmas festivities. Got talking to the manicurist about being fed up with the dating challenge. She told me she had a dream a few years back that she was running on the treadmill at the gym except there was a rainbow at the end of it, and she reached it just before she woke up. The next day, she met her husband on the treadmill next to her at the gym. Wow, some people have all the luck. I told her about the dream I'd had about me and Ace sleuthing.

'That's a pretty obvious dream,' she said.

Was it? I had no idea what it meant. How intriguing. 'What do you mean?'

'You're looking for a reason to be with him. That's the sleuthing on behalf of your friend. You're wearing matching outfits because you want both of you to feel the same way, and you help your friend get rid of her cheating husband, which means you two are together for a good reason and outcome. See?'

OMG. Was that right? Was my subconscious telling me to go for it? Was I dreaming of a new life with Ace? I always thought it was cheesy, but I could see me and Ace going for walks wearing cute, coordinated clothes. I can picture us holding hands as we watch TV like that couple on Gogglebox. And the image of me using the second basin is so clear in my head. This woman was wasted as a manicurist.

'But then it could be,' she continued, 'that you're fed up with your life and you want a career change. You're hoping your friend will help you get a new job with a lovely uniform and that'll make you happy.'

That interpretation was unlikely.

'Or…'

What was she going to dream up now?

'Did you have beef that night by any chance? It could be that. I get terrible indigestion after beef,' she continued with her useless dream translations.

'Or…'

I zoned out. It was lovely to dream of a future with Ace, but it wasn't a dream that was likely to come true.

Thursday, 5 December, 11.30pm

Went to the Xmas party at Material Build where I met THO in the summer, but luckily, he wasn't there. We were given goody bags containing their New Year desk diary (yippee), a tea towel (double yippee), a small spirit level (dull but useful), and a tiny chocolate Father Christmas (eaten in taxi home).

Friday, 6 December, 11.30pm

Ace surprised me with tickets to the Kenwood Christmas Light Trail, where we had a magical, enchanted, fairy tale evening. We wrapped up warm and walked arm in arm down the sparkling paths and displays of cute lighted rabbits, owls and deer. When we reached the enormous Christmas tree, I closed my eyes and suggested making a wish. On opening them, I found him watching me with affection, and I wished it was the look of love instead. I blushed and hoped he thought it was redness from the cold.

'I asked for happiness. What about you?' I said.

'Something similar.' I didn't dare ask if it involved me.

Then we heard Christmas music, so I took his hand, and we had a little slow dance. I longed to be kissed but when the song finished, he stepped back casually, and the moment was over. I just couldn't read the signals. Later, under the mistletoe, he gave me a peck on the cheek.

'For luck,' he said and winked. I didn't want just a lucky peck. Not while my body was all atingle.

At the end of the trail, I zoned out while we warmed up with hot chocolate topped with whipped cream, lost in erotic fantasies of the combination of whipped cream and Ace.

I went home dizzy with questions. Was tonight a friend date or something more? Ace's touches and affection seemed so romantic surrounded with twinkling lights, but there was no flirting or playful touching. My optimistic heart says he's falling for me, but my head says I'm imagining romance where there's only platonic love. For now, I'll cherish our sparkling evening, but I'm longing to know if it meant as much to him as it did to me.

P.S. The lovely Kenneth and Valentina have asked me to go back and work on upgrading the rest of the house. Yay! That should revive the bank balance next year. I'm sure I'll get a feature with that project in one of the glossy magazines. Double yay! Maybe one day, *Elle Decoration* will do an 'At home with leading interior designer Sophia and her musician partner Ace'.

THIRTY-THREE

The Father

Monday, 9 December, 7.30am

HOPING today's coffee date will be good. Just a nice normal date, having a lovely chat and being interested in each other. Too much to ask for?

11.30pm

That is definitely the last date this year. It wasn't normal. There was no lovely chat. There was no interest. But there was violence.

The Father arrived for our coffee date – with his daughter! I didn't want to meet the family quite so soon, but he was apologetic and said his daughter's mum had an emergency and couldn't pick her up from school. Before I could say let's rearrange, his phone rang, and he excused himself and went outside to take the call. Rude.

'Would you like a drink?' I asked the daughter, thinking I hadn't signed up for this.

'Chocolate milkshake please and … a tuna melt and plain crisps.'

She'd obviously been taught to express her needs. Good for her. I went to the counter.

'Are you going to have sex with my daddy?' she asked when I returned with a full tray.

'Erm … aren't you a bit young to be asking that question?'

'I'm seven. I know all about sex. Mummy says Daddy's always having sex. With lots of different women. I think it's something to do with his trousers. Mummy says he can't keep his zip done up.'

I turned mute.

'Mummy says that's why I have so many siblings with their own mummies. Are you going to have a baby brother or sister for me?'

'No. I can tell you categorically that's not going to happen.'

I peered through the window at The Father, who was having an intense conversation. Probably with one of the mummies.

'So … what's your favourite subject at school?'

'I'm seven. You don't need to talk to me like a child.' That told me. 'But my favourite thing of all time is judo. I can throw you over my shoulder if you like.'

'Thanks for the offer, but no. Has your daddy taken you to a date before?'

'Yes. Do you want to know what happened?' I nodded. 'This,' she said, and kicked my shin under the table.

'Ouch. What did you do that for?'

'To show you what I did. I didn't like her either,' she snarled.

I watched her eat in silence. The Father came back after twenty minutes. Twenty minutes. I would have gone after five minutes if I wasn't babysitting.

'This was a mistake. I'll leave you with your delightful daughter,' I said, narrowing my eyes at her.

Tuesday, 10 December, 11.30pm

I wonder if I was played and fooled by a seven-year-old. It's quite possible she'd been manipulated by her mummy to say those things. I have no idea about The Father's backstory. And I don't want to know. I'm done. I've failed the dating challenge. I didn't meet my dream soulmate and I certainly didn't have sex fifty-two times. I'm going to enjoy the build-up to Christmas and New Year, and not think about dating. I'll do it next year. Who knows what will happen then?

P.S. Does developing a massive crush on one of your best friends count towards the dating challenge? And what if it's more than just a crush? The more I think about Ace, I realise how perfect he would be for me. We're best friends anyway and we get on so well. And now I have feelings of the vagina throbbing kind for him too. Perfect, right? But does he have longings of the hard type for me?

Thursday, 12 December, 11.30pm

Texted Sara to see if they're coming to Mum and Dad's for Christmas. It's time to forgive and forget. She replied, 'No, we're at home this year.' I was so disappointed. I hate not seeing her, and I so miss Jack and Charlotte. I have their presents all ready and would love to see their bright beautiful young faces on Christmas Day.

THEN, Sara asked me how I was, and I nearly fell off my chair. We actually had a nice chat. She even laughed when I told her about The Dog Lover and The Father. Maybe next year will bring reconciliation.

THIRTY-FOUR

The Hot One Revisited

Friday, 13 December, 5.30pm

WHOA. A text from The Hot One.

> Hi Sophia, how are you doing? Long time, no hear xx

I stared at the screen for a minute, started typing, stopped, restarted and finally persuaded myself I shouldn't reply. He texted again ten minutes later.

> I understand if you don't want to talk to me. I know I behaved badly. I miss you. Will you give us another chance? Let me explain what happened? I want to see you. xx

I don't know how I feel about this at all. I'm so torn. He was awful to me, and sensible Sophia would tell him to take a hike. But at the same time, the thought of being near him again is so inviting. Doesn't everybody deserve a second chance? He made a mistake and hadn't realised until now. Would I be depriving myself of what could be an amazing relationship by holding a grudge? Or am I making excuses for him? And then there's Ace.

What if he is interested in me romantically? I don't want to ruin my chances with him by seeing The Hot One. Then again, if Ace isn't interested, what then? I don't know what to do.

11.30pm

I reached for my mobile a hundred times, typed a few words, then deleted them. In the end, I didn't reply. I'll sleep on it. If I can sleep. He's stirred up all sorts of emotions in me. Apparently, all that pushing him into oblivion didn't work. He's still hanging around in my heart. And in my vagina! I still want him, but I also resent him for what he did. I don't know if I should forgive and forget, or even consider speaking to him. What I do know is that I'm writhing in my bed right now thinking about what I could do to his hot body next to me.

Saturday, 14 December, 8.30am

I'm seeing Ace today. I'm going to try and forget about The Hot One and concentrate on spotting any giveaway signs from Ace.

10.30pm

Went shopping for a Christmas tree with Ace. I picked a massive seven foot tree despite Ace protesting it wouldn't fit in his car. Cue four feet of Christmas tree jutting out of the sunroof. On the way to my house, I told him about the text from The Hot One and was quite startled by his vehement reaction.

'I can't believe you're giving the time of day to that idiot. How can you even think about him after what he did? Please tell me you're not getting back with him,' he said, letting out an exasperated breath and flexing his jaw. He was even more angry than he was with Jude on my birthday. I couldn't help but wonder if he's concerned just as a friend, or if the thought of me reconciling with The Hot One has provoked jealousy.

'I haven't replied to him and I'm not going to,' I protested.

'Good,' he said with finality, and continued white knuckling the steering wheel.

There was a bit of an atmosphere in the car but when we got home, we dragged the tree up the stairs while Winnie kept running between our legs and making us laugh. She's too cute for words and made us forget about earlier. Joy was cleaning in the kitchen when we walked in. She groaned her usual reluctant hello, but then noticed Ace behind me and transformed into a ray of sunshine.

'I make coffee for you?' she asked Ace as I picked up my chin from the floor. Those were five words she'd never uttered to me before. She brought in the coffees as we were unwrapping the tree, and stroked Winnie for a while.

'Very good tree,' she said. So much positivity in one day. I thought she fancied Ace but he's a bit old for her. I spotted her smiling and looking at him through the ajar kitchen door.

'You come here for Christmas?' she asked Ace, as though it was her habit to engage in chitchat. I should have left my chin on the floor.

'No, I was thinking of going away,' he replied.

'Maybe you come here for Christmas.'

What the hell was going on? I hoped she wasn't angling for an invite so she could be with Ace. Then, I remembered it would be Ace's first Christmas without Kelly. And without his dad.

'I'm going to Mum and Dad. Why don't you come? They'd love to see you. It's been ages,' I said to Ace, not making eye contact with Joy.

I was quite excited when he agreed. It'll be lovely to spend Christmas with him and great to have him to talk to if things are still difficult with Mum and Dad. They'll have to behave themselves if Ace is there. After he'd gone, Joy came over and started helping me with the tree decorations. I could feel she was building up to saying something. Maybe she did fancy Ace and wanted to ask about him. She doesn't usually talk about her love life, so I assume she's single.

'Do you like Ace? He's handsome, isn't he?' I fished.

'Yeah, very handsome.'

Bother. Joy coming onto Ace was the last thing I needed.

'You know he's fifty-seven?' I asked.

'Yes, good age.'

I wanted to throttle the newfound joy out of her. I'll make sure she's not around next time he comes over. I couldn't bear it if she worms her way into his heart. I need to find out how he feels about me, not lead him into the arms of an alluring young entrepreneur. As she walked towards the kitchen, I scowled at her back but had to catch myself when she came back and resumed decorating. I sat on the sofa watching her back. I couldn't look her in the eye.

'Look, Joy, there's something I should tell you. It's about Ace. The thing is, we've been friends forever, but now I think I might have feelings for him, and I have a suspicion that he feels the same way about me. You know I've been searching for someone for a long time and now ... now I think he might be the one I want. So ... what I'm saying is ... I don't want him distracted by anyone else. Do you understand?'

After what felt like hours, she turned round, and I held my breath.

'I hang Christmas hookers?' she asked, holding up a bauble. After taking out her earbuds.

11.45pm

Just got another text from The Hot One wanting to meet and begging me to let him explain. He's even suggesting going away together for Christmas. Now I can't sleep. He's in my head again. I can't help comparing him to Ace. If I'm honest, he was distant and non-committal whereas Ace is caring, reliable, honest and everything a woman could want. But then I'm remembering being with The Hot One and how great it was. I'm so confused.

Sunday, 15 December, 11.30pm

Bought all the presents for Mum and Dad so I can execute my cunning reunion plan. Ace is letting me order a surprise costume for him for Leila's NYE party. One cute costume ordered. Then I video-called Ace to show him the decorated tree. I set up the phone on a stand, put on a tinsel halo, climbed a ladder behind it and peeped over the top of the tree, pretending to be the angel. Then I lost my balance and pushed the tree over. It took me two hours to put everything back, but it was worth it to hear Ace laughing so heartily at my performance.

P.S. I've been failing at pushing The Hot One into oblivion.

Monday, 16 December, 8.30pm

Whoa! Just had a hot under the collar sofa dream about Ace that turned into a nightmare. I dreamt I'd ordered him a tiny pair of Speedos for his NYE costume. He strutted around in them at the party while all the women stared with lustful eyes and whispered 'budgie-smugglers, budgie-smugglers, budgie-smugglers.' Then a cockatoo flew in and pecked at me in my hammock. What could that mean?

11.30pm

I was getting hot and bothered about the Ace dream earlier, so I started scrolling social media to distract myself. A message popped up saying, 'Undercover Dust Bunny who you might know is on Instagram', so I tapped but the account was anonymous. The bio said, 'Queen of Clean, Duchess of Dust, Empress of Elbow Grease. Bringing you the polished truth in a world of mess. Spilling the dirt while I clean yours. Unmasking the world one mop at a time.'

It had twenty-seven thousand followers and looked like a hilarious account of the life of a cleaner dishing the dirt on their clients, so I followed the account. I was about to return to scrolling when I saw a picture of a Christmas tree that looked very much like mine. Closer inspection revealed that indeed it was mine. I scrolled down to find a picture of Leila's deflated plastic man. It must be Joy! Under the Christmas tree, she had commented, 'I think my favourite client is in love. Fingers crossed it work out this time. She deserve to be happy.' A tear rolled down my cheek. I scrolled down and there were other posts gushing about me. All that bravado and judginess is all an act. And I'm her favourite client. Another tear fell onto my phone.

I texted her.

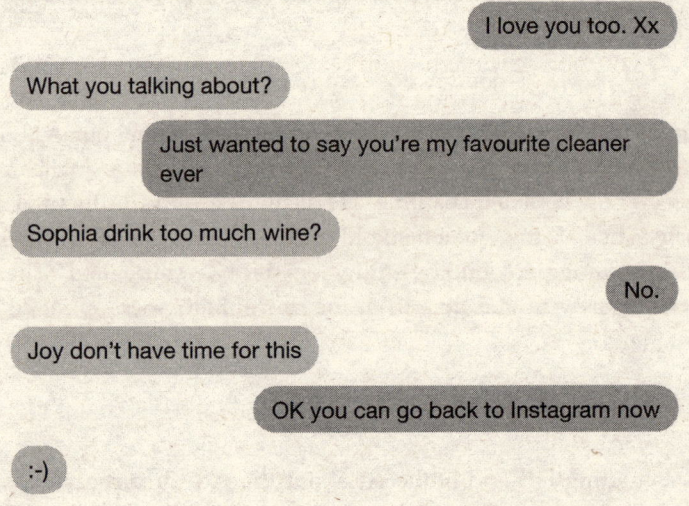

I love you too. Xx

What you talking about?

Just wanted to say you're my favourite cleaner ever

Sophia drink too much wine?

No.

Joy don't have time for this

OK you can go back to Instagram now

:-)

Tuesday, 17 December, 11.30pm

The dating challenge is a lost cause now and it seems I'm condemned to singledom forever. But there are still two weeks to go before the year ends. Could there be a last-minute reprieve? Could Ace forge ahead and sweep me off my feet? I admit, I rather like that idea, but I don't know how to engineer it without risking being rejected. But then, what if I gave The Hot One another chance? He's keen to get back together again, so maybe…

Wednesday, 18 December, 7.30am

Meeting Ace in a bathroom showroom today to look at options for his flat. Will he still want two basins? Or worse still, one huge lovey-dovey-let's-share-everything basin? I'll quiz him discreetly about Jacqueline. She could seriously scupper my romance prospects.

11.30pm

I didn't need to ask about her. Ace turned up with her.

'I hope it's OK to crash your shopping trip,' she said. 'I was feeling a bit down and Ace invited me.'

'Yes of course. Though I don't know if showing you bathrooms is a good way of cheering you up, but I'll do my best,' I said. I couldn't help thinking that if she and Ace are an item, I'd be deflated, disappointed and desolate, especially after allowing myself to acknowledge that I have feelings for him. But I don't want to be jealous and bitchy. It's not my style. I'm all for being sisterly and I'm not going to forget who I am. I decided to bury my feelings along with my hopes of romance with Ace and to carry on as if nothing had happened. Actually, nothing has happened. I've been dreaming of romance with Ace but have no idea how he feels about me. I let my imagination run wild. I'll just have to suck it up.

'I won't go into it, but it's my ex-husband. Anything to stop me thinking about him is good.'

'If you need a girly chat, I'm here,' I said. Ace smiled and winked at me, pleased.

I think I got her wrong and allowed my feelings for Ace to affect my judgement. She was good company and had some interesting design ideas. But when it came to choosing the basins, I made an excuse about making a call and left them to it. I'm sad but I'll try and be happy for them.

More texts from THO today. He's certainly persistent. I've had more texts from him in the last week than I did the whole time we were together. He may be my last-minute reprieve if Ace is with Jacqueline now, though it would feel like I've settled for second best. I haven't come this far to accept the runner-up. I wish there was no Jacqueline to distract Ace, and no The Hot One to confuse me. I suppose there's no harm in meeting him for a coffee.

Friday, 20 December, 11.30pm

I'm probably being stupid, but I've agreed to meet The Hot One for lunch on Sunday. I know I shouldn't, but he's been so persistent, and he keeps reminding me of the lovely times we had together, so I finally cracked today. It's lunch. Nothing more. I want to hear what he has to say. It's possible I didn't realise how bad things were for him when we were together. And just thinking about his body gives me goosebumps.

Saturday, 21 December, 11.30pm

Leila was surprised about Ace and Jacqueline. She doesn't think she's his type either, and thought it was probably just Ace being Ace and helping someone in need. I don't know and don't want to ask. He must be wondering why I haven't made any comment about the two of them though. He may not be ready to go public yet.

Then I told her about The Hot One and she completely blew up at me and said she couldn't believe I was even considering seeing him again after the way he treated me. I was so tempted to remind her of how she stuck her head in the sand about Jude but decided not to go there. Am I being ridiculous to consider it? Should I not forgive him? Everyone makes mistakes. I shouldn't punish him, and myself, for one mistake.

Sunday, 22 December, 2.30pm

Just back from lunch with The Hot One and I'm … happy. My bedroom was a disaster zone when I left to meet him. I built up a pile of abandoned outfit options in the corner of the room before settling on casual but sexy pale blue jeans, nude high heel boots, a pale pink jumper, and a winter white fur coat. My GHD was still hot from straightening my hair when I decided to put in giant rollers for a wavy look, which I then combed out as soon as the rollers were discarded. I had to look my best to let him see what he'd been missing, and I felt confident when I arrived at Le Petit Bistro. I stood at the entrance, took in the room with my best pout and smouldering eyes, then strutted towards him, tossing my tousled tresses. In my head I was striding in slow motion to Marvin Gaye's 'Let's Get It On'.

He was so handsome in a blue cashmere sweater and expensively ruffled hair. We made a good couple. All those feelings of yearning came flooding back. I sat opposite him and thought the sexual chemistry was still there. Cue massive vagina throbs. He said he wanted to explain how he was feeling back in August, so I let him talk and listened.

'I'd been working hard and making so many personal sacrifices for the partnership. That day when we were due to go to Valencia, they told me it wasn't working out. They said they had concerns about my commitment to the firm. Had concerns? I couldn't believe it after everything I'd done for them. I was in shock at first but then I was raging, and I had no bandwidth for any other emotional demands. That was why I ended us, but now things have settled down, I regret it. I want you back, Sophia.'

'But you dumped me by text and…' I started to say. The rowdy group of women at the next table looked at each other, stopped talking and started eavesdropping.

I wanted to tell him he'd been aloof from the beginning and how much he'd hurt me by finishing it the way he did, but he interrupted me and carried on talking about what a terrible time he'd been through. He went on to tell me he'd changed his strategy at work, and he was working smarter to get himself noticed and finally it was starting to work, and the CEO was pleased with him.

'So, that's it. That's what happened. But I hope you understand the reasons. Can we forget about it and pick up where we left off?' He smiled and winked at me.

I thought, is that it? You've made your excuses and you think it can all be OK again? No asking me about what I'd endured or how I felt at the time? Not even an actual apology? The man was a complete narcissist. How could I not have seen that before? Then a thought.

'Have you seen anyone else since we broke up?' I asked.

'Yes, but it didn't work out,' he said, furrowing his brows.

'She dumped you, didn't she?'

'She didn't mean anything. It's not relevant to us.' He looked sheepish and couldn't keep eye contact.

'Was it by text?'

He put his hand through his hair and fidgeted, staring into the distance. One of the women at the next table guffawed.

'It was, wasn't it? Oh my God. I think it is relevant. I think your ego was dented and you thought, who can I go to who wants me and can make me feel better about myself? I know, I'll try Sophia.'

He shook his head from side to side again, sighed and played with the stem of his wine class.

I smiled to myself.

'I'm really glad I came today. When I walked in earlier, I thought you looked hot, and I still wanted you.'

He looked up at me and leaned forward.

'I needed to see you and hear your explanation and decide if I should give us a second chance. To understand how you feel about me. And thank you for being honest about your other relationship. That was helpful. But now that I know the reasons why you broke up with me, and why you now want to get back together again, I realise that … how can I put this? You're self-obsessed, cowardly and a complete knob.' There was a hush at the next table.

I stood up, put on my coat, and picked up my bag, then took a last sip of my red wine.

'Have a nice life,' I said, and poured the wine over his head.

He pushed his chair back to duck the stream of red liquid, but it was too late. As he dabbed his hair with a napkin in disbelief, I turned for the door and breezed out to the sound of clapping and whooping from the women at the next table.

I'm smiling to myself as I write. I feel free and light, as though a weight has been taken off my chest. He hurt me and I resented him for it, but it took me a long time to stop having feelings for him. Now, I don't care anymore that he dumped me, and I don't keep wondering what's wrong with me. It's not me. It's him. I know now that it was the exterior I'd fallen in love with, not the man. I loved his looks and his body and mistook that for loving the whole man, when deep down I must have known he didn't want me.

I can see now that he was never interested in a real relationship. I'm so relieved that I no longer have any feelings for him and can see him for the thoughtless and selfish man that he is. The Hot One, you have been sent to oblivion forever. The clouds have lifted, and the sun is shining. The future is bright.

Monday, 23 December, 11.30pm

Ace texted earlier.

Hey, looking forward to Xmas day. Should I bring anything?

No just yourself.

OK. Will bring booze!

Unless you want to bring Jacqueline?

No, why would I bring her? Can't wait for Christmas Day. x

Phew. What if he'd said yes and brought her? Did I imagine they were in a relationship? Thinking back, I didn't see any tell-tale signs of togetherness. No intimate glances or touching. Perhaps it was all in my jealous head. Christmas Day is looking more promising. And what should I read into 'Can't wait for Christmas Day'? Does it mean what I think it means? Could I allow myself to hope for that? After seeing The Hot One, I know now it's Ace I really want.

Tuesday – Christmas Eve, 9.30am

Going to Mum and Dad's today. Last time I visited, the atmosphere in the senior Stone household was so cold, Frosty the Snowman could survive indoors over Christmas. I'm going to knock some sense into them and stop the madness.

11.30pm

Move over Esther Perel. Sophia Stone has a new career in marriage counselling. When I arrived, Mum was busy in the kitchen avoiding Dad, and he was in his lounger doing his sudoku. As usual. Was he always this obsessive or is it old age? I knew I was going to try and reconcile Mum and Dad, but didn't know it would take all day.

Round One – I ate half of my lunch in the kitchen with Mum and half in the living room with Dad because they refused to sit together. I tried talking sense into each of them, but they wouldn't budge. I despaired and had two mince pies.

Round Two – After lunch, Mum moved to the dining table to read her book. Progress. At least they were in the same room. In the afternoon, I made tea and opened the Christmas cake I'd brought. I was ready with my speech.

'Mum, Dad, I need to talk to you,' I said, turning from one to the other at opposite ends of the room. 'I've had a tough few months and I'm looking forward to spending Christmas with you. And this'—I pointed at their full-of-misery faces—'won't do.' They fidgeted and said nothing. 'Come on, you're being childish. Why don't you give each other a hug and say sorry?' Now I know what having squabbling kids must be like.

Dad stared at his shoes and Mum went back to the kitchen. I despaired and ate all the triangles in the Quality Street tin.

Round Three – Conversation over dinner was stilted and channelled through me, but at least they sat at the same table. As soon as we finished, I went in for the kill.

'I know you love each other. Before all this nonsense with the modelling and dancing started, you used to hold hands over the radiator while you watched TV in your armchairs. Don't tell me that's not love after sixty-odd years.' They each studied their empty plates intently like naughty children being chastised. My heart brimmed over.

'You're being stubborn and making each other miserable. I know you don't really want to carry on like this, and I've had enough of the tension.'

'Tell your mother to apologise and stop her modelling shenanigans and I'll consider it,' Dad said.

'Tell your father to apologise and stop dancing with that Consuela woman and I'll consider it,' Mum said.

When Dad didn't say anything, Mum slammed the door and went upstairs, and Dad busied himself on the iPad. I despaired and had a large piece of Christmas cake.

After about an hour, Dad went upstairs. I could hear their voices, so I listened at the bedroom door. He said he was feeling lonely and left out when she did her modelling and that's why he went dancing with Consuela, who is happily married and only dances with Dad because her husband is in a wheelchair. Dad just made more of it to make Mum jealous. Mum thought he was being disapproving of her modelling, then she became jealous of Consuela, and it all got out of hand.

Round Four – They came down an hour later looking more relaxed with each other. I took out their presents from my bag. 'Here, I want you to open your Christmas gifts.' They both sat on the sofa, and I could see they were excited, and started unwrapping.

'Dad, I got you a new mobile with a good camera. I know you

love sudoku and it's good brain training, but you could do with a new hobby.' He grinned and started taking out the pieces.

'Mum, you get a year's subscription for two to a new ballroom dance class, so you can BOTH enjoy dancing again. Without Spanish distractions. And a lovely Latin dance dress. You can model it and Dad can photograph you in it. Treat it like a photoshoot for both of you.'

Mum was delighted with her dress. She disappeared upstairs while I helped Dad with the mobile. When she reappeared and swished the fringing on her dress, he beamed and took a few photos. She went over to him.

'You look magnificent,' he said as he showed her the images.

'And you have a talent for photography. You could photograph me in different outfits, and I could put them on … what's that internet site for photos, Lovely?'

'Instagram?'

'Yes, that's it. Me and your father could be the new Instagram sensations,' she declared. Where did she learn to say that?

'Does that mean you won't be doing any more modelling for that photographer?' Dad said.

'It was getting too tiring anyway, going up to London and hanging around a studio all day.' She kissed the top of Dad's head. He beamed. But there was still something left unsaid. The elephant in the room.

'Does that mean you won't be dancing with Consuela anymore?' I asked.

'Not when I have a beautiful wife to photograph and dance with.' He hugged her. So romantic and cheesy. I filled up. I can only dream that I'll be loved up like them in my eighties. Maybe next year things will change for me.

And so it was that peace was restored in the senior Stone household (that sounds like a fairy tale's ending). They needed a nudge to stop being stubborn. I'm not despairing anymore but I think I deserve a few more yummies from the Quality Street box before going to sleep. I wonder if there are any blue coconut ones left.

Wednesday – Christmas Day, 7.30am

Dad still carries on the tradition of filling our Christmas stockings with gifts if me or Sara is staying on Christmas Eve. I woke up to more chocolate, beautifully wrapped soaps, and a pearl hair clip in mine. I wonder if he dressed as Santa like he usually does. I was so exhausted after the marriage counselling day I slept like a log and didn't hear him come into my room. It's great to see Mum and Dad being back to their usual happy selves.

As for me, I'm VERY excited about seeing Ace later, but trying to hold it together, hoping there is nothing between him and Jacqueline. I love Ace, have done forever, but now I think I have a different kind of love for him. I KNOW I have a different kind of love for him. The kind of love where I could contemplate giving myself fully, revealing my soft core, and not holding back. Now that I don't have The Hot One squatting in my brain, I can see more clearly. I cannot believe I even considered getting back with The Hot One when there was a chance I could be with Ace instead. Ace would win hands down, on every front. There is no comparison. Ace is the whole package, not just a handsome face, or a fit body. Not just beautiful outer packaging (although that's pretty hot) but beautiful inside too. In fact, he's everything I said I wanted in my ideal man in the dating apps:

- Articulate – He can even rap!
- Adventurous – We had so much fun in Cuba.
- Glass half-full – Always. He sees the best in people and in every situation.
- Smells nice – Mmm, yes.
- Energetic and fit – Oh yeah.
- Intelligent – He has a first-class degree and speaks three languages.
- Youthful – Well, he hasn't retired to buy a pipe and slippers. He's joined a Latin band!
- Sexy – Have you seen him in a Speedo?
- Confident – He sure strutted his stuff in that Speedo.

- Funny – Have you seen his dancing?
- Attractive – And then some.
- Open-minded – Well, he might not be up for a threesome but neither am I.
- Bonus superpower – Have you seen him in a Speedo?

I can also add kind, considerate, generous, honest, protective, loyal, talented, trustworthy, compassionate, and more.

If we were to get together, wouldn't it be perfect? We're already best friends, and I've loved spending more time with him lately. I wish I knew how he feels. I don't want to make a complete fool of myself, but then why break the habit of a lifetime?! I'd be devastated if he rejects me. In Valencia, I had the excuse of being vulnerable and drunk when I kissed him, but what would he say if I did it again?

I hope Santa will give me the best present ever this year. I'd better get up and help Mum and her sous chef. She seems to be cooking for an army and not just for the four of us, but when I mentioned it yesterday, she told me to stop fussing.

Thursday – Boxing Day, 9.00am

It was lovely to have Mum and Dad being a team again and cooking Christmas lunch together. I tried to help but they said I should relax as I'd already done enough to make it a happy Christmas, so I spent quite a long time getting ready for our guest. I put on my flowy red chiffon dress with red tights and red velvet ankle boots. I was smiling and standing proud in the mirror but inside I had a million butterflies fluttering. I was so looking forward to seeing Ace but apprehensive about his feelings for me.

Floaty and rosy-cheeked, I welcomed Ace and Winnie, and was serving drinks when the doorbell went. Who could that be? My wondering was followed by shock and confusion when I opened the door to find Sara, Laurence, Jack and Charlotte standing before me. I nearly dropped my prosecco. They were all smiles and bearing presents. I was so chuffed to see the kids. Sara was acting like nothing had happened. We hadn't seen each other since she walked off after admitting to sleeping with The Traitor. Yes, she was nice the last time we spoke on the phone, but I wasn't expecting this Sara. The old lovely, sisterly Sara.

I went to the kitchen to get glasses and asked Mum if she knew Sara was coming. Then I remembered her enigmatic smile when I'd questioned the quantity of food.

'If I'd told you, it wouldn't have been a surprise,' Mum said. She can be so annoying.

I didn't want the day spoilt with another row, so I chatted to Ace on the sofa, but Sara kept looking in my direction. My heart sank like a lift with its cables cut when she asked to have a word in private. I was dreading another confrontation.

'Look, Sophe, I have something to say.' She took in a big breath. We were standing in the middle of her old bedroom, surrounded by framed photos of our childhood.

'Don't start anything please. Not today,' I said.

'Just let me say what I have to say. Please.'

I deflated onto the single bed and waited for whatever was coming.

'I know I've been awful to you this last year. In fact, I've been horrible to everyone including Laurence, the kids, and Mum and Dad.'

'No argument from me on that.'

'After our fight when you had your accident, I had a meltdown at work and my boss suggested counselling. She thought I had anger management issues, apparently flying off the handle with my colleagues over the smallest things and making the practice atmosphere toxic.'

'Are you saying that was my fault?' Was she going to pin everything that was wrong in her life on me?

'No. Just let me finish.'

She said the counsellor made her understand that it was all about her feelings of guilt. She felt guilty about what she did to me and to Laurence. She was angry with herself but took it out on the people she loves. All that time she was carrying this massive, awful secret and it was too much.

'I realised that honesty was the only way out of the mess. I had to be honest with myself, with Laurence and with you. So I told Laurence about that night,' she said.

'Oh my God,' I gasped. 'How did he take it?'

'He was devastated at first but honestly, he's been brilliant.'

'I suppose he couldn't take the moral high ground when he'd been having an affair.'

'That's another thing … erm … he didn't have an affair. I told you that because I didn't want to tell you the real reason.' Another deep breath. 'I had a miscarriage and…'

'I know. Mum told me.'

'So much for Mum keeping a secret,' she said.

'Don't be angry with her. She had to tell me. You were being so awful to me, she wanted to explain why. She didn't know there was another reason too.'

'Do you hate me?'

'Yes. No. I don't hate you, but there have been times when I was so furious I wanted to come over and scream in your face. You slept with my boyfriend, right under my nose. Do you know what that did to me? My sister, who I adored and trusted with my life up to that moment, with the man I loved, while I watched TV downstairs. How could you hurt me like that when you knew what that kind of betrayal would do to me? You tore my heart apart. I was broken for a long time.'

'I know. There's no excuse and I'm so ashamed. I think I went bonkers for a while. I couldn't cope and I lashed out. It was unforgiveable. I'm truly sorry.'

'And I can't believe you thought I wouldn't understand about the pregnancy. You should know me better than that. You should have known I don't have it in me to resent you for what happened,' I said.

'I know. In the confusion and misery of what happened, I forgot who I was. I felt like I'd killed my baby deliberately. I made a mistake and I paid for it, as did Laurence. He was devastated. Please believe me, I didn't do it on purpose, honestly.'

'I believe you, and I'm so sorry about the baby. It must have been a horrible experience. To me, it felt like somehow you blamed me. That it was my fault you had a miscarriage, and it was my fault you slept with The Traitor.'

'You're right. I think in my distressed state, I needed someone to blame, and you were an easy target, even if it made no sense to hold you responsible. You didn't deserve any of it.'

She said that after the miscarriage, things got awful with Laurence for a while, and that night when she came to my house, she drunk herself silly to kill the pain of the misery.

'I've stopped drinking now. I've been a cow to everyone. I want to make amends and start by acknowledging what I did and apologising. To you, in particular.'

'You should have told me. About all of it…' I hesitated. I'd had enough of being mad at her and wanted it to be over, and to go back to being loving sisters. 'I can't talk though. I bottled it all up too. We're a right pair of uptight bitches,' I said, smiling. 'How are things with Laurence now?'

'We've had a difficult time, but I think we're going to be OK. We have a new regime at home. I let Laurence and the kids help around the house, so I'm not a martyr anymore.'

I snorted.

'Yes, you can laugh. I do have some self-awareness.' She paused. 'I know I don't deserve it, but will you forgive me?'

Tears trickled down both our faces, and all I could think was how great it would be to have my sister back. Yes, she'd done a terrible thing to me, but she was in pain and vulnerable at the time and made a mistake. She deserves a second chance. I reached out to her, and we hugged for a long time.

As we pulled away, she said, 'What about you-know-who? Ever wonder what might have happened if you were still together? I mean if I hadn't messed things up for you.'

'Things were probably messed up already. Apparently, he moved on from me pretty quickly and shacked up with somebody else. If I'm honest, I don't think he loved me, so you probably did me a favour.'

She sighed and wiped her nose. 'Let's go and enjoy the party, but you need to fix your makeup first. Mum wouldn't approve of the Marilyn Manson look.' We both laughed at my reflection in the dressing table mirror.

'Hey, you missed out on the Christmas stocking fillers last night,' I said, as I tried to salvage my carefully applied makeup.

'Is Dad still doing that?' She paused. 'What's going on with you and Ace? You look different around each other. Cosy. If I didn't know different, I'd say you were together.' I told her about my growing feelings for Ace, and about him and Jacqueline.

'He's a good man. He'd be perfect for you, and he'd look after you. As for Jacqueline, it sounds like they're just friends.'

I can't believe I've been so blind to his charm all these years. I suppose we haven't been single at the same time since our early twenties, but now we're both free. Is it possible he loves and wants me too? I wasn't warming to the idea. No, I was burning up with it.

The rest of the day was a picture-perfect Christmas. The tree was twinkling, Winnie jumped around being cute and golden, we all ate and drank too much, we laughed a lot, and the kids played with their new gadgets. And of course, me and Ace cosied up like the best friends that we are, but he didn't know that all I wanted for Christmas was to take him upstairs and jump him. I wonder if my constant state of flushed breathlessness gave it away.

AND IN OTHER ROMANCE-RELATED GOOD NEWS: JACQUELINE HAS GONE BACK TO HER HUSBAND. SHE NEVER WANTED THAT SECOND BASIN.

The spark of love for Ace is starting to turn into a flame. But how to ignite it fully? My increasing longing for Ace is bittersweet. There's a bit of me that still doesn't believe he wants me, and I don't want to make a move and lose him altogether.

11.30pm

It's been a quiet but lovely day today, just me and Mum and Dad eating chocolates and watching crap TV. I wonder how many more Christmases I'll have with them. Still feeling warm from the glow of yesterday. But only five days left of the year. When will my last-minute reprieve come?

Friday, 27 December, 11.30pm

Decided to stay another day with Mum and Dad. He hasn't stopped taking photos of Mum, and I had to set up an Insta account for him. He's already posted twenty pics. I've created a monster.

Saturday, 28 December, 11.30pm

Boozy brunch with Grace and Leila today. Grace has been busy setting up her doggie dating business. Woof, woof. I'm so pleased for her. She's calling it Canine Cupids.

I need to think about my priorities for next year. Back in January, I threw myself into dating with the determination and enthusiasm of Sheriff Woody, but gradually turned into Mrs Potatohead with missing bits. I went from being as enthusiastic as Bugs Bunny with a bag of carrots and ended like Winnie the Pooh without honey. I searched for Mr Darcy and found Mr Wickham.

The Opera Buff introduced me to operatic sex, The Fetishist taught me to love my feet, and Mr Delicious put me off sushi for life. And The Hot One … he made me miserable for a while but taught me to never ignore the red flags again.

Along the way, I had my hopes raised and dashed, there were some fun moments, and my heart got broken. I was open-minded to all sorts of people. I welcomed new experiences and any opportunities to meet men. I realised I wanted love after all and wanted the dating project to work. But none of it came to anything. Did I waste a whole year searching and being preoccupied with finding the next date? After all that effort, could I end up with the person who's been in front of me the whole time? I probably needed to meet all those men to understand exactly what I want. It took the many dates to open my eyes and my heart and to prepare me for real love. I know now Ace is the one I want. The only one.

I told Grace and Leila about how I've been feeling about him. They were pleased and excited for me but not surprised. They both knew I'd started to have feelings for Ace but was being ridiculous and refusing to acknowledge it.

Tuesday – New Year's Eve, 6.30pm

Sooo excited about Leila's party tonight. After last year's foil frock fiasco, I'm going for comedy value tonight and wearing an octopus outfit. The best part, though, is that I can control the arms with a thread pull system. I'm going to enjoy dancing with that. Ace doesn't know he's going to be a crab. We can make a delicious seafood salad together. Is tonight going to be the night of my reprieve?

PART XIII
January

THIRTY-FIVE

The Last Man

Wednesday – New Year's Day, 11.30pm

HAPPY NEW YEAR! So much to write about but no time or energy to do it.

THIRTY-SIX

The Last Day

Thursday, 2 January, 7.30pm

NYE SEEMS like a long time ago and feels like it might have been a sofa dream, but I'll try and remember everything that happened. Ace came to my house to put on his surprise costume.

'Interesting outfit,' he said, inspecting the crab costume he'd taken out of the packaging. 'Are you trying to tell me something?'

'No! I thought it might be fun for both of us to go as seafood.'

'You're weird,' he said and laughed.

He came down a few minutes later head-to-toe in red, with crab eyes on top of his head and pincers for hands. Super cute.

'Hello Octopussy,' he said.

I tested the arm controls on my octopus outfit and put all eight of them around Ace. We had a moment when we were up close and stared into each other's eyes, but I blushed and tried to pull away. I got the control strings tangled up and he had to kneel and free himself from below before untangling me. Then our taxi came. I had trouble getting into the car with all my arms and it took me a while to get settled in the back seat. The driver watched us in the mirror and shook his head and smiled.

'Let's go be seafood,' Ace said.

The party was in full flow when we arrived. Cement Man and

his wife were surveying the room in matching sand-coloured safari suits. I congratulated them on their marriage and meant it. Dick Pick Man was – you couldn't make this up – wearing an inflatable dick outfit, with two giant balls at his ankles and the tip of a penis over his head. I can confirm, like his picture, his outfit was circumcised. Leila was floating around being the perfect hostess in a red traditional Iranian costume with a full skirt, gold thread and jangling coins. Her new boyfriend followed her like an adoring puppy in a lawyer suit. I so admire her resilience and capacity for finding love. Grace and Ajay and the kids had come as sunflowers and were super cute standing in a smiling bunch. Izzy was happy with her new man – a fitness instructor she met at the gym – in matching eighties shell suits.

Near midnight, there was an insistent knocking on the door. Grace opened it to find a drunk and dishevelled-looking Jude wanting to come in. She tried to persuade him to leave but he pushed past her and started looking for Leila. As he went around the room shouting for her, he left a trail of hush.

'There she is, my beautiful wife,' he said, and tried to kiss Leila, but she pulled back.

'What the hell are you doing here?' she asked under her breath as people watched.

'Come on, babe. It's New Year's Eve. I know you still love me. I've come back to you.' He tried to grab her hand, but she pulled away again.

'Get out, Jude. You're not wanted here,' Leila said firmly, though I could see she was flushed and tearing up.

'I've been miserable without you. I know you miss me. You want your toy boy back, don't you, babe?' He lurched forward at her. At this, Leila's new man stepped in.

'Are you deaf? She doesn't want you here. Just be a good fellow and leave,' he said.

Jude snarled and waved him away, then noticed the man was holding Leila around the waist.

'It didn't take you long to replace me, did it? You bitch.' He staggered towards the lawyer to punch him but missed. There was a mass intake of breath, then relief when there was no punch back, just a pitying smirk.

'Come on, Jude. Can't you see you're upsetting everyone? Just go,' Ace said.

Jude turned to Ace, and only then became aware the party had stopped to watch.

'What are you all staring at?' he sneered. 'You're all as bad as each other. You're all tossers.' He turned to Leila again. 'You're an old bag who thinks she can buy young men with her money.' I was next. 'And you're a saddo who can't get a man.' Then it was Ace's turn. 'And you, you're pathetic. You've been mooning over her for forty years but don't have the guts to admit it,' he said, pointing at me. He searched around for other people to attack and could only see Grace and Ajay holding the kids protectively in a bunch of sunflowers. 'And you and your fucking happy family. You make me sick.' He scowled like a jackal, then walked off and out of the door.

Everyone was quiet and shocked. True to form, Cement Man and his wife looked petrified, Dick Pic Man stood erect, and The Divorcee had passed out on the sofa. Leila's coins jangled as she sobbed, but her lawyer was doing a good job of consoling her, and they were soon kissing. I knew she'd be OK. It took a few seconds before a more subdued chatter resumed.

I realised I'd been holding my breath, and as I took in some air, a rush of adrenalin flooded my body. My knees went soft, and I had to steady myself on the drinks table. Could it be true? Has Ace been in love with me all these years? Have I been oblivious to the signs? And the last few months, while my feelings for him were coming up through my inner core and into my limbs and breathing out through my skin, I still hadn't quite believed it. I couldn't take it in.

I looked at Ace standing expectantly across the room, then ran to the bathroom by default, locked the door and sat on the loo. It was New Year's Eve after all. Tears burst out of my eyes, but I realised this time I wasn't mourning for lost love or feeling like a spare part. These were tears of surprise and joy. The ones that ooze inner happiness but usually dare not appear. There was a knock at the door, and Ace calling my name.

'Are you OK?' he said as I opened the door and let him in. The New Year countdown started. Ten, nine…

'Is that true? What Jude said? Do you like me?' I asked.

'No, I don't just like you.' He hesitated. 'I love you.'

I tried to speak but all I managed was, 'When?'

'After I knew it was over with Kelly, I wanted to tell you, but then we had our first brunch of the year, and you were all excited about the dating challenge and meeting lots of men…' he trailed off.

I put my hand to my mouth, stunned.

'I tried to tell you in Cuba, but I couldn't work out if you felt the same way. I took a chance and sent you the Valentine card…'

'That was you?'

'Yes, I thought you knew, so when you didn't mention it, I assumed you weren't interested. I didn't want to ruin our friendship and lose you altogether, so I kept quiet. Then after Valencia, I hoped the kiss meant something … but you wanted to forget about it. It's always been you, Phia. I've been in love with you for as long as I can remember.'

He searched my face for clues, with desperate expectant eyes.

I took in a deep breath of spicy oil burner and said, 'I think I started to wonder about my feelings for you after Valencia, but I didn't want to acknowledge them. I'm too scared of being hurt again, so I blamed it on being drunk and vulnerable. I didn't want to lose you.'

'I'm scared too, but you have to take a leap sometimes and right now I feel like I can grab your hand and we can fly together. I won't let you fall. I'd never hurt you.'

'Promise?'

'I promise.'

'I've been dreaming about us and not just the sleuthing dream.'

'I've been waiting so long for you to look at me and love me. I know it's hard, but you can't hide your feelings forever and lock your heart away in a cage. I want the carefree Sophia back.'

'I want her back too. Will you help me find her?'

'Yes, if you'll let me. But…' He furrowed his brows and took a deep breath. 'What about that guy you were dating? Did you go out with him again? Do you still have feelings for him?'

'Yes, I did go out with him. Just once, and I'm glad I did. It made me realise he didn't deserve my love, and I have to confess I compared him to you in my fantasies. And that's when I knew he wasn't worth a hair on your head. He's nothing to me now. Whereas you … you're everything.'

The cheering outside was dying down and I heard the first few chords of 'Vivir Mi Vida'. He took my hands (the ones at the end of the non-octopus arms) and led me into a confident slow salsa dance.

'Wow, you've been practising. You've got moves, Mr Ace.' I pulled him in close.

'Well thank you, Ms Sophia. But I want to hear about your fantasies about me,' he said, raising an amused eyebrow.

'All I'm willing to divulge is that they involved Speedos, budgies, cockatoos, a hammock and an invisible man.'

'You're weird,' he said with an indulgent smile.

'Anyway, what you need to know is that I only want sex with you,' I said deadpan.

He looked away from me, downcast. 'I want no part in your dating challenge.'

I pulled him back by his chin.

'I meant I want to have sex ONLY with YOU. Tell me again how you feel about me.'

'I love how you always want to help, even if it involves having my hair sheared. I love how your eyes smile when you dance. I love how you boycott restaurants if the chairs are not stylish enough, and I love how you pout after your first sip of fizz. I love you, Sophia Stone.'

'That's lucky … because … I love you too.'

I pulled the string, put all my arms around him and pressed

my lips onto his. It was the sweetest and sexiest kiss and it made me shiver all over. It was the only place I wanted to be. It felt like home.

'Wait a minute. Who did you think the card was from?'

Gulp.

'Never mind that,' I said and pulled him in for another kiss.

I didn't know I had an Ace-shaped hole in my heart until it was filled so well that you'd think he'd been there forever. There's no cement talk, no listing of pizzas, no deceit, no sushi, no lack of commitment. There is requited love and yes, many orgasms. Oh, the orgasms. I love everything about him, and best of all, I finally feel adored. Properly and unconditionally. This is going to be the best year yet, and I plan to make that second basin mine. I have a new life and I'm going to squeeze the pips out of it. I am now the Joint CEO of Couples United.

Acknowledgments

My brilliant creative writing teacher, Deana Luchia, without whose support and encouragement this book would not have been written.

Claire Moffett, for going above and beyond in reviewing the earlier manuscript versions.

My lovely writing group and beta readers, Raquel Cassidy, Sarah Linklett, Vanessa Tenn, Leonie Whittingham, and Louise Woodcock, for their amazing support and valuable feedback.

Julie Williams for offering to read the first draft and promising to tell me if it was no good – full disclosure, she liked it.

Helen Lederer and Comedy Women in Print Prize for welcoming me into the comedy women family and giving me a lift up the ladder.

Charlotte Ledger, Arsalan Isa, and Caroline Kirkpatrick for helping me to elevate this book to its fullest potential.

Book Club Questions

1. Consider the symbolism of Sophia's "disappearing act" on New Year's Eve. What does this reveal about her emotional state?

2. Analyse the family dynamics at the New Year's lunch. How do these interactions shed light on Sophia's character and background?

3. How does Sophia's honest self-reflection and body positivity challenge traditional narratives around ageing and beauty?

4. Consider the broader social and cultural context of a sixty-year-old woman embarking on a dating journey. How might Sophia's choices challenge societal expectations and stereotypes around ageing and sexuality?

5. Sophia's struggles with past relationships, and the fear of starting again, are relatable for many readers. How did these elements impact your reading experience?

6. How do you perceive the role of Sophia's friends in her life and their influence on her decisions and self-perception?

7. Sophia's journey is filled with self-discovery, humour, and some embarrassing moments. Which moments resonated with you the most, and why?

8. How well do you think the protagonist handles the surprises, twists, and turns in her dating life?

9. Which was your favourite date and why?

10. Sophia's openness to new experiences led to a few unusual situations, from the opera buff's matador moves to the foot fetishist. If you were Sophia, would you have been open to some of these new experiences? Where would you draw the line?

If you loved *Aged to Perfection*, you may also enjoy *One Bed*, the hottest forced proximity romance set in Santorini!

Rising star author Bea Williams needs a vacation.

And her godmother's snug Greek island retreat is the perfect place to use as an escape from her writer's block.
Until she finds she's going to have to share her idyllic one bed cottage with *him* – Gibson Caddell, one time childhood friend and a great big, drop-dead-gorgeous red flag.

As the sun sets on Santorini, Bea's thoughts soon turn to something much more pressing – there's two of them. And only one bed…

Available now in paperback, ebook and audio!

The author and One More Chapter would like to thank everyone who contributed to the publication of this story...

Analytics
James Brackin
Abigail Fryer

Audio
Fionnuala Barrett
Ciara Briggs

Contracts
Laura Amos
Laura Evans

Design
Lucy Bennett
Fiona Greenway
Liane Payne
Dean Russell

Digital Sales
Lydia Grainge
Hannah Lismore
Emily Scorer

Editorial
Janet Marie Adkins
Laura Burge
Kara Daniel
Charlotte Ledger
Ajebowale Roberts
Jennie Rothwell
Helen Williams

Harper360
Emily Gerbner
Jean Marie Kelly
emma sullivan
Sophia Wilhelm

International Sales
Peter Borcsok
Ruth Burrow
Colleen Simpson

Inventory
Sarah Callaghan
Kirsty Norman

Marketing & Publicity
Chloe Cummings
Grace Edwards
Emma Petfield

Operations
Melissa Okusanya
Hannah Stamp

Production
Denis Manson
Simon Moore
Francesca Tuzzeo

Rights
Helena Font Brillas
Ashton Mucha
Zoe Shine
Aisling Smythe

Trade Marketing
Ben Hurd
Eleanor Slater

The HarperCollins Distribution Team

The HarperCollins Finance & Royalties Team

The HarperCollins Legal Team

The HarperCollins Technology Team

UK Sales
Isabel Coburn
Jay Cochrane
Sabina Lewis
Holly Martin
Harriet Williams
Leah Woods

eCommerce
Laura Carpenter
Madeline ODonovan
Charlotte Stevens
Christina Storey
Jo Surman
Rachel Ward

And every other essential link in the chain from delivery drivers to booksellers to librarians and beyond!

ONE MORE CHAPTER

One More Chapter is an
award-winning global
division of HarperCollins.

Subscribe to our newsletter to get our
latest eBook deals and stay up to date
with all our new releases!

signup.harpercollins.co.uk/
join/signup-omc

Meet the team at
www.onemorechapter.com

Follow us!

@OneMoreChapter_

@OneMoreChapter

@onemorechapterhc

@onemorechapterhc

Do you write unputdownable fiction?
We love to hear from new voices.
Find out how to submit your novel at
www.onemorechapter.com/submissions